A PLACE BEYOND COURAGE

A PLACE BEYOND COURAGE

Elizabeth Chadwick

SPHERE

First published in Great Britain in 2007
by Sphere

A CIP catalogue record for this book
is available from the British Library.

ISBN: 978-1-84744-051-8

Typeset by Palimpsest Book Production Limited,
Grangemouth, Stirlingshire
Printed and bound in Great Britain by
Mackays of Chatham plc, Chatham, Kent

Sphere
An imprint of
Little, Brown Book Group
100 Victoria Embankment
London EC4Y 0DY

An Hachette Livre UK Company

www.littlebrown.co.uk

Acknowledgements

I'd like to take this page to say thank you. Since *A Place Beyond Courage* is my seventeenth novel, many of the usual suspects are involved, but it doesn't diminish my gratitude. Without their input, I'd have had considerably more hassle to finish the work. Indeed, without them I probably wouldn't have this great job.

So thank you to my agent Carole Blake and Oli Munson at Blake Friedmann who have shared so much of the 'John Marshal' experience with me. To the editorial team at Little, Brown – Barbara Daniel and Joanne Dickinson for letting me get on with my work in my own way, and to Richenda Todd for letting me get away with nothing – which I truly appreciate when I am too close to the narrative to see wood for trees – or to tell north from south!

I would also like to thank Alison King for showing me John FitzGilbert the man, and taking me beyond the brief hints provided by chroniclers and poets.

I am grateful to Angela Kennedy and Frank Garton for talking to me about living with a visual disability.

My husband Roger continues to be totally good-natured and amenable concerning my obsessions with various medieval men, but as he's known me since I was seventeen, I guess he's used to my foibles by now – but my love to him anyway for understanding!

My thanks must also go out to fellow friends and professionals in the RNA and the various online communities including Friends and Writers, Penman Review and UK Novelists, who aid my writing efforts by ensuring that my frequent moments of procrastination are fun and profitable – in that I can always learn something new.

Les proz e les vassals
Souvent entre piez de chevals
Kar ja li coard n'i chasront

The brave and the valiant
are to be sought often between the hooves of horses
for never will cowards fall down there

L'Histoire de Guillaume le Maréchal

KINGS OF ENGLAND

THE CONTINENTAL DYNASTIES 1066–1216

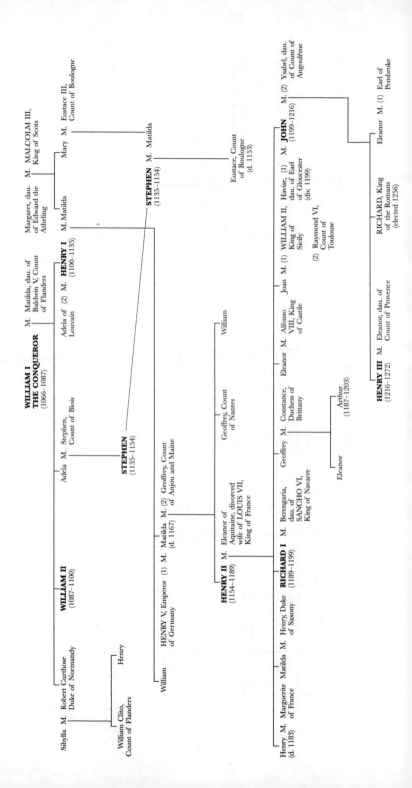

MARSHAL FAMILY TREE

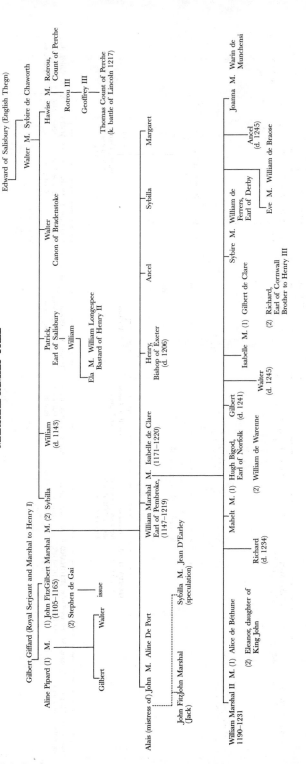

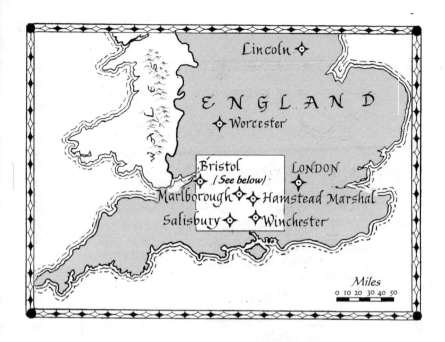

Lincoln

E N G L A N D

Worcester

Bristol
(See below)

LONDON

Marlborough   Hamstead Marshal

Salisbury   Winchester

Miles
0 10 20 30 40 50

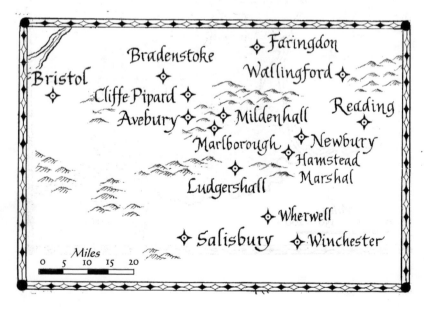

Faringdon

Bradenstoke

Wallingford

Bristol

Cliffe Pipard

Avebury   Mildenhall

Reading

Marlborough   Newbury

Hamstead
Marshal

Ludgershall

Wherwell

Salisbury   Winchester

Miles
0   5   10   15   20

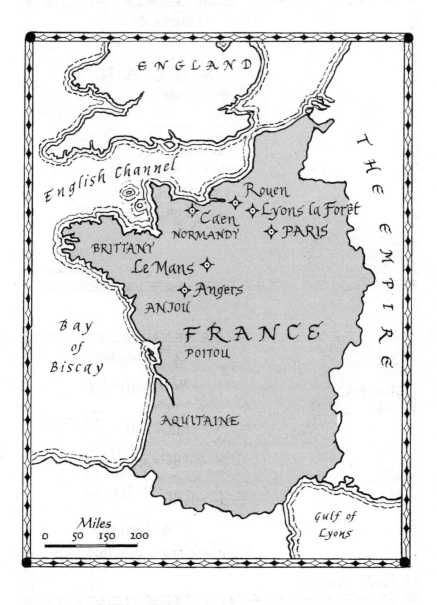

1

Vernon-sur-Seine, Normandy, Autumn 1130

'Why,' John FitzGilbert asked with icy displeasure, 'does the list say palfreys when the beasts I've just seen in the stables are common nags?' He cast his deputy a penetrating look from eyes the hue of shadowed water.

'My lord?' A muscle ticked in the fleshy pouch beneath the man's left eye.

Tresses of autumn sunlight swept across the rushes carpeting the great hall of King Henry's hunting lodge and trailed the edge of a trestle table, illuminating the lower third of a parchment covered in a scribe's swift scrawl. A strand of gold touched the back of John's hand and twinkled on the braid cuffing his tunic. 'One's spavined, another's got mange and the chestnut's old enough to have carried Moses out of Egypt!' He stabbed a forefinger at the offending entry on the exchequer roll. 'It says here that Walter Picot renders five palfreys in payment of his debt to the King. If those creatures out there are palfreys, I'll salt my boots and eat them.'

'My lord, I—'

'No excuses, Ralph. Return these sorry beasts to Picot and make him replace them with others fit to the

1

description. If he refuses, report to me and I will deal with him. I'm not in the habit of giving house room to other men's leavings.' Leaning back from the table, he laid his hand to his sword hilt in deliberate emphasis. As King Henry's marshal, he was responsible for discipline in the hall and a sword was part of his daily apparel rather than an accoutrement of ceremony and war. 'Of course,' he added, rubbing a reflective thumb over the smooth curve of the pommel, 'if I find out that Walter supplied five good palfreys and someone has been using my absence from court to line his own purse by switching them for nags . . .' He let the sentence hang unfinished.

Ralph licked his lips. 'I am sure it is not the case, my lord.'

John raised a sceptical eyebrow. Leaning forward again, he placed his hand upon the parchment, arching long fingers over the words. 'I expect absolute loyalty and competence from my men and I reward it generously. Play me false or let me down and I will find out – and if you live to regret it, you will be unfortunate. Understood?' John was barely five and twenty, but had won the right to be the King's marshal by more than heredity. Three years ago, he had defended a challenge to his position in trial by combat and settled the matter so convincingly that no one had questioned his abilities to fight or administrate since.

'My lord, I will attend to the matter,' Ralph answered, pale and set-lipped.

'See that you do.' John picked up the parchment and studied the next entry concerning quantities of bread for feeding the royal hounds. Usually he would have delegated the scrutiny of such lists to a subordinate but having been absent from court dealing with personal matters of estate in the wake of his father's death, he needed to stamp his authority on his office like a seal impressing warm wax.

'Christ, how much bread does a dog—?' He stopped and looked up as a shadow blocked his light. 'My lord?'

'Never mind that,' said Robert FitzRoy, Earl of Gloucester, standing over the trestle, arms folded, the sun streak now warming his blood-red tunic. 'Come outside. There's something you need to see.'

John mentally sighed. It was pointless telling Gloucester he wanted to finish assessing these accounts before he went anywhere. As the King's eldest son, albeit bastard born, Gloucester wielded a powerful influence at court. It was in John's interests to be accommodating; besides, the man was a friend, ally and sponsor.

He pushed to his feet. Gloucester was tall, but John topped him by the length of an index finger, although the Earl's broader frame made them look much of a size. John picked his hat off the board and tucked it through his belt, thereby conceding he was unlikely to return to his accounts this side of the dinner hour.

'My cousin Stephen has a new horse.'

Pinning his cloak, John stepped around the trestle. 'Take those tallies to my chamber,' he commanded over his shoulder to Ralph, 'and I want to see the military service receipts for the months I've been gone. I'll expect a report on what's been done about that walking dog meat in the stables before noon tomorrow.'

'Yes, my lord.' His deputy bowed, sweat beading his brow.

John quickened his pace to catch up with Robert, his stride long and confident.

'They know you're back,' the latter remarked with amusement.

Mordant humour curved John's lips. 'They had better do.'

'You've found foul deeds hidden in the murk?'

John's smile deepened, putting creases in his cheeks, showing where one day harder lines would develop. 'Not as yet. Some questionable horses and dogs that appear to be eating best wheaten bread in suspicious quantities, but nothing I cannot handle.'

'And the women?'

'Nothing I cannot handle there either,' John said casually.

Robert laughed aloud and set his arm across John's shoulders. 'I should hope not. Ah, it's good to have you back!'

The courtyard was a churn of noisy, organised chaos, signalling the imminent departure of the hunt. Amid misty clouds of breath and pungent aromas of horse and stable, nobles were mounting up or conversing in groups as they waited for their grooms. Dogs snuffled underfoot, or, quivering with anticipation, strained on taut leashes. John observed the rib-serrated flanks of a white gazehound and thought about the accounts he had just been reading.

A crowd had gathered to watch a ruddy fair-haired man putting a powerful roan stallion through its paces. Robert and John joined the group and stood with arms folded to watch the performance.

'Spanish,' John said with an appreciative eye and felt a twinge of envy. As the King's marshal, he owned fine horses himself but a beast of this calibre was too rich for his purse. However, it was standard fare for Stephen, Count of Mortain, King Henry's nephew and so high in favour that he was flying above most other folk at court. Not that Stephen was haughty with other men because of it. John had heard Henry's daughter, the Empress Matilda, remark with contempt that Stephen would drink water with the horses like a common groom rather than quaff wine out of a precious goblet as a man of his rank ought to do.

Stephen made the horse rear and paw the air. A broad

grin lit up his face and his eyes sparkled with pleasure. He brought the roan down to all fours and dismounted but only to spring back into the saddle facing backwards. Then he scissored round to the fore and swept a flourish to his appreciative audience. He was so exuberant that it was impossible not to be caught up in his high spirits and John began to laugh and then applaud with the rest of the crowd.

Gloucester cupped his hands to shout at Stephen, 'Have you ever thought of performing such tricks for a living?'

John glanced sidelong at the Earl, noting that his mirth was tinged with asperity. There was an edge of rivalry between Gloucester and his cousin Stephen. Both were magnates; both were close kin to the King. All the time they were slapping each other's backs and drinking together in the hall they were jostling for position and favour.

'Many times!' Stephen called back cheerfully. He gathered the reins and settled the horse, patting its neck, tugging its ears. 'But then I would lose the joy.'

'John has to earn his crust keeping the court concubines in order. I haven't seen any diminishing in his enthusiasm for the task, and it involves just as much sleight in the saddle as yours!' Robert retorted.

Stephen gave a knowing grin. 'I wouldn't dare to compete with the anvils and hammers of a royal marshal on that score!' he quipped, to the laughter of all, for everyone knew these were the time-honoured symbols of a marshal as well as a euphemism for the male reproductive equipment. John's reputation in the latter department was somewhat notorious and he did nothing to play it down. Now he merely flourished a sardonic bow.

Stephen's attention focused on a point beyond his audience. 'The King is here,' he said. 'Best mount up or you'll be left behind.' He nudged the roan towards a stocky, grizzle-haired man who had emerged from one of the lodging halls and was setting his foot to the stirrup of a handsome bay. A heavy gold clasp pinned his short hunting cloak at his shoulder. Two swaggering young men – Robert de Beaumont, Earl of Leicester, and his twin brother Waleran, Count of Meulan – accompanied him. They were cronies of Stephen and treated with suspicion by Robert of Gloucester because of their intimacy with his father the King. Meulan had proved a traitor in the past, but the King had forgiven him his transgressions and welcomed him back at court. Beaumont, the more circumspect of the two, cast an observant glance around as he took his courser's reins from a groom. John thoughtfully assessed their proximity to Henry. This was another area where he needed to focus following his absence. Every subtle change and nuance had to be taken into account in order to survive and advance at court.

Stephen greeted them all with natural bonhomie. John thought – with further admiration for the Count of Mortain – that such ebullience was also a way of opening doors and disarming men of their caution.

'You're riding out with us,' Robert told John as he called up his mount and set his foot to the stirrup. 'I've had your horse saddled.' He snapped his fingers to a groom who led forward John's freckled grey courser.

John tugged his hat from his belt and pulled it down over his blond-brown hair. 'Thank you, my lord,' he said with muted enthusiasm.

Robert chuckled. 'You don't mean it now.' He tossed John a boar spear, which the latter caught mid-haft with a lightning reflex, 'but you will in a while.'

Cantering along a forest trail, the first autumn leaves glimmering from the trees in flakes of sunlit amber, the ground firm but springy under the grey's hooves, John realised

6

Robert had been right. The powerful surge of his horse was exhilarating and the rich colours and deciduous scents of the autumn woods filled him with sensual pleasure.

The King was hunting hard, pushing his horse and the dogs to their limit, his cloak bannering out behind him and his body curled over his mount's neck like a wave. The beaters flushed a boar from a thicket and Henry was after it like the devil in pursuit of a soul, one hand to the reins, the other hefting a spear. John spurred after him with the rest of the hunt, ducking under tree branches, forcing his way through thorny bramble thickets. The thud of hooves upon forest mulch, the belling of hounds and the hard breath of his horse were a joy to his ears. Count Stephen pushed past him on his new roan, the Beaumont twins charging behind accompanied by the King's cup-bearer William Martel. Robert of Gloucester scoured their heels, his mouth set in grim determination. Prudently, John reined back and gave room to Henry's constable, Brian FitzCount, lord of Wallingford. John was his deputy in the household and careful to keep on his good side. FitzCount acknowledged John's courtesy with a flash of teeth and a fisted wave as he spurred on amid a flurry of dogs.

The hunting horn sounded to John's left, but veering with the wind. He pivoted the grey towards it, but hastily drew on the rein and adjusted his grip on his spear as the undergrowth before him rustled with vigorous motion. An instant later three wild pigs broke from a deep thicket of bramble and ivy and charged past him so closely that his horse plunged and shied. He saw earth-smeared tushes, coarse rusty hair and the moist gleam of snouts. Controlling his mount with the grip of his knees, he grasped the spear like a javelin and cast it with all his strength, piercing one of the boars behind the left shoulder to the full depth of the iron blade. The pig leaped and fell in a thresh of limbs and deafening squeals. The spear haft snapped off, leaving a bloody stump in the wound. John drew his sword and manoeuvred the grey cautiously towards his victim. Even mortally injured, a wild boar was capable of eviscerating a dog and slashing a horse's leg to the bone. The boar struggled to rise, failed, shuddered and was still.

As John dismounted, the forest around him filled with running dogs, beaters and huntsmen on foot. In the distance, a horn was blowing for another kill – probably acknowledging the King's success. He gazed at his own prize and, as a dog-keeper whipped the hounds to heel and his heartbeat slowed, he suddenly grinned like a youth.

By the time the main hunt had turned back to investigate the second blowing of the mort, John was watching two beaters heave his prize across a pony's back.

'You outdo us all,' King Henry told him, his smile exposing a crowd of chipped, life-worn teeth. His own trophy dangled limply over a pack saddle.

'Sire, I was fortunate and I had little choice.'

'Perhaps not, but it won't harm your reputation for being a dangerous man to cross. Anyone who tackles a boar on his own deserves whatever fate deals to him – in your case, John FitzGilbert, an accolade.'

'Thank you, sire,' John replied with a grave bow. 'Indeed, it was three,' he added as he straightened, 'but I am sorry to say that two escaped my spear and ran off in that direction.'

Henry laughed and his eyes shone with a huntsman's relish. 'Then you have a grain of prudence and it leaves more for the chase.' He gestured to his attendants and spurred off in the direction John had indicated, the hunting horn blowing the away.

Stephen started to follow his uncle, but paused to lean

8

down and slap John's shoulder. 'Well done!' Genuine admiration gleamed in his blue eyes.

'It was the heat of the moment,' John said with modest dismissal.

'Proves you don't need a Spanish horse to make an impression,' Gloucester remarked acidly as he turned his own horse.

Another boar and two roebuck later, the hunters stopped at a pre-arranged clearing to replenish their energy with the victuals the King's attendants had gone ahead to prepare.

The hunting party fêted and teased John for bringing down a boar single-handed. He shrugged off the praise because he knew any of the others would have done the same, and open boasting was not in his nature; nevertheless, he was quietly pleased.

He was crouching by the firepit, toasting a chunk of bread on a pointed stick, when Gloucester sauntered over to join him. 'You know my sister is still in Rouen,' he said casually after a moment.

John turned the stick, drawing the bread a little away from the heat. 'No sign of reconciliation between her and Geoffrey then?' Shortly before he had left court to attend to his dying father and the affairs of his estate, the King's daughter Matilda had quarrelled with her new husband, the adolescent Geoffrey of Anjou. The youth had sent her home to Normandy, saying he refused to live with such a termagant, let alone bed with her and beget an heir.

Robert turned his mouth down at the corners. 'She's still saying that hell will freeze over before she'll go back to him and he's saying the same about having her back.'

'And your father?'

'Gnashing his teeth in private but still striving for diplomacy. There's not a lot he can do without agreement from either side, is there?'

John removed the toasted bread from the stick. He had had some dealings with Matilda, who liked to style herself 'Empress' and remind everyone that her first marriage had been to the ruler of the Holy Roman Empire, by implication a real man of dignity and standing, not some spotty count's son more than ten years younger than herself. That the youth's father was now King of Jerusalem had not mellowed her attitude one whit. 'No, but there are certain pressures he can bring to bear.' John glanced eloquently towards the King, who was deep in conversation with Stephen of Mortain. The two stood close together in relaxed camaraderie, mirroring each other's body movements as they ate and drank. 'He needs to.' John bit into the crisp, brown crust. 'He has no direct male heir from his marriages and even if he is hale for the moment, he is not young.'

Robert rubbed the back of his neck and scowled. 'Everyone swore to uphold my sister's right to the throne. We've all taken oaths of homage to her.'

'With your father watching every move of every man, who would dare to refuse? Without him, it might be different.' John had been in Rouen for the oath-taking in the great cathedral. His father had been alive then and had sworn allegiance, but the lands they had of the Marshalsea were insignificant and it was the pledges of the magnates that had mattered to Henry.

'What are you saying?'

'That if your father wants Matilda to sit in his place, it would be useful if there were a well-grown grandson or two by the time he starts to feel his years. Like it or not, my lord, men look to be ruled by another man, not a woman.'

Robert made an impatient sound, but his gaze flickered towards his father and Stephen.

10

John speared another piece of bread and held it to the flames. 'He's using Stephen to exert pressure on her, but sometimes you can't tell who's hunting whom. Every creature preys on something weaker than itself or aligns itself to take advantage.'

'You included?'

John gestured around. 'Look at the trees. Winter strips them bare. You can see every knot and crevice, every rotten branch and strong limb. But clad them in green and it is harder to tell. Depending on the season, they are the same but changed.'

'What kind of answer is that?' Robert snapped. 'You talk in foolish riddles.'

John watched the bread begin to turn brown and said quietly, 'Your grandsire was bastard begotten, but he wore a crown. Some say that—'

Robert stepped back as if John had struck him, colour flooding his complexion. 'I know what "some say" and if you are one of them I have misjudged your friendship. I will never take that road. Never!'

John pulled his stick away from the fire. 'You misjudge me no more than you misjudge yourself, my lord.'

Robert looked away. Adjusting the set of his cloak like a cat grooming ruffled fur, he stalked off without another word. John attended to his toasted bread and thought that Robert was vehement because the notion of reaching for the crown appealed to him at some deep level where he would never admit to it. Since childhood, it had been instilled in him that his father's heirs were those born of legitimate marriage. The world had changed since his grandfather, William the Bastard, had ruled Normandy and seized the English throne. Robert had lands, titles and great wealth. His mother's relatives were all welcome at court. His father loved him dearly and kept him deep

11

in his counsels. Even without a crown, the rewards were great and Robert's moral code would keep him walking that straight path, a willing servant to his father's will. Nevertheless, John supposed it was a great temptation to eye the gilded road running parallel and think that, but for the grace of God and the words of a priest, one might have been treading the miles of one's life shod in the purple of kingship. John knew which road he would have taken, but then it was easy to imagine from a distance and a different perspective.

John had been nineteen years old when a crone at the September fair in Salisbury had studied his hands and told him he would beget greatness – that one day a son of his would rule England. John had laughed in her wizened face. He was the son of a minor household serjeant who had thrust his way by cleverness, diligence and loyalty into the position of royal marshal. John had the ambition and ability to build on such foundations, but he was certain they didn't come with a crown attached. The memory of that prediction brought an arid smile to his lips. Dusting crumbs from his hands, he rose from his crouch by the fire and went to question the kennel-keepers about the eating habits of the hounds.

The feast that followed the King's return from the hunt continued deep into the night and John was kept busy in his role of marshal of the court, maintaining order with his mace of authority in hand. Men who desired audience with the King had first to pass him and his ushers. If Henry made a request to talk with a particular person, it was John's duty to see it done. Conversely, if the King wished to avoid someone, John and his men were responsible for making sure Henry was not troubled. Sometimes there were objections, which was why John wore his sword and cultivated a dangerous air. People didn't notice how young the King's marshal was. What they saw was the speed of his reactions and his ability to anticipate trouble and nip it in the bud.

By the time Henry retired to his chamber with a few select members of the court, including Robert of Gloucester, Stephen of Mortain and the Beaumont brothers, the moon was a high white sliver in a star-spun sky. John's ushers had dealt with several drunkards, quelled a brawl between two young hotheads, disarming them of knives in the process, and escorted a bishop back to his lodging after he tripped over Waleran de Beaumont's dog and cracked his head on a trestle.

Satisfied that all was under control, John left the hall and walked to his one-roomed lodging near the stables. A glance as he strolled revealed that the lamps were still burning in the whores' domicile, but that was nothing unusual. Business would continue late into the night. He contemplated stopping by for a word, but decided it could wait until the morrow. He had a pile of tallies and parchments waiting his attention without adding the concerns of the court concubines to the workload.

Like the horses, the dogs and the hawks, the royal prostitutes came within the marshal's remit. John had to see the women fed, clothed, housed and paid for out of the exchequer. Many of the women were looking to become permanent mistresses and there was always fierce competition to join the royal household and seek such an opportunity. John was never short of applicants, although few won past his exacting standards. He well knew the tastes of the King and his magnates – his own come to that. A court prostitute had to have more than fine looks and the ability to give a man the ride of his life. She had to be socially adept and adaptable, and utterly, entirely discreet.

John sometimes thought it would have been easier to collect a bucket of hens' teeth than find women of sufficient calibre.

Arriving at his lodging, John dismissed his chamberlain and squire. Most of his waking hours were spent in company, but he enjoyed moments to himself when he could snatch them. They gave him time to recoup and reflect; to be still and think at leisure. He draped his cloak across his coffer and hung his swordbelt and scabbard on a wall hook. A flagon and a cup stood on a trestle under the shuttered window together with the pile of tallies and parchments from this morning. He poured wine, moved the lamp until he was satisfied with the fall of light upon his work area, and sat down with the sigh of a man letting go of one thing and preparing to tackle another.

He reached for a document lying to the side of the others, its lower edge tagged with Henry's seal. This one was personal business, not a routine matter of palfreys or bread for the hounds. His inner vision filled with the memory of the blushing girl he had seen at mass in the cathedral at Salisbury when he had been home attending to his father's affairs. Aline Pipard's father was recently deceased too, and John had now bought her guardianship, which gave him the right to administer her estates and eventually sell her marriage to whomsoever he chose.

Sipping his wine, he contemplated the document, wondering if she was going to be worth the fee he had paid for her. He hadn't decided what he was going to do about the guardianship – sell the marriage on, or take the girl to wife himself. His father and hers had long been acquainted. He had known Aline from a distance since she was a little girl, but his association with her amounted to no more than a few casual meetings and glances in passing. His purchase was less concerned with family ties than with the available revenues from the Pipard lands and the knowledge that a bird in the hand was worth two in the bush. His acquisition was something to fall back upon should lean times arise. Thoughtfully, he rolled up the document, tied it with a length of silk cord and, having set it aside, commenced work on the routine lists and tallies waiting his attention.

John was on his second cup of wine and had just trimmed a fresh quill when a soft tap at the door interrupted him. He considered ignoring it, but the work was boring and he was in a mood for distraction – probably a female one to judge from the sound of the knock. Leaving his work, he went to open the door and was pleased to discover his assumptions correct. Without a word, he stood aside to let the woman enter the room. She moved to the hearth with fluid, deliberate grace and turned to wait for him.

He dropped the latch, fetched another cup and poured her wine. 'Mistress Damette,' he said courteously. 'To what do I owe this pleasure?' He addressed her by her working name. Her real one was Bertha and she was the youngest of six daughters belonging to an impoverished knight from the Avranchin. It was three years since she had left the enclave of court whores to become the concubine of an Angevin baron.

She responded with a throaty laugh and a knowing look as she accepted the wine. 'You owe it to the fact that you are the King's marshal and I am in need of employment.'

'I gathered as much.' He picked up his own half-finished cup and leaned with feigned nonchalance against the trestle. 'What happened?'

She pursed her lips at him. 'Crusade. He took the Cross and forswore women. He was selling everything he could to raise the money to go and fight for Christ, so I grabbed my silks and furs and left before he had a chance to sell them too.' Her voice developed a sultry edge. 'Otherwise, I'd be here in naught but my shift.' She put the wine down, unfastened her cloak and draped it across the coffer on top of his own. The tight lacing of her gown accentuated every line and curve of her figure.

John looked her up and down. She had burnished dark hair and eyes to match. Lamp and firelight glanced upon orbit and satin cheekbone. His father had originally been responsible for admitting Damette to the court enclave and she had occasionally shared the senior marshal's bed, but never his. He had been a youth learning his trade back then, and even if she was of his years, she had been a deal less innocent. 'An interesting notion,' he said, 'but you know the ways of the court and I'm afraid that "naked under the cloak" is one of the less original ploys these days.'

Her eyes gleamed. 'I think you'll find I have more to offer than that, my lord.'

'Such as?'

She stepped up to him, dipped her forefinger in his wine and slowly rimmed his lips. 'Experience.' She trailed her hand languidly down his body from breastbone to groin, her touch lighter than a breath. 'Skill.'

Lust surged through him, hot and heavy as molten lead. 'You know the rules; the dues owing.' He set his arms to her waist and pulled her against him. The supple pressure of her body was exquisite.

'Oh yes, I know them . . . my lord marshal,' Damette breathed. 'You will have no cause for complaint on any score . . . I promise you.'

Languorous in the aftermath of twice-taken release, feeling as if all sharp edges and discontents had been smoothed

16

out, John folded his hands behind his head and studied the rafters. 'How did you know to call me "my lord"?' he asked curiously.

'Because your deputy told me your father was dead . . . I am sorry for that.' Damette raised herself on one elbow. A rosy flush darkened her breasts and throat, revealing that the pleasure had not been his alone.

He said nothing. She hesitated, then leaned over and cupped his face on the side of her hand. 'I am not sorry you have his position though.'

The haze of satisfaction cleared from his eyes. 'It's no use casting your line in my direction, sweetheart; I'm not a man for taking mistresses. I know too much to be snared by such bait.'

She laughed and bent to kiss the corner of his mouth. 'You may have the face of a sinning angel and a way between the sheets, but I'm not angling beyond mutual interest. You would demand too much – and so would I.'

'That's about the measure of it – especially the last part.' He stroked her hair to keep the moment light, then sat up and reached for his clothes.

'You shield yourself from people, don't you?'

John donned his shirt, rapidly followed by braies and hose. 'Show me a courtier who doesn't.' Padding from the bed, he returned to the trestle and the pile of work still waiting. He was tired, but he had learned to cope without sleep long ago. His father had been wont to say that the time to slumber was in the grave, and John had embraced the philosophy with a whole heart. He looked across at her. 'I don't have to shield myself,' he said. 'The face I wear is the face beneath.'

She rolled on to her stomach and turned towards him, slender ankles raised and crossed, dark hair spilling around her shoulders. 'You'd be surprised.'

'At what?' He sat down and began work.

'At what does lie beneath when you are put to the test. Can I stay until morning?'

'As long as you're quiet.'

'I promise not to snore.'

'That's not what I meant.'

She made a face at him and John almost laughed, but managed to preserve an offhand demeanour.

Borrowing his comb from the coffer, she began to tidy and braid her hair, completely unselfconscious in her nudity. John occasionally glanced and admired. Firm, full breasts; long legs. Damette wouldn't stay long among the whores. She would attract another patron soon enough.

She worked at a tangle. 'I know you do not want me to interrupt you,' she said, 'but you might be interested to know I spent two nights with Geoffrey of Anjou.'

John lowered his quill and eyed her sharply.

'He's a handsome youth, the Empress's husband,' she said. 'Fast to the finish as you'd expect of his years, but a fresh bolt in the bow as soon as his first one's spent.' She gave him an eloquent smile before contemplating the ends of her gathered hair. 'He says he's thinking of going on pilgrimage to Compostela and that he won't have his wife back for all the gold in England.'

'You're certain he said that?'

'Of course I am. He's still too young to have learned discretion. If a man has finished futtering and does not wish to sleep, then often he wants to talk . . . and I am a very willing listener.'

John shook his head. 'Henry won't let him go to Compostela, at least not until this impasse over the marriage has been resolved. He needs his daughter and Geoffrey to beget heirs.'

'Then perhaps Geoffrey is forcing the King's hand, or

18

perhaps he is teasing. I gained the impression he's the kind who likes to throw sticks in the fire for the pleasure of watching them burn.' She secured her braid with a red silk ribbon.

John gave her a speculative look. 'You didn't want to make a bid to become Geoffrey's mistress then?'

She wrinkled her nose and laughed. 'Oh no, he's far too fickle. For the moment he's a prickly youth who needs stroking and reassurance – although when he grows up, he might be worth it.'

John continued with his work for a while, although his mind was split between the parchments and tallies of the marshal's accounts and what Damette had said.

'I could be very useful to you,' she offered, as if sensing the periphery of his thoughts. 'Your father always considered that the things I heard and saw were a great asset to him.'

John studied a tally without focusing on it. He realised now how much his father had protected him in keeping him away from Damette when he was Geoffrey of Anjou's age. 'Then I too will be happy to consider.'

'And the fee?'

'Negotiable.' He put his head down over his work. She plainly knew just how far to push, for she lay down with her back to him and, pulling the coverlet high over her shoulder, at least feigned sleep.

John poured more wine and toasted her huddled form, his eyes lighting with dour humour. If nothing else, tonight's interlude had informed him that he was most certainly back at court.

2

Abbey of le Pré, Rouen, Autumn 1130

'Compostela!' Matilda, dowager Empress of the Holy Roman Empire, and currently cast-off wife of the seventeen-year-old Count of Anjou, spat the word with angry laughter. 'Now I know my husband truly is mad!' The word 'husband' was uttered with disgust, as if she had been eating greens and discovered a slug. 'What's he going to do there? Pray for Saint James to intercede and grant an annulment to this hellish marriage? Jesu let me add my prayers too!' Spots of fury brightened her cheek-bones and brought a dangerous glitter to her eyes.

Leaning against the wall near the door, his rod of office tucked into his belt, John admired her even while being overjoyed she was not espoused to him. Small wonder her marriage to a youth more than a decade younger and of lesser rank was foundering and sinking as swiftly as the ship that had drowned her brother ten years ago. He had told Robert of Gloucester what Damette had said, and Robert was now telling his sister before he escorted her across the Seine to dine with their father at the Tower of Rouen.

'He won't do it.' Robert looked uneasy. 'It's a threat, a whim. He wants to twist the knot a little.'

'Then let him hang himself with it, I care not.'

'Geoffrey has a duty even as much as you do yourself. Our father won't let either of you off the hook, you know that.'

She scowled at her brother, encompassing John with the same look. 'Do not prate to me of duty. I was eight years old when I left my nursery for my first wedding at my father's behest. I married Geoffrey of Anjou because my father wished it. Do you think I would have undertaken either match of my own accord? At least the first time I was an empress and I had respect from my husband and his people. This second marriage is a . . . a vile travesty!'

Robert looked uncomfortable. 'Geoffrey of Anjou will grow up.'

'Into what?' she retorted with a curl of her lip and glared contemptuously at John. 'I suppose you heard the piece about Compostela from one of your whores?'

John bowed his head. 'Where would the court be for information, madam, without the digging of prostitutes and priests?' he asked in a bland voice.

Her eyes narrowed and John braced himself for a tirade, but it didn't come. Instead, she faced her brother. 'I won't go back to him, Rob.'

'Not even if circumstances were different?'

'This marriage has brought me low enough already,' she said bitterly. 'I do not see how circumstances could be different. Geoffrey did the repudiating. Let him do the begging now. If he prefers Compostela and his whores then let him lie in those beds, for he certainly won't lie in mine.'

Her voice was hard with anger and resentment. John thought that if she pitched it lower and used its music, it would be a devastating weapon rather than a hostile instrument, but he doubted that compromise and softness were in her nature. He admired Matilda for her courage, and

21

knew she was dear to Robert – although perhaps such affection was allied to the amount she would have to rely on her half-brother when she inherited Normandy and England.

Matilda stalked away to her maid to have her cloak arranged and pinned.

'At least there's a glimmer of hope,' John murmured to Robert. 'She did say "let him do the begging". That means she's prepared to reconsider should he make an approach.'

'You think so?' Robert looked wry.

'Geoffrey's advisers won't permit him to let Normandy and England slip through his hands, and if it means reconciliation with his wife, then so be it. As you say, he has some growing up to do, but he's not a fool.'

Robert smiled. 'More insights from your informant?'

'It's not all the gossip of whores,' John said tautly.

Robert's smile deepened. 'I know that. You wouldn't be my father's marshal if your wits weren't as sharp as an awl. The way you weigh up men and situations in my father's hall is enviable.'

A bleak smile entered John's eyes. 'It's not enviable,' he said, 'it's necessary.'

Raised upon a windswept mound, Salisbury cathedral faced a rolling landscape populated by ancient stone circles and footpaths that had existed time out of mind. A bitter east wind dappled with snow was sweeping across the Downs and the sky over the church of the Blessed Virgin Mary, with its great new east end, was a lowering grey.

A large congregation filled the long nave but the press of bodies did little to warm the atmosphere. Hacking coughs, red, streaming noses, damp sleeves attested that the usual winter diseases and chills were performing their circuit of misery as December advanced further into darkness.

Aline Pipard tucked her frozen hands under her arms and curled and uncurled her toes which were half-numb and half-burning with swollen, red chilblains. Making an effort, she concentrated on the ritual of the mass which Roger, Bishop of Salisbury, was conducting. His presence was something of an event since he was usually dealing with affairs of state and the royal finances, leaving the administration of his flock to subordinates. Rumour ran that investigations at the exchequer had exposed unto-ward dealings and laxness, and that the Bishop was under a cloud at court, if not exactly in disgrace.

The vapours wisping heavenwards from the censers bore the aroma of frankincense – one of the costly spices brought by the Three Magi to the Christ Child in Bethlehem. Aline's imagination twirled aloft with the exotic, resinous scent. She imagined herself kneeling in worship at the manger in the stable and being bathed in the holy glow surrounding the Virgin and child. *Hosanna in excelsis. Benedictus qui venit in nomine Domini. Hosanna in excelsis.*

Aline adored churches, adored the rituals, the objects, the stories. Even today in the biting cold, she found comfort and solace just by being in God's house. *Pater noster, qui es in coelis: sanctificetur nomen tuum: adveniat regnum tuum: fiat voluntas tua, sicut in coelo, et in terra.* Yesterday, on arriving in Salisbury, she and her mother had learned from Lord Walter the sheriff that King Henry's marshal, John FitzGilbert of Hamstead, had officially purchased the right to her wardship and marriage. There had been a letter from FitzGilbert himself, and a gift of a set of prayer beads. They were made of amber and each one glowed like a globule of hard honey. Lighter than glass or stone, they were warm like a residue of summer as she slipped them through her fingers. Aline had been overwhelmed but uncertain what the gift betokened. Was it a symbol of esteem? Did he mean to marry her, or remain her warden? Following the standard salutation at the beginning of the letter, he had promised to care for herself and her interests with all diligence and duty, but the words had been set out in formal language and the beads were the only personal part of his communication. *Et ne nos inducas in tentationem: sed libera nos a malo.*

She had known John FitzGilbert from a distance since she had been a tiny girl at her mother's knee and he had been an adolescent, accompanying his father to their family on a matter pertaining to the exchequer. She had been struck dumb with shyness before the strangers. The youth's smile and his coltish good looks had tied her being into knots of wonder and embarrassment. She had seen him intermittently since then and he still had that effect on her. The most recent occasion had been here this summer when he was home from court dealing with his affairs following his father's death. He had been talking to Sheriff Walter after the mass. No longer a youth, but a grown man, tall, long-limbed and graceful. His hair was warm brown at the nape and sides, but the summer sun had flashed it with white-gold through crown and fringe and the striking looks of his adolescence had held their promise and matured into virile masculine beauty. As if sensing her scrutiny, he had glanced in her direction. Their eyes had met and she had gasped and looked away in flustered discomfiture. She had not dared raise her head lest he was still gazing at her in that stomach-dissolving way. When he turned to leave, she had risked a peek at his retreating back, both relieved and bereft at his going.

Now came the news that he had bought the right to her lands and her marriage. He had sent her these prayer beads and flooded her timid heart with emotions she had no experience to map. *Domine, non sum dignus ut intres sub*

24

tectum meum; sed tantum dic verbo, et sanabitur anima mea. As she prepared to go forward and take communion, she grasped the paternoster like a talisman and was beset by both longing and fear. Should she pray for him to come and make her his wife, or should she pray that he remained with the King and beguiled her imagination from afar? *Deo gratias.*

Outside the cathedral, the snow had dwindled to tiny white flakes, not much larger than scurf, but cheek-stingingly cold. Aline and her mother bent their heads into the wind and, servants in tow, hurried towards the nearby castle where the sheriff had offered them hospitality and a bed for the night before they returned to Clyffe. Lord Walter had also been in church for the mass, accompanied by his wife and several of their offspring, ranging from his two eldest sons who were almost grown men, to his youngest daughter, a bright little girl of six years old. Aline avoided them. The Salisburys were as boisterous as dogs. However, aware that God was watching, she put a smile on her face as the child skipped past, her plait of brunette-bronze hair bobbing from side to side. The notion of bearing John FitzGilbert children such as this made Aline's stomach leap and churn and she fiddled nervously with her beads. He had touched them; he had chosen them.

A sudden cry followed by shouts of alarm made her spin round, her heart in her mouth. An elderly man making his way from the cathedral had fallen over a chunk of dressed stone left by one of the masons working on improvements to the castle. Aline stared at the jagged twig of bone thrusting through the punctured skin and the blood welling round the wound. The queasy feeling in her stomach intensified. She looked away but it was too

25

late; the image was branded upon her vision. She faltered, saliva filling her mouth.

'Oh Aline, not now!'

Her mother's dismayed cry seemed to come from a tunnelled distance. She felt a tightening grip on her arm as her legs buckled. She was dimly aware of being half carried into one of the dwellings of the castle complex. Someone sat her on a bench and pushed her head down between her knees. The stink of burning feathers filled her nostrils and she retched, bringing up bile and watery spittle into the floor rushes.

'Lady Cecily, I am sorry your daughter is unwell,' she heard a woman say in a concerned voice and as Aline's focus returned, she saw that Lord Walter's wife, Lady Sybire, was standing at the side of the bench.

'It is nothing.' Her mother made an embarrassed gesture of negation. 'She will be all right by and by.'

Beneath Lady Sybire's quiet scrutiny, shame flooded through Aline. The sight of blood made her sick and no one understood. They all thought her weak and foolish. She had tried to control her aversion but to no avail.

The sheriff's wife lightly touched her shoulder. 'I will have someone bring you wine,' she said, then looked round as a commotion heralded the arrival of the injured man, being gently borne by two companions. 'You will excuse me.' Inclining her head, she whisked away to deal with the matter.

'I'm sorry, Mama,' Aline whispered. Swallowing on tears, she made a determined effort not to look in the wounded man's direction.

'Hush, child,' her mother said, her voice gentle, but edged with irritation. 'You must find it in you to deal with these things. What will your warden think of you? You have to prepare yourself for the future.'

26

'Yes, Mama.' Aline felt cold and shivery. Her father had never had much time for her, but providing she stayed out of his way in her chamber or at her prayers, he had not expected more. The notion of what might be required now terrified her.

A servant came from the lady Sybire with a flagon of hot wine and the offer of a quieter, private chamber for Aline to recuperate, which Cecily accepted with alacrity.

'You can learn much from watching Lady Sybire,' she told Aline as they sat down upon another more ornate cushioned bench arranged before a glowing central hearth. 'She is a great lady.'

The heat from the logs made Aline's chilblains tingle and her cheeks burn. The wine warmed her vitals and took the edge off her panic. 'I do not think she likes me, Mama,' she said in a small voice.

'Tush, child,' Cecily replied with impatience. 'She knows neither of us beyond a few words in church and her husband's dealings with your father, God rest his soul. I suppose though she'll want to know more about you now you're the ward of the King's marshal. He is a neighbour after all, even if an absent one.'

Her mother's mention of John made Aline fumble for her new prayer beads, but to her horror, they were no longer at her belt. Uttering a distressed cry, she leaped to her feet and frantically searched the bench and the floor, but there was no flourish of colour, no gleam of honey among the rushes.

'I had them in the other hall!' She searched again, frantic, unable to believe they were gone. 'I know I did, I know it!'

'You must have dropped them.' Her mother laid a soothing hand on her shoulder. 'Calm yourself, daughter, we'll find them.' A note of censure entered her voice.

'They won't turn up for tears and weeping. You should not become so distraught over trifles.'

Aline wiped a panicky hand across her eyes and, striving for composure, started to retrace her steps.

The soft lustre of the amber beads caught little Sybilla's eye as she passed a bench in the main hall. The sheriff's youngest daughter swooped on them with a child's magpie delight, and immediately realised they were the ones belonging to the young woman who had swooned when the man fell over and broke his arm.

The beads glowed like golden water and felt warm and tactile. There was a lovely tassel of gold silk in the middle and a hanger to fasten them to a belt. Sybilla was entranced. She had a feminine adoration of jewellery and trimmings. On a wet afternoon, she loved nothing more than to sit on her mother's bed and riffle through the rings and brooches, belts and buckles in her enamelled jewel casket. Sybilla had no trinkets of her own apart from her bronze cloak brooch and assorted hair ribbons. Her mother said she was too young to own such fripperies and the time would come all too soon when she was grown enough to have a lady's responsibilities and therefore a lady's privileges.

Gazing upon the beautiful set of beads, Sybilla felt an enormous temptation to run to her bed and hide them under her pillow. No one would know; they would be her secret treasure. Perhaps God had meant her to have them by making her the finder. Then again, perhaps Satan was tempting her. She was old enough to know the Ten Commandments and that coveting and stealing were wicked sins. If she took the beads and her mother found out, the punishment would be terrible. Being whipped and denied dinner would be the least of it. She would probably be

28

barred from playing with the jewel casket ever again too.

Sybilla was still deliberating the merits and disadvantages of desire versus honesty when the young woman and her mother returned to the hall. Clearly distraught, the former was searching the floor, stooped over and taking small, slow paces. The mother followed, looking too, eyes screwed up as she struggled to focus. Guilt flashed through Sybilla. With a pang of regret but also a feeling of relief, she approached the women and held out the beads. 'I found these,' she said. A small, righteous glow warmed her stomach.

The young woman fell on them with a joyful cry. 'Thank you, thank you!'

'I told you they would turn up,' the mother said with a roll of her eyes.

'They're very pretty.' Sybilla's gaze was wistful as she watched their owner secure the beads to her belt and stroke them possessively.

'The King's marshal sent them to me,' the young woman told her. 'He's my guardian.'

Sybilla considered the statement with interest. She knew about guardians because her father often had to deal with such matters and she had heard him speaking to her mother about this heiress or that with lands in wardship. She wondered if their guardians sent them presents too. Perhaps it was a good thing to have a guardian.

The mother reached into the purse hanging from her belt and producing a silver halfpenny gave it to Sybilla. 'You're a good girl,' she said.

Sybilla curtseyed politely as she had been taught, and thanked the woman, but the small piece of coin didn't warm her hand as the beads had done and she went to drop it into the bowl of a beggar sitting outside the hall door where it fell with a soft, cold clink.

3

Northampton, September 1131

John paced Northampton castle's wall walk and inhaled the scent of dying leaves and woodsmoke on the sharp midnight air. He was glad to be wearing his fur-lined cloak rather than his lighter indoor one as autumn began to encroach. The leaves were turning, the swine had been herded into the woods to feed on pannage in preparation for the November slaughter, and mushrooms were integral to every meal.

He spoke to the guards, checked that all was well and looked out over a sward populated by the tents and pavilions of men unable to find lodgings in castle, town or auxiliary buildings. John and his officers had been toiling like ants to ensure the smooth operation of their particular concerns. Thus far, everything was running as easily as oiled fleece through an experienced spinster's hands, but one had to be constantly alert for snags and tangles. Although most folk were abed by now and those who weren't had legitimate reasons for being on the prowl, John hadn't allowed the men on duty to relax their vigilance.

The King was holding a grand session of pleas on the morrow and John knew he was going to be busy beyond belief. Still, it would be a lucrative time too, and he was expecting to prosper via the gratuities that would flood the marshal's coffers. For every baron paying homage to the King, John was entitled to five and a half marks. There were lesser tariffs for lesser men, but all owed a fee to John which came as extra to his salaried marshal's wage of two shillings a day.

Having performed a circuit of the battlements, he descended to the ward and strolled to have a word with the porter who was sitting by the door, a pair of mastiffs couched at his feet. The dogs were accustomed to John and forbore to growl but he didn't encourage their familiarity because they were guard dogs. Besides, they had a tendency to slobber.

'All quiet, my lord.' The porter rubbed the jowls of the nearest mastiff. A glint entered his eyes. 'Apart from the comings and goings of folk in search of beds other than their own, of course.'

John half smiled. 'There are always those.'

The porter sniffed the air. 'Rain before dawn,' he announced with the experience of one who spent most of his time outside officiating at doorways. John glanced skywards and made a face. That would mean a crowded hall and short tempers among men forced to wait outside. Mud, damp and the stink of wet wool.

One of the dogs rumbled in its chest and a ridge of fur rose and darkened along its spine. The other lunged to its feet, its muzzle on a level with John's hipbone. The porter ordered it down with a terse command and the mastiff sat on its haunches and stared into the night, its body quivering. 'A bed-searcher,' the porter said. 'Hector can smell 'em a mile off. He knows the scent of a bitch in heat.' He gave a salacious wheeze into the collar of his hood.

31

John smiled wryly at the porter's crude but apt assessment and, bidding the man goodnight, moved off into the dark, as quiet as a shadow himself. The guards stood aside for him as he entered the great hall. A few lamps burned to light men's paths to the privy but the rafters were in darkness and the hearth was banked for the night, not even an ember's glow filtering from beneath the close-fitting cover. There were moments of brighter light like stepping stones where a few souls were keeping late hours in the alcoves allotted to them. A couple of knights belonging to King David of Scotland were playing a protracted game of merels by a stub of candle and someone's squire was sitting cross-legged on his pallet, mending a piece of harness. John picked his way between these islands of light to his own pallet-space, which was divided off from the others by a curtain of heavy Flemish wool. With sleeping room at a premium and so many magnates in residence, even the King's marshal had to bed down in the hall tonight.

Damette was waiting for him as he had suspected she would be. However, given that she was now the mistress of the King's cup-bearer William Martel, he did not expect her to warm his sheets. Rings adorned her fingers tonight, and jewelled pins secured her veil to her hair. She smelled delicious: given other circumstances, he would have devoured her whole.

'I hate those dogs,' she said with a grimace. 'They always growl.'

'It's their duty.' He reached out to stroke one of the dark braids shining below the hem of her veil. 'You are late abroad.'

She gave him a conspiratorial look. 'Since my lord has gone visiting, I thought I would too.'

'Gone visiting where?'

'To the Earl of Leicester's lodging with Meulan, de Senlis and the Bishops of Winchester and Salisbury.'

'A regular conspiracy,' John said with a curl of his lip.

Amused scorn glinted. 'You expect anything else at court and you the King's marshal? Henry is going to make everyone swear an oath on the morrow to uphold the Empress's right to inherit when he dies. Many are not pleased.'

He didn't insult her by asking if she was sure. She wouldn't be here otherwise. It puzzled him for a moment as to why Henry was intending to make men reiterate the oaths they had taken four years ago during the preparations for Matilda's wedding to Geoffrey of Anjou, but then realisation dawned. 'She's going back to him, isn't she?' he said. 'She's returning to Anjou.'

Damette regarded him with smiling annoyance. 'Oh, you're too quick! Yes. She's received a letter from her husband requesting her in humble language to return to him. He wants to heal the rift.'

John lifted a cynical brow. 'Rather say he doesn't want to lose her dower and the prospect of one day being lord of Normandy and England. I suspect he's had some stiff words of advice from his counsellors. I cannot see Geoffrey of Anjou being humble of his own accord.'

'I don't know about that, but you'll hear the rest on the morrow in the hall – and you'll have to add an Angevin party to those already staying here. He's sending an escort to bring her back with all ceremony.'

Inwardly John groaned at the notion of finding yet more sleeping spaces in an environment where men were already packed together like herrings in a barrel.

She gave him a sympathetic smile and stroked the side of his face. 'It's a great pity you're not a man for permanent arrangements, my lord,' she said with a regretful sigh.

'I am afraid that whatever else I bring to you from now on will be a favour from me to you, not an obligation.'

John curbed the retort that without his help, she would be plying her trade on the streets of Rouen and should William Martel tire of her, she would need his help again. Life was always fluid at court and the rules that applied one day might change the next. 'Then I hope you are as generous to me as I have been to you,' he said. Taking her hand, he turned it over and kissed the inside of her wrist.

'I will bear it in mind.' She withdrew from his grasp. Her gown swished over the floor rushes and, moving between pools of light and shadow, she was gone. John exhaled and lay down on his rope-framed bed. He didn't want to sleep. Her visit had set him on edge. His body needed a woman and his mind was turning like a dog on a spit wheel. Where in the name of God's lance was he going to put the representatives of the Count of Anjou? And what were the implications of renewing the oath of allegiance to the Empress?

Uttering an impatient growl, he left his pallet and went in search of his ushers and deputies. If he was wakeful, they could be wakeful too. There would be time for swiving and slumber later when the Empress had gone on her way.

Crossing the ward, he saw William Martel emerging from Robert of Leicester's chambers. Martel noticed him too and stopped, his expression freezing. John nodded his head in courtesy and strolled over to him. 'God's greeting, messire.'

'Do you never sleep, Marshal?' Martel's belligerent tone revealed his discomfort. His stance was aggressive with shoulders back and legs planted apart.

The creases showed in John's cheeks, although he didn't smile. 'I find it instructive to prowl the night hours,' he said. 'It helps me to think and, besides, it's my duty to be on guard. And you, messire, do you not sleep either?'

Martel shrugged. 'I'm for my bed now.'

'Ah.' John glanced at the doorway from which Martel had emerged and hoped Damette was quick on her feet. 'Sometimes it is useful to burn late candles with men of a like mind.'

A muscle flexed in Martel's jaw. 'What of your own mind, FitzGilbert? With whom would you burn wax to the stub?'

'Most likely myself on the King's business, but if not, then with one of the whores. We're not so different, are we?'

Martel fixed John with a narrow gaze, which John returned implacably until the other man yielded and, disengaging, walked swiftly away. In a contemplative mood, John continued towards the gatehouse.

Matilda wore her empress's crown to take the oaths of allegiance from the gathered barons. Strings of pearls dripped from the gem-set circlet at her brow. Her face was as smooth and cold as marble and her dark eyes were guarded. John watched men give their promises and wondered how many would keep them when Henry was dead. The atmosphere was edgy. He had warned his men to be on the lookout for trouble and to stamp down hard on any minor incident before it could escalate.

When it came his own turn to kneel to Matilda, he went forward confidently, set his hands between hers and swore his oath in a strong, firm voice. But the words tasted strange in his mouth and, within himself, he was deeply uneasy. Her lips were soft as she gave him the kiss of peace, closed mouth to closed mouth. Somehow, he had expected them to be hard and unyielding. He wondered

35

what it would be like to bed such a woman. Would all that cold pride melt like hot wax when kindled, or was her element stone? The notion of having her rule England as Queen and Normandy as Duchess filled him with disquiet, yet what alternative was there? He was the King's marshal and depended upon the royal goodwill for his status and livelihood.

The feast following the ceremony was a strange affair. Men's voices were loud with bonhomie and upon his great chair at the dais table King Henry smiled and appeared to be genuinely pleased with the oath-taking and its re-iteration of his intention to have his daughter succeed him. Matilda's expression remained inscrutable. Whatever her feelings about returning to Anjou and her young husband, she was keeping them to herself.

'You look troubled, John,' said Robert of Gloucester, pausing to speak on his way to the latrine.

John grimaced. 'So would you if you'd had to find sleeping space for all those Angevins without ruffling the dignity of others.'

'You always manage.'

John lifted one eyebrow. He was good at what he did and most of the time could perform his duties with only one hand on the reins, but it meant that expectations were high. *Don't worry, John can do it*, was both a compliment and a concern. 'Actually,' he said, 'I was wondering how many here today will hold to their oaths in the future.'

Robert tugged his earlobe and looked uncomfortable. 'Only God and men's consciences will tell you that. At least my sister is returning to her husband. There is hope for a good outcome and my father is much pleased.' He glanced towards the dais where the King was laughing at something his Queen had said, although his gaze was fixed hungrily on Isabelle, the sister of Waleran and Robert Beaumont.

Certain rumours concerning Henry and Isabelle were rife and probably true. What price advancement and royal favour? Not having a sister, John didn't have the option of finding out. 'That is reassuring to hear, my lord,' he said politely.

Robert gave him a look and continued on his way to the latrine and John sighed. When men such as himself and the Earl of Gloucester, who were staunch to Henry's wishes, had their doubts, and when others joined to mutter in little enclaves in the dark of night, it made for an uncertain future. He had kept his knowledge about last night's gathering to himself but with a feeling of deep unease. Sooner or later, he would have to decide with which pack to run, and hope not to make the wrong decision.

4

Hamstead, Berkshire, Autumn 1132

John's fortified manor at Hamstead guarded the river valley of the Kennet midway between Marlborough and Reading. He had been born in the chamber above the timber hall that his grandsire had built in the year following King William's great survey of England. The place had been improved upon and renovated by his father, when funds permitted, and John had maintained the fabric. However, he had plans that extended the buildings far beyond their current modest proportions. His ambition was to see a fine castle marking the skyline one day.

His arrival was the signal for a bustle of activity. The hall was swept and the bed linens hastily aired. Servants stuffed the undermattress on the great bed with fresh sweet hay and shook and plumped up the top one of goose down. Sconces and candle holders were cleaned of old deposits and fresh candles set in their sockets. The best napery was fetched from the linen coffer and draped upon the lord's table in the hall. The silver-gilt cup his father had used was set at John's right hand. He should have been well satisfied, but sitting alone in his chamber later that night, a flagon to hand, a brazier warming his feet and his ponderings lit by the scented yellow glow of good beeswax candles, he was restless.

While engaged about the King's business, his days were so busy that he had little time to think beyond his occupation. Here, without the constant flurry of tasks and with only his servants and retainers for company, he felt as if the walls had expanded and put him in a place of echoes and dusty memories. He needed something to colour the gaps and lessen the shadows.

Planning the future, deciding how to develop his influence and prosperity, helped a little, for he enjoyed devising strategies. Anticipating and being one step ahead was something he did well. But building the future meant building for future generations too – as his father had done, and his grandfather before.

Until recently, he had never thought beyond his immediate physical need for a woman – as a pleasure and a necessary release. Being in charge of the court whores meant that he never had to go without. But since his father's death and his purchase of the wardship of Aline Pipard, his mind had turned towards more permanent arrangements. It would be satisfying to have a wife sitting opposite him now, plying her embroidery, a son in the cradle and another one growing in her belly. Robert of Gloucester had several offspring. Stephen had been waxing lyrical about his own small sons, Baldwin and Eustace. The Empress Matilda had returned to her young husband in order to fulfil her father's wishes for the succession, and expected a child in the spring. Everyone he knew was marrying and begetting future generations. Over the last year, he had made several bids at court for heiresses to lands more extensive than the Pipard estates, but others with greater resources and influence had offered more. It had been hinted at, although not openly said, that he was aiming too high; that he might be the King's marshal, but not of sufficient rank to wed the women whose hands and estates he sought. Without promotion from Henry, he had reached a level above which he was never going to rise. He was a royal servant: a big fish in a small pool to those outside the world of the curia – and a minnow challenging pikes to the denizens within it.

He reached for the flagon and realised he had drunk the contents to the lees. It wasn't good to drink alone, but tonight he hadn't particularly wanted to socialise with his men and he had had no intention of bringing one of the servant girls or village women to his chamber. They wouldn't know what to talk about or how to behave, and bedding with one from such a small community would only lead to complications.

John rose to his feet and wove unsteadily to his bed. It was an effort to remove his boots, but he didn't call for his squire or chamberlain. He was seldom in his cups and didn't want them to see him stripped of his usual grace and control. He flopped down on the sun-bleached sheets, the two mattresses yielding to his weight. Rolling to his side, he closed his eyes and decided that on the morrow he would put in hand a visit to his ward at Clyffe.

In the small timber church at Clyffe, Aline crossed herself before the altar and rose from her knees. It was a distance from the manor, which had no chapel of its own, a matter about which her father had been wont to grumble, but he had never done anything about it. Nevertheless, Aline tried to attend confession at least once a week and mass as often as she could. She frequently thought that had she not been an heiress, she would have chosen the religious life. There was order in prayer. The rhythms and repetitions were soothing and calmed her soul. To be a

40

nun, to wear Christ's ring on her finger, that would be a fine thing.

Followed by Edith, her maid, she returned reluctantly to the world outside and allowed the waiting groom to help her up on to the pillion position of his cob while Edith mounted her donkey. The sky was threatening rain and a chill wind blustered across the Downs, whipping her veil about her face like the wings of a bird. Shivering, Aline huddled inside her cloak.

As the cob plodded through the timber gateway of the manor house, Aline noticed the fine palfreys tethered by the trough and her stomach leaped. As far as she knew, they were not expecting guests, and she didn't recognise any of the horses.

The two smartly equipped serjeants standing with the beasts saluted her and Edith as they rode past. Once into the courtyard proper, Aline allowed the groom to lift her down from the cob, brushed pale horse hairs from her gown, and hurried into the hall. Then she stopped in her tracks, her limbs suddenly gelatinous, for John FitzGilbert was standing by the fire talking to her mother. Her heart began to pound. She wondered if she could escape to the upper chamber without him seeing her, but even as she hatched the thought, he looked up and trapped her in the straight intensity of his stare.

Her mother's tone was gentle but peremptory. 'Aline, come here, child. Your guardian is here to pay his respects and see that we have everything we need.'

Swallowing on panic, Aline advanced to the hearth and, keeping her gaze on the tiles around the firepit, dropped a deep curtsey. 'My lord,' she whispered, before her throat closed.

She felt her arm taken in a firm grip, drawing her to her feet, and then a finger beneath her chin, tilting her face towards the light from the unshuttered window. 'Aline,' he said.

She raised her lids, met his gaze and felt it burn her. It took every iota of her will to hold her ground but she stiffened her spine and clutched the comforting smoothness of the prayer beads he had given her.

He lowered his hand and gestured. 'I see you have the gift I sent to you.'

'Yes, my lord,' she answered in a high, strained voice.

'She treasures them,' her mother intervened again. 'They are never off her person.'

He walked to the window and looked out, arms folded.

Pale with anxiety, Aline glanced at her mother. The older woman shook her head and made a calming gesture.

John turned round and gave the sigh of a man reaching a decision. 'I am of a mind to make a marriage of this wardship and join the Pipard lands to my own. If your daughter is willing, then I desire to make a formal betrothal.'

Aline gasped, feeling as if she had been punched in the solar plexus.

'My lord, forgive us, this is sudden,' Cecily said.

Through her shock, Aline saw his lips curve in a grim half-smile. 'Not that sudden. You have known of the possibility for more than two years. Nevertheless, I am prepared to wait a while longer and give you time to adjust.' Returning to the women, he took Aline's hand. 'Are you willing?'

Aline swallowed and darted a frantic look at her mother. Was she willing? The latter made a shooing gesture behind John's back and nodded. 'Y . . . yes, my lord, you do me great honour,' Aline said. There was no other possible answer. When she wasn't dreaming about being a nun, her thoughts were both pleasured and troubled by images

42

of this man who had arrived out of nowhere and was now proposing to make her his wife.

'Then I am content.' He raised her captured hand to his lips and kissed her fingers in the manner of a courtier. 'Do you go and dress in your finest and I will give you a ring and a vow to go with it.' He released her, but Aline stayed where she was, rooted by shock.

'Go to, child.' Her mother stepped forward and propelled her towards the stairs. 'My lord Marshal will think you a lackwit!'

Aline managed another abashed curtsey to John, then fled towards the stairs.

'Best go with her,' John said with a tilt of his head, 'or else she'll be bolting herself in her chamber and refusing to come out.'

'I am sorry, my lord. My daughter . . .'

'. . . is shocked, I can see that.' He looked rueful. 'You say you are willing to wait . . . for how long?'

John briefly pondered. 'Depending on the whereabouts of the court, let us say next summer?'

Cecily let out a sigh of relief. 'You are generous, my lord. It has been one of my greatest fears – and hers – that you would sell her marriage to a stranger on the moment. You do not know how grateful I am.'

'It is not generosity but common sense that stays my hand. I would no more take her to wife now than I would ride a colt into battle. It is as clear as daylight she needs time to prepare.'

'Nevertheless, thank you.'

She curtseyed and hurried away. John returned to the window and sat upon the cushioned bench beneath the sill. Aline Pipard was a frightened girl, plainly less adult than her actual years. Tongue-tied, nervous. Yet despite his reservations at her lack of maturity, he acknowledged

43

that it was part of her appeal. There was no artifice in her blush and utter innocence in the darting glances she cast at him from those wide eyes. She stirred the part of him that was jaded by the pretence of the court and the subtle ways of the women who made their living by stalking its corridors. There would be neither pretence nor artifice with Aline. He spread the silk tassel of the cushion and studied the fanned-out threads. If he made a marriage with her, it wouldn't be all of his life, either. Far from it. The court was his work, his prestige and his livelihood, but to have her purity in which to cleanse himself of the murk appealed to him. Give her a little longer to grow up and she would have to do. He was sufficiently pragmatic to realise that a greater marriage was unlikely to happen.

5

Oxford, March 1133

An hour before sunrise, John quietly left his bed, his movement stirring a faint aroma of musky perfume from the
sheets. Earlier in the night it had been occupied by one
of the new concubines – a chestnut-haired girl called
Celeste who was still on probation. She was unpolished,
but a fast learner with endless legs, a dazzling smile and
a sharp wit. Another one who would go far and no doubt
wind up as some man's mistress, perhaps even the King's.
Rumour had it he was starting to tire of Isabelle de
Beaumont – although not of the company of her twin
brothers who were still deep in his counsel.

He swilled his face in the ewer, dressed, and left his
lodging which huddled in the shadow of King Henry's
new tower. A stiff breeze blew from the north, making
the day seem more like winter than the first week of spring
and he shivered as he crossed the bailey.

The gates were still shut, but a greening light tinged
the eastern sky and the porter was poking his fire to life
in order to put his frying pan over the coals. John's gaze
sharpened as he saw that Brian FitzCount, lord of
Wallingford, was keeping the man company. Being Henry's

constable, FitzCount was nominally overseer of the marshal's department, although to all intents and purposes he let John run it as he wished. FitzCount was the bastard son of Alain Fergant, former Count of Brittany, and had been raised at the Norman court where Henry treated him like a son.

John approached the fire and bowed in greeting. 'You are abroad early this morning, my lord.'

'I must be if I am ahead of you,' answered FitzCount with a dry smile. 'I have never known a man to need so little sleep – except perhaps your father. I still remember him wagging his finger at me when I was a squire and telling me sleep was for the grave.'

'It was a favourite saying of his.'

'He spoke a deal of common sense.' FitzCount rubbed his hands together then held them out to the fire with a sigh. 'Even so, I wouldn't usually abandon my bed this early, but I have duties at Wallingford.'

John nodded but said nothing. Brian was lord of Wallingford in respect of Maude his wife. Despite being more than six years wed, they had no heirs and conducted their marriage from a distance, but John supposed FitzCount had to put in an appearance now and again and hope sons would come of it. Everyone knew FitzCount was devoted to the Empress and she to him, even if their behaviour towards each other was exemplary. Not even the hardened court gossips could find a trace of scandal. But the way they looked at each other was revealing: the acknowledgements, the things that did not have to be said, because they were already known.

'I hear you are to be married, Marshal,' FitzCount said.

John watched the light brighten in the east. 'Yes, my lord, before the court returns to Normandy.'

'Will you bring your wife across the Narrow Sea with you?'

'Would you bring yours except on necessary occasions?'

FitzCount made a face. 'Probably not. Court and domestic hearth are like drinking ale and wine together. They don't mix.'

The sudden beating of a fist on the outside of the great doors caused both men to jump. Cursing, the porter abandoned his breakfast preparations and went to slide the bolts and unlock a small door cut into the bigger one. The royal messenger, who had been waiting outside, stepped over the threshold leading a blowing nag, its saddlebags fat with sealed parchments. John knew him well. He was nicknamed Absalom because of his silky long hair, although unlike his biblical namesake, he had yet to come to grief by getting it tangled in a tree. Currently he was wearing it in a neat, almost feminine braid, but there was nothing feminine about the sword at his left hip or the jut of his jaw. Absalom was as tough as a peasant's toenails. FitzCount had stiffened at the sight of him, which didn't surprise John. There could only be one reason for this dawn apparition after an obvious ride through the night.

Absalom gave them a dazzling grin. 'Great news, my lords! The Empress was delivered of a son at Le Mans on the fifth day of March. He has been christened Henry, for his grandsire. My lord the King has an heir, as he desired!'

'God be praised!' Colour flushed FitzCount's throat and face. 'The Empress herself, she is well?'

John's gaze flickered to his companion as he heard the betraying anxiety in his voice.

'Yes, my lord,' Absalom replied. 'She is in good health and recovering well. The baby is not big, but he's robust

47

and strong. I saw him in the cradle before I set out. The Empress desired me to see him so that I could make report to the King her father. He has red hair like his sire . . .'

'Such hair runs in the Empress's family too, on her father's side,' said FitzCount.

'That explains it then, my lord.' Absalom chuckled. 'Norman lion, not Angevin fox.'

FitzCount laughed, and taking a ring from his little finger gave it to Absalom in token of thanks. The messenger bowed, touched his forehead, and led his horse towards the stables.

'Good news indeed.' FitzCount blew out between puffed cheeks. He clapped his hand to John's shoulder, visibly struggling with emotion.

'It makes the road ahead a little more certain,' John replied. 'You will excuse me, my lord. With such news abroad there is bound to be high celebration. I had better warn my men.'

FitzCount swallowed and withdrew his hand from John's shoulder. 'Of course,' he said and busily adjusted the fastening of his cloak as if it were a closure on feelings he should not have revealed. 'And I have a day's ride to Wallingford ahead of me.'

'Then God speed you, my lord.'

With a brusque nod, FitzCount departed, and John turned to his own duty.

6

Winchester, Midsummer 1133

In a small private chamber in Winchester castle, Aline suffered her attendant women to make the last tugs and tweaks to her wedding gown before she went to chapel. The fabric was a soft blue wool, embroidered at the hem with a pattern of circles worked in silver thread. Her hair, unbound as a symbol of her virginity, had been combed and smoothed until it shone like polished pinewood. A chaplet of fresh white dog roses and columbine crowned her brow and her cloak was pinned with a beautiful brooch of delicate blue enamel work. She had been sick twice already that morning and her mother had dosed her with a ginger tisane to settle her stomach before pinching her cheeks hard to give them some colour. 'You can't go to your marriage with a face like a new cheese,' she had said, fussing around Aline like a housewife about to take a heifer to market.

John's position as the King's marshal meant that the marriage was being celebrated at court. Aline had never been to Winchester and had been overwhelmed at the size of the town and the constant hurry and bustle, so different from her own quiet existence at Clyffe.

Winchester was the seat of England's treasury and John had told her the town was second only in size and importance to London. Rather than filling her with wonder, the detail had made her feel small and inadequate. Her only experience of such large gatherings had been occasional visits to Salisbury Fair and the cathedral, which hardly compared to Winchester with the court in residence. Aline felt like a stranger in a foreign land peopled by assured, sophisticated inhabitants, who could see straight through her, knew she was not one of them and scorned her for it. She was trying her best not to disgrace herself or her future husband, but knew her best was not good enough.

'You look beautiful,' said Sybire of Salisbury, who had stopped by to wish Aline well.

Aline swallowed and thanked her in a tight, small voice.

Sybire laid a compassionate hand on Aline's sleeve. 'Don't worry,' she said with a maternal smile. 'John knows what to do; he's been at court since he was a squire. Let him guide you and everything will be well. It's daunting, I know, but it will pass.'

Aline whispered her thanks, grateful for the reassurance. Behind Sybire, she saw two women exchange glances and smirk at each other as if Lady Salisbury had said something amusing or ironic. Their looks, their barely concealed titters, knotted her stomach. She wondered what it was they knew that she didn't. Women had been offering her advice all morning, and much of what they said had increased her fear. To be certain of conceiving a son on her wedding night, she should eat plenty of parsnips and sleep on the right-hand side of the bed. But it wasn't parsnip season and what would she do if the right-hand side was the one preferred by John? Ask him to move? Holy Mary, she was not sure she dared ask him anything!

Her mother had had a quiet word with her concerning

50

the physical obligations of a wife and Aline was not entirely naive. She had seen animals mating, and even people once, although her glimpse of the latter had been fleeting and the couple fully clothed with most of their congress hidden. She was anxious about that aspect of marriage, but more worried about pleasing John and doing the right thing. Her mind was a vast empty space when it came to thinking about things to say to her new husband. What kind of conversations were they going to have? She needed someone to tell her what to do, to murmur instructions at each stage of the game, but instead she was being launched, oarless, on to a heaving ocean and expected to stay afloat. The thought that she would soon be mistress of her own household filled her with dread. She knew she was going to make some terrible mistakes.

An usher arrived to escort the bridal party to the cathedral. Aline forced down a retch and, with her mother and the other women in train, followed him from the palace. She concentrated on putting one foot before the other, using the feeling of the stony ground under the thin kidskin soles of her shoes to anchor her to reality.

John was waiting for her in the cathedral's porch. At his side, resplendent in a chasuble of glittering white and gold, stood Henry, Bishop of Winchester, brother to the Count of Mortain. Aline took a single frightened glance, then gazed at her feet. Step, step, step. She was afraid to look up beyond darting glances. John was so tall, so handsome – a distant stranger to her, and familiar with this world as she was not. He was surrounded by other clerics and courtiers, all talking quietly and at ease with the moment, but all Aline could see in her fear was a blurred glitter of colours, silks and jewels. She groped for the prayer beads looped at her belt and clutched the smooth, warm pieces of amber for reassurance.

Robert of Chichester, Dean of Salisbury, stepped forward to stand representative for her family. His expression was kindly and taking her hand, he gave it a gentle, reassuring squeeze. 'Courage, daughter,' he murmured.

The kindness in his voice made Aline want to burst into tears, but at the same time, it stiffened her resolve. There was no way to go but forward. Taking a deep breath, and the final steps, she let him bring her to John's side.

She knew what she had to say. Even in her state of high anxiety, she managed to stutter '*Volo*' in response to the Bishop's question concerning her willingness to take John for her husband and keep him in sickness and in health. But still her voice was small and soft and seemed to lose itself against the imposing and colourful backdrop. John's in contrast was firm and strong. His hand was steady and dry as he slipped a gold, sapphire-set band on to her right index finger and said, 'With this ring I honour you. With my body I wed you.' The ring fitted her finger perfectly. Aline shivered, for the vows they were making were irrevocable before God.

Once the pledges had been spoken and witness borne to the contractual aspects of the bond, the gathering entered within the church to celebrate a wedding mass. Aline relaxed a little. The familiar rituals were balm to her soul. Her fingers moved with certainty over her prayer beads. She admired the rich church furniture, the beautiful colours of the mural, the purple silk altar cloth; she inhaled the wonderful scent of incense. She listened to the Bishop's voice rising towards God, declaring that matrimony was an honourable estate, and suddenly, amid all the conflicting, worrying emotions, felt a bright thread of happiness. She peeped several glances at John and thought how fine he was. Her husband ordained by God and sanctioned by the Church.

52

Following the mass, John took her hands in his and kissed her, but in formal ceremonial manner with lips closed. Restrained and refined. Others crowded to embrace and congratulate them, very few known to Aline. She blushed and kept her head down and eyes lowered. A stubby forefinger chucked her beneath the chin and she found herself being appraised by a stocky, grey-haired man clad in a short green mantle. The people around her, John included, all knelt and she realised belatedly that this must be the King. Mortified, she started to curtsey, but he prevented her with a hand under her arm and gestured everyone else to rise. He had not been present at the wedding, but had obviously come from other business to well-wish. He kissed her soundly on both cheeks, leaving a damp imprint and the feel of his beard. 'My marshal is a fortunate man in his bride,' he said with a twinkle in his eye. 'May your union be blessed and fruitful.'

'Thank you, sire; it is as God ordains, but we will do our best,' John replied with a smile in his voice. Blushing furiously, Aline looked down again.

John found it strange to be sitting in the place of honour at his wedding feast, and not officiating as he would usually be doing in such circumstances. His deputies were charged with the task, but it was difficult to refrain from giving them orders and he could not prevent his gaze from wandering around the hall, assessing areas where trouble might occur and watching who entered and who left.

Making an effort, he turned his attention to his bride. She was wilting like a plucked bluebell, but he was not surprised since she was unaccustomed to being the centre of attention. John had marked the shy, anxious glances she kept darting at him and hoped she was not going to fall over the edge into hysteria when it came to their wedding night. He was used to forthright women who knew the moves with practised thoroughness. He had been keeping her cup well filled, but since he didn't want her drunk out of her skull, or sick to the stomach, he had been judging her intake keenly – and his own. His experience with women was extensive, but frightened virgins were not a part of it. Should such creatures enter the lists of the court prostitutes, their innocence was the preserve of magnates and bishops – or the King.

At least there was to be no formal bedding ceremony. John had chosen to take Aline back to his lodging on Scowrtene Street close to the castle. He owned the rents of several houses there and kept one for his own use when he was in the city. From what he had seen of Aline, there was no reason to doubt her innocence; he did not need witnesses to her virginity, and she would cope better without the palaver of public observance.

'A toast my lord to you and your new bride. Waes hael!'

'Drincheil!' John gave the traditional response and raised his cup to the salute made by Patrick FitzWalter, second son of Wiltshire's sheriff. The young man's hazel eyes were glassy and his smile inane. Had John been on duty, he would have been herding him unobtrusively towards the door or the latrines. Patrick had a bearish arm around his youngest sister. "S a good thing to show Sibby off at court,' he slurred. 'Make a fine marriage prize herself some day, won't you, my chicken?'

'I remember you.' Aline's gaze lit with sudden interest on the girl and she gave her a sweet smile. 'You found my beads when I lost them at Salisbury. Do you like marchpane?'

'Yes, my lady.' The child answered with a polite curtsey.

John congratulated himself on his judgement of his wife's wine consumption. She was relaxed enough to speak

54

of her own accord but that speech was clear and her fingers were dextrous as she broke a piece off the subtlety on her salver and handed the sweetmeat to the child.

Sybilla took it and thanked her, then thanked John too. Unlike Aline, who had only taken quick blushing glances at him all day, the girl gave him a measured look from brown eyes flecked with tawny and green. Her appraisal amused John, for it was the kind of stare he would have bestowed upon someone he was weighing up, not necessarily to their advantage. When she looked down, he suspected it was out of courtesy and not because she was shy or embarrassed.

'Has your father anyone in mind?' he asked Patrick.

The youth shook his head. 'Not yet. Her sister married the Count of Perche last year.' He swayed on his feet and, swallowing a belch, pinched the child's cheek. 'She'll be a worthy prize, though, when the time comes.'

Sybilla pulled away from her brother, giving him a straight stare too, although aggrieved rather than assessing. John folded his lips on the urge to laugh. 'I have no doubt,' he said when he had control of his expression.

Lady Salisbury arrived and, looking irritated, took charge of her daughter and sent Patrick outside, telling him that his brother William and some of their mutual cronies were looking for him.

'Formidable woman,' John remarked to Aline. 'I wonder if I could recruit her to my household.'

Aline looked alarmed before quickly dropping her gaze. 'I don't think it would be allowed,' she whispered.

'It was a jest.'

She reddened. 'Oh.'

He said nothing, but poured another quarter-measure into her cup.

*   *   *

55

In the balmy summer evening, sweet with birdsong and scented with honeysuckle, Sybilla was bubbling with the excitement of the occasion as she and the other wedding guests accompanied John FitzGilbert and his bride from the castle to the marshal's house on Scowrtene Street. All were on foot, save the bride and groom, who sat together on a dappled-grey palfrey, its harness festooned with ribbons and flowers. He was astride with his bride perched on the crupper, her hands gripping his belt and a queasy smile fixed on her face. Torch-bearers illuminated their way, although there was still enough light to see by. Sybilla thought the flares looked pretty and added to the magical atmosphere. Everyone was in high spirits and there was much singing and merriment en route. Fortunately, the horse was docile, and plodded along as if on a dusty country lane. Robert, Earl of Gloucester, played the role of squire, with a hand to the bridle, and led the singing in a rich, deep voice.

Not everyone was capable of walking in a straight line. Sybilla was glad Patrick wasn't among the company, for he had been behaving like a boor. The last cup of wine had felled him. Her oldest brother William had dragged him away to a corner of the hall to sleep it off.

Sybilla skipped along the road, holding her mother's hand and performing little dance steps, her eyes alight with pleasure. She hadn't eaten the piece of marchpane Aline had given her, but had stowed it in the small leather pouch at her belt to enjoy later along with her memories of the day. She had loved every moment, the more so because she hadn't seen her big sister's wedding, which had taken place in France. The King's marshal and his bride looked like two figures from a stained-glass window and she had imagined Hawise and Thomas looking like that too. Sybilla hoped that when her own wedding day came, she might have a fine new gown, a chaplet of flowers for her hair, and ride to her new home on a beribboned grey horse.

The procession arrived at the house. John's servants had opened the doors and lamplight spilled over the threshold in a welcoming pathway. Sybilla watched John dismount from the grey, then raise his arms and lift Aline down in the strength of them as if she were thistledown. The gesture elicited aaahs from several of the women. Aline flushed and stared at the ground.

John turned to his well-wishers and flourished them a bow. 'My thanks for your good company,' he said. 'But now, as you will all understand, my wife and I desire to be alone.'

There was laughter, a few sparking jests, raised eyebrows. John gestured to his servants and they came out bearing cups of hot, sweet wine imbued with spices. 'A final cup to wassail you on your way and for you to wish us Godspeed tonight!' he said and, having raised one of the cups on high, took a token drink, then presented it to Aline to sip from the same place. Her complexion on fire, she did so, to good-natured applause and shouts of approbation. Sybilla thought when a cup was passed to her that the drink tasted ambrosial – honeyed and hot, with a hint of cloves. She closed her eyes to savour the flavours on her tongue, rather than drinking it down like the adults were doing.

John took the cup back from Aline and handed it to an attendant. With a light hand at his bride's waist, he bowed again to his guests and went into the house, closing the door, shutting off the path of lamplight. Shouts, laughter, ribald comments bounced off the timber walls and barred threshold, but after a brief chorus, the guests started to leave, either returning to the castle or back to their own lodgings. Sybilla gave her empty cup to a servant with a smile and a thank you as she had been taught. Her mother was always saying that good manners were not only a duty, but also a tool to make the road ahead easier. As she reached for her mother's hand and set off back through the dusk, she looked over her shoulder. She was tired, but there was still an excited, happy feeling in her stomach. Today had been special – a memory to put away and treasure, sweet as a piece of marchpane subtlety.

It was quiet in the bedchamber once Aline's two maids had curtseyed and left, closing the door behind them. Clad in her chemise, her hair freshly combed to her waist, Aline stood alone in the middle of the room and looked round. The shutters were bolted, but candles of clean-burning beeswax cast a warm golden light upon the furnishings. She could hear John talking to his men in the room below, the rumble of his voice made indistinct by the thick wooden planking on the floor. The thought that this was his bedchamber when he stayed in Winchester, the intimacy of it, made Aline tremble

A plain wooden coffer stood against the foot of the bed. There was a bench covered with fleece-stuffed cushions, two long poles for draping clothes, hanging hooks, an empty wall niche, shelves containing sheaves of parchment, quills and inks. A trestle and bench stood near the window, positioned to obtain the best of the light. Everything was tidy, ordered, in its place. She longed to touch and investigate, but dared not.

Tentatively she approached the bed she was soon to share with John. Kneeling on the sheepskin rug at its side, she clasped her hands beneath her chin, looped her prayer beads through her fingers, and prayed, asking God for the strength to help her be a good wife and please her husband. She felt lightheaded and nauseous from the unaccustomed quantity of wine she had consumed . . . from anxiety too. She wondered if she should climb into bed and pull the sheets up to her chin. If everything in this room was in its place, would he expect her to be waiting for him there, in her place too?

She heard him bidding his men goodnight and it was too late to act. As he entered the room, he stared at her on her knees at the bedside. Although he said nothing, Aline felt as if she had done wrong and stood up in guilty haste. She could feel the soft sheepskin between her toes, the smooth warmth of the beads in her hands. Running them through her fingers for comfort, she swallowed and hoped she wasn't going to disgrace herself by being sick.

He sighed as he removed his belt and laid it across one of the coffers. 'I assume your mother has told you what to expect?'

'Yes, my lord.' Her voice emerged as a tight squeak. She dared not look at him because she knew she would dissolve in a puddle of terror.

'And you were praying for the strength to see it through?'

'I always pray at night, my lord. I . . . I was asking God's help to make me a good wife.' She stared at the sheepskin and fumbled ever more desperately with her beads.

'Then let us hope God hears and answers you,' he said after a pause, 'but since we must shift for ourselves on the practical matters, I suggest you shed that chemise and get into bed – if you have finished your prayers.'

Now she did look up, her eyes widening in shock. 'You . . . you want me to take off my chemise?'

He nodded. 'Easier now than tangling with it under the bedclothes.' He removed his tunic and folded it neatly beside his belt.

'My mother said that . . .' She bit her lip. 'I thought . . .'

'You thought what?'

Aline started to tremble. 'I . . . I know my duty, my lord, I will not shirk it, but the priests say lust is one of the seven deadly sins . . . and . . . and I do not want to court that sin.' She saw him grimace. 'I have angered you . . .' she whispered.

He made a gesture of negation and his voice softened. 'I am not angry at you, but I can think of a few well-fed, lustful prelates I'd take pleasure in throttling. Forget them; forget your mother. I'll not have them in this chamber with us tonight.'

'No, my lord.'

'Well then, the sin of lust aside, I have the right to see what kind of bargain I have made – as do you.' He stripped his rings and placed them in the wall niche. 'You should count yourself fortunate – Lady Marshal. If we had stayed at the castle, you would have been put to bed in front of a host of baying witnesses and I would have had to bed you with naught but a curtain between your modesty and their eyes and ears. Here at least we have privacy.'

Aline flinched at the images conjured by his words. She would have died if she had had to do that. She knew he was speaking the truth. The bawdy jests and rough-housing of some celebrants at the feast had terrified her to the point of tears. One of them had been blaspheming about a cock crowing thrice before dawn, and he hadn't been talking about St Peter's betrayal of Christ.

He was staring at her expectantly, but she was rooted to the spot. She couldn't do as he wanted; she just couldn't. Not in front of him like this.

John came over to her. With swift, gentle fingers, he unfastened the ties at her throat and pushed the chemise down off her shoulders. Mortified, Aline gasped and grabbed the falling garment, but John caught her hands and unfolded them from their grip on the linen. 'No,' he said, 'let it fall.'

She closed her eyes, tears seeping from under her lashes. Quivering with fear and embarrassment, she felt the chemise puddle at her ankles. There was a long silence in which she imagined him staring at her. Did she please him? Is this what he wanted? Her own breathing was shaky with distress, but she could not hear his. Then she felt his open palm against the side of her face, warm and steady. His thumb brushing her tears.

'Is it really that terrible?' he asked.

She said nothing because answering was beyond her.

His voice gentled and he removed his hand. 'Go, get into bed.'

She scrambled to do as he said and pulled the covers up to her chin. He looked at her inscrutably, then, heaving a sigh, unlaced his own shirt and pulled it over his head. Aline pressed her lips together and turned to study the plaster frieze painted on the wall beside the bed as if it were the most fascinating thing she had ever seen.

She heard him cross the room and blow out the lantern on the coffer. Returning to the bed, he also snuffed the large night candle on its wrought-iron stand, plunging the room into darkness. Her heart caught in her throat and she didn't quite suppress a squeak of alarm as she felt his weight on the other side of the mattress.

'I hope you are less afraid of the dark than you are of seeing men and women as God intended,' he said wryly. She heard the rustle and whisper of him shedding the rest of his clothes in the dark and then the draught of air as he lifted the covers and got in beside her. She took short, shallow breaths, hardly daring to move, wondering fearfully what he was going to do next. Would it be better if she could see? Keep the light but close her eyes?

61

He broke the silence with a sigh. 'We both have a duty,' he said. 'The marriage must be consummated. Do you understand?'

'Y . . . yes, my lord.' Her words hardly stirred the air. She felt him turn towards her, his hand against her hair and then on her neck, sliding to cup her shoulder. 'I swear to you I will do my best not to hurt you.' The covers rustled as he leaned over and began kissing her on brow, eyelids, cheek, mouth corner, and then finally on the lips. Her stomach tensed until she felt as if it were touching her spine. She didn't know how to answer him. What was she supposed to do? Clumsily she tried to kiss him back and, with great daring, set her arms around his neck. After a moment, she decided that she quite enjoyed the kissing and the closeness. She curled tentative fingers in the hair at his nape. However, when he stroked her breasts, she jumped like a startled deer. Her mother had never said that her husband would do this; she had only spoken in the broadest terms about the deed itself, but Aline could hardly ask John if this was a necessary part of the rite. It must be, if he was doing it. Then he lowered his head. As his lips tugged on her nipple, she felt a sharp flicker of sensation that arrowed directly to her loins. She gasped and tightened her fingers in his hair as new, bewildering feelings tingled through her body. This had to be the sin of lust against which priests were always warning folk to be on their guard. If she followed the path he was illuminating for her it might lead to hell. But oh, it was so nice to be held and caressed and soothed.

He stroked her rib cage, her belly, her thighs, and then, softly, with one finger, the forbidden place between her legs. She gave a cry of protest at this new intimacy. She had never put her own hand there, would not have dared.

'Hush,' he murmured. 'Hush, it's all right.'

But it wasn't all right because the feelings had reached a new pitch and she was scared she was going to dissolve, or that God would strike her for her wantonness. She could feel the sweat on his skin, and her own where their bodies touched . . . it was carnal, indecent . . . and, God forgive her, it felt wonderful.

There was a sudden, cold draught as he drew back and knelt up. He was doing something, she wasn't sure what, but his breathing grew harsh and swift. He lay over her again, kissing her, whispering reassurances in her ear, nuzzling her throat. She felt a blunt, hot nudge at the juncture of her thighs, followed by a slow, firm invasion that made her arch and gasp. Then he was over her, taking his upper weight on his forearms while his hips thrust forward, pressing into her body. She shook, trying to control her breathing while discomfort warred with flutters and twinges of the lust feeling. He pulled back a little, pushed once, twice, then a more forceful third time that made her whimper. His breath caught, he shuddered, and Aline shuddered with him. After a long pause, he sighed, kissed her throat, eased from her body and lay down.

Aline bit her lip, feeling ashamed, knowing she would have to go to confession and own up to the sin of wanton lechery. There was a hot seep between her thighs. She was glad it was dark so she didn't have to see it. Her mother had told her there would be blood as a sign of her virginity, and that the man's seed itself consisted of purified blood. She didn't want to think about that aspect, or the disturbing, shameful response of her body to his touch.

'Did I please you, my lord?' she asked in a small voice. 'Did I do it right?'

There was a long hesitation before he answered and his voice was devoid of inflection. 'You did your duty as a wife.' The mattress shook as he left the bed. An instant

63

later, sparks flared from a strike-a-light and, from the tiny flame kindled on dry tinder, he relit the night candle. Aline squinted at him. His back was turned. His body was long and straight, lean at the hip. Her cheeks flamed. She tried to tell herself that it was just as Adam must have looked in the Garden of Eden. Then he turned round and her eyes widened. Dear God, *that* had been inside her! Adam surely never had one of those! She looked away in shock.

John had noticed the direction of her stare. Swiftly but without undue haste, he donned his braies and tied the waist belt. 'You'll become accustomed in time,' he said drily. 'I am made no different from any man, and that includes the priest who hears your confession – and Christ himself, come to that.'

Aline gave a dismayed squeak.

'You think me blasphemous? I am only trying to put matters in perspective. Do you want some wine?'

Aline wordlessly shook her head. He sighed and, returning to the bed, sat down beside her. Gently he pushed a strand of hair away from her face and tucked it behind her ear. 'It has been difficult for you, hasn't it? I can understand that. I don't have sisters, but I know women well enough. You should sleep.'

'Have you . . . have you finished with me, my lord?'

He winced. 'It's hardly what a groom wants to hear on his wedding night, but yes. I will not trouble you again . . . unless of course you want to trouble me.'

She looked down but not before he had caught the flash of dismay in her gaze. 'I thought not,' he said and donned his shirt.

'You . . . you are not staying?'

He shook his head. 'I am not tired and I have work to do.' He picked up her chemise from the floor and handed it to her. 'Here, put this back on, if it eases you to sleep in your clothes.'

Aline clutched it to her bosom and her eyes filled with gratitude. 'Thank you, my lord, thank you!'

'Don't make a fuss over trifles,' he said, and left the room.

As he closed the door behind him, Aline scrambled into the chemise and tied the lace at her throat, as if in so doing she could hide from herself. She didn't dare to look at the sheet, because she knew she would be ill. There was a dull throb between her thighs and she skittered away from the memory of his body within hers. She had done her duty according to God's will. Latch on to that thought and use it for comfort.

Kneeling at the bedside, clutching her prayer beads, she closed her eyes and resumed her prayers, asking the Virgin to make her a good wife and help her cope with the changes that being married was going to bring.

John sat down on the bench before the hearth in the main room and signalled to one of the men for the wine jug. They were looking at him askance, and he didn't blame them. He'd have been surprised too, had he been one of their company.

'I surely didn't expect to see you this side of the dawn, my lord,' said his cook Walchelin as he obligingly poured a goblet and handed it to John. He moved with a lop-sided twist, the result of a horse falling on him when he had been one of John's serving serjeants. Since he was no longer fit for active duty, but owned skill with a ladle and could drive a baggage cart, John had found him a new niche in his household. His tongue was as robust as his cooking. 'Which shows how many virgins you've had in your life,' John said grimly, and drank.

65

Walchelin cupped his chin. 'How many have you had then, my lord?'

'A surfeit,' John replied, and took his goblet outside. Winchester was mostly dark under the cover of an overcast starless night. The breeze was warm and smelled of imminent rain with a ripe undercurrent of midden. The occasional light flickered in a house where the shutters had been left open. The shoemaker next door was working late over his leather. Muted by distance he heard a woman shouting and what sounded like a pot crashing against a door. His lower lids tensed in brief sympathy. Not that any woman had ever hurled a pot at him, although many would perhaps have liked to.

Drinking his wine, he grimaced. The consummation had been awkward, but he had expected no less. He didn't understand why men should think the taking of a virgin such a wonderful experience. Aside from knowing that any child begotten of the deed would be of their siring, and the virile feeling of being the taker of innocence, there was far more pleasure to be had from an experienced woman who knew her business. Initiating Aline had been like dancing with someone who had no idea of the steps . . . and who was afraid to try them out in case she fell over – or worse, started enjoying herself. He hadn't mistaken her response when she dropped her guard, but he wasn't sure he had the patience to keep on coaxing her. Then again, it was his duty to bed her until he got her with child, as it was hers to open to him. Remembering her horrified stare as she looked at him, still erect and naked, he didn't know whether to laugh or curse. He had wanted innocence and had well and truly received it. A door slammed and another pot crashed. John toasted the sound and drained his cup. Done was done. For better or worse, he had a wife, her lands and a marriage bed.

7

Hamstead, Berkshire, August 1133

John entered the bedchamber and moved smartly aside from the door, allowing two attendants to carry out a large coffer and a weapons chest. Aline sat on a bench watching the activity with a wan and miserable face. Her eyes were heavy-lidded and the delicate skin beneath them was shadowed with blue. The last two mornings she had been sick on rising and queasy for much of the day. It was too early to be certain she was with child, but the symptoms were suggestive.

John picked up his thick cloak from the back of the bench. He didn't need it now while the summer temperature was vying with the inside of a charcoal clamp, but it would be protection against the stiff breeze mid-channel on the sea crossing, and if the court over-wintered in Normandy, it would be essential.

Aline reached for his hand, her eyes liquid with tears. 'I don't want you to leave,' she sniffled.

John mustered his patience. 'I must. The King commands my presence in Normandy and I have responsibilities to over-see. I can't leave them to others. God knows, I've delegated enough these past two months. I will return when I can.'

Aline looked at him like a kicked puppy.

'You can cope,' he said, his tone brusque with irritation because he felt guilty and because she was being a milksop. 'Other women do. My mother often had to run Hamstead and Tidworth on her own when my father was away at his duties. You can have your own mother to stay if you wish, you know that.' He withdrew his hand and used it to cast the cloak over his other forearm. 'Surely you won't miss me to that extent? If you speak two words when I'm by, it's a miracle.'

Aline blew her nose on a screwed-up piece of linen. 'I feel safe when you're here,' she said. 'I feel protected.'

'You'll be protected in my absence. There are knights and serjeants enough to garrison my halls and provide escort should you want to travel. The country is peaceful. Who is going to want to harm you?' He stared at her in growing perplexity.

She bestowed him another drenched look. 'I know in my heart nothing bad can happen while you're here. Crossing the sea is dangerous. You think me ignorant, but I know the story of the *White Ship* and how King Henry's son and all his courtiers were drowned . . . What if there's a storm?'

John rolled his eyes. 'Good Christ, I could walk out of here and a roof tile drop on my head and spill my brains, but that's no reason to skulk in the bower and never venture outside. I've been crossing to Normandy and back with the court since I was fifteen years old and I'm still here to tell the tale. God will do what God will do and the rest is in the hands of a skilled captain and a sound ship, both of which I intend employing.' With an effort, he swallowed his annoyance. They had been married for two months and he had already discovered she was the kind to allow worries to grow out of all proportion to

68

their size. 'Besides,' he said, attempting to lighten the moment, 'I have a gentle, God-fearing wife to pray for my safekeeping. That must count for something.' He touched her damp cheek. 'Will you come down to the bailey and see me on my way?'

Biting her lip, she stood up and came around the bench. John took her hand and kissed it. In truth, he thought, it was going to be a relief to return to the court and a different way of life. One could have a surfeit of innocence. Aline was forever taking herself off to church to confess her sins, foremost among them those of fornication and lust. She would grow upset if he wanted her body on a Sunday, or a saint's day. She was still shy of being naked before him and would look away rather than see him unclad. She preferred the act of procreation to happen in the dark with chemise and shirt separating skin from skin, and to be over as quickly as possible. John had found it quite stimulating at first, with its reminders of adolescent encounters in hedgerows and desperate fumbles behind hayricks with alehouse wenches. Nevertheless, for an experienced courtier whose appetites these days were more sophisticated, the novelty had soon paled. Added to which Aline would lie under him as passive as a warm corpse and not reciprocate even while she made herself available to him, because then she was doing her duty and not sinning.

The sun beat down on the courtyard like a hammer upon an anvil. John looked at the baggage cart with the three cobs harnessed in line and Walchelin the cook sitting on the driving board, whistling tunefully. The knights and serjeants were assembled and quietly waiting John's word. Everyone knew his place and duty. The buildings basked complacently in the heat. Amid his satisfaction with such order, John felt as if he was stifling too. There had to be more to life. He could manage it all this with his eyes closed. He was only marking time.

He turned to Aline. 'We are going to have more than this one day,' he told her as his groom brought his horse. 'This is only the beginning.' His voice rang with ambition and its cadence wasn't for her benefit alone. If the spirits of his parents still lingered within these sun-drenched timbers and stones, he wanted them to hear and to know.

'Yes, my lord,' she said meekly and gazed up at him with a mingling of worship and uncertainty. Tears still glinted at her eye corners.

He lowered his gaze to her slender waist. 'With God's will and good fortune, your part is already in hand,' he said.

She blushed and suddenly her delightful, shy smile peeped out. John pulled her to him to kiss her in farewell. Her lips were soft, her body supple against his. If only the rest could be like this.

They were still kissing when one of the knights shouted in alarm. John spun Aline behind him and reached for his sword, but the danger wasn't physical. The knight was pointing skywards where a dark shadow had begun eating into the disc of the sun, creeping over the courtyard turning everything to twilight.

'Dear God, Holy Virgin Mother!' Aline wailed, dropping to her knees. 'It's the end of the world!'

John's heart was still pounding in response to the threat of danger, but his rational mind was in control and he was remembering a late-night discussion at court between himself, one of Henry's chaplains and Grimbald, the royal physician, who was interested in all manner of phenomena. 'Enough!' he snapped. 'I have never seen such a thing before but I have heard of it. It's an eclipse; it'll pass over.'

'But it's a sign from God!'

He shrugged, simulating more nonchalance than he felt. The twilight was deepening, washing the world in violet and grey 'What of it? So are rainbows and thunderstorms.'

Aline gripped his sleeve. 'Don't leave me,' she entreated. 'Don't leave me now. We must go to church and pray!'

'What?' He gave her an exasperated look.

'It's a sign from God. We must go to church and pray or something terrible will happen, I know it will – my lord, I beg you!' Her eyes were huge with terror. She clasped her other hand to her belly as if shielding the new life within.

John felt her fingers gripping him hard enough to bruise. Others were panicking, crying, falling to their knees and crossing themselves. Through his impatience, he knew she was probably right. He dare not set out until the eclipse had passed. It might indeed be a sign from God – a portent like the hairy star that had brought his grandfather as a young serjeant from Normandy to England, and on Hastings field had begun the rise of his bloodline. He reminded himself that portents which were evil to some were beneficial to others.

The population of Hamstead decamped to the small timber church of Saint Mary, and there knelt with the village priest, the latter exhorting God not to visit any murrains, plagues or ill fortune on his loyal flock. Aline promised a new cross and a silk cover for the altar. John bit his tongue as he thought of the cost and told himself that it would be good for his own status to provide for the church. If it kept Aline busy and happy, so much the better, and it would honour his mother and father too.

The shadow continued to cross the sun, eventually covering it in a perfect dark disc, like the curfew lid on a banked hearth. Rays of light beamed out from behind

71

the black circle. Standing in the church doorway, staring at the frightening, awe-inspiring sight of the flaming corona like a bright iris ringing the pupil of an eye, Aline still half thought the end of the world might be nigh, or that an angel might suddenly appear. Still with her hand upon her womb, she remembered Mary and the annunciation, then worried that such a thought might be blasphemous and dropped it like a hot cake.

Gradually the shadow passed from the sun. Light dazzled on the left-hand side; colours sharpened; the grass became green again and the red returned to John's tunic and her gown. Weakness and gratitude swept through her at God's great mercy. John had been right; it had passed over. Her awe for him increased. She knew she made him impatient at times, but he had yielded to her wishes and gone with her and everyone else to pray. She wanted him to stay but knew now the shadow was gone, he would leave. At least she could begin work on the altar cloth. Even if she didn't have the silk for it in her coffer, she could prick out a design and experiment with a few stitches.

An hour later, when John kissed her in farewell again, she managed not to cry and cling, although she was still terrified that she might never see him again. It was a struggle, but she bade him Godspeed like a proper wife, her only entreaty being that he write to her and tell her he was safe. He assured her that he would. Searching his eyes, she saw they were both the colour and distance of the horizon, and realised with a pang of bereavement that his mind was already far away.

Aline spent the months of her pregnancy sewing the new altar cloth for Saint Mary's. She ordered new church furniture for the altar from the goldsmiths on Calpe Street in Winchester. John paid for the refurbishment without quibble and, although he was in Normandy, his agents conducted the transactions with smooth efficiency. Letters arrived via his messengers – usually for his stewards and constables, but there was always a small personal note for her and sometimes a gift – a new ring, a silver brooch, a gold cross set with red spinels. Aline had her scribe write back to him, but didn't know what to say. Apart from expressing her gratitude for the gifts, giving him sparse particulars concerning her pregnancy and detailed minutiae about the improvements to the church, she left it to the scribe to compose the necessary courtly flourishes. His absence meant she had their bed to herself and didn't have to worry about the sin of lust, although a few times her dreams had betrayed her and she had awoken with a dull melting ache in her pelvis. On those occasions she had gone to confession and done penance, hoping that she hadn't been the victim of an incubus.

In late February, John paid a swift visit to Hamstead to see to the business of his estates, but since it was Lent, he slept apart from her. Besides, she was in her sixth month and, with her slight frame, already as round as the moon. He told her that the Empress Matilda, who was visiting her father, was also with child. 'But about a month behind you.'

'How old is her firstborn?' she had asked as they sat before the fire in their chamber. For once, after a busy day dealing with matters of estate, John was at ease and content to lounge on the bench beside her, drinking spiced wine and contemplating her burgeoning figure with a satisfied air. Aline savoured the moment while worrying what to talk about to keep him interested.

'Henry will be one year old next month.' John studied the wine in his cup. 'To say the marriage had such inauspicious beginnings, they're making up for lost time now.'

'I will pray for her.'

He arched one eyebrow but did not follow up on the remark. 'The King is very taken with his grandson,' he said, 'inasmuch as one can be taken by an infant of that age. I can't say that I'm struck, but then I'm not kin.' He smiled at her belly. 'I dare say I'll dote on my own.'

Aline flushed and gave him an uncertain smile.

'I look at him and I wonder if he'll be our next King,' he mused. 'Some men say so, but it's a perilous long way from cradle to throne and who knows what kind of man he'll make – apart from a red-haired one.'

Aline didn't know what to say. Red hair was not a good sign in a man or a woman. It spoke of volatile humours and fickle behaviour. She hoped her own baby wouldn't be born with it.

'As to his mother . . .' John grimaced and tossed the lees on to the fire where they hissed and steamed. The sudden move made Aline squeak with surprise. 'Well, let us hope men are never called upon to uphold the oath they were forced to swear to her,' he said, and his words had been the end of the quiet time, for after that he had grown restless and had gone to walk the defensive perimeter of the manor with the dogs.

On a fine morning in early May, Aline went into labour. At the onset of her travail, she was afraid but strangely resolute. The bible said that the pain was a punishment for Eve's sin, and thus she knew she was fulfilling God's will by suffering it.

Her mother had come to Hamstead for the confinement, and she rubbed Aline's back while soothing and distracting her with murmured assurances and endearments. A brisk midwife and her assistant were in attendance, and a wet nurse recommended by Sybire of Salisbury had been engaged.

Although Aline's build was slight, she was supple, and stronger than her thistledown appearance suggested. The midwife was cheerful and had no qualms. Before noon, Aline was bearing down, pushing with all her might to expel the baby from her womb. The pain was bad, but not unbearable, and by focusing on the blessed Saint Margaret and immersing herself in prayer, Aline managed to block out the higher levels.

'Ah,' said the midwife, her hands busy between Aline's spread thighs. 'Here we are. What have we got?'

Aline felt a slippery, gushing heat and heard a sudden wail, high-pitched and fractious.

'A boy, a fine boy!' the midwife cried with triumph, holding aloft a smeared, bloody object resembling a very young, freshly slaughtered piglet. Aline's eyes lost focus and the room began to spin.

When she revived, the baby was being washed in a large copper bowl and her women were fussing around her in concern. Another bowl, covered with a cloth, was being borne away from the bedside and linen rags had been packed between her thighs in the same wise as when she had her menstrual flow. She was given a reviving drink of wine, sweetened with honey.

Tears pouring down her face, her mother leaned over the bed to kiss her. 'Oh Aline, my daughter, my daughter. You have given your lord a fine son. Praise be to God!' Cecily turned to take a towel-wrapped bundle from the midwife. 'He's perfect.'

Aline took a dubious look. It hadn't resembled a baby when it emerged from her body. She was assailed by the same feelings that had struck her on her wedding night.

75

It had seemed impossible for that *thing* to fit within her body. Now it seemed equally impossible that the consequence, this baby, had come out of her. There shouldn't have been room, but of course there was. How great were God's miracles.

She was reluctant to take him from her mother and hold him, but forced herself. He was still as pink as a piglet, but the blood and slime were gone. His breathing was swift and snuffly and his minute fists were clenched either as if to resist the world, or grasp it tightly. His eyes were the hue of dark slate and it gave her a jolt for they were so much like John's. A pang went through her, of pride, of dawning triumph. She had succeeded. She had given a thing of worth to the marriage through her own striving. 'He is to be named Gilbert,' she said in a trembling voice, 'for my lord's father.'

'I will have the chaplain draft your lord a letter straight away!' Cecily wiped tears from her cheeks. 'Oh, this is a day for celebration.'

Aline found a tired smile. She knew John would be greatly pleased at the birth of a son . . . and she was pleased with herself too for she had fulfilled her duty. She touched the baby's soft cheek, still disbelieving. 'I wish John were here now,' she said.

The atmosphere in Rouen was as tense as a primed trebuchet. The June day had been as hot as the heart of a bonfire and in the aftermath of sunset, the western skyline wore the heat like a dull purple bruise. John stood on the battlements of the Tower of Rouen, trying to catch a hint of breeze and looking out over the glitter of the Seine, busy with a traffic of barges and cogs. Not being on duty, he had discarded his tunic and rolled his shirt-sleeves back to his elbows. The locals and the irreverent called this section of the battlements Conan's Leap, after the occasion when King Henry as a young man had lost his patience and thrown a baron over the walls to his death. John could well imagine Henry doing the deed. Affable though he was, his temper was like the swift kick of an angry destrier when provoked, and he was as strong as one too.

Hearing footsteps, John turned to regard Robert of Gloucester as he joined him on the wall walk. Gloucester was still wearing his tunic, but had unpinned it at the throat. A gold and garnet cross flashed on his breast as he stopped beside John and leaned one shoulder against the stonework. He too narrowed his glance in the direction of the busy river before sighing heavily down his nose.

'How are the Empress and her new son faring?' John enquired.

Gloucester grunted. 'The baby is well; a fine little fellow to say she took so long to birth him, but my sister has a fever.' He made a face. 'It was too soon after the first. She'd hardly been churched before her belly was ripe again. A woman needs more time than that to recover.'

'I am sorry . . . Is she very sick?' John's tone was diffident and tactful.

'She's not out of her wits, not rambling, or at least I think not. She and my father were having a vigorous argument about where to bury her when I left. He says the cathedral, she wants the abbey at Bec-Hellouin and insists it's her dying wish that counts, but he's being stubborn – says as her father it's his right to choose and she won't be able to do anything about it if she's dead.'

Standing upright, John rubbed his sunburned neck. 'I know little about women and childbirth except that it is a dangerous business, but I do know that while your sister is strong enough to argue with the King, there is hope.

77

She will fight to the last stand, and surely this is not it.'

'No,' Robert said doubtfully and looked sideways at John with troubled eyes. 'But what if she does succumb? What then?'

'She has two sons to succeed her.'

'Yes, and what happens when a country's heirs are little children?'

'They will need a guardian; someone to govern until they can take the reins for themselves.' John returned Robert's look. 'A benevolent uncle, for example.'

'Hah!' Robert shook his head. 'I sometimes feel like a lion charging a flock of carrion crows.'

'Yes, my lord, but that is one of the annoyances of being a lion, not a crow.'

Robert snorted with grim humour. 'You always manage to put situations in a nutshell.'

John opened his hand. 'My position at court dictates that I observe all who come into the King's presence, and note what manner of animal they are . . . or what they think they are. It's not always the same thing.' He watched the dusk darken over the river. Several of the craft bobbing there had now kindled lanterns at their prows. It might be better if Matilda did die, he thought, for then Robert could rule in her stead in the name of her sons. Of course, Henry might name one of his nephews his heir instead. Stephen of Mortain or Theobald of Blois – Stephen especially. Henry had engineered his marriage to Matilda of Boulogne and in doing so, joined Stephen to the ancient English royal line. There were many who thought Stephen should be the heir. Not that John would say so to Robert; he was too diplomatic and he knew very well that Robert considered Stephen one of the carrion crows.

Robert sighed. 'No,' he agreed. 'How is your own wife?' he asked after a moment.

John knew Robert was enquiring to be polite, but perhaps also out of need for distraction and reassurance. 'Well enough, from the letters I received, and my son is thriving.' He felt an unexpected warmth at his core as he said 'my son'. 'Providing the Empress recovers, I plan to be at Hamstead for my wife's churching ceremony.' He watched bats flit through the last of gloaming and the sight made him smile a little. A colony of them had made their roost in the rafters at Saint Mary's in Hamstead and Aline had screamed to see them hanging there. She wouldn't have made a good wife for Noah.

'I am pleased to hear the King's daughter has made a full recovery,' said Walter, sheriff of Salisbury. 'Bearing a child is always hazardous for a woman. I thank God that my wife birthed all of ours without mishap, and that your own lady has been safely delivered.' He smiled at his wife on his left, and then at Aline on his right. The latter reddened and looked down.

'Indeed, my lord,' John replied and signalled an attendant to refill the cups. They were feasting in the hall at Hamstead, following Aline's churching. All was quiet at court and with the Empress's life no longer in danger, he had been able to spare a fortnight to attend to affairs at home. He had noticed that the bats no longer inhabited the chapel. Even the swallows' nests had been poked out from under the eaves. The altar sported an ornate new cross and embroidered cloth, and the pillars had been repainted in fresh, bright colours. He had also noticed a new statue of the Virgin and Child occupying a wall niche. The blue of its robe had matched the blue of the new gown Aline had worn to the thanksgiving mass for her safe delivery and purification after childbirth. He had made a mental note to rein back her spending on the church.

Sense and reason in all things. The next order of the day was improving Hamstead's general fabric and defences.

'I hear the Empress's eldest son has red hair,' Lady Salisbury remarked to him.

'That is so, my lady,' John replied, 'and a temper that surely comes from his grandsire.'

Sybire smiled. 'And the new little one?'

John managed not to shrug. A baby was a baby and he had seen little enough of Prince Geoffrey. A swaddled scrap lying on a lambskin and crying fractiously. 'More like his mother,' he said.

'I always think that such children are blessed,' Sybire said with a glint of mischief. 'I wish that all of mine took after me.'

'God forbid!' Walter growled, but humour sparked in his own eyes.

John smiled politely. He didn't want to imagine having a son who grew up like Aline. Many scholars were of the opinion that a woman was only the vessel and that most of the newborn's essence came from the father, but he wasn't going to get into that kind of discussion with his guests. He glanced towards the wet nurse who was suckling Gilbert at her breast and felt a lurch of emotion, but then it was different when the child in the cradle was your own. Even if he felt no great outpouring of love, there was still pride in having begotten an heir, the powerful instinct to protect and the knowledge that here was the future. Not only could he be ambitious for himself, he could plan for his son. He had always been careful with the whores at court, only spilling himself inside those who were barren or who knew how to prevent conception. He had nothing to offer a bastard child except a place at his hearth, and he didn't want that responsibility. But a son and heir was a different matter.

The Salisburys' youngest daughter was watching with fascination as Gilbert nursed. She had the gawkiness of late childhood as if someone had stretched her limbs on a tenter frame. Her masses of rich brunette hair were plaited in blue ribbons and her hazel eyes were as wide as goblet rims, taking everything in.

'The King himself is in good health?' Lord Walter asked.

It was a common question these days. Men were nervous. John turned his focus from the girl and fixed it on her father. 'Indeed so, my lord, and very pleased with his grandsons.'

'I swore my oath to the Empress,' Walter said, tugging at his luxuriant whiskers, 'but I am hoping those little boys grow fast and that their grandsire stays hale.'

'Amen to that.' John raised his cup in toast.

The old man gave him a shrewd look. 'You must hear rumours at court, my lord Marshal. You are in a position to know most of what goes on.'

John drank and set his cup down. 'Rumours are like pebbles on a beach – so many of them that you pick the one that attracts your eye. But whether it has value or not . . .' He shrugged. 'It is rare to see a piece of gold among the stones.'

'But a man who knows the beach has more chance than a stranger.'

'In this case, there is nothing I can tell you that you do not already know, my lord.'

Walter gave a mirthless smile. 'I would hate to play chess with you.'

John said nothing. He didn't need to, for the silence was not uncomfortable. Walter of Salisbury was too wily a diplomat for that and so was he. Even if he was growing old, Walter wielded tremendous influence and authority throughout Wiltshire. He had the support of the people too, for his father had been an English thegn and his family was one of the few to have survived the upheaval of the Norman invasion.

'The Bishop of Salisbury will never accept the Empress as Queen. Neither will Waleran of Meulan, or Henry of Winchester,' Walter opined after a moment.

'Well then, my lord, it seems to me you have at least seen your stones, if not picked them up.'

'I didn't say I liked the look of them.' The sheriff bestowed a hard, shrewd stare on John. 'What of your own?'

'I stand back and wait. Who knows what the next tide will push into the shore?' John watched the sheriff's daughter take Gilbert from the wet nurse and cradle him in her arms with natural ease, her face alight with pleasure.

'Probably more stones,' Walter said.

John laughed in dour acknowledgement.

'Speaking of which, I see you are going to be busy with your outerworks if those cartloads of timber in the bailey are any indication – or are you collecting firewood in anticipation of a hard winter?'

John looked wry. Despite his encroaching years, Walter of Salisbury remained as observant as a hawk. 'The defences are in need of renovation,' he said with a casual wave of his hand. 'Nothing more than that.'

Walter folded his hands on the trestle and pressed his thumbs together. 'I have no quarrel with ambition, my lord Marshal,' he said quietly. 'A man must do his best for his sons, so that they may do the best for theirs when the time comes. Providing you do not interfere with me and mine, I wish you well.'

'Then we are of the same mind,' John said.

* * *

As John unbuckled his belt and laid it across the coffer, Aline saw him frown at the dust there. She had meant to tell one of her women to see to it, but had forgotten in the hectic rush to prepare the hall and the chapel for her churching and the feast. At least that seemed to have gone well and their guests had enjoyed themselves. Most of the conversation had been beyond her, but then it was men's talk.

She watched John strip his rings and place them in the wall niche, then his tunic brooch and the jewelled cross from around his neck. Just looking at him stopped her breath. He had spoken little to her since his return, but had seemed genuinely pleased by their infant son, and proud.

'I told Father Geoffrey that I would ask you about a new silk chasuble for him,' she said in a breathless rush.

He swung round. 'Do you know how much a single ell of silk costs?' he asked. 'I don't dress in silk to serve the King.'

'He's serving God,' she said in a small voice.

'Yes, but God sees people, not their clothes.' He made an impatient gesture. 'Silk is wasted on a priest who is not going to further our family. By all means let him dress to suit his station, but he's hardly a bishop, is he? You wouldn't clad a beggar in the robes of an earl.' He came to the bed and stopped beside her. Aline's stomach clenched with a mingling of fear and anticipation. 'I need to do something about Hamstead itself. Better new walls and defences than gauds for the clergy.' He reached across to examine the cloth of the bed hangings. 'Come to that, we need new curtains for the chamber. These are full of moth holes.'

Aline swallowed. 'I was thinking of our souls.'

'Our souls will be saved because I dress my priest like a court whore?' John gave a bark of laughter. 'Oh, that is funny!'

Aline gasped in horror. 'You should not mock!'

'*I* should not mock?' he snorted. 'God on the Cross, woman, if cladding a common priest in silk is not a mockery, I don't know what is. Small wonder he was all over you at the dinner table. He knows when his daily bread has honey on it.' He clamped his jaw.

'Don't be angry,' she whispered tearfully. 'I'm sorry.'

He closed his eyes for an instant. Then he sighed and looked at her. 'Aline, you do not know,' he said with laboured patience. 'I wish you did.'

'Know what?' She searched his face, feeling desperate.

Very gently, he removed the pins from her wimple and unfastened the brooch at her throat.

'I . . . please, I . . .'

'No more,' he said, kissing her. 'It's late. Stop being sorry.'

Aline closed her eyes. The candles were still alight. Perhaps if she didn't protest about that, it would atone for annoying him. Perhaps she shouldn't have mentioned the priest's robes as soon as they retired. It was so important to her – but obviously not to John. He didn't see things in the same light. Determined to be a good wife, she let him disrobe her and take her to bed. She even managed not to hide herself from his gaze.

He was slow and thorough, making a banquet of his pleasure, and she spread herself for him, eager to please. It had been a long time since they had lain together and she had not realised how much she ached to have him touch her. Even if it was a sin, her body answered the smooth motion of his. He kissed her as he moved within her and she writhed, digging her fingers into his arms, holding on to him for dear life.

When it was over, he stroked her hair and continued to nuzzle and kiss her. Torn between guilt and ecstasy, Aline lay in his arms, scarcely daring to move.

From beyond the curtain in the antechamber, Gilbert started a hungry wailing. The nurse's rope-framed bed creaked as she left it and shuffled over to the cradle, her voice pitched to a soothing croon. Aline had been glad to give the duty of breastfeeding to the woman. Some said it was essential a child should be nourished from his mother for the first weeks of his life at least, but Aline hadn't liked the feel of the baby suckling at her breast, especially when she thought of the detail that a mother's milk was formed from purified blood just like the essence in a man's loins. Feeling squeamish and afraid, she had been glad to give Gilbert to the wet nurse and bind up her breasts. She loved him, of course she did, but preferred others to do the handling.

His cries quieted to soft squeaks and then a sudden spluttering cough as he choked. She heard John give an amused grunt at the sound. He eased his arm out from beneath her and quietly left the bed. Aline reached for him in panic. 'Where are you going?'

He glanced round at her, his lids heavy with satiation, his expression and posture relaxed. 'Only to blow out the candles,' he said. 'I don't need to see to sleep.'

Aline lay in the dark with his arm around her, his palm loosely spread across her belly, and his breathing quiet at her neck. She tried so hard to please him, but it was difficult when she knew nothing of men . . . of this man. He lived a different life beyond the small boundaries of Hamstead, Tidworth and Clyffe, one populated by royalty, great magnates and bishops. What did she know of such a world, except for a few faint glimmers? Perhaps she should learn, but she didn't want to; it was too daunting.

When she woke just before dawn, Gilbert was crying again to be fed, and the place at her side was empty.

8

Lyons-la-Fôret, Normandy, November 1135

A crisp silver frost glittered on the roof shingles of the hunting lodge and a red dawn was rising out of the trees as the King set out to hunt with his courtiers. Watching him leave the hall, John noticed the bounce in his stride and heard his laughter as Robert of Gloucester said something amusing. There was no sign of the irritation that had gripped him earlier that week on hearing that the Empress's husband and some malcontent Norman barons had been fomenting rebellion along his borders. Henry was keen to go to England and instead was having to stay in Normandy and keep an eye on his troublesome son-by-marriage. John suspected the vigour of the hunt was what kept the King's temper from erupting; besides which, he could use the chase for informal discussion with his advisers without too many eavesdroppers.

John had joined yesterday's gallop through the forest, but today he had matters to attend to. Henry still wanted to be in England for Christmas if possible and that involved organising stopping places on the road, hiring horses, carts and drivers, making sure there was accommodation for the royal household and sufficient fodder and provisions en route. If the King decided the situation in Normandy was too critical to leave, then Christmas would be spent in Rouen, and that meant John had to plan for both contingencies. Leaving the hall, he went out to the stables in search of the head groom, who would tell him how many horses he was expecting to feed over the next three days and at whose expense.

Two small children were jumping on the frozen puddles in the yard, making crazed fretwork patterns, their squeals as loud as colours on the raw silver air. Nearby a messenger stood picking his teeth with a dagger while he waited for an attendant to saddle up his mount. Straining in the traces, a cob hauled a two-wheeled cart into the courtyard. A pungent smell of raw fish struck John like a wet slap of sea spray. The cart's interior was lined with straw, but even so, a trail of odorous moisture dripped from baskets of lampreys, oysters, mussels and assorted fish. John grimaced. The King was particularly fond of lampreys, although God alone knew why. John disliked eels in any form. Even smoked they failed to inspire his palate. He watched the cart rattle off in the direction of the kitchen quarters. If the oysters were fresh, they'd do, cracked open with the edge of a broad knife and swallowed whole.

He spoke to the groom, went on to the keeper of the hounds, then the head falconer. He sent messengers out, and received messengers in with details of supplies and news about accommodation. He checked the tallies as to who was eating in the hall, who was on duty and who wasn't, then took time to make a quick meal of bread and cold venison, washed down with decent wine, before going to sort out the ushers, the guards and the collection of petitioners hoping to put their pleas before the King. Some women were parading at the gate, eyeing up

87

the soldiers and swinging their hips. John took in the tawdry copper rings on their fingers, the unpinned neck-lines of their gowns and the flash of dirt-spattered calves. One had increased the length of her braids with horse hair, but the colours were badly mismatched and the effect was jarring and incongruous. John knew a certain bishop who had a penchant for sluts, but since he wasn't currently at court, he had no demand for such women in the enclave. Even had they possessed the silver to bribe their way in, he had his own reputation to maintain. 'No,' he said to the guard. 'If the off-duty soldiers want to take their chance, fair enough, but I don't want them in the hall . . .'

'My lord.' The soldier dipped his head to John and began moving the women along with the haft of his spear. They squawked and protested like poultry, but John well knew how to deal with hens and lightly laid his own hand to the hilt of his sword.

The hunt returned as the winter sun was setting in streamers of molten gold, casting long shadows over grass and stone. The dogs ran low-tailed and panting; the horses steamed as if drawn out of a boiling cauldron. Grooms came at the run to take bridles and prepare to rub down the sweating, mud-caked beasts. Waleran, Count of Meulan, flung from his stallion, waited for his twin brother to dismount, then, arm in arm, the pair of them headed off to the hall. Robert of Gloucester was grinning too as he leaped from his own horse and hastened to hold his father's bridle.

'I can manage,' Henry growled. 'I could still outride any man of you here, if I chose – and make a night of it while you were all snoring exhausted in your beds.'

'I do not doubt it, sire,' Robert said diplomatically. 'If I hold your rein, it is only out of respect.'

Henry grunted as he set his foot on the bailey floor. 'You're a good son.' He slapped Robert's arm, then noticed John, who immediately flourished a bow. 'You should have come with us, Marshal.' Henry indicated the three stag carcasses occupying the baggage cart that was rumbling into the courtyard through the open gates.

John bowed again. 'Sire, I doubt I would have been able to keep up.'

Henry snorted. 'I don't believe that, FitzGilbert. You're always well ahead of the chase.'

In fine mood, the King walked on into the hall, arm in arm with his son. John followed them. A glance at the cart of bloody carcasses informed him that venison in its various forms was going to follow fish on to the menu for the next several days.

Saving a few lamps kept burning so men could see their way to the privy, the hall was in darkness, the fire banked and covered. John glanced over the sleeping forms of the servants and retainers. The dark mounds under blankets formed a familiar landscape and the mutters, snores, and pockets of soft conversation reassured him all was well. Stepping lightly, he went to the door, spoke with the guard and slipped outside. The weather had warmed during the evening and, although still bitter, was damper and misty. The ice in the puddles had turned to liquid and there was a slick of mud underfoot. John hoped none of the morrow's supply carts would get bogged down. The winter months were a perennial nightmare for such incidents.

He was passing the royal apartments on the way to his lodging when the door opened and one of Henry's attendants ran out and collided with him.

'Apologies, my lord!' The youth's expression was

89

frightened and preoccupied. 'The King is not well. I have to fetch his physician.'

'Not well?' John caught the young man's arm as he prepared to run on. He recognised him as the dogsbody attached to Rabel, Henry's chamberlain. 'How not well? He was hale enough when he retired.'

'Sick,' the servant said. 'Puking up his guts. Bad fish, Master Rabel thinks.'

John let him go and went to the door the youth had left open in his haste. Henry's chamber boiled with activity. A lackey was tugging fresh bedsheets out of a coffer; another was airing a clean chemise in front of the fire and all were exchanging worried glances as they went about their duties. A pile of soiled bed linens had been deposited near the door and was sending up a vile waft that made John hold his breath and move away. 'Take that to the laundry,' he snapped at a lad who was pumping bellows at the hearth. 'Now.'

Henry was kneeling over a slop bowl, doing exactly as the messenger had described. A blanket had been draped across his spasming shoulders. His complexion was the hue of his nightshirt. The sight filled John with alarm. The King was close to seventy years old and anything of this ilk was dangerous.

'What are you doing here, FitzGilbert?'

John swung to face William Martel. Henry's cup-bearer had materialised out of the darkness, still fumbling to fasten his belt, his hair standing up in untidy tufts. A scowl furrowed the space between his brows.

'My rounds,' John replied. 'When folk are abroad in the middle of the night, it is my duty to know their business.'

'That's as may be, but the King's chamber isn't in your remit. You attend to your duties and leave me to attend mine.'

90

John decided Martel was in a temper because he had just woken up and had arrived to find his domain invaded by another court official with whom he was on tepid terms at best. 'Make sure you do,' John said and, with another glance at the King, went back out into the murky night. He didn't think the court would be moving on the morrow. He retired to his lodging, but only to wash, shave, and change his shirt and braies. Sleep could wait.

Throughout the night, people came and went from the royal apartments: Grimbald the physician, the Beaumont twins, the Bishop of Rouen, Henry's chaplains and Robert of Gloucester. John worked steadily, making lists and tallies while keeping his ears and his door open. He offset the discomfort of the dank November evening by spreading his spare cloak over his lap, keeping the fire going in the small central hearth and warming a jug of wine on the embers.

A little before dawn, a bleary Robert of Gloucester put his head around John's door. 'Do you never stop?' he asked irritably.

'Not when there's work to be done.' John left his seat at the trestle and went to pour hot wine from jug to goblet. 'How is the King?'

'Sick.' Robert took the cup from him. 'Very sick, if I am being honest. He's still purging even though there's nothing to bring up. He shouldn't have eaten so many lampreys.'

'Anyone else been taken ill?'

'Not that I'm aware, but it only takes one bad fish, and he gorged on them. You know how fond he is. Martel ate one from the same dish and he's not suffering.' He bit his thumbnail. 'I am wondering whether to send a messenger to my sister in Anjou, but perhaps it's too soon. We've all had nights like this.'

91

John agreed politely that they had.

As Robert drank he glanced at the parchments on the board. He read the list and his eyes narrowed with anger.

John faced Robert without chagrin or apology. 'It's as well to be prepared,' he said in a pragmatic voice. Someone had to think about a sturdy cart to bear a coffin and decent horses to pull it, rather than the usual jades used for haulage. Then there was the matter of salt to pack the eviscerated body, the coffin itself, the silk for the shrouds. They didn't just materialise out of thin air.

Robert heaved a grim sigh. 'Yes, you're right, but I pray your forethought is in vain, because God help us all if it is not.'

When Robert had gone, John methodically tidied the trestle, told his squire not to disturb him except for a dire emergency, and went to lie down on his pallet. Now that he had completed his preliminary work and had the latest details on the state of the King's health, he could afford to rest for a few hours. If this was Henry's death struggle, John knew he would soon have no time for sleep at all. Henry's powerful personality was what glued his barons together. No one would dare to flout his authority while he gripped the reins of government in his fists, but with him gone there would be mayhem.

The rain sluiced down the roof shingles, dripped off the eaves and splashed into the courtyard, filling the puddles, creating a muddy brown sauce through which men paddled, grimacing. The yard poultry huddled in the lee of buildings, fluffing up their feathers and grumbling. If people had to cross from one building to another, they ran, splashing their hose and soaking their shoes.

John stood sentinel in the King's chamber, acting as usher, his mace of office resting in the crook of his arm.

The sound of the rain formed a backdrop to the happenings in the room, not soothing or soporific, but monotonous and irritating, heightening tension.

Henry lay in his bed, propped upright against a mass of pillows and bolsters. His formerly robust and ruddy features were sucked-in and cadaverous and his stare, socketed in purple shadows, was glazed and unknowing. His chest heaved with the effort to breathe.

'Sire.' The Earl of Leicester leaned over Henry and grasped his hand. 'Will you name your successor so that those gathered here may do your bidding? We need to know.'

Henry closed his eyes. His swallow was audible to all in the room. 'I am not dead yet,' he said in a rusty voice. 'I am the King.'

'Yes, sire, but . . .'

'But nothing. Robert, are you there? My son?'

'Sire . . . my lord father.' Gloucester shouldered Leicester roughly away and knelt at his father's side.

Henry gathered himself. 'Take money from the treasury in Rouen and pay all my officers what is owing to them. Give them their Christmas robes – whether I am here or not.'

'I will see it done, sire.'

Henry gave a faint nod. 'Do it now, as soon as you leave the room. Also, you know it is my wish to be buried at Reading . . .' His hollow gaze fixed on the nobles gathered around his bed. 'I hold all of you, on your oaths, to bring me there and see me interred . . . all of you.'

Listening to him, John pondered the mingling of astute political acumen and delusion. On one level, Henry had accepted he was dying. Forcing his magnates to stay together on oath until they had brought him to Reading Abbey meant they would have to remain in each other's company and work together. Yet refusing to name his successor revealed that Henry was not ready to relinquish power until the bitter end . . . and that was dangerous.

'Sire . . . we need to know,' said Waleran of Meulan. 'Will you tell us whom you intend to succeed you?'

Henry closed his eyes and turned his head aside on the bolster, abjuring all contact. 'You should not have to ask,' he said.

John remained on duty for the rest of the day, not always in the chamber, but on the prowl like a restless beast. Already the shadows were darker and there were things in them that prickled his nape. When he finally returned to his lodging for a moment's respite, his senior knight Benet de Tidworth was waiting for him in the company of Walchelin his cook, the latter armed with a platter of hot griddle cakes, and both men looked grim.

John's gaze snapped from one to the other. 'What's wrong?' Taking a griddle cake, he bit into it.

'Tell him,' Benet said with a jerk of his head.

Walchelin hitched the linen apron knotted at his hip. 'I was talking to one of the King's cooks. He says he thinks Henry was poisoned.'

In the middle of swallowing, John almost choked. He coughed hard and recovered. 'Someone was always bound to make that comment. Why should it be more than rumour?'

'Because the man who gutted the fish was a stranger, my lord. He'd been hanging round the kitchen door begging for work and the cook took him on for a penny. Not been seen since, has he?'

John shrugged. 'Surely that's the way of casual hire. With the King sick, he'd not stay around to face inevitable accusations.' He gave Walchelin a keen stare. His cook enjoyed gossip, but he wasn't a fool, and Benet was the most dependable man he knew. 'What makes you think he's a poisoner?'

'The cook saw him talking to William Martel in the privy later in the day and Martel gave him more silver.'

The prickling at John's nape extended down his spine. 'That doesn't mean he poisoned the King's dish.'

'No, my lord, but Martel was the one who brought the lampreys to the table.'

John went to pour himself wine from the flagon. 'Why should Martel desire the King's death?' He had to stop himself from sniffing suspiciously at his cup. 'He even ate from the King's plate, so I've been told.'

'That I don't know, my lord. I'm only telling you what I've heard.'

'There are many reasons why Martel might have been exchanging silver in a latrine.'

'Yes, sir, but I thought you would want to know all the same.'

'I do, and thank you.'

Walchelin gave a brusque nod. 'Do you not want these, my lord? They'll soon be cold.' A wounded expression filled his eyes.

John shook his head. 'No offence to your skills,' he said, 'but suddenly I'm not hungry. Share them around the men – and I trust you to keep your own mouth shut unless you're putting food in it.'

Walchelin took the platter and bowed out. Benet looked at his lord. 'You believe him then, sire?'

John drank. 'I believe that a chance-come lackey was employed to gut fish and that William Martel had cause to pay him in secret, but as to the rest . . .' He contemplated the cup. 'Before you can accuse, you need proof.'

'Are you going to say anything?'

95

John met Benet's knowing, shrewd stare. 'What good would it do?' he said after a long pause. 'Martel is Henry's cup-bearer, not a great lord. If he paid a hireling to poison the King's dinner, then someone higher up will have paid or promised Martel.' He finished his wine and set his cup down. 'Even if it is true, the deed is done. I'll poke a wasp's nest when I have to, but otherwise leave well alone. I don't want to die with a dagger in my back or face down in a puddle of poisoned wine. This conversation never took place.'

Benet nodded and compressed his lips as if setting a seal on the command.

'Better find the cook with the loose tongue and tell him if he wants to keep it, to put it behind his teeth.'

'I'll see to it, my lord.'

When Benet had gone, John poured himself a second measure of wine, and stood at his lodging door, staring out at the rainy courtyard. His expression was composed and his hand steady as he drank, but he was thinking fast and contemplating options and consequences. Walchelin's news, in hindsight, didn't surprise him. In a game of chess there was always a moment when someone made a decisive move.

Robert of Gloucester emerged from the sickroom, his broad shoulders slumped with weariness. Seeing John standing in the doorway, he walked over to join him.

'He won't last much longer.' He rubbed his hands over his face. 'He still won't name his successor, but surely there is no choice. Surely he desires his own grandson to wear the crown one day. Why doesn't he speak?' His voice was heavy with frustration and weariness.

'Before his grandson can wear a crown, the Empress must do so first and with Geoffrey of Anjou as her consort,' John said. 'Your father knows such a detail sticks in men's gullets. Why else twice-bind them with oaths?'

Robert looked grim. 'There's little left of him now that's knowing or rational, but you would think after he made men swear, he would cling to that instinct. Instead he . . .' He broke off and shook his head. 'He keeps saying, "Stephen's a man, Stephen's a man."'

John gave him a keen look. 'He's named Stephen?'

'No. When he's asked to confirm he intends Stephen to follow him, he doesn't answer. It's as if he can't bring himself to do it. Anyway, Stephen is his father's second son. Theobald is before him in line.' Robert's mouth twisted as if he had tasted something so bitter it was unpalatable. 'My sister is the rightful heir and her son after her. My oath is to them, and I hold by it.'

John had felt a jolt go through him at Robert's mention of Stephen. He didn't believe Stephen was capable of murdering his uncle in order to seize power, but he did believe he was ambitious enough to take it should someone pave the way for him. There were plenty of such men at court, including some attending the deathbed.

'You say nothing?' Robert's tone quickened. 'You swore the oath too.'

'So did most men here,' John replied, 'but oaths can be absolved if sworn under duress, as everyone knows. There are certain bishops who believe that being ruled by a woman goes against nature and you will find plenty of the magnates feel the same way.'

'You included?'

John gave a humourless smile. 'I am the King's marshal and until your father dies, my loyalty is to him. Once he is gone, I hope to serve his successor, but whether it be man, woman, or babe in the cradle remains the choice of other men.'

Robert's upper lip curled. 'You mean you'll bury your

conscience. Tell me this: if he names my sister, will you serve her?'

'I will give my oath to the anointed sovereign,' John said neutrally.

Robert looked disgusted. 'I thought better of you. Well, I tell you, neither Stephen nor any of his cronies will receive a welcome in my strongholds. I'm putting Dover and Southampton on alert as of now.'

'In your place I would do the same, my lord. I would hope for the outcome I want, but be prepared for it to go the opposite way and to have the wherewithal to bargain at my disposal.'

'So it comes down to price. Would you have me sell my honour?'

John shook his head. 'No,' he said. 'No man should do that, but he should expect to receive due payment for what he is worth.'

In the dull, cold dawn of an early December morning after three days of hard struggle to stay in the world, Henry, King of England and Duke of Normandy, died without openly naming a successor. He had not spoken since the previous evening, and had said nothing significant even then, for words had been almost beyond him and all coherence gone. Robert of Gloucester wept over his body and he was not alone in his grief, but others exchanged knowing glances, in which there was an equal mingling of relief and apprehension. And for some there was triumph and a burden of guilt.

Returning to his chamber, John gazed around the room as if it belonged to a stranger. Osbert, his chamberlain, had left food, wine and washing water to hand. Everything was the same and yet it seemed distorted – as if visual perception had been knocked awry. Probably just tiredness, he told himself as he sat down in the barrel chair near his bed. The clean, crisp sheets beckoned him, but he didn't want to lie down – not after seeing Henry's last struggle and knowing what he knew.

He had been born when Henry was the King. He was thirty now and had never known a different rule. He and his father had risen from the ranks of the serjeantry on the back of reward and promotion for efficient, unquestioning service. Now all that effort was threatened. He possessed more lands than his father had done, and he had wealth and chattels hoarded from the good years, but there was no guarantee of continuing favour.

In sombre mood, he drew his sword from its scabbard and inspected it. The weapon was as much a part of his authority as the rod he bore in the hall when keeping ceremonial order. The blade was Cologne steel with a grip of plaited silk cord over a core of padded whalebone. The King had presented it to him at his knighting nine years ago with a gilded scabbard and belt. Since then he had used it in trial by combat to put down two challengers for the Marshalsea. The grip had been bound in green back then, but, after succeeding in the arena, he had changed it to blood-red. He had not been challenged since, but still he kept the edges oiled and sharp and he wore it as a matter of course to maintain familiarity with its weight and remind men that his authority was borne out by more than just words.

A soft tap on the door roused him from his contemplation. He rose from his chair and went to lift the latch, the sword still bare in his hand. Damette's gaze widened at the sight before she slipped past him into the room. Raindrops gleamed like crystals on the fur collar of her cloak. 'Already preparing for war, my lord?' she asked.

John sheathed the blade. 'Just testing my edge.' Having

99

closed the door, he leaned against the coffer and folded his arms. 'I wondered how long you would be.' He watched her help herself to his wine. 'You might as well drink it while I can still offer you the best.'

She studied him over the goblet rim. 'You're a cat, John,' she said. 'You'll land on your feet.'

'A cat? Safer to be a wolf these days.'

'You think so? I say a fox would be better.' She sipped daintily. 'Emma's crying buckets in the whores' lodge. She thought she was going to be his permanent mistress and now he's dead. Silly wench; he only wanted her because she was a fresh tumble.'

John's mind filled with the vision of a creamy-skinned country girl. Big blue eyes, bigger breasts, about as much wit as a plantain leaf. He eyed Damette. 'So where has your own lord gone galloping off in such haste?'

'You saw him?'

'Riding out on a fast courser as if a devil clutching a basket of lampreys was snapping at his heels.'

Colour swept into her face. So she knew as well.

'I suppose he's ridden to the Count of Mortain?'

'As far as I know.' She made a rapid recovery. 'Others will have gone to the Count's brother – Theobald is the eldest, after all, but it is Stephen who will succeed.'

'Does Stephen know?'

'About what?'

He folded his left hand towards himself and scrutinised his fingernails. 'Baskets of lampreys.'

She shook her head. 'He's not the kind to deal well with such information.' She put her empty cup on the trestle against which he was leaning, and rested her hand there, close to his hipbone. 'I had better pack my coffers.'

John made a gesture of negation. 'The court won't be moving for a few days yet. The King's body has to be

100

prepared for burial and his magnates have sworn to escort him to Reading and see him interred.'

She trailed her hand over his hip close to his groin, raised it to run up his arm and finally laid her palm against the side of his face. 'No, but the court of a dead king is not the same as that of a living one. I will not tarry, and neither should you if you want to remain a king's marshal.' She rose on tiptoe to kiss him slowly on the mouth, using her tongue, then drew back. 'The weather is calm for a sea crossing if you're of a mind.'

With a farewell glance over her shoulder, she went to the door and quietly let herself out. He tasted wine and felt the lingering, moist imprint of her lips on his. A week ago, life at court had been predictable and mundane, the routines settled for the winter season. Now, suddenly, the world had tipped upside down, scattering certainty like spilled beans, and it was every courtier for himself.

Sybilla drew back her arm and threw the stick as hard as she could so that it splashed well out into the river. The two dogs, already wet from the last bout of fetching, plunged into the water and paddled in pursuit, tails ruddering the surface. They were strong swimmers and although it was December, there hadn't been too much rain and the Kennet still flowed within its bounds.

Her family's manor of Mildenhall lay two miles east of Marlborough, close to the Salisbury road, and they visited it at least a couple of times a year, usually in late spring and late autumn before returning to Salisbury for Christmas. The manor raised fine geese and other poultry and her mother liked to select the ones that would dress the feast table herself, as well as gifting some to the clergy and favoured vassals.

The yellow hound, having won the race for the stick,

waded on to the bank and shook himself vigorously. His brindle companion sloshed out after him and tried to snatch the prize, thus initiating a tussling match punctuated by ferocious growls, of which Sybilla took little notice, for it was all show and no substance. As the dogs vied over the stick, Sybilla heard horses on the track and, looking round, saw a party of riders approaching the manor. Whistling the dogs to heel, she went forward to greet them and recognised the lady Aline, wife of John FitzGilbert the marshal. She had an escort of serjeants with her and a woman attendant. A nurse rode with Aline's infant son in her care, all bundled up and warm in a side pannier. Sybilla curtseyed as her mother had taught her and murmured words of welcome.

Aline nodded in return. Sybilla thought she didn't look very well. Her face was pinched and pale and there were dark circles beneath her eyes. She looked nervously at the dogs as if she expected to be set upon.

'They don't bite,' Sybilla said, to which Aline gave a faint smile that immediately faded from her lips.

'My horse has cast a shoe,' she replied in a slightly breathless voice. 'Do you have a farrier here?'

'Yes, my lady,' Sybilla replied. 'He's at the manor now, shoeing the plough oxen. My mother will be pleased to see you.'

'And I her ...' Aline's voice was hesitant and uncertain.

Sybilla brought the guests to the manor, walking cheerfully beside Aline's limping palfrey, glad for the novelty of having guests to entertain.

Aline looked at her curiously. 'Your mother lets you out on your own?' she asked.

'I took the dogs for a walk,' Sybilla said. 'It's one of my duties.'

Aline blinked and looked a little taken aback. 'Does she not worry about you?'

Now it was Sybilla's turn to look nonplussed. 'She knows I am safe with the dogs to protect me. She knows where I go; I have to tell her.'

'How old are you, child?'

Sybilla tucked a stray tendril of hair behind her ear. 'I was eleven years old at the feast of Saint John, my lady.'

'Eleven,' Aline repeated and bit her lip. 'I wish I . . .' She swallowed and looked as if she was going to cry and suddenly Sybilla was glad to arrive at the palisade entrance leading into the manor courtyard.

One of Aline's escorting serjeants helped her down from the mare and the animal was led away to be shod. The men trooped into the main hall and Sybilla took Aline, her women and the baby to the domestic chamber on the floor above, accessed by a steep outer staircase. Her mother smiled to see Aline and, abandoning her sewing, rose to greet her with kisses on either cheek, before sitting her down by the hearth with an offer of hot wine and griddle cakes freckled with dried fruit.

The nurse settled Gilbert on her knee and gave him one of the griddle cakes to chew while Sybire commented with admiration on how much he'd grown since last she had seen him.

'He's walking now, and chatters like a magpie,' the nurse said proudly.

'I can see his father in him,' Sybire said, 'but there is much of his mother too.' She smiled round at Aline, and then her face fell with consternation. 'My dear, what is it, what's wrong?'

Sybilla's gaze widened in shock as their guest burst into tears and began to weep as if her heart was broken in pieces. Sybire sat down at her side and took Aline in her arms.

103

Through a storm of tears, Aline sobbed out the detail that her mother had died at Clyffe three weeks since of congested lungs and she was returning from lighting candles for her soul at the cathedral in Salisbury. 'It was what she wanted. She asked me to . . .'

'I am so sorry,' Sybire said, 'we did not know, God rest her soul. You should have sent a messenger.'

'I . . . I did not think . . . everything was too much . . .' Aline wiped her eyes on her sleeve.

'Have you written to John?'

Aline nodded tearfully. 'But he is with the court and I do not know when the news will reach him. I never know where he is and he's been gone so long . . .' Her voice developed a cracked, thin edge. 'They told me in Salisbury that the King is supposed to be returning to England before Christmas, but they said that about the autumn too and it never happened . . . without God, I would be alone . . .'

Sybire hugged and comforted her, but also pointed out with gentle asperity that she had her son to cherish and nurture, and the responsibility of a household and estates to run in her husband's absence. Aline said little to either remark; she just shrank in her seat. As the storm of tears passed, she withdrew into herself and stared into the fire, one hand shaking on the wine cup, the other toying with the string of prayer beads looped at her belt. Sybilla found herself gazing at them intently. Even though it was five years ago, she still remembered discovering them in the hall at Salisbury and being tempted to take them for her own. It was one of those vivid recollections that would stay with her always, just like her memory of the torchlit walk from castle to house on the day Aline married John FitzGilbert.

Aline declined the offer of a meal and a bed for the

night and as soon as a servant arrived to announce that her mare was shod, she was in haste to be on her way. Sybilla had been playing with Gilbert and had to hand him back to his nurse so that he could be settled in the pony's pannier, which was lined with sheepskins to keep him snug and secure. The heat from the fire and the cold of outdoors had turned his little cheeks a shiny apple-red and, in contrast, his eyes glowed like silvery flints. Apart from a glance at him to make sure he was safe, Aline paid him no more attention than any other piece of baggage.

'I will have prayers said for your mother and I will light candles; she was a good and gentle lady,' Sybire said as she and Sybilla stood at the gate to make their farewells.

'Thank you, my lady, you are kind.' For a moment Aline's chin dimpled, but then she pulled herself together, and with a brief nod to her hostess, rode out with her escort.

Glancing at her mother, Sybilla saw that she was watching Aline with the pursed lips and narrowed eyes she usually bestowed on her children when they fell short of expectations. 'What's wrong, Mama?'

Sybire shook her head and sighed. 'Nothing, child, nothing.' She set her arm around Sybilla's shoulders and kissed the top of her head. 'Come,' she said, and there was a hint of sadness in her voice. 'We have candles to light, and while we are about our prayers, we should say one for Lady Aline too – for she is in need of strengthening and comfort.'

9

Tower of London, December 1135

John's tension relaxed as he passed through Aldgate with his mesnie and entered the city of London. The ambler hired yesterday in Canterbury was stumbling, for he had pushed it hard to reach the city before sunset. Not that there was any sign of sun. The sky was overcast with rain threatening in the wind and his riding cloak and boots were splattered with mud.

Arriving at Dover, he had discovered that Stephen had been there ahead of him but the constable, under orders from his lord, Robert of Gloucester, had refused him entry, having been told that under no circumstances was he to open to Stephen, Count of Mortain ... who was not King of England, whatever he might claim. Staying only to hire horses, John had followed Stephen's trail to Canterbury, to find that Gloucester's men had rebuffed Stephen's attempts to enter that city too, and Stephen had been forced to head for London.

John had silenced the anxious muttering of his men. He had been anticipating such a response. Canterbury and Dover might have closed their gates to Stephen, but London was a different matter. Mortain had a good rapport with its citizens and Gloucester's influence did not extend there.

Once through Aldgate, he followed the city wall and ditch for a short distance, ignoring the urchins who were poking about on its periphery. Some of the cheekier ones clamoured for silver and went ignored, although Benet, who was always soft where youngsters were concerned, threw them a loaf from his rations.

'It was going stale anyway,' he said sheepishly to John who shook his head and restrained himself from remarks about encouraging vermin.

The guards on duty at the Tower's outer gate were cautious about admitting John and his men and a soldier was sent for further orders. John contained his impatience; a few more moments wouldn't matter. He eyed the equipment of the men, assessed their attitude and composed his own thoughts.

The soldier returned at the run, which John thought interesting. Either he was eager to his job, or those inside the keep had reason to be keen.

'My lord, the Count of Mortain bids you welcome.' He flourished a bow that had not been present before. Grooms came to take the horses and an usher brought John and his men to the hall. From there, John on his own was escorted to the royal apartments on the third storey – rooms that had last been used by Henry in the full expectation that he would return to enjoy them again. Now Stephen of Mortain, his brother the Bishop of Winchester, and William Martel, together with various senior members of their retinues, occupied them.

Lips tight with displeasure, Martel scowled at John, who ignored him. Stephen was a trifle shadowed around the eyes, but his smile bore its usual undisciplined vigour and he sprang to his feet and greeted John with much back-slapping and bonhomie, as if they were equals meeting in a tavern for a gossip over wine.

John bowed but omitted to kneel or tender homage. Stephen's good humour remained, although his companions glowered at the temerity.

'My uncle's marshal,' Stephen said. 'Have you come to swear your allegiance to me?'

John gave Stephen a direct look. 'That I cannot say, my lord, until I know more. I followed you from Dover and Canterbury, and the welcome there was not as warm.'

Stephen shrugged. 'I expected no less. The Earl of Gloucester has strong influence in those parts, but I trust to win him round.' He cleared his throat and his fair skin flushed. 'I do not deny we gave our oaths to uphold the Empress, but the King absolved us of them on his deathbed.'

It was the first John had heard of such a thing. As far as he knew, Henry had been incapable of anything on his deathbed except dying.

'It is true,' William Martel concurred. His eyes locked with John's, challenging him to disagree.

'It is also true that England and Normandy will not settle under the rule of a woman with an Angevin stripling for a consort,' added Stephen's brother, Henry, Bishop of Winchester. 'There will be war. It is ridiculous to think that a woman could govern.' The supercilious flare of his nostrils and the contempt in his voice made it obvious what he thought of such a notion.

John acknowledged the point with a dip of his head. 'From what I hear, the lords in Normandy, including Robert of Gloucester, are going to offer your brother Theobald the crown.'

Stephen exchanged looks with Winchester. 'Not for long. As soon as they realise I have England, they'll give

108

me their allegiance.' He pointed to his breast with his index finger. 'Henry groomed me for the kingship, and my wife is of ancient English stock. Theobald's isn't.' He continued to smile at John, albeit less broadly now. 'I don't know you well, FitzGilbert, but you have always been a loyal king's man and my uncle only employed the best. That trial by combat you and your father fought against de Hastings and de Venoiz for the Marshalsea was the talk of the court for weeks – the way you put de Venoiz down. I'd never seen such speed and purpose. I'd like to harness those skills to my own cause.'

John recognised flattery and he recognised praise, but allowed neither to turn his head. He knew he was fast and he knew he was good. He also knew his own worth and was not susceptible to the valuation others put upon it.

Genuine curiosity filled Stephen's eyes. 'What makes you come to me and not my cousin the Empress, or my brother?'

'Call it a direct way of seeing, my lord. I used my initiative . . . like many others.' He shot a sidelong glance at Martel, who was still sulking. 'If you are set to become King of England, you will need the services of a proven marshal.'

Stephen nodded. 'That is so, but on what terms, I wonder?'

'My lord, I am open to suggestion.'

Martel's upper lip curled with hostility. 'Everyone knows you're a crony of the Earl of Gloucester and he has closed his castles against my lord.'

John pinned Martel with the stare he reserved for men who were making a nuisance of themselves in the King's hall. 'I may have an affinity with the Earl of Gloucester but I owe him no allegiance. King Henry *was* my lord and I served him faithfully. I swore an oath to his daughter, we all did, because it was what he desired and because we had no choice. I am an honourable man, but a practical one too.'

Stephen considered him. 'If you are willing to kneel, and swear to me, then in my turn I am prepared to nurture your ambition and reward you well, but I require your absolute loyalty, not an oath given on a whim.'

John didn't hesitate. It was either kneel or walk away and he hadn't pursued Stephen halfway across southern England to do the latter. 'My liege,' he said, affording Stephen the greater title and, dropping to his knees, offered his oath of homage.

Snow was flickering down out of a sword-grey sky when the lookout told Aline that her husband and his troop had been sighted on the road. He had sent an outrider, to give her time to prepare, and Aline had been in a state of panic ever since. She had had the fire in the bedchamber built up and water set to heat, knowing he would want to bathe. Clothes had been turfed out of the coffers and set to air, although she was dismayed to find that moths had been busy again. There was only a gluey pottage in the cauldrons, no new bread and the hens were hardly laying because of the time of year.

The bower was a mess, the chests open, belts and shoes strewn where she had left them. An empty cup stood on the night table and yesterday's burned-down candle stubs had not yet been replaced. She hadn't noticed such shortcomings before: it wasn't in her nature and she was no good at chivvying her women; but now, as if through John's eyes, she perceived the neglect and was filled with panic. If only her mother was here, but she wasn't . . . and thinking of her only made Aline's throat close with grief and panic. 'See to this,' she commanded the maids, waving her hand around the room. 'I don't care what you do; just make sure it looks tidy for my lord.' She swallowed her fear. It would be all right. If he did comment, she would excuse the domestic chaos by citing her grief over her mother's death. It wouldn't be a lie.

She opened the shutters covering the window of the upstairs chamber and squinted out. The troop was riding into the courtyard, churning the wet snow to mud. Breath and horsehide steamed. Her eyes lit on John and she watched him dismount with the lithe grace of a cat. Her stomach rippled with fear and anticipation. Behind her, her women had been galvanised into action – as much by their anxiety over the lord's return as by their mistress's orders – and were attempting to make the room look cared for, at least at a superficial glance. Aline closed the shutter and hurried down to the hall to greet her husband.

He entered the room on a moist, chill wind, his hair and cloak starred with snow and his garments spattered with hard travel. Hastily she curtseyed. 'My lord, welcome.'

He raised her to her feet and gave her a formal kiss on the hand and then the cheek. His lips were cold, but she tingled where they touched. He appraised her from head to toe. 'You look like a nun,' he said.

Aline hadn't thought about her gown. It was her everyday one, of simple dark grey wool, adorned on the breast by a silver cross. Her wimple was of good but plain linen and completely concealed her hair. 'I can change if you wish it.'

He shook his head. 'No matter.' His gaze turned to the nurse who had brought his son from the hearth.

'Ball,' said Gilbert, holding out to his father his toy made of soft leather strips stuffed with fleece.

111

John reached to take it and Gilbert immediately snatched it back with an emphatic yell of 'No!'

'A strong sense of possession already.' John's proud grin made Aline's stomach contract. 'He's a fine boy, Aline.'

She glowed at his praise.

'I have some news for you,' he said. 'Indeed for everyone, in fact, but first I need to wash and shed these travel-soiled clothes.' He strode towards the stairs. Aline hurried after him, hoping her women had managed to set the bedchamber into some semblance of order. As she entered the room, her eyes darted round it with worry, and then relief. Clothes had been flung over poles or stuffed into coffers which were all now closed. The coverlet had been pulled over the bed and smoothed, the hangings tied back. Fresh candles adorned the spikes.

John removed his cloak and handed it to a maid. 'It needs brushing and hanging to air,' he said, adding wryly, 'but not too near the fire.'

Aline winced. She had managed to singe one of his cloaks by doing just that. He sat down on the bed and she hastened to help him remove his boots, as a good wife should.

'King Henry is dead,' he announced. 'It's not common knowledge yet, but it soon will be.'

She leaned back, mud on her hands, and looked up at him. 'Dead?'

'Of a bad gut five days since. When I left the court, they were preparing the body for its journey to Reading.'

She crossed herself. 'God rest his soul. I will have candles lit and prayers said for him. We should have a mass—'

'God's blood, woman, leave the mummery for a moment! He's dead; his soul can wait a prayer and a candle. What is important is that Stephen, Count of

112

Mortain, has claimed the crown and, barring an obscure mishap, he's going to be the King – and I am to serve him as his marshal.'

Aline gave him an uncomprehending look. She struggled with conversations of this kind for they had little to do with her life. Decisions about how many hens to kill for the pot and whether to change the rushes in the hall were taxing enough without considering the alien world of the royal court. Plainly though, she was expected to say something. 'Is that a good thing, my lord?'

'Well, it's certainly better than a kick in the teeth,' he said. 'It means I'll have more lands than those I hold now and a greater part to play. If I do well for Stephen, he will reward me with estates and the custody of castles.'

The final three words caused Aline's stomach to wallow. 'Castles?' she said faintly. She groped for a towel and wiped the mud from her hands.

'I haven't been told which yet, but I have my hopes. In the meantime, I'll set about fortifying this place in earnest.' He unfastened his belt and removed his tunic, his eyes agleam.

'Why?' Fear jolted through her. 'There isn't going to be trouble, is there?'

He gave a pragmatic shrug. 'Times are not as certain as they were and a prudent man prepares for all eventualities.'

A maid brought him a bowl of hot water and John washed his face and hands. As he dried himself, he cast her one of his long, straight stares. 'You are the mother of my son, Aline, the wife of the King's marshal. I need you to be steadfast.'

Aline swallowed. 'Yes, my lord,' she said, desiring nothing more than to hide in a corner and hope everything would go away.

113

'You . . . you heard about my mother?' she ventured. 'I had my chaplain write to you . . .'

She saw him frown, and make the effort to return from his own concerns. 'Ah yes . . . I wrote you a reply, but it's still in my baggage.' His expression softened. 'I am sorry.' He put his arms around her. 'I mean it . . . Have masses said for the soul of King Henry, and for your mother too if it will comfort you, and I will give alms in her name now, and each year on the feast of Saint Cecilia.'

Aline laid her cheek against his breast and struggled not to weep. He had said he wanted her to be steadfast. 'Thank you, my lord, thank you.'

Above her, she heard him sigh. He tilted up her chin, kissed her damp cheek and mouth corner, then sought a fresh tunic. She saw him notice the jumbled state of the coffer contents, but he said nothing. Aline dug her fingernails into the palms of her hands, and swore to try harder.

10

Oxford, Spring 1136

John was not usually one to linger in latrines, even ones which had recently been cleaned out and spruced for the King's visit, but just now, the waft of sewage was more acceptable than some of the verbal excrement with which he was being forced to deal. Already he was feeling nostalgic for the decorum and discipline of King Henry's enclave.

Stephen's court was packed. Magnates, barons, bishops, archdeacons: all vied with each other for a place at the new King's table; clamouring for a share in the power and wealth that was currently being portioned out in much the same manner as the venison, boar and swan at the high table. King Henry had kept a tight fist on his strong-boxes and coffers, leaving his treasury piled with wealth just begging to be spent. Stephen, on the other hand, enjoyed luxury and delighted in distributing largesse. There was nothing wrong with that if you were on the receiving end, but prudence would have been of more use to John when he and his men were trying to keep order.

The Archbishop of Canterbury had objected to the

King of Scotland's seating position at the high table, because he said it should be his, and David of Scotland was annoyed because the Earl of Chester had been given lands in his claim, namely Carlisle. Their men had taken sides and as the wine sank in the barrels, the exchanges of abuse had become more than verbal. John's forearm was bruised where he had blocked a punch from a belligerent Scots baron, who had been wading into Chester's chamberlain who he said had tripped him up and called him a boy-loving ferblet. A knight of Waleran of Meulan's household had joined in and John had had to summon his two burliest serjeants to help subdue the fracas.

Since it had been quelled and John was on top of the matter, Stephen hadn't noticed, but John was beginning to think it time he did. Despite his show of munificence at this great Easter gathering, Stephen had yet to bestow anything on John other than his standard wage of two shillings a day and vague promises. John understood that first he had to prove his loyalty to Stephen. It was not as if he had ever made a point of fraternising with Stephen's camp before King Henry's death. Beneath the bonhomie, he knew Waleran of Meulan and Robert de Beaumont were suspicious of him and undecided. William Martel was openly hostile.

He had been at court continuously since December, setting up the new Marshalsea from the remnants of the old, constructing a solid framework. He had attended Henry's funeral at Reading and had watched a tearful Stephen lay his shoulder to the coffin. Significantly, Robert of Gloucester had not been present, pleading delays in Normandy. How much longer he could hold off swearing allegiance to Stephen when most others had done so was a frequent point of conversation in guardroom and alehouse.

116

John had ridden north with Stephen to the Scots border, where the latter had negotiated a peace with King David, a peace that this Easter feast was supposed to be cementing, but where policing the rivalry of the different factions was giving John a thundering headache.

Walter, sheriff of Salisbury, limped into the latrine for a piss and complained to John about the state of his knees. 'Be glad when it's summer,' he said. 'My body's wearing out faster than an old mill grindstone. I'd leave things to my sons, but they're still striplings and I wanted to test our new King's mettle for myself.' Having emptied his bladder, he adjusted his clothing, eased himself down on the seat and, folding his arms, lingered to talk. 'Different from Henry, isn't he?' John nodded. 'Wears his thoughts on his face,' Walter continued, 'and mostly they're of the happy-to-see-you kind. Reminds me of a friendly dog – wagging his tail, eager to please. Henry would bite off your bollocks if he thought you were overstepping your authority.'

John smiled at the crude but apt analogy. 'No bad thing,' he said.

'Indeed not. You knew how far you could go . . . and how far everyone else could go as well. Now it's every man for himself and devil take the hindmost. Good horseman though,' he admitted judiciously, 'and knows the business end of a sword.'

Bonhomme, John's youngest usher, appeared in the latrine doorway, panting from his run. 'My lord, the Earl of Gloucester's just ridden in with his mesnie. I thought you should know!'

'Interesting.' Walter of Salisbury rose laboriously to his feet. 'This is going to ruffle some feathers.'

John didn't answer except by way of an eloquent look. With a nod to Bonhomme, he strode from his malodorous sanctuary back into the murky waters of the court.

Robert of Gloucester was dismounting in the court-yard, surrounded by several knights and a troop of Flemish mercenaries armed to the teeth. John eyed up the leader of the latter group, one Robert FitzHubert, small in stature but as broad as a barn with muscles bursting his hauberk and the kind of neck that almost wasn't there. You'd have to find his throat before you could cut it.

'Welcome, my lord.' John flourished a bow and beckoned grooms to take the horses.

Gloucester didn't smile and his eyes were guarded. 'Perhaps not the right word in the circumstances, John. We shall see. Being as you are here, you may as well conduct me to the . . . to the King.' His mouth contorted on the word.

John appraised the knights and mercenaries. 'Your men will have to disarm.'

Gloucester scowled. 'I know the routine. Being absent from court doesn't mean losing my memory.' He gestured and the knights and mercenaries began handing over their weapons, although FitzHubert was plainly disgruntled by the demand.

'No, but last time you were at court, it was your father's.' John set out for the King's chamber, holding his rod of office before him.

News had already run ahead and instead of waiting in the dignity of state to greet the Earl of Gloucester, Stephen was already on his feet and striding across the chamber, arms wide. 'Cousin!' he cried, beaming from ear to ear. Inwardly John grimaced. Either Stephen was playing a brilliant game of bluff, or the man was a buffoon.

Gloucester bent one knee to Stephen and bowed his head. John wondered what it had cost him to do that. Stephen immediately raised him up and kissed him heartily on both cheeks.

118

'I am glad you have come. This truly makes today one for celebration and rejoicing!'

Robert forced a smile in return. 'I am pleased to be here, cousin, but you will understand why I took my time to come to you.'

Stephen's smile remained, but it fixed a little at the corners and John did not miss the assessing glitter in his eyes. Not quite the buffoon then. 'Indeed, my lord. You are an honourable man and I rejoice that you have chosen this path. Come, sit, take wine.' He gestured to the dais table where he had been drinking and discussing affairs with his senior magnates. 'Waleran, make a place. William, the flagon.'

The lord of Meulan shifted sideways on the bench, making room. His own smile was wide, but he had a way of clenching his teeth that made it hard to tell if it was a snarl or a grin. Martel fetched the wine and poured it, his expression watchful.

Gloucester hesitated. His head had remained down, but not so much in deference as in preparation to do battle. 'Cousin, if I give you my allegiance, it is with the proviso that if you take away any of my lands or act dishonourably towards me, I have the right to renounce that allegiance.'

Stephen gave him a man-to-man nod. 'Any of my vassals has that right,' he said. 'There has to be trust between us.'

'Yes, there does,' Gloucester agreed in an arid voice, 'and part of that trust is knowing precisely where we stand from the beginning.'

'I am surprised at you, John,' Gloucester said in a reproachful voice. 'I never thought you would be so quick to do homage to Stephen.'

119

They were standing in the courtyard in the spring dawn. The King wanted to go hunting and the horses were being saddled up. John was assessing horse fodder requirements, given that Gloucester had arrived with his retinue and the Bishop of Salisbury had left on episcopal business. He watched the groom lead out Stephen's roan courser. 'What else could I have done?' He gave a practical shrug. 'Some of my lands are held by serjeantry of my post as King's marshal and the ones that are not are still in England. Whoever controls the country controls them. If I had sworn for the Empress, I would have lost everything. I have neither castle walls behind which to hide and fight nor the resources to resist. What could your sister give me in recompense when all she has to her name are a few border fortresses in Normandy still holding out for her?' He had started to breathe hard. Until now, he had not realised how much anger and anxiety had built up inside him. 'Yes, I took the oath to serve the Empress as my Queen when the time came, but again I had no choice. None of us did except to obey your father. He never confirmed his wish when he was dying. All he said, and you heard him, was: "Stephen's a man."'

'Even so, that vow was made, twice over by some, and to my sister, not to Stephen.'

'The Archbishop of Canterbury has absolved all men of that vow,' John said. 'It was obvious even from the start that it was untenable.' He looked at Robert's tightening jaw and angry eyes. 'If you are so strongly opposed, what are you doing here? Should you not be with the Empress? From what I heard, you lingered in Normandy to offer the crown to Stephen's brother, not put the Empress on the throne.' He stalked into the stables and looked at the empty stalls. A youth was forking soiled straw in a desultory fashion that earned him a rapid clip around the ear.

Robert had reddened at John's words. 'That is not true. I said in all the councils that my sister's son should be the next King.'

'A child of three?'

Robert's flush deepened. 'His mother could sit in regency, guided by trusted advisers. There is nothing wrong in such a plan. It is what my father intended.'

'Except he could not bring himself to utter the words on his deathbed. And if you are saying that Matilda could have sat in regency, you are saying she is not fit to be Queen in her own right.'

Robert threw up his hands. 'I cannot swim against the tide. My sister is full capable of ruling England and Normandy. The only bar is men's acceptance of her sex and the belief she could possibly have it in her to govern. Be honest, John. If Matilda were male, would you have bent the knee to Stephen?'

'No, but then this situation would never have arisen, would it? We would all have been certain.'

Robert looked morose. 'When my nephew is grown up, how will I look him in the eyes and tell him I gave his birthright away – that I did not fight for him?' His voice was harsh with self-disgust and suddenly John felt smirched too.

'There are many years between now and then,' he said. 'You say you cannot swim against the tide. Even less can I and we're only a mile out from shore as yet. I hazard it's going to become rougher and deeper for all as time goes on.'

A few weeks later, John remembered his conversation with Robert of Gloucester as he drank wine from a flask before the walls of Rougemont Castle at Exeter. Its castellan, Baldwin de Redvers, had rebelled against Stephen. After Henry's death, de Redvers had declared for the Empress, but had lost his nerve and come later than anyone else to yield grudgingly to the new King. Egged on by his advisers, Stephen had refused to accept the latter's tardy homage. Baldwin had fled to Rougemont and now he, his troops, his wife and sundry rebels were holed up in the city defying Stephen with every fibre and dried-up sinew of their beings even as their water supply dried up in the desiccating summer heat.

John thought the siege interesting from a tactical viewpoint and had been watching and learning with keen interest and natural aptitude. During his employment as King Henry's marshal, opportunities to practise the theories of battle strategy had been few for Henry had usually chosen diplomacy over war and mostly been successful. John knew he had the coordination, speed and skill for individual combat, that he was an efficient quartermaster and organiser, but there was more to being a good commander than that, and he was taking pleasure in testing his strengths and improving his weaknesses; mentally putting himself in the position of the besieger and the besieged.

Earlier in the day, de Redvers had sent some of his officers out under a banner of truce to negotiate terms, but Stephen had looked at the state of them, gaunt with hunger, lips drawn back from dry gums with thirst, and refused to bargain. The end was obviously near and agreeing to any terms but abject surrender would be both foolish and weak. Robert of Gloucester had argued that agreeing to let the garrison leave unharmed as de Redvers was requesting would mean a cessation of the fighting so they could be within the castle by nightfall, but Stephen, bolstered by Meulan, Martel and his brother the Bishop of Winchester, had chosen to stand firm on his initial decision.

The knights had been escorted out of the camp and Stephen, dusting his hands and looking pleased with himself, basked in the approval of those barons who had counselled him to be stern, but John was troubled. Having observed the manner in which the King listened to the differing advice and having seen the expression on Robert of Gloucester's face, he could tell trouble was brewing.

Thirst quenched, he handed the flask to a squire and, hands on hips, watched the crew of a trebuchet prime their machine to hurl another boulder at Rougemont's ruddy sandstone walls. A woman alone and on foot emerged from Rougemont's gatehouse and crossed the ditch. Her rich brown hair blew loose around her shoulders and as she drew closer, John saw that her feet were bare.

'God's blood,' swore Benet softly, his eyes growing round. 'He's only sent his wife now!'

'I thought de Redvers was a fool earlier when he sent those suffering knights to treat for terms, but he knew what he was doing,' John said with admiration.

Benet looked puzzled. 'He did?'

'Think about it. De Redvers has resisted Stephen for three months. That's not the mark of a fool, but a strong soldier. He deliberately sent his men in a desperate condition to play upon the sympathies of the lords not as committed to the King as Martel or the Beaumonts. Now he's increasing the discomfort and putting more pressure on Stephen's conscience. To send his wife into the enemy camp barefoot with her hair unbound and no women to attend her is a fine strategy. Many here are her kin. Seeing her humiliated and reduced to begging will appal them and fuel their unrest against Stephen and his advisers.'

Benet gave a judicious nod. 'I hadn't thought of it like that.'

'De Redvers certainly has.' John stored away the tactic for further perusal. He couldn't imagine Aline doing the same as de Redvers's wife. She would probably hurl herself from the battlements first – if she hadn't already descended into madness.

He went to escort the woman into camp and silenced the jeers of some of the King's Flemish mercenaries with a quelling glance and a hand to his sword hilt. He was no soft-heart but there was such a thing as courtesy.

Adeliza de Redvers was shaking, and when he offered her his arm, she leaned on it with gratitude, but she was resolute too, and John admired her courage. It wasn't going to hurt her cause either, he thought, that she was a beautiful woman.

When they came into Stephen's presence, Adeliza fell to her knees and hung her head, so that her masses of thick brown hair concealed her face, but there was no mistaking her tears and the trembling of her body. The soles of her feet were dusty, grass-stained, and she was bleeding from a cut on her heel.

'Beau sire, I beg you to show mercy to my lord husband and the garrison. Let us surrender the castle to you and leave with our lives!' Her voice cracked and broke. 'I ask not only on behalf of the men, but of their dependants, their wives and little children. Will you make orphans or corpses of us all?' She wept harder and Stephen's own face started to crumple with distress. He plucked a napkin off the trestle and stooped to her.

'Oh, in the name of God!' snapped Henry of Winchester. 'Can't you see you're being played for a fool,

124

brother? It's just another ruse by de Redvers. First he sends us his bravely suffering knights, and when that doesn't work, he uses a woman!'

Stephen's eyes narrowed. He rounded on his brother. 'Henry, enough! I full know the situation, but that doesn't mean I've lost my manners.' Gently he raised Adeliza to her feet and sat her on a camp chair. Then he had a squire bring her bread and wine. She dabbed at her eyes and thanked him in a quavery voice.

'I understand how distressed you are, my lady,' Stephen said, looking distressed himself. 'These are difficult times for all, and especially, as you say, for innocent women and children. It grieves me to see you in this condition.'

'Then I pray you, my lord, show mercy . . .'

'I am not unmoved by your plea, but I cannot yield.' His mouth twisted and he looked round at the others in the tent. 'If I do, I send out the message to others that I am not prepared to do what I must.'

'Doing what you must is murder.'

She had gone too far. Stephen drew himself up, his nostrils flaring. 'The terms must remain the unconditional surrender of your husband and his men. I can give no guarantees.'

Adeliza put down the wine she had been about to sip and pushed the bread away. 'Then there is no more to say, sire,' she answered bitterly, tossing the napkin down on the trestle. 'You are famous for your courtesy, but perhaps it is mere gilding over dross.' She rose and, straight-backed, her hair swaying at her waist, walked from the tent. Stephen gave an indecisive grimace, then gestured John to go after her. 'See her safely through the camp, FitzGilbert.'

'Sire.' John bowed out in her wake.

'I do not need your help,' she said to John in a voice

125

filled with loathing. 'What does it matter if I receive consideration now if I am going to die at your hands within a few hours or days?'

'You will not die, my lady,' John answered. 'The King will not allow it.'

'But he will allow others to be cut down by your swords or hanged on gibbets,' she flared at him. 'He will give his mercenaries leave to do what mercenaries do when they overcome an enemy.'

John took her arm as she stumbled. 'It's not over yet,' he said.

She didn't reply. He halted on the periphery of their camp before he came within arrow range of the castle walls. Adeliza pushed her hair out of her eyes and faced him. 'Do you have a wife and offspring?'

'Yes, my lady, I do.'

'Then look to their safety because no one else will. And look to your back also, because someone will put a knife in it one day.' She gave him a wet, angry stare. 'At least my husband can go to his maker with his honour intact. How many in your own camp can say the same?'

Maintaining a bland expression, refusing to be drawn, John bowed to her. 'You will be safe from here, my lady.'

'I know that, messire. I am returning to those I trust. I cannot say the same for you.'

'As you will have it, my lady,' he said and returned to the camp. She was right, but then such was the nature of life at court.

At the King's pavilion, the Bishop of Winchester, the Beaumonts, Martel and the King's mercenary captain William D'Ypres were arguing with Robert of Gloucester, Miles of Hereford and Brian FitzCount as to whether the Exeter garrison should be allowed to ride out in honourable retreat or not. Stephen stood in the middle of the disputing factions looking as bewildered as a child caught at the centre of a parental row.

'Sire.' Gloucester opened his hands towards Stephen in a pleading gesture. 'If you hang and mutilate the men behind those walls, you will sow the teeth of the hydra. How many of your own men will stay with you when they see their own kin brought to this? Take his castle in surrender, let him go overseas and count yourself well rid of him. What harm can he do if he has no lands or revenue?'

Gloucester's voice and words were eloquent. John watched Stephen dither and vacillate and saw the weakness in him. Faced with a dilemma, Stephen could not choose. John knew from his own duties at court that to appear indecisive or not in command was fatal. One of the first lessons his father had taught him was that even if you were unsure of your ground you never let it show on your face. You never let the talking go on for too long either – and never after you had given your decision.

He had to leave to deal with the matter of some missing tallies and a supply cart of arrows that had been expected but hadn't arrived. By the time he had sorted that out, a messenger was hurrying from the direction of the royal tent towards the horse lines and the council had broken up.

'He's letting them go,' Gloucester said as John joined him outside the tent. 'As he should have done at the start without this circus. Those men have fought to a standstill; they deserve better than to swing. Too many have relatives in our camp – there would be a riot among our own troops if it came to executions. This way, we take Exeter and honour is satisfied all round.'

There had been a great deal of talk about honour, John noticed. It was as if Matilda's ghost lingered at the council tables and men had to say the word loudly to drown out their guilty consciences. Still, he doubted that Baldwin de Redvers slept any more soundly at night for having kept his oath . . . and the earth was going to be a hard pillow while he made his way to whatever succour he could find overseas.

De Redvers left Exeter to an exultant fanfare of trumpets from Stephen's heralds. Some portions of the King's army jeered, shook fists, threw clods and excrement at the line of men and women departing the castle. John stood at the front of the line to watch the garrison pass, his face expressionless, but he allowed his men to cheer fellow soldiers who had held out against the odds and had been defeated through dry wells, not lack of prowess. No one under his command threw anything save water costrels and loaves of bread. De Redvers rode his destrier, one of the few horses still alive, and his wife rode pillion behind him, her hair now decently veiled, and her feet shod in slippers of fine dyed leather. The troops belonging to Robert of Gloucester and Brian FitzCount greeted the draggled, parched refugees with a massive roar of approbation, as if de Redvers had won a great victory. Perhaps he had, John thought. He had a strong suspicion that Adeliza was right; it wasn't over.

11

Hamstead, Berkshire, Autumn 1137

They were slaughtering pigs for winter salting and the yard by the kitchens was occupied by the industry. Aline had retired to her chamber and barred the shutters but the sound of the squeals still filtered through the timbers and made her feel sick. She fancied she could smell the basins of dark blood that stood waiting to be mixed with oatmeal and fat and turned into puddings. She wouldn't go anywhere near the kitchens for the next several days until all evidence had been packed away in barrels, hung in smoke houses or put in store.

Rohese the nurse was telling a story to three-year-old Gilbert. Aline raised her head from embroidering crosses on a pouch and managed to find a smile as Gilbert's voice piped up, interrupting the story with a question. He was a beautiful little boy and she was so proud of him and her achievement in bearing him – he was her gift to John of their marriage. Yet she found it difficult to connect with him on an intimate level. Rather than have him run to her for cuddles and reassurance, she wanted to join him and be a child again herself, to be praised and loved as a child. Being a grown woman was much too complicated and demanding.

Her duty remained to bring more offspring to her union with John, but when he had lain with her before going to Normandy in February, her womb had not quickened, and he had been absent on campaign since then. She had worried that her failure to conceive was a sign of God's displeasure and had done extra penance and confession to cleanse herself. It might be a sign too that John had displeased God, but she could do nothing about her husband's relationship with his maker; that was up to him.

Agnes, one of the women who served in the hall, put her head round the door. 'Madam, your lord is home from Normandy. The troop's just riding in.'

Panic flooded through Aline. Usually John sent word ahead so that she could at least be half prepared; even then she was frequently caught out. She couldn't go out to the courtyard to greet him, not with those dead pigs strewing the kitchen yard and the ground all bloody. Now Agnes had mentioned it, she could hear the clop of hooves, the shouts of men. She bundled her sewing aside and rose to her feet, wondering which way to turn, but before she could gather herself, John was striding into the room. Seizing her by the shoulders he gave her a hard kiss on the mouth.

She staggered as he released her and, pressing a hand to her tingling lips, stared at him with widening eyes. He laughed, and her astonishment increased because she had never seen him so exuberant. He went to his son and crouched to the child's level. 'Bones of Adam, you've grown!'

Gilbert, not having seen his father since the spring, pressed his face against Rohese's skirts.

'Have you been good while I've been gone?'

'Good as gold.' Rohese gently ruffled Gilbert's hair. 'He is no trouble.'

130

John smiled. 'I was always trouble – so I've been told!'

Aline struggled to recover her wits. She barely recognised her husband. The John she knew was laconic and understated, like a hunting cat. The man who had returned from Normandy more resembled an excited hound straining at the leash. She sent Agnes, who was still goggling in the doorway, to fetch food. There was plenty of hot water available owing to the slaughtering, but she wasn't sure about bathtubs. Most of them were probably in use for holding pig parts.

'W-was Normandy successful, my lord?' she ventured and went to pour him wine from the jug on the coffer by the bed. It had been standing since last night, but hopefully wasn't too sour.

John's high spirits lost some of their ebullience. He gave his cloak to an attendant. 'Normandy, sweetheart, was hell. If there was ever a reason to stay at home, then these past months have been it. I've seen a deal of hard fighting and put some bad nicks in my sword. I'm going to need a new blade before the next campaign.'

Aline put her hand to her mouth. She hoped he wasn't going to tell her about his battles. 'You weren't injured?' she asked faintly.

'Not beyond bruises, and I didn't lose any men. The Angevins weren't much of a challenge – a rabble in fact.' He took the cup from her. 'We swept them back over the border like whipped curs. What finished them off was the fact that they had no idea how to dig proper latrines. Once they went down with the belly gripes, they were easy meat.' He made a scornful face. 'Geoffrey of Anjou and the Empress will have to do better than that if they intend claiming Normandy and England.' He drank and looked round the chamber. Aline hoped he was familiarising himself with home rather than noticing the cobwebs in the rafters. 'The hellish part was the fighting among our own troops,' he added. 'There was close to open war between the Flemish mercenaries and the Norman lords. William D'Ypres and Robert of Gloucester almost came to personal blows over their men and an issue of stolen wine.'

She wrung her hands. 'Y-you weren't involved?'

He shook his head. 'I've more sense. As long as they kept the brawl in the camp and didn't bring it into the court, it was none of my business. Let their line commanders deal with the matter. But now Gloucester and D'Ypres hate each other. Even if they've shaken hands in public, they haven't set their differences aside and Gloucester's stayed behind in Normandy. Adeliza de Redvers was right about knives in the back.' He took another mouthful of wine and grimaced before thrusting the cup into the hand of his squire. 'Hugh, go and find a fresh flagon. I've drunk enough vinegar in the field without having to drink it at home too.'

Aline flushed and muttered an apology. 'It's been standing . . . If I'd known . . .'

He waved an impatient hand. 'No matter.' The gleam returned to his eyes. 'Stephen has finally fulfilled the promise he made to me at his coronation. He has given me custody of his castles at Marlborough and Ludgershall as well as the manors of Wexcombe and Cherhill. Finally, I'm being rewarded.'

Aline stared at the fierce exultation on his face. This was what he had wanted from the beginning and was something she had dreaded. 'That is great news, my lord,' she managed to say, but her voice was small and thin. She found it difficult enough coping with what they had. How was she going to manage as the wife of not only the King's senior marshal but also a royal castellan?

Marlborough was a powerful fortress. Ludgershall was smaller, but on a level with Hamstead. She fought for composure. If John had castles, then the castles were bound to have chapels. His increased standing would mean he would be able to do more for the church. To have given them this much, God must surely be smiling on them.

'Stephen doesn't trust Brian FitzCount. He wants me to guard the road to Wallingford and the route to Devizes. If I have control over all the valley of the Kennet, nothing will escape my notice.'

She gnawed her lip. The political doings of this baron and that were above her head and didn't interest her, unless they impinged on her daily life. 'What about your duties at court?'

His squire returned with a fresh flagon and John's silver-gilt cup, which he had unpacked from the baggage. 'I'll be there for the great occasions,' he said. 'I'll have to go for the Christmas season, but I have some useful deputies trained up and they're capable enough unless there's great upheaval.' He took the filled cup from the youth. 'I'll show my face enough for men not to forget it, but Stephen will expect me to take some time away to stamp my authority on my new responsibilities.'

She smiled at him to hide her failing courage. At least he would be home, she thought. It would be reassuring to have his protection and the servants would obey with more alacrity. During his absences, their performance was always less enthusiastic.

That night, she was bold, removing her chemise without prompting and steeling herself to the exposure of candle-light. John looked at her with a smile in his eyes as he removed his shirt. 'Do I take it that absence makes the heart grow fonder?'

133

She looked at the exquisite bones of his face, that toned, masculine body. 'I have missed you,' she whispered with a blush. 'And Gilbert should have a brother.'

He didn't reciprocate and say that he had missed her, but he was tender when he took her in his arms. 'It has been a long time, hasn't it?' he said.

At Salisbury, Sybilla was helping her mother sort out bolts of fabric for making new gowns. They had indulged in a buying spree in Winchester last week. As well as fine linen for undergarments and gossamer weaves of the same for veils, there were yards of madder-red Flemish twill, dark green thickly napped wool for cloaks, and a beautiful mid-blue Lincoln cloth with a pattern of tiny lozenges self-woven throughout. Sybilla ran a covetous hand over the last fabric, which was her favourite. Her mother watched her and smiled.

'Yes,' Sybire said. 'The blue will suit you, with embroidery of beads if you want it as your Christmas dress? And perhaps this for everyday?' She indicated another bolt the greenish-gold of a ripe pear. Sybilla nodded delighted agreement to both while her mother clucked her tongue. 'You can't wear that brown for much longer. Your ankles are beginning to show. At this rate you're going to be as tall as your brothers.' There was exasperation and pride in her mother's voice.

Sybilla was kneeling, so the widening gap between the hem of her gown and her shoes didn't show but it was the same with her sleeves where several inches of white wrist linked her cuffs to her hands. She had turned thirteen years old at midsummer and her body had begun a determined change into womanhood, although she had yet to start her fluxes. She certainly didn't want to become as tall as William or Patrick. The latter had bumped his head on the stable door yesterday and sported an enormous bruise in the centre of his forehead, thus causing him to remark that it was more dangerous living at home than it was campaigning in Normandy.

The door banged open and her father stumped into the room, favouring his right leg. The winter damp was playing havoc with his ageing joints and, in consequence, he was irascible with everyone. Patrick and William were still abed, catching up on sleep after the rigours of the battle-camp. Sybilla knew a part of her father's crabbiness stemmed from his frustration at not having been able to serve in Normandy with the King. His worsening knees meant he now struggled in a soldier's role and had to rely on his sons.

'What's wrong now?' Lady Salisbury set the chosen bolts of cloth to one side and went to store the others in the fabric cupboard.

He limped over to a coffer and picked up the walking staff that was lying across it. 'I've just heard that the King has given John FitzGilbert custody of Marlborough and Ludgershall and enriched him with the manors of Wexcombe and Cherhill.' He looked daggers at his wife as if it were her fault. 'Why can't he do the same for us? Why couldn't he have given those keeps and manors to me? Good Christ, when my sire was the greatest English thegn in these parts, FitzGilbert's grandsire was a common stable serjeant.' His indignation rose as he spoke and spittle foamed on his grey moustaches. 'In the name of God, why give him Ludgershall?'

Sybilla had heard similar invective from her father before. He was always disgruntled when others received preferential treatment for what he viewed as fawning at court. He was very proud of his English blood and the fact that it went back to long before the Normans came

135

to England, their family being one of the few that had survived the upheaval of the Conquest years with its lands intact.

'John FitzGilbert is a clever man,' her mother said neutrally.

Walter glared. 'Too clever for his own good.'

'Patrick says he fought a duel to prove himself.' Sybilla spoke up.

'Hah, any dolt with the fast arm of youth can wield a sword and look convincing. John FitzGilbert has the Devil's own luck and knows how to manipulate situations, but sooner or later he'll have debts to pay, and then we'll see what manner of man he is.' Anger and opinion vented, he shook the staff he had come to fetch and stamped from the room.

Lady Salisbury sighed and shook her head. 'One of the most important lessons you need to learn as a woman is the virtue of patience when dealing with oxen,' she said.

Sybilla gave a puzzled frown. 'I thought Papa liked John FitzGilbert?'

'It's not so much that, my love, as seeing our family stand still while other men who are good at pushing themselves forward at court are given privileges.'

Sybilla looked thoughtful. She could understand it wasn't fair. 'Why was he so cross about Ludgershall?'

Her mother closed the clothing cupboard. 'Ludgershall used to belong to your English grandsire, Edward, but when he died, the King took it into his own hands. Your father thinks it should still be ours, not handed out as a favour to a courtier. His knees have been troubling him too, which makes him feel old and unable to do things. He hates having to send your brothers to fight in his stead.' She came to stroke Sybilla's rich brunette braids. 'Sometimes when people are in pain and cannot do the things they want, they lash out at others who they feel are more fortunate. If you can understand that and learn to cope with it, then it will be a great asset to you.'

Sybilla nodded thoughtfully. She had not thought about such things before. Of late, her mother had taken to speaking with her in a woman-to-woman fashion and Sybilla sensed that the free days of childhood were nearing an end. No one had mentioned betrothal yet, but it was like a distant scent on the breeze – tantalising and worrying at the same time.

They were carrying the bales of cloth to the trestle for cutting when her brother Patrick sauntered into the room, stretching and yawning after his long slumber. He was as tall and as indolent as a young lion. The campaign in Normandy had put a new assurance and swagger in his stride. Having greeted his mother and sister, he deliberately tugged Sybilla's braid.

She rounded on him with a yelp, anger flashing. He laughed, lifted her off the floor, swung her round and plonked her down. 'God, you're as heavy as a sack of flour. What have you been eating while I've been away? Too much pudding, I'll warrant. Hah, you're even growing dumplings on your chest!'

'Patrick, enough!' their mother snapped.

Sybilla inhaled the pungent heat of his armpit as he stretched again. She thought about kicking him in the shins, but there wasn't enough room to run away; the mood he was in, he would catch her and, in the guise of play-fighting, tickle her until she was bruised.

'And be mindful of your father,' Lady Salisbury warned. 'He's in a sour mood.'

'What's riled him now?' Patrick lounged over to the

cutting trestle and absently fingered the bolt of Lincoln weave.

Fetching her shears and a box of pins, her mother told him about John Marshal. Sybilla saw Patrick grimace.

'Don't you like him either?' she asked her brother. Whenever Sybilla thought of John Marshal, she remembered his wedding day in Winchester and the lovely torchlit walk to his house. She remembered the sweetness of marchpane on her tongue and the scented summer air. She had seen him on a few occasions since then, including the churching of his wife after their son's birth. He had always seemed pleasant and courteous – refined, she thought – unlike Patrick.

'It's not a matter of that,' Patrick said. 'Certainly I'd rather have him at my back in a fight than a band of Flemings or troops led by Meulan.'

'Why?'

'If John Marshal says he will protect your back then he'll do it and not back down. He's as hard as horseshoe nails. He'll hold his ground and fight like one of the Devil's own – which means he'll hold on to Ludgershall like a baiting dog with its jaws clamped in a bull's nose. I wonder how he got it approved. He must have sneaked it under the noses of Martel and Meulan.' A narrow glint entered Patrick's eyes. 'It means he'll be a closer neighbour now . . . and richer than he was.'

'I hardly think he will do much visiting,' Lady Salisbury said. 'Even with Marlborough and Ludgershall, he won't be paving his sideboard with golden salvers.'

Patrick gave a sour grin. 'If he did, he'd only be accused of having stolen them from the King.'

12

Ludgershall, Wiltshire, June 1138

In the sweltering June heat, John blotted his brow on his forearm and watched the masons at their toil, building new defences, raising a new hall, replacing timber with stone. The trundle of cartwheels, the tap of busy hammers, the sound of industry and progress were sweet to John's ears and he was enjoying himself immensely. His duties at court were fulfilling and there was satisfaction in doing them well, but there was little joy. He had to be constantly on the lookout for traps set by rivals, and for situations that could escalate in a moment from minor squabble to full-blown squall. Here, within his own jurisdiction and with licence to expand as he chose, he had discovered happiness and he was still getting to grips with it, like one of his squires learning a new skill.

His son was busy in the company of the masons, helping them mix the mortar. John grinned to see him following the men around, aping their actions, his small features set in serious lines of concentration, a purloined measuring rod in his hand. Four years old was perhaps a little young to be revealing firm traits as a castle-builder, but good for constructing solid foundations.

He glanced beyond the child as the guard on duty at the gatehouse blew three blasts on his horn, warning of visitors. John clapped stone dust from his hands and crossed the foundations to the entrance as a procession of riders with dogs and hawks trotted through. His gaze sharpened as he recognised William and Patrick of Salisbury, the sheriff's two oldest sons. They swung down from their sweating coursers, gave the reins to grooms and advanced to greet him. 'Neighbour,' said William, extending his hand.

John took and clasped it firmly. William was about six years younger than himself, slender and dark-haired like his mother. A reasonable tactician, John knew from Normandy, and an astute courtier when he had to be. Patrick, but recently into full manhood, more resembled the sheriff, being of a wide, muscular build with a ruddy complexion and broad cheekbones. He was the better soldier too, but less useful at the diplomacy. Their sister was with them and had been helped down from her mount by one of the attendants. She stood expectantly behind Patrick's broad, turned back and when neither of her brothers said anything, she cleared her throat.

Patrick glanced round. 'Oh, our sister Sybilla,' he said as a definite afterthought.

She curtseyed.

'My lady, you are welcome,' John said with a slight bow, applying the manners of the court even if she was just a girl and he was wearing a sweat-stained shirt with sleeves rolled back and dust-powdered hose and braies. 'What brings you to Ludgershall?' he asked William.

The latter flashed a smile. 'A stray hawk,' he said blandly. 'A fine peregrine. I didn't want to lose her, and she fetched up in those oaks yonder. Being as we were so close, I decided to pay a visit, lest we were seen from afar and you should wonder.'

John raised an eyebrow. 'Indeed I might have done.'

William sucked in his cheeks. 'You are busy, I see.'

More feigned nonchalance. John was well accustomed to this kind of sparring at court. The circling and sniffing like two dogs uncertain whether to wag tails or to bite. 'Indeed so. The King entrusted Ludgershall to me on the understanding that I would improve the defences.'

Patrick stirred his toe in the dust. 'You know this place used to belong to our grandfather Edward?'

'How could I not, when my parents grew up knowing your grandsire as the sheriff? Some of the villagers here still remember him.' He gave the brothers a mocking smile. 'The old woman who keeps the fire in the hall claims she used to warm his bed furs long ago when she was a toothsome wench.'

'Hah, does she?' Patrick gave a short laugh. Sybilla smiled but kept her gaze lowered to show she was a modest, well-brought-up young lady.

'I also know your father wasn't happy about the King's gift of this place to me,' John said. 'I have ears.'

Patrick eyed him narrowly. 'It should belong to us,' he growled. 'Our family was its custodians long before The Bastard came from Normandy with his baggage of hangers-on.'

William had the sense to nudge his brother and give him a warning look.

John half smiled. 'Things change. Any forester will tell you that old wood has to go to make way for vigorous new growth.' Turning, he gestured to a bench set in the shade of the old Saxon hall. 'You look as much in need of watering as your horses. Come and take some wine.' He sent one servant running to bring a pitcher and cups,

141

another to fetch Aline, and summoned Gilbert from his play to present him.

'Fine boy.' Patrick cast his eyes over Gilbert as if he were a hound pup of dubious parentage. Sybilla smiled and admired the mason's rod the little boy was holding.

'I'm starting him young,' John said. 'By the time he's ten, he's going to be the best castle-builder in England . . . except for his father, of course.' His sardonic tone of voice earned pained expressions from the brothers.

Aline joined them, her belly a taut dome on her slight frame. John watched his wife greet their guests in such a soft voice that they had to strain to hear her. Her gaze darted nervously and, as always, she toyed with the amber beads that never left her belt. Sitting down, she became little more than a shadow at the trestle. Watching her struggle, John wondered why he had bothered to send a servant to fetch her. The Salisburys' little sister already had more assurance than Aline and was barely an adolescent.

Patrick leaned back and toyed with the stem of his goblet. 'I can see you're turning this into a fine fortified site, my lord . . . but on whose behalf, I wonder? It's no secret that you and the Earl of Gloucester have always been on excellent terms.'

John fixed Patrick with one of the hard stares he used on upstarts at court. 'I owe my service to the King, not Robert of Gloucester. If you are implying my loyalty is compromised, either you have a reason, or you are deliberately setting out to insult me.' *Or you are stupid.* He didn't add the last remark, but put enough of it in his stare to make Patrick's cheekbones flush red.

'So the news hasn't reached you then?' William said in the tone of a peace-maker and once more glared at Patrick.

'News about what?'

'Robert of Gloucester has renounced his oath to Stephen and gone over to his sister. He's given her all of his castles in Normandy and they are mustering an army to invade England. There's going to be war, and men have to decide where their loyalties lie. Given the circumstances, we are bound to ask. This may be the last time we ride abroad without our mail and in gentle company.'

Aline made a dismayed sound and pressed one hand to her mouth and the other to her belly. John folded his arms. 'No, I hadn't heard,' he admitted, 'but I am not surprised. It has been in the air since Normandy. My lord of Gloucester has been discontented for a while.'

'Well, now he's openly rebelled. There's war in Normandy and it'll likely spread to England. The lands you command stand on the edge of Gloucester's territory and you will be in his path should he choose to strike north.'

John rubbed a considering palm over his jaw. 'What you say is true, but it is also speculation. We all stand in the path of someone, do we not? I am in your father's . . . or perhaps he is in mine?' He raised his brows at his guests.

Patrick finished his wine, banged down his goblet and rose to his feet. 'You will find it wise to give us leave to pass if you desire to keep the peace.'

John rose too. 'Providing you grant me the same courtesy, I see no need for conflict,' he said pleasantly.

Sybilla curtseyed to Aline and then to him, but John responded without really noticing her. His mind was on what William had told him and the fact that his visitors had had plenty of opportunity to look around the new works at Ludgershall and would now report to their father on everything they had seen.

John saw his guests back on their horses and to the

143

gateway. 'I hope you don't lose your hawk again,' he said to William, 'but if it flies this way, I am sure we can find you a warm welcome.' His tone was bland and, because of it, filled with meaning.

William was not slow on the uptake. 'Thank you, my lord. We will bear it in mind.' With a final look around the compound, he rode off with Patrick, his sister and their retainers. John watched them leave and pondered. Aline joined him, and he heard the soft, monotonous click, click of the beads through her fingers.

'There's not going to be war, is there?' she asked in a frightened voice.

He twitched his shoulders. 'What will be, will be. I do not doubt Robert has gone over to the Empress. He wasn't happy to swear for Stephen in the first place. He was always foremost in his father's council chamber, but now he has been pushed aside in favour of others. In truth I don't blame him.'

'But what if he comes to England with an army?'

John clung to his patience. 'If Robert of Gloucester lands in England with an army, then grant me the wit and ability to deal with whatever happens.' He saw that her hands were trembling. Her ability to cope, always shaky at the best of times, scattered like dry sand in a breeze at the notion of facing war and violence. 'It's not as if there's an army on our doorstep,' he said. 'If it helps you, go to church and pray awhile.'

An expression of relief crossed her face and she almost ran from his presence to do as he suggested. Grimacing, John returned to the trestle, poured himself another cup of wine, and sat down to do some serious thinking.

On the edge of the foundations, Gilbert had settled down with a pail of water to build himself a castle moulded from mud with stones pressed into the sides for decoration. John watched his play and wondered if he was doing the same thing. All it would take to destroy it would be a wilful foot, or a sudden thunderstorm.

13

Bristol, August 1138

The King's campaign tent was a lavish affair of heavy linen canvas, waxed for protection against the weather, and lined with hangings of embroidered Flemish wool. New green rushes cut from the banks of the river Avon strewed the floor and a heady green scent filled the tent space, making it smell almost like a fresh stable.

Having just returned from a foraging trip, John was still wearing his armour. An angry red scratch threaded the back of his wrist and his chausses were bloodstained. Usually he would not have entered the King's presence thus attired, but he had been late to the meet, and his appearance was a timely reminder to others that the blade at his hip was for more than just show. The subject under discussion was how to make Bristol capitulate.

'Treachery is spreading like a canker,' Stephen growled, the usual good humour absent from his expression. 'By taking Bristol, I will cut out the core of the tumour, but how can I do that when the town is still receiving supplies by the river?'

'You should blockade the estuary, sire,' advised the Earl of Leicester. 'Sink obstructions at the harbour mouth –

boulders, rubble, tree trunks – anything to prevent the boats from getting through.' He bared his teeth. 'Once the citizens begin to starve, they'll not be so defiant.'

'We could build a dam and flood the town,' Martel suggested.

Stephen pinched his upper lip, considering. 'I have also thought to build siege castles to prevent use of the bridges across the city.'

John was sceptical. The building of siege castles was usual procedure and a sound tactic, but the other notions seemed ambitious folly to him. 'Sire, it would take tons of material to make an impression on a channel that deep. We would have to find the boulders and trees in the first place and then transport them, with no guarantee of success. The tides and currents are powerful and would wash most of the work away. What was left would be neither use nor embellishment.'

'An expert, are you, FitzGilbert?' sneered Martel.

John gave him a cold stare. 'As much as you are, my lord,' he retorted. 'The people to ask would be the local fisherfolk and merchants, but since they are the ones bringing in the supplies, you'd have to catch one first and hope he'd talk and tell you the truth. As to the issue of transporting tree trunks and boulders, you'd have to find strong enough carts and horses and decide how many you'd need. At least part of that is within my remit. If the King chooses to blockade the harbour, then I will do my best to find him what he needs.'

Martel glowered at him. 'Your words might seem like common sense to many, except we know you are a close friend of Robert of Gloucester.'

John refused to be riled because he knew Martel was angling for just such a response. 'That accusation is as stale as mouldy cheese, as well you know, my lord. The

147

Earl of Gloucester is indeed my friend, but I am not bound in his service and my oath of fealty is to the King. If pointing out the shortcomings of a suggestion is treachery, then where are we bound?'

'Marshal's right, on all points,' said Brian FitzCount. 'I have seen men who should know better look at me in the same way for saying what has to be said. First we must know the depth of the channel and how much material will have to be rolled into the river and if it is likely to stay. Ideas are good, but the wherewithal to fulfil them has to be addressed.'

Several others nodded in FitzCount's wake while de Beaumont and Martel fought their corner, stressing the need for a blockade to prevent supplies coming into Bristol.

'You have the garrison at Bath,' John said. 'If you build the castles at the bridges and use Bath to keep Bristol pinned down, then you are free to move elsewhere. There are other rebellious lords around you – Ralph Luvel and FitzJohn at Cary and Harptree. They are easier targets and will prevent the soldiers from becoming frustrated.'

Stephen narrowed his gaze in thought. 'It seems to me I have two choices. One that if it works will give me Bristol in the palm of my hand, but if it doesn't, will be a waste of time and effort I can ill afford to expend. The other won't give me Bristol, but it will keep its garrison pinned down and harassed. It should not be difficult to secure Cary and Harptree and, as my marshal says, the men need a taste of success. I say we take the second option. Prepare to strike camp.'

Riding to Cary, John was aware of a heightened sense of danger. It didn't come from the King, who was highly pleased with him. Stephen had been delighted at John's contribution to the discussion about what to do at Bristol.

For part of the journey, Stephen rode with John and presented him with a row of expensive enamelled silver pendants for the brow- and breast-band of his stallion whilst hinting at rewards for his service greater than such trifles.

Such intimations goaded John's ambition, but they goaded other men too. Martel's followers muttered in corners, but stopped as soon as John approached. De Beaumont was ignoring him. William D'Ypres had been giving him the kinds of looks John would have used himself on men not welcome in the King's hall. He was aware of being isolated, of being pushed out and put in a dangerous position on the edge of the shoal. He had a modicum of protection in the neutrality and mild friendship of men such as Geoffrey de Bohun, Brian FitzCount and Hugh Bigod of Norfolk, but he knew how precarious his position was.

Some young knights belonging to the entourage of William Martel were laughing, making loud jokes and tossing a wine flask from one to the other. John rode with a set expression, determined not to let his irritation show. He would never allow his own men to drink and behave like unruly children when on progress. Suddenly, a brightly painted spear hurtled past John's head, missing him by a fraction, and skittered along the side of the road. John's palfrey shied and nearly threw him, although by clinging to the reins and saddle, he managed to keep his seat. Behind him, the shouts and guffaws increased.

Furious, he pulled out of line and gestured his squire to pick up the spear and give it to him. Grasping the haft, he spurred towards Martel's cluster of knights, but they turned their mounts and rode away at a gallop, still laughing. John drew rein. His heart was pounding against his rib cage and his grip on the spear haft was slippery with cold sweat.

149

'Drunken young fools,' muttered Benet. 'Are you all right, my lord?'

'Yes,' John said, although he wasn't. This was no sottish horseplay. He had been sent a warning, and it made his spine crawl. Next time, even if it looked like an accident, they wouldn't miss.

'Good spear,' Benet said drily. 'Your gain, their loss. I say keep it.'

John looked at his knight and felt some of the sick tension leave him. He found a tight smile as he hefted the weapon. 'I intend to,' he said. 'In fact I'm going to fly my banner from it when we pitch tent. If they want it back, let them come and ask me for it.' He looked at the lance head. It was made for killing boar and the tines were barbed. A blow from this would grant no easy death.

Martel bestowed on John a look of scornful astonishment, as if he thought the latter's complaint was mere carping. 'It was horseplay that got out of hand,' he said with a dismissive gesture. 'I'll see it doesn't happen again.'

John nodded stiffly and controlled his temper. He was standing outside Martel's tent as Stephen's army finished pitching camp in the sinking afternoon. Beyond their lines, Ralph Luvel's timber keep rose against the roseate skyline. He had expected just such a response from Martel and thus was prepared for it. 'If you do not, my lord, I will. As the King's marshal, it is within my remit to discipline the troops on the road. A more suspicious man might take their behaviour for treachery.'

'Be careful what you say, Marshal.' Martel drew himself up.

'Be careful what you do,' John retorted, meeting Martel stare for stare. 'Don't underestimate me. I have your measure down to the final dreg in the cup and the last lamprey on the salver.'

Martel laid his hand to the hilt of his sword. 'If you have an accusation to make, then do it. Otherwise hold your peace.' A dark flush rose from his throat and into his face.

John looked pointedly at the fist Martel had made around his sword grip. 'I can see that you are holding yours,' he replied. 'Tell your men. I assume they obey your orders.'

Sybilla knelt on the floor, using one of her outworn shoes to play tug of war with a hound pup. Her brothers had returned from the Welsh Marches an hour ago and, having washed and eaten, were sitting in the private chamber, regaling their father with all their news, most of it good from the sounds of it. Sybilla knew her brothers considered it unseemly for a woman to listen in to masculine conversation, so she was being circumspect. The pup was a good distraction. As long as her brothers thought she was just playing with her dog, she'd be allowed to remain as an extension of the surroundings.

Bristol was still under guard from the garrison at Bath and the castles at Cary and Harptree had surrendered. Shrewsbury had rebelled and been retaken. The Scots, led by the Empress's uncle King David, had been defeated by the English barons of the north in a decisive, bloody battle at Northallerton the week after the Assumption of the Virgin. Also, Ludlow had been given to one of Stephen's Breton mercenaries along with the right to marry its widow. Sybilla's ears pricked up because the widow's name was Sybilla too.

'Lucky bastard,' Patrick grumbled. 'We don't get given castles and widows.' There was a petulant note in his voice.

'Joscelin de Dinan is related to the Counts of Brittany,' said her father, 'and he's a strong soldier. I don't envy him holding Ludlow for Stephen. It's not going to be an easy ride – and neither is that woman.'

There were some salacious masculine chuckles. Sybilla wondered why her namesake was not considered an 'easy ride'? Was she difficult in the bedroom? She knew when men spoke of mounting and riding women, the connotation was sexual. But it did have other meanings too.

'Put her in a scold's bridle and she'll be easy enough,' said Patrick. 'Show her who wears the chausses like we've been showing the other whoresons who've declared for the Empress. Her plans have come to naught this year.'

'Women never know when to give up,' Walter said wryly. 'Mark me, she'll keep trying. All she needs is somewhere to land. Stephen will have to watch all the ports, and still keep the garrison at Bristol pinned down.'

'I heard a rumour that John FitzGilbert was thinking of defecting to the Empress when she lands,' Patrick announced.

There was a brief silence. Sybilla stopped playing with the puppy and turned round to stare at her father and brothers.

William snorted 'Where did you hear that?'

'I was playing dice with some of Martel's knights.'

'And you believed them?'

Patrick made a face at his brother. 'Why shouldn't I? Martel's got his finger in every pie at court. His woman used to bed with John FitzGilbert and she's a known spy. Who knows what she sees and hears in the course of a night's work.'

Sybilla's eyes widened. The pup took advantage of her distraction to seize the shoe out of her hands and nestling it between his paws, began to chew in earnest. The last she had heard about John FitzGilbert and his concerns was that his wife had recently borne another son they had christened Walter after Lady Aline's father, but this was much more interesting!

'I can't see the King's marshal jeopardising the castles he's just received in order to rebel in favour of the Empress,' her father said, looking sceptical. 'He's too shrewd for that.'

'And shrewd enough to see where he stands if Robert of Gloucester does invade. He's on the edge of Gloucester's territory. It might make more sense to form an alliance with him than withstand his assault.'

'And then he'd have us to contend with for a start,' her father said.

'We might be able to get Ludgershall back.' Patrick's eyes gleamed. 'And who knows what might happen to Marlborough . . .'

'Indeed, but let us not get too far in front of ourselves.' Her father made a settling motion with the palm of his hand. 'Still, there's no harm in being vigilant. If John FitzGilbert does make a false move, we'll be ready to deal with him.'

Looking at her father and brothers seated around the fire, Sybilla thought they looked a little like the hounds from the pack to which her pup belonged. Eager for the chase, pulling at the leash, anticipating a kill.

14

Oxford, June 1139

'Christ on the Cross!' John muttered to his usher, Bonhomme. 'I need eyes in my arse today.' Hand on sword hilt he gave a passing soldier a hard look. The court gathering in Oxford was a large one, involving many of King Stephen's tenants-in-chief and a goodly salting of the most important ecclesiasts, including Bishop Roger of Salisbury and his nephews the Bishops of Lincoln and Ely. Finding suitable lodgings for so many would have been awkward at the best of times and this wasn't one of them with the country on a knife edge and rebellions still flaring up like little marsh fires all over the place. Bristol was still defiant, bloody but unbowed, and rumours continued to grow that the Empress was planning to invade England with an army of Normans and Angevins. Men's swords were quick to clear the scabbards and tensions were rife.

'Indeed it's bad,' Bonhomme agreed with a glint of morose relish. 'Like being in the midst of six hostile dog packs all at once. Someone's bound to get savaged before the day's much older. Speaking of which . . .' He gave an infinitesimal nod towards the courtyard.

John swore under his breath, then bowed as Roger, Bishop of Salisbury, approached the King's hall. The elderly prelate was leaning on his crosier and not walking well, although that could have been due as much to his bulk as the condition of his legs. In the June heat, he was glistening with sweat as if someone had basted his face. Behind him, amid an assortment of deacons and clerics, the Bishops of Ely and Lincoln walked in jewelled magnificence like living marchpane subtleties. Rumour had it that Alexander of Lincoln was in fact Roger's son rather than his nephew and there was indeed a resemblance about the noses, although Bishop Alexander was of slighter build.

Salisbury presented John with his ring to kiss – a fat sapphire set in a hoop of gold. His flesh puffed around it like pastry. John and Bonhomme knelt to perform obeisance. Salisbury's breath wheezed in and out of his chest and the incense of his sweat hung in the air with breath-stopping pungency. The Bishop had a mistress of a similar size to himself, although he had left her behind at Devizes. John hoped their bed was a sturdy one.

'I don't know what I'm doing here, FitzGilbert,' Salisbury said as John rose to his feet. 'At my age the court no longer holds the attractions it used to. I'm as much use as a colt on a battlefield.' He gave a phlegmy laugh. Behind the smile, behind the superficial crinkling of his eyelids, John saw the pride, the fulsomeness, the anger. Roger of Salisbury had ruled England in the old King's day, acting as the justiciar when Henry was out of the country. Together he and Henry had built the exchequer and made it into an efficient department for collecting revenue. Money had flowed into it and stayed. Stephen had inherited a treasury brimming with silver and was setting out to spend it like water.

155

'The King would not have summoned you to court had he not thought it necessary, my lord,' John said.

Salisbury snorted. 'You're not naive, Marshal. If he has summoned me to this gathering, and my nephews with me, it is not because he desires to fold me to his bosom – but he needs me nonetheless. How else will he stay solvent?' The last word was spoken with superior contempt.

He moved on into the hall and, as he did so, straightened up and walked tall. Bonhomme puffed out his cheeks so that for a moment he almost seemed to be aping the Bishop.

John looked amused but quickly sobered. 'Yes,' he said. 'It's a warm day and set to grow warmer yet. Stand upright and don't make faces at the King's barons.'

John returned to his own lodging room before the dinner hour, intent on donning his best tunic and more formal attire for the later court sessions. Walchelin, his cook, was sitting on an upturned bucket by the door, performing the dual duties of guarding the house and preparing a pottage for the men.

'Visitor,' he said succinctly. 'Didn't want to be seen loitering in the street.' He made an eloquent gesture with his hands, describing a feminine outline.

John answered with a raised eyebrow and entered the house. Damette was sitting in his chair, her hands folded in her lap, but as he entered the room, she sprang to her feet. A gown of crimson silk clung to her figure, accentuating her curves as Walchelin had described. Her braids had been augmented by additions of false hair in the latest style, woven with silk ribbons, and dangled almost to her knees. Rings glittered on every finger and a gold brooch the size of a griddle cake adorned her mantle at the shoulder.

John flourished his hand towards her attire. 'If I may say so, you would outdo the sugar subtleties at a Christmas feast – but in an entirely edible way.'

She made a gesture of her own, sweeping aside his flippancy. 'I shouldn't be here,' she said. 'If William finds out, he won't be pleased.'

'And it wouldn't do to put William's nose out of joint,' John replied sarcastically, thinking that he'd enjoy doing so and using force. Then he looked at her face. 'What is it?'

She bit her lip. 'John, you're in danger. Keep away from Roger of Salisbury and his nephews if you value your position and the King's favour.'

He felt the space between his shoulder blades go cold. 'What?'

'There's going to be trouble. Waleran of Meulan has been brewing poison for Salisbury for weeks now. He's told the King that Salisbury is going to declare for the Empress and turn over his castles to her and her knights.'

'I suppose he has evidence for such claims?' John folded his arms. 'How is he going to prove such a thing?'

Damette shook her head. 'He doesn't need to prove it; the King will listen because he's afraid. Salisbury rules the finances. You've sat at the exchequer yourself. You know the kind of power he commands. He has most of the sheriffs in his pocket too. He has served his purpose and people want rid of him.'

'By "people", I assume you mean the likes of the Earl of Leicester and his brother, and your own paymaster.'

'Who else would I mean?' A look of urgency crossed her face. 'It's not good, John. If you're not careful, they'll make you part of it. You keep too close an eye on what goes in and out – you see too much . . . You know too much. They'll bring you down with him if they can.'

Her words struck through him like a thin bolt of lightning, but he maintained an impassive countenance. 'Thank you for the warning. I'll bear it to the fore.'

She made an exasperated gesture. 'You don't understand. The game's afoot. Waleran has hired men to do his bidding. It's going to happen today. Salisbury and his nephews are in grave danger, and so are you.'

'Do you have details?'

Damette shook her head. 'William wouldn't say and he'd have grown suspicious if I'd pressed him. I shouldn't be here now; I have to go.' She gave him a long, steady look as if bidding farewell to something she would not see again. 'Have a care, John.' She kissed the index and middle fingers of her right hand, placed them to his lips, then left in a rustle of silk and a subtle waft of musk.

John let out his breath on a hard sigh. He wasn't surprised that Roger of Salisbury was about to be tackled. He had served his purpose and he was too powerful – both of which were strong reasons for bringing him down. He was like a fat spider at the centre of the treasury, guarding the stockpile of wealth that others wanted for their own use, weaving strands of sticky silver thread to enmesh men. Rumour abounded that his castles were stuffed to the rafters with coin and plate. His web extended everywhere and the sheriffs were indeed mostly his appointees. It was inevitable that others would try to break the strands and use webs of their own to net power and influence for themselves. If men of lesser degree became tangled up and suffocated along the way, what did it matter – especially if such men were not allies?

Salisbury had never evinced interest in the Empress's cause though. Indeed, years before, he had argued strongly against her being Henry's successor. Were John ever to point the finger of suspicion at the individual responsible for King Henry's demise, it would be at Roger of Salisbury. But suspicion wasn't proof. As Damette said, it was as well to keep clear.

Accompanied by Benet and a serjeant John set out for the court. He had warned his men to be on their guard and to mind their own business as far as possible.

'There was never this kind of trouble in the old King's day,' Benet muttered for the tenth time as they entered the High Street and turned towards the castle. He eased the leather lining of his hauberk around his throat.

'Well, those days are unlikely to return, so best keep your sword girded and your eyes keen,' John snapped.

They passed the lodging house that had been commandeered by the entourage belonging to Roger of Salisbury. John quickened his pace but as he drew level with the entrance, one of Meulan's knights staggered from the hall into the street, lurched into John and fell at his feet, blood spurting from the severed stump of his right hand. From the interior of the lodging came the clash of weapons and the sound of men locked in combat. Swearing like a common footsoldier, John ripped off one of the wounded knight's hose bindings and lashed it around the forearm, reducing the gush to a dribble.

Two more soldiers ran out of the door, one bleeding from a broken nose, the other with a huge tear in his quilted tunic through which the fleece stuffing poked like a cloud. Together they picked up the injured knight at John's feet and dragged him away. Benet and the serjeant drew their swords. So did John, a dark stain marring the sleeve of his court tunic and his hands glistening with blood.

The fighting erupted out of the lodging and into the street with a vengeance. John recognised knights belonging to Waleran of Meulan, Alain of Brittany, and the Bishops of Salisbury and Ely. Damette had been right but he had not expected things to move with quite such immediacy. Swords clashed. No one was carrying a shield and the shriek of metal on metal was one that ripped up the spine and lodged between the teeth.

One of Salisbury's knights saw John with his sword bare in his bloody hand and leaped on him with a howl of 'Treacherous bastard!'

John hastily parried and parried again, his blade taking the punishment of what were intended to be killing blows. He turned his wrist, stepped and, with a hard twist and flick, sent his assailant's weapon spinning out of his hand, then levelled his sword at the knight's throat.

'Now why should you call me that?' John snarled.

'You're in league with them, aren't you?' panted the soldier, teeth bared. 'You're part of the plot to overthrow my lord the Bishop!'

'I am part of nothing!' John bit out. 'What's happening here?'

'We were here first; it's ours, bought and fairly paid for!' The knight's expression blazed with indignation.

'This started as a quarrel over lodgings?' John asked incredulously.

The knight curled his lip as if he thought John was calling him an idiot. 'Yes,' he sneered. 'A quarrel over lodgings. Think that if it eases your conscience . . . my lord Marshal.'

'So it's not an argument over who gets the best house, the Bishop or the lay lords?' asked Benet as he, John and the serjeant continued towards the palace.

'No,' John said grimly. 'Roger of Salisbury and his family have been controlling too much for too long, and

160

that includes who gets the best of everything. Also, they know too much.'

Benet said quietly, 'So do we.'

John glanced at his knight. 'The knowing in itself is not dangerous. It's the failing to anticipate and act that is. You have to be several moves in front of your opponent if you want to survive.'

Benet wiped his palm across his lips. 'Let's hope you are then,' he said.

The repercussions of the brawl at Roger of Salisbury's lodging fanned out from the initial incident like ripples from a large boulder dropped into a pool from a height. John had not long arrived at the King's hall when the men of Meulan and Brittany came complaining to Stephen that they had been set upon when they went to the Bishop's lodgings to discuss the fair distribution of sleeping space in the town. They brought their wounded, including the knight who had fallen bleeding at John's feet. Since John's first rough and ready treatment, the wound had been cauterised and dipped in pitch. Whether or not the knight would live was in the hands of God. One of Meulan's soldiers was already dead of a sword wound to the groin.

'You have to show the Bishop of Salisbury that he is not above the law!' snarled Waleran of Meulan in a voice full of righteous anger. 'He must be brought to heel. Who knows how much he has stolen from the treasury over the years to build his castles, enrich himself and buy men in important positions at court?' He stared around the gathering, his gaze resting longer than necessary on Brian FitzCount, Miles of Gloucester – and on John.

Stephen drew himself up. 'It is indeed disgraceful behaviour. Marshal, have the Bishop of Salisbury brought

161

to me to answer the complaint. And bring the Bishops of Ely and Lincoln too. Let them all answer to me for the violent behaviour of their men. I will not have my peace disturbed in this disgraceful manner.'

Stephen was not a good actor. There was nothing spontaneous about this. The emotion curling in the air like smoke was of triumph, not anger. John had no love for the overweening Bishop of Salisbury and his slew of hungry relatives, but there was a bad taste in his mouth. If a man as great as the chancellor could be brought down by the pack and torn to pieces, what chance did he stand? Bowing to the King, he set his hand to his sword hilt and strode out to perform his duty.

News of the order for the arrest had flown ahead. Roger of Salisbury and Alexander of Lincoln had been slow to act, refusing to believe the King would go so far as to command seizing them and their goods and thus both men were easily apprehended. Nigel of Ely, having a swifter awareness of his situation, had fled by the time John arrived at his lodging.

'Do we give chase?' Benet asked as John prowled around the Bishop's chamber. Two travelling chests stood against the wall, one stuffed with fine silk vestments and goldwork. John eyed it with sour humour and ordered his serjeants to set the chest aside and guard it well. Aline could have her silks to clad her priests and it wouldn't cost him a penny. And if he was giving it back to the Church, he wasn't robbing from it. 'No,' he said. 'The King has Salisbury and Lincoln. The Bishop of Ely has too great a start and we'd only exhaust the horses to no good purpose.'

Benet eyed him sidelong. 'But at least the King would know we had tried.'

John shrugged. 'The King only knows what he wishes to know. Even if we set out on fast coursers, we would not catch up with the Bishop of Ely. Either Stephen will accept my decision as the right one, or he won't. I do know I am not going to go chasing my tail halfway to Devizes today.'

'What about all this?' Benet gestured round at the chests, the household items, including the cauldron that was still simmering over the hearth, the bed hangings, the wall embroideries. More proof that Bishop Nigel was riding light. A glint of metal caught John's eye where a jewelled cup had rolled under a bench. He retrieved it, studied the gems clawed in its base and looked impassively at Benet. 'If the King only knows what he wishes to know,' he said, 'then his marshal only sees what he wishes to see.'

Sybilla supervised the draping of the tablecloth in the private chamber, checking to ensure the bleached, embroidered linen was unstained and properly arrayed with the corners even. Then she fetched the silver-gilt aquamanile from the sideboard. As a child, the water container had always fascinated her with its horse-shaped head and wonderfully worked whorls of mane. She had always thought it a pity that it only came out on special occasions and she had sworn to herself that when she had a household of her own, she would use such objects every day and take pleasure in them. Today wasn't exactly special as such, but since her mother had left her in charge of arranging the solar for the return of her father and brothers from the royal camp at Devizes, she had taken liberties. After all, the return of the family menfolk safe from the battlefield was cause for celebration. They had received notice, her father's heralds having set out at dawn while the baggage camp was making ready to march and her father and brothers were still talking to the King.

'Is it true what they're saying in the kitchens, mistress?'

Sybilla turned to the cook's wife, Gytha, who had entered the chamber bearing a basket of spiced apple fritters that were a particular favourite of Lord Walter's. Gytha had been Sybilla's wet nurse and the affection between them still ran deep, defying – to an extent – conventions of rank. Sometimes Gytha would come to the private chamber and tell stories from her vast repertoire, and Sybilla loved to spend time in the kitchens and dairy. Knowing how to knead dough or fashion pastry might not be essential to her education, but her mother let her do it, reasoning that a wife who had a broad knowledge of what went on in the domestic quarters would be better qualified to run a household than one who shut herself away in the bower and learned little but stitchery.

'I don't know what they're saying,' Sybilla replied. 'You probably know more than I do anyway. You hear all the best gossip.'

Gytha's eyes twinkled amid the seams and wrinkles. 'Suppose I do, young mistress, but the best gossip isn't necessarily the truth.' She set the platter down on a serving trestle. 'They're saying that the Bishop of Salisbury's had all his powers taken away, except those ordained by the Church. Stripped o' the lot.' She raised and lowered her hands in emphasis. 'All of it gone. Put his son in chains and threatened to hang him in front o' his mother and the garrison at Devizes unless they surrendered. Not that I'm saying those Bishops didn't need bringing down off their high horses – because they did.'

'My father says that priests should lead by example.' Sybilla repositioned the aquamanile.

'Hah!' Gytha snorted. 'If folk followed the Bishop of

Salisbury, we'd all be in a fine stew!' Then she gave a bawdy chuckle.

Sybilla stifled a giggle. She probably shouldn't know that a stew was another term for a brothel, but growing up with three brothers had considerably broadened her education. The Bishop of Salisbury had a concubine who dwelt in his castle at Devizes and with whom he sported in luxury when he wasn't busy at the exchequer board raking in the coins or promoting his friends and relatives to high positions.

Gytha ran her tongue around her teeth. 'They say they found four hundred thousand silver marks in the strong-boxes at Devizes – imagine such a sum!'

Sybilla couldn't. She had sometimes seen the silver in their own coffers and witnessed manorial payments on rent days, but had never set eyes on a hundred marks in one place together, let alone four hundred thousand. 'They were probably embroidering,' she said. Her father's heralds knew how to tell a good story at the kitchen door in exchange for bread.

'Who knows?' Gytha said, deliberately looking mysterious, not prepared to diminish the tale.

Through the open shutters, they heard shouts from the guards on watch and the horn blew to signal the arrival of the troops. Gytha sped back to the kitchens and Sybilla hurried to finish the solar preparations, plumping the cushions on the bench, placing a bowl of dried rose petals on the coffer. She sang as she worked for she loved creating comfort and order for the pleasure of herself and others. That Salisbury's menfolk would take it for granted, she understood with resignation. The main thing was that it pleased her.

The troop had been riding hard and was sweaty, sun-roasted and floured with dust. Sybilla and her mother greeted the men with jugs of watered wine and cool, wet napkins. Her father's forehead glowed like a beacon against his thinning silver hair. He was gasping in the heat and limping badly from his stiff joints, but the grin on his face was as broad as the sun as he eased down on the solar bench and mopped his face.

'Is everything well, my lord?' Sybilla's mother asked, her tone demure but her eyes filled with avid curiosity.

Walter laughed. 'If you're the Bishop of Salisbury, Lincoln or Ely, then no, everything is not well, nor ever likely to be again.' He told them in more detail what Gytha had told Sybilla.

'Is it true about the four hundred thousand marks?' Sybilla wanted to know.

Her father shook his head. 'I don't know about that, my chick. Certainly there were plenty of chests of silver and some fine jewels and plate. All in the King's coffers now. Makes you wonder how Salisbury obtained it in the first place – not by any honest means, I warrant. He must have been milking the exchequer for years.' He looked at his wife. 'The King has put Devizes into the hands of a constable.' He gave a smug grin. 'The bishop's palace at Salisbury has been given into my custody.'

A flush brightened her mother's face and she leaned to kiss his ruddy cheek. 'Oh, that's wonderful news!'

His grin became a chuckle. 'It's good for the moment,' he said, then sobered. 'But times change, and we need to seize the luck when the wind blows it our way.' He held out his arms for Sybilla to kiss him too. Patrick and William smiled and looked full of themselves.

'The Bishop and his kin are not the only ones who have lost the King's favour.' Walter mopped his brow again. 'I always knew the honeymoon would not last. It

166

looks as if the King is beginning to regret giving Ludgershall and Marlborough to his marshal.'

Lady Salisbury's eyes widened. 'Has he turned traitor?'

'Let us say he isn't trusted at court by those who matter. Rumour has it that FitzGilbert is only waiting for Robert of Gloucester to land and he'll declare for him. He was in the field at Devizes and marshalling, but he was being frozen out by the King and his cronies. Mark my words, there's a rift looming. If you build castles of sand, then someone is bound to knock them down.'

15

Marlborough Castle, Wiltshire, September 1139

Hands on hips, John watched the supply carts roll into the castle bailey. There were barrels filled with sheaves of arrows, mail shirts, bags full of spare rings and rivets. There were ash-stave spears cut from specifically felled trees in Hamstead's park, shield bosses and blanks, coils of chain, hogsheads of pitch, tuns of wine, more barrels of salt fish and pork. And still the carts rumbled in. Not for nothing did John have a reputation as one of the most skilled quartermasters in England and Normandy.

He had increased the fortifications apace at Hamstead and the building at Ludgershall was going forward too. His grip on the valley of the Kennet was so strong now that nothing moved without his knowledge.

Aline crossed the ward to join him, picking her way timidly between the supplies being unloaded and carried off into storage, jumping as someone dropped a barrel with a loud bang. The staves split and a bundle of arrows spilled across the yard.

'Why are you doing this?' she asked in a high, frightened voice. 'I don't understand.'

He threw her an exasperated look. 'I have already told

you. It is because I am a grain caught between two mill-stones and I intend those millstones to crack before I do.'

Except for fear, her eyes were blank. John mustered his patience. 'Look,' he said, slowly and clearly, 'Baldwin de Redvers has landed an army in the name of the Empress and taken Corfe. Robert of Gloucester and the Empress are still in Normandy, but will soon land somewhere on the south coast to lay claim to the crown – yes?'

Aline nodded.

'I control the approaches. Any army landing on the south coast cannot afford to have me either in front or behind them. I guard the road to Brian FitzCount's fortress at Wallingford, and Wallingford defends a strategic crossing of the Thames.'

She nodded again, looking uncertain.

'Stephen expects FitzCount to defect to the Empress the moment she sets foot in England, so Stephen needs to be within striking distance of Wallingford. To do that he has to have control of Marlborough.' His gaze narrowed. 'He seems to believe that I intend defecting too. He may well come here and try to take this place from me – and I'm not about to let him do that.'

Aline clutched her prayer beads. 'But couldn't you tell him you are loyal?'

He gave a bleak laugh. 'I could, but being believed is a different matter when others are constantly pouring poison about me into his ears and blocking up all access save to their own ambitions. I could easily have been brought down with Bishop Roger in June. It would have suited certain members of the court very well indeed.'

Her voice rose a notch. 'But if Stephen comes and you open the gates and surrender, he will know you are true.'

John clung to his patience. 'If Stephen comes to Marlborough, acknowledges my loyalty and confirms me

169

as its castellan before a slew of witnesses, I will open the gates to him and serve him to my last breath. If he demands my submission and the return of this castle, he leaves me no option but to bar the way to Wallingford. The choice is his.'

Another cart rumbled into the bailey and riding behind it were three tough-looking soldiers – mercenaries to judge from their appearance. Leaving her side, John went to speak to them, intent on recruiting if they were of the right material. A forlorn figure, Aline made her way back to the keep and sought the comfort of her chaplain.

Five days later, John was breaking his fast in the great hall when his constable interrupted the meal with the news that King Stephen was approaching at the head of an army.

The news surged through John like fire but he showed no reaction on his face. He picked up his cup, finished the contents and unhurriedly rose to his feet. 'Close the gate,' he commanded. 'Get the archers to the battlements and bring out the spare sheaves. We've drilled this often enough. You know what to do.'

Aline laid a hand on his sleeve, arresting him as he prepared to go and don his hauberk. 'Don't do this,' she whimpered. 'Don't defy the King. You mustn't fight, dear Holy Mother of God, you mustn't!'

John tightened his lips. 'I have no choice. I am not going to hand over this castle for him to bestow on one of his cronies. Do your duty. Prepare hot water, splints and bandages. We are going to need them.'

Her face drained of colour. 'I . . . can't. I . . .'

'Then tell your women to do it and go and pray,' he said curtly, and somehow managed to refrain from shaking her. A good battle captain had control and knew where to position each man. Aline was a weak reed; he couldn't rely on her except as a conduit for prayers. Prising her grip from his arm, he left the trestle and hurried to don his armour.

As he had suspected, as soon as Stephen arrived beneath Marlborough's walls, he sent forth envoys, demanding John hand over custody of the castle or face the royal wrath. It did nothing for John's optimism that one of the envoys was William Martel, and another Hervey de Leon, husband to Stephen's bastard daughter, and plainly the intended new castellan for Marlborough.

'Tell the King I will not yield this castle,' John replied with frozen courtesy when he met the men at the gate in the outer defences. 'I have done everything he has asked of me and served him well. I have not broken faith.'

'But you are breaking it now,' Martel pointed out, eyeing the burly soldiers guarding the entrance, their hands gripped around spear hafts and sword hilts.

'I was not the first to do so. Tell the King to confirm to me the lordship of Marlborough and I swear to serve him faithfully. Should he refuse me and demand I yield this keep into another's hands, then let him fight me tooth and nail for every inch of ground.'

Martel looked down his nose. 'The King will not be given an ultimatum by one of his servants.'

'And I will not be told my business by another one,' John retorted.

Martel's bony face flushed. 'I will give him your message,' he said, tight-lipped, and turned his horse. De Leon had not commented throughout the exchange, but his gaze ranged the walls of Marlborough with a possessive air that made John's hand twitch at his sword hilt.

Once Martel and de Leon had ridden away, John climbed to the battlements. He knew Stephen would decline to accept his fealty. If Stephen's weak good nature made him vacillate, Martel and de Leon would stiffen his resolve.

John had had trebuchets assembled on the wall walks, and two great picks like giant beaks for tearing attackers off siege ladders. Mounds of sling stones were stockpiled against the hoardings together with staves, spears and barrels of arrows. He paused beside a pair of arbalesters from Ghent, whom he had recruited during the siege of Bishop Roger's castle at Devizes.

'Shoot anything that comes in range unless it's bearing a flag of truce,' he said. 'Keep the whoresons pinned down.' He made a circuit of the wall walks, checking positions, making sure that every man knew his part and was alert. He briefed his senior knights, and paused to watch Stephen's camp disgorging its supplies.

'There's a trebuchet,' said Benet. 'And two perriers. Ladders too.'

John nodded. 'Make a note of what you see, and how Stephen has set up his guard posts. I want to know every move they make.'

John was dozing on a pallet in the bailey gatehouse when Stephen's men attacked in the grey light before sunrise. At the first blare of the horn, he was up from his mattress, on his feet and into his hauberk. Buckling on his sword, he ran out to the wall walk and began issuing commands as the siege ladders slammed against the palisade timbers. A few gestures, some rapid orders and the missiles began to fly at their assailants: arrows, stones, chunks of timber. John seized a gaff and went to help pry a ladder off the palisade and send it crashing into the ditch with its burden of men. He grabbed his helmet from his squire and set it on his head, over arming cap and coif.

172

'Is this supposed to be a surprise attack?' he scoffed. 'God, I've seen better stealth from a feast-day parade!'

'Arrows!' someone shouted as a shower of dark flights swooped overhead and rained down on the bailey, skidding on roof slates, lodging in the thatch that John had had thoroughly soaked during the night.

'Bastard!' snarled Benet.

'He's trying to pin us down and distract us so he can bring his ram close enough to the bailey gates.' As a second arrow storm whickered overhead, John ducked along the palisade boards to help at another point where a ladder had gone up. A stone from the palisade perrier flung outwards towards Stephen's soldiers and there was a satisfying thud, following by dismayed and furious expletives from the besiegers.

As the first of Stephen's men reached the top of the ladder, John knocked him off it with his shield, used his sword on the second, then left it to Benet and a serjeant to finish the deed and throw the ladder down into the ditch.

The dawn brightened and the sun rose in a fiery ball. Mist layered the area below the ramparts like the finest linen as John fought to keep King Stephen from gaining the bailey. Arrows flew between the camps in a continuous rain, Stephen's tipped with burning pitch in the hope of firing the bailey buildings. John had bucket chains at the ready. When a shed caught fire, the blaze was immediately extinguished. He used fire arrows of his own when Stephen tried to bring forward his ram and directed the perrier on the wall to lob stones at it, until Stephen was forced to order a retreat.

Shoulders heaving, John stood beside his banner on the battlements and watched the royal troops withdraw. He took the cup of watered wine his squire offered and drank with gratitude for his throat was on fire. When he removed his coif and arming cap, his hair clung to his scalp in sweat-drenched tendrils.

'How long before they come again?' gasped Benet.

'Afternoon, mayhap,' John answered as he recovered his breath. 'They may try again before dusk, then again tonight unless we can maul them badly enough to think twice. They've lost more men than we have. Their ram's damaged and they're going to have to repair the ladders too.' He blotted his brow on the cuff of his gambeson. 'If they bring up their trebuchets, they'll break through, but the keep's well protected.' He gestured behind to the masonry wall ringing the castle mound.

'You expect them to break through?'

'Depends how long we can hold them. Stephen won't sit here for ever. Either he'll want to negotiate terms or he'll grow tired and leave. I know him; he won't stick.' He handed the cup back to his squire. 'Put the reserves on watch and stand the men down.'

Throughout three days of incessant assault and counter-assault Aline had moved from Saint Nicholas's chapel to bower and back to chapel, trying to pretend she didn't hear the shouts and screams of battle, the whump of the trebuchets, the crash of stone, the sporadic assault of fire arrows. She kept the shutters tightly closed in her chamber and had her chaplain read to her aloud. She couldn't bear this constant knife edge. They had wounded men and two had died, but she had not gone to help tend the injuries, knowing that it would make her ill. John had not asked it of her either. She knew she was failing him, but even for duty, she could not face up to the sight of broken bones and mangled flesh. The most she had managed was to make bandages and funeral arrangements. She

174

had lit candles and prayed because that was what she did best. She felt drained by the anxiety of being under siege. In her mind's eye, she imagined herself running out to the King, weeping that she was sorry, that it was all a mistake and he could have Marlborough if only he would let them leave in peace. John, on the other hand, seemed to be revelling in the challenge. Aline had never seen his true mettle before, and the sharp, incisive warrior prowling the keep was even more the stranger than the man who occasionally shared her bed and sat at table with her in the great hall. If she had barely known him before, now she was at a complete, bewildered loss.

Despite John's determination, it was inevitable that the King's forces would eventually break through the first line of defence. John was prepared; indeed, the first barricade had held a couple of days longer than he expected, and even if Stephen's troops did take the bailey, they would gain little. John retreated behind the ring wall protecting the castle mound. It meant that conditions were cramped, but he could still launch an attack from the inner wall walk and the battlements.

'Are we going to die?' little Gilbert asked him. Fear glistened in his big eyes and there was a tremble to his chin.

It was a damp autumn morning, grainy with mist, and John was breaking his fast in the great hall before heading to the battlements.

He looked at his son. 'Eventually, yes,' he said, 'but not yet, God willing. What put that thought into your head?' He wondered if the child had fixed on the notion because of the handful of men who had been killed on the walls, and the talk of the soldiers about the push and pull of battle.

'Mama said we were.'

175

John gave Aline a hard look and she shrank from him. Her face was ghost-white, her bones sharp beneath her skin and her eye sockets bruised from lack of sleep. Her hands shook as she crumbled the bread on her dish and ate none of it. He could imagine her self-indulgent hysterical outburst and its effect on the child. 'No one is going to harm you or your baby brother while I am by,' he said quietly, 'nor your mother. If I have to yield this castle, you will be allowed to leave without being harmed; I promise you that.'

Gilbert fixed him with an anxious gaze. 'Does that mean we're not going to win?'

John sighed and looked at the trestle. This was more difficult than talking to his knights. 'It means I have planned for everything that might happen so I don't have to worry. If God chooses differently then so be it, but I have generally noticed that God helps those who help themselves.'

Aline's lips quivered. John inclined his head to her. 'I give you leave to retire, madam,' he said frostily. 'I can see you are unwell.'

As she rose to her feet, he noticed how loosely her gown hung on her body. She was as emaciated as an over-wintered heifer. The willowy slenderness of her wedding day had become gaunt and brittle, and the shy, sweet gentleness had mutated into something self-pitying and barren. He nodded at one of her women to go with her and signalled the nurse to take care of Gilbert. Then he lifted his cup to finish his wine.

One of the watch soldiers entered the hall and hastened to the dais, hand on sword hilt to stop the weapon from banging at his side. 'My lord, my lord, come quickly,' he said. 'They're leaving!'

John put his cup down and hastened from hall to battlements. Peering down he saw that the trebuchets were being dismantled and loaded into carts and the tents demolished in haste. Already some of Stephen's troops had ridden off and what they were seeing was the slower baggage-cart detail preparing to leave, although still protected by knights and footsoldiers.

'We've beaten the bastards. Hah, we're too good for them!' a serjeant shouted and clapped a companion on the back.

Along the ring wall, John's men were jeering and shouting. A couple of the archers loosed arrows, but in exultation rather than hope of hitting an enemy. John smiled with the men, but his eyes remained calculating as he studied the activity. 'I agree we're too good for them,' he told Benet, 'but we certainly didn't defeat them and they hadn't tested the half of our mettle yet. Something has happened to make them leave.'

'Perhaps the Empress has landed, or the Earl of Gloucester?'

'Very likely. It has to be something important to make Stephen abandon the siege without another push. Don't stand the men down. Keep them all on alert.'

'Yes, my lord.'

An hour later, Stephen's army had gone, leaving behind smoking firepits, latrine middens, bits of broken equipment it would have burdened them to carry and two whores who had decided to try their luck in Marlborough rather than follow the army. Neither woman was clean or attractive. John would certainly never have admitted them within the gate when he had been Henry's marshal, but he was interested to find out what they knew and he had them brought to his chamber.

The women looked around, plainly impressed by the luxury of their surroundings and ill at ease to be out of their habitual territory of hovel, tent and guardroom and facing the lord of the castle and his senior knights.

John folded his arms and leaned against a trestle. 'I grant you leave to ply your trade among my soldiers,' he said, 'but before you go about your business, I need to know where your former employers are bound.'

The whores exchanged glances. 'I don't know,' one of them said, screwing up her face in thought. 'Said something about the Empress and some castle called . . . Ar . . . Ard . . . summat.' She looked at her companion for aid, but the other one just shrugged and twiddled the end of her straw-coloured braid.

'Arundel,' John supplied. 'Was it Arundel?'

'Aye, my lord, that were it.' The whore gave an enthusiastic nod of recognition but didn't attempt to say the word after him. 'Empress has landed there, and her brother, so I heard.' She wiped a grimy sleeve across her nose. 'The King's troops're going to lay siege to them.'

John dismissed the women to whatever trade they could pick up. 'We are all at a crossroads,' he said to his knights. 'I can ride after the King and throw myself on his mercy – although I doubt mercy is what I would receive. I can go on crusade until all this resolves itself, and hope that if a Saracen doesn't put an end to my life, I'll have something to return to.' He drew a deep breath. 'Or I can go to the Empress and offer her my services.' The words sent a ripple down his spine. Eight years ago, the notion of swearing fealty to a woman had filled him with deep unease. Even now, it went against the grain, but he knew there was no choice if he and his family were to survive.

'And what of us?' Benet asked.

John gave him a steady look. 'Either stay with me or renounce your oaths and leave now. If you stay, I expect your loyalty to the death. If you go, I promise not to have my archers shoot you in the back on the way out.'

Benet said quietly, 'I am your vassal, sire. My eldest son is your squire. My father served yours; my grandsire rode beside yours against the English on Hastings field. I would be dishonoured if I abandoned you.' Abruptly he knelt to John, his hands extended in the gesture of paying homage. 'I will double my oath to you, my lord. Where you ride, so do I.'

Like a breeze rippling through corn, the others bent the knee too until John was the only one standing in his solar. He found himself having to swallow hard, which was ridiculous. He prided himself on his control; his ability to remain collected whatever the pressure. He was tempted to tell them all not to be so stupid and get up, but their gesture demanded one of equal gravity from him. They were making a pact and it had to be sealed. 'Then I had better be careful where I ride,' he said. Stepping forward, he took Benet's clasped hands between his own palms and gave him the kiss of peace, and thought it a strange thing to call such a gesture when they were in the midst of an escalating war.

16

Salisbury, October 1139

'Idiot!' spat Walter of Salisbury, striding into the domestic chamber. 'Purblind, stupid idiot. If Stephen ever had brains, they trickled out of his ears when he became King!'

Sybilla looked up with a start from the braid belt she was weaving on her frame. Her father had gone out into the town shortly after sext to talk business with some of the merchants and burghers, but either the discussions had not been amicable, or something else had seriously upset him. He was red in the face, almost purple in fact, and his eyes were ablaze.

'What is it?' Patrick rose from the bench where he had been drinking wine. He had recently returned from business at their manor of Mildenhall. His older brother was still elsewhere, also dealing with the affairs of the estate.

'What do you think?' Walter unhitched his belt and threw it at a coffer. It missed and struck the floor with a thud. 'Stephen had the Empress trapped in Arundel and the fool has only gone and let her go. What is wrong with the man? He could have ended it now in one fell swoop, but no!' He kicked a leather foldstool out of his way and threw himself down in his barrel chair, breathing hard.

'What do you mean, he's let her go?' Patrick asked. 'Where?'

'Hah, here's the rich part!' Walter's jaw worked. 'Only to Bristol. Only to the Earl of Gloucester's chief castle in the region, the one that Stephen's been trying to take for more than a year.' He wagged his finger. 'Why couldn't he have kept her holed up at Arundel?' He made a sign of slitting his throat. 'He even provided an escort for her when she asked him for it. He hasn't got the brains not to piss into the wind!'

Sybilla listened with interest. They had heard all about the Empress and her brother landing at Arundel at the invitation of the old King's wife and her new husband who had promised them succour. Robert of Gloucester had ridden on to Bristol to gather more troops, and Brian FitzCount of Wallingford had immediately defected to the Empress's cause. But then Stephen had arrived at Arundel, trapping her there.

Patrick cupped his chin in thought. 'Arundel is not exactly an easy nut to crack. What if Stephen got himself bogged down in a siege there and the rest of the country under Robert of Gloucester rose against him? What would he do then? What would people think of him, besieging two women, one of them the old King's wife? I'd say he's been clever.'

'Clever!' his father spluttered. 'God's balls, your own wits must be addled too! How can it be clever to have something in your fist and then let it go!'

'Because he's making the situation seem less than it is. He's telling everyone he's not bothered by the Empress's landing. She's a weak and foolish woman. What happened to Arundel? Did he make them yield as part of the terms?'

'Yes, but that isn't the point.' Walter struck his fist on the side of the chair and the hue of his face darkened.

'You have your enemy in your hand, you don't let her go!'

'That's as may be, but with them both in Bristol, he doesn't have to keep his left eye on that and his right on Arundel. He can deal with them in a single place.' Patrick opened his hands. 'I think he's weighed up the odds and made a shrewd move, myself.'

'And I still say he's an ass,' his father scoffed. 'That move looks as shrewd to me as picking a cauldron off the fire with your bare hands.' He shook his head. 'Nor do I know what he was thinking not to finish the siege at Marlborough. It'll make FitzGilbert twice as arrogant now, the whoreson.'

'He was committing too much to it in time and men.' A gleam lit in Patrick's eyes. 'Besides, we can take care of that for Stephen.'

Walter made a rude sound through pursed lips. 'Do you think I have the time and resources to besiege Marl—' A look of astonishment suddenly crossed his face. He stared down at his left hand, tried to move it. 'I can't . . . I c . . .' His words slurred and gobbled together while saliva dribbled from the side of his mouth. Sybilla looked at him in shock. Patrick strode forward and grabbed their father as he fell.

'Fetch Mother,' he cried. 'Quickly!'

The command, the urgency in his voice, galvanised Sybilla and she ran.

Sybilla sat at her father's side, holding and rubbing his limp left hand. He was conscious but confused, and couldn't focus properly. The left side of his face dragged downwards and he had little movement down that side of his body. Saliva shone at the corner of his mouth and more dribbled out as he struggled to speak but made only

182

garbled, nonsensical sounds. Dutifully, Sybilla wiped away the spittle on a napkin. Ralf, their physician, said he had suffered a seizure – too much choler, he said. Her father had always had an imbalance in that area. Ralf had bled him to try to redress some of that imbalance, and had said that either her father would recover over the next few days, or he would die. The best they could do was to try to spoon bland foods into him if he could swallow, and keep him quiet.

Patrick came to stand at the foot of the bed. 'It's not good, is it?' he said with a grimace.

Sybilla glanced round, but her mother was seeing Ralf out and taking more instruction from him. Wordlessly she shook her head. Her father had always been a constant in the background of her life. Big, warm, strong. Someone she could run to for protection when her brothers' teasing got out of hand; someone who gave her security. Nothing bad could happen while he was around to save her. But now something bad had happened and to him. Even if he did survive, the physician said he would be permanently weak on the damaged side. He wouldn't be able to conduct affairs as sheriff for a while and certainly not lead men in battle or take major decisions. It would be up to her brothers to do that from now on. Sybilla shivered. A bitter wind of change was blowing through their household, and it frightened her.

17

Bristol, October 1139

'Well, my lord Marshal. You come to do me homage and put yourself at my command?'

John knelt at the feet of the Empress. Her voice was as cold and strong as the channel current beyond the castle walls. She was wearing the crown she had brought from Germany, its pearl strings beaded with opalescent light. The hand John kissed was well tended and rich embroidery shone with a diffused gleam upon her wine-red gown. She looked older, with lines pursing her mouth and a new hardness in her eyes.

'Domina, I do,' he replied in a neutral tone. Even if he was here seeking her favour, he would not humble himself beyond the standard formalities. He had three strongholds to offer her and control of the Kennet valley. He possessed the abilities to fight and administrate. He needed her, but equally she needed him.

'And how do I know you will not change your mind as you changed it before?' Her voice remained cold, but she flicked her fingers, bidding him rise. 'You were swift enough to break your oath to me and swear for Stephen.'

John stood up. 'Because, Domina, I cannot change

my mind even should it be my greatest desire. I have enemies at Stephen's court who would see me dead rather than restored to favour. I will not couch my reasons for being here in falsehood. You are my only chance of survival. Stephen has shown he has neither the strength nor the inclination to curb those around him who wish me ill.'

Dark amusement filled Matilda's eyes. 'Fairly said, but you must realise why I am suspicious. No one at my father's court would play chess with you because you were devious and always several moves ahead.'

'I am not several moves ahead now, Domina. I am backed into a corner.'

She nodded to herself. 'Indeed you are, but still dangerous. Tell me, what happens if matters change and you find yourself with room for manoeuvre? Which road will you take? I am not prepared to offer you a bolt hole only to have you scuttering back to Stephen the moment he extends you a pardon.'

John contained his irritation at her tone of voice and choice of words. If he couldn't cooperate with her now, he might as well throw himself from the battlements and have done. 'I will not waver, Domina,' he said. 'I did not break faith with Stephen; he broke faith with me. Had the men on whom he relies for counsel not made it clear they would rather see me dead than continuing in my post, I would still be his man. I served your father to the best of my ability and held by my oath. If I swear to you now, only my death will unbind that vow.'

She exhaled through her nose and leaned back to contemplate him. 'It may well come to that, and I may well demand it,' she said. 'Very well. I am prepared to take a chance and make you my marshal. Others here speak well of you and they will be depending on you to

185

keep your oath.' She gazed briefly at Brian FitzCount and Robert of Gloucester.

'I will not fail,' John reiterated. He knelt again and placed his hands between hers, and she leaned to give him the kiss of peace. Her smell was clean and astringent, and her hands were strong. He wondered what it would be like to lie with her. Even in the bedchamber, he doubted she would yield an inch of control. FitzCount might know, but on balance he thought not. And then he wondered how he was going to adapt to being ruled by a woman and decided the only way was to imagine her rule as an extension of her father's.

That afternoon, while he was sitting at dinner with his new allies and familiars, Robert of Gloucester joined him between courses. 'It's good to have you with us,' he said, smile lines creasing his eye corners. 'We're going to need you and every good man we can recruit.'

John glanced around the great hall. As well as Brian FitzCount, Miles the sheriff of Gloucester had renounced his fealty to Stephen, as had his son-in-law Humphrey de Bohun. But it was still more of a frugal gathering than a feast. 'We are a little thin on the ground,' he said.

'Others will join us.' Gloucester gave a confident wave of his hand. 'Men desert Stephen daily. Like you, they don't trust his justice or his strength. He's too easily swayed by those around him – as you have cause to know.' He pressed John's shoulder. 'At least my sister, for all that she is a woman, has a mind of her own and will not be ruled by the likes of the Beaumont brothers, or persuaded by the opinions of toads like Martel. And in the fullness of time, her son will inherit and we'll have a king again.'

'I know how strong-willed the lady is, and I will serve her as I have said,' John said, managing not to sound irritated. 'You do not need to convince me further. Had I been of two minds, I would not have come at all.'

Gloucester gave a wry smile. 'Then I am glad you are of single purpose and that you are here.' He moved on to talk to other men, giving each a moment of his time and words of hope and encouragement. John well recognised the ploy for he was accustomed to do the same among his own troops. To keep men keen and alert to your bidding, you had to win their confidence and approval. He noticed the Empress did not stir from her own place, but presided over the affair with regal formality, every movement and mouthful taken with her dignity in mind. But then she had Robert to apply the common touch – or as common as she required. He doubted Gloucester would go and rough it with the soldiers in the guardroom as was Stephen's occasional wont.

Following the meal, the Empress retired to her chamber. John replenished his cup from a pitcher left standing on a side trestle and relaxed his tense shoulders. As he took the first swallow, Gloucester's mercenary captain, Robert FitzHubert, joined him. The man was a few years older than John with a florid complexion. He lacked height but was so muscular that he walked wide-legged and his arms were forced away from his body by his bulk. The effect was compounded by thick leather vambraces worn at both wrists.

'So you're the lord of Marlborough now?' FitzHubert said with a wolfish glint in his eyes.

John politely confirmed that it was so. He didn't particularly want to socialise with FitzHubert but, since the mercenary was one of Gloucester's senior soldiers, he allowed tact to prevail.

'I hear you took on King Stephen and held out against him.'

'I did what I had to do.' John drank the wine, wondering where this was leading and how soon he could make his escape.

FitzHubert rocked back and forth on his heels. 'I admire you for it. Takes a hard man to stand in the gale.'

John said nothing, but he noted the outsize spurs clipping FitzHubert's fancy leather boots and the belligerent language of the man's body. He was well aware that FitzHubert was sizing him up and assessing his chances. Beneath his urbane façade, John's hackles rose.

'This conflict is an opportunity for men like us to succeed. We can become lords of substance with lands and castles.' FitzHubert clenched his fist and forearm under John's nose. 'Whatever I have gained is by the strength of my own endeavour.'

It would have been more comfortable to take a step back from FitzHubert, but John held his ground. 'Strength is a useful thing to have,' he agreed blandly, not adding that the intelligence and guile to harness that strength was even better. FitzHubert must have a glimmer of the latter traits or he wouldn't be so high in Gloucester's esteem, but that didn't mean he was consummate. Even a wild boar had natural cunning.

The mercenary gave a wide smile that didn't reach his eyes. 'I can see we are men of a kind,' he said.

John swallowed his wine and sincerely hoped not.

18

Ludgershall, Wiltshire, March 1140

John looked at the foal, newborn and still damp but on its feet, albeit staggering like a drunkard. The groom had summoned him to say the mare was nearing the end of her labour, and he had been present to witness the birth, as had his eldest son.

'A fine colt,' the groom announced, looking pleased. 'Be your heir's first destrier, my lord.' He winked at Gilbert.

John gave a grunt of amusement. 'You're a bit premature, Godwin, but I'll keep it in mind.' The foal delighted him. Its mother, of Catalan destrier stock, had been a gift from the Empress when she had taken him as her marshal. Since the role of the marshal had originally been that of horse master, it had suited her sense of occasion, but rather than a destrier, she had chosen to gift him with this Spanish mare, in foal to a Lombard stallion. The result, now seeking its dam's udder, was equine royalty.

The mare swung her head and licked the infant with long strokes of her muscular tongue, making him totter and wobble. His coat was dark, but would change as he grew to become the same snow-silver hue as his dam's.

Watching the mare, John thought that there were never

enough horses. Finding beasts of the required quality in sufficient numbers was a logistical nightmare. He often lay awake, staring at the rafters, making tallies in his mind, trying to balance what came in against what went out, and not succeeding. With Henry that had never been a problem; there had always been the resources and a steady flow of income into the exchequer. Matilda's wherewithal was in kind and often by way of promises taken on trust, and John knew how ephemeral promises were. But this one at least had the potential to be fulfilled, and the mare was young and would produce more offspring.

'Can we show Mama?' Gilbert asked.

'Later,' John replied, knowing that the sight of the after-birth would make her queasy. Nor did she like to go too near horses in case they bit or kicked. She would appreciate the foal better when it was out in the paddock with its coat dried out to a charcoal fuzz. She was the same with new-hatched chicks, grimacing at their wet feathers but cooing over them once they were fluffy balls of down.

With a parting look at mother and son, he nodded to the groom and took the boy back out into the stable yard in time to see one of his huntsmen arrive at the gallop, his horse sweating hard.

'Men, my lord,' he said without preamble. 'Moving up the valley on the Devizes road.'

'Whose?' John asked, equally to the point. 'How many?'

'About fifty. From the direction, I'd say they belonged to Gloucester. Blue and red shields.'

John thanked the man and summoned Benet. 'Ready the men,' he commanded and hastened to don his mail and sword.

Aline watched him with miserable eyes as he shrugged into his hauberk. 'What if they attack you?'

John jumped up and down to aid the descent of the

190

mail over his body until the hem swished at his knees. 'Then I'll be ready for them.'

'Won't it be safer to stay here?'

He shot her a straight look from under his brows. 'If I don't challenge those who trespass on my territory, I am storing up trouble for later. A friend would send a herald to tell me of his presence on my lands, so I must assume until I know otherwise that this man and his troop are either ignorant, ill-mannered or enemies.' He latched his scabbard to his belt.

'I wish you wouldn't—' she started to say, then pressed her lips together.

'Believe me, you are better protected than if I stayed behind my walls and pretended to be deaf.' He tucked his helm under his arm and left the chamber, mail jingling as he strode.

As the air settled behind him, Aline sat down on the bench, feeling weak-legged and sick. He was so confident, so assertive. She tried to absorb his mood and motivation but they were so alien to her nature that not even a vestige would stick. All she knew was that the more he rode out and the more he risked himself, the higher became the chances of disaster. She still had nightmares about the siege at Marlborough. To have mercenaries and knights assaulting their walls with battering rams, trebuchets and fire arrows had unravelled her. She could not bear to think of it happening again. And the wounded . . . dear Holy Mother, the wounded. She pitied them, she wept for them, but she could not stomach the sight of their injuries. Even when they mended there were scars and mutilations that made her ill to look upon, yet look upon them she must, or spend every waking moment in the bower.

John said he had a duty of care to his men. He saw them

paid on the nail, fed, equipped and housed. If they died, he found their families a living within his domicile, and if they were too maimed to return to active service, he gave them alternative employment. It was one of the reasons his men followed him with such unquestioning loyalty. Aline admired him for it too, but it did not prevent her from hating to see the human cost of warfare under her nose.

The church was her solace and she relied ever more on her faith, although her entreaties were usually to the Virgin who was softer and more accessible than Almighty God. She felt the Virgin might lend a sympathetic ear to her pleas and understand her revulsion at the sight of blood and suffering. 'Holy Mary, keep him safe,' she whispered, clutching her prayer beads. 'Let him come home unhurt.'

John rode hard, hit the Devizes road and caught up with his trespassers five miles beyond Ludgershall. It proved to be a mercenary troop led by Robert FitzHubert, who reined in and flashed a hard smile when he saw John advancing in his dust.

'God's greeting. You have come to join us, my lord Marshal?' He spread his hand to encompass his men who were all watching John and his troop with wary eyes and hands close to weapons.

'I have come to see why a band of armed men is riding through my territory without acknowledging my presence,' John said coldly.

'Ah.' FitzHubert slackened his rein and removed his helm by its nasal bar. He polished a mark on the steel with the cuff of his gambeson. 'I saw no need to trouble you.'

John wasn't taken in by FitzHubert's casual manner. Common protocol and good manners dictated that the mercenary should have sent a scout to report on his movements through an ally's lands. 'And that in itself is troubling,' John said.

'Then I apologise, my lord. If I had known how keen you were, I would have called to pay my respects.'

John raised an eyebrow at that. He didn't relish the thought of entertaining a man of FitzHubert's ilk in his hall. 'The courtesy of a messenger would have sufficed.'

FitzHubert made a contrite gesture that was expansive in execution and short on sincerity. 'We're heading to Devizes under the Earl's orders to ruffle a few feathers. If we can take the town, so much the better. If not, then there are plenty of birds to be plucked in enemy territory.'

'As long as you do no plucking in mine, I wish you good fortune.'

FitzHubert looked wounded 'You are my ally. I would not dream of touching a single ear of wheat in your fields, or laying a hand to your villages.'

'If you did I would bury you,' John said, tight-lipped. 'Send a messenger next time.' He clicked his tongue to his stallion and turned for home. The space between his shoulder blades was sensitive with unease. It was the same feeling he had had on the day when the young knights of William Martel's mesnie had thrown a lance at him on the road to Cary.

With sadness and pity, Sybilla watched her father's head nod. Saliva dribbled from the slack left side of his mouth. She had been playing dice-chess with him, but the effort of having to concentrate had worn him out. A thick woollen blanket covered his knees and, although the day was warm, he was enveloped in several layers of clothing. He had regained some of the use in his left side, but it was permanently cold, as if a part of him had died and was clinging

193

like mistletoe to the living part for sustenance. His speech had improved, but it was still difficult to tell what he was saying, and he made a dreadful mess at mealtimes, so he ate the simple pottages and frumenties that were all he could manage in his chamber with only his immediate family and closest attendants to witness his struggle. The duty of caring for him had fallen mainly to her for her mother was unwell with a persistent and bloody cough that had sapped her strength and vitality. Her brothers were constantly absent on the affairs of the family. Her father still tried to have his say in what happened but it was inevitable that his opinions were pushed aside when he couldn't articulate them properly. With warring factions on their threshold, the need was for active, forceful warriors, not a seizure-damaged elderly man.

'Oh Papa,' she said sadly and summoned one of the maids to help her bear him back to his bed. He was too tired to do more than mumble and slur as she and the woman laid him down and drew the covers over him. She squeezed his good right hand, remembering the times when it had engulfed hers with all the power of a bear. Now her own strength was almost enough to break his.

As he fell into slumber, Sybilla left the bedside and wandered to the window embrasure. She felt as restless as the burgeoning spring outside. She was almost sixteen years old and in tune with the season. Her brothers had spoken of betrothing her to this friend or that ally, but it had gone no further than words and speculation. Restless though she was, Sybilla had no desire to wed with any of the names so far mooted. She knew the difference between the courtly love portrayed in songs and stories and the reality of daily life, but she at least wanted to be able to live in companionship with her bridegroom when the time came. She heaved a sigh. Her parents were ailing, her brothers strutting hither and yon in their armour. There had to be more than this. These days not even travelling musicians visited because of the danger on the roads.

Gytha entered the room bearing a bowl of sops in wine for Lord Walter and a platter of honey cakes for Sybilla. 'Devizes has fallen,' she announced breathlessly. 'Just heard it from a messenger at the kitchen door.'

'What?' Sybilla turned and stared. 'To whom?'

'Some mercenary called FitzHubert in the pay of Robert of Gloucester. Took it by stealth in the middle of the night using leather scaling ladders.' Gytha clucked her tongue and shook her head. 'So that means Devizes is in rebel hands. Too close for comfort, if you ask me. It's bad enough having that hellspawn John FitzGilbert at Marlborough without this.'

Sybilla took a honey cake from the platter and bit into it. 'Salisbury won't be threatened,' she said with more confidence than she felt. 'It's too well defended. Even if my father is ailing, my brothers are seasoned warriors. Nothing like that will happen here.'

'Mayhap not,' Gytha agreed, 'but it still frightens folk to think on it, especially those who can remember the long peace of King Henry's time. It doesn't look as if there's going to be peace in Stephen's, does it?' She gave a brusque nod and left the room. Sybilla sighed and finished the honey cake, although she barely tasted it. Once, Gytha would have protected her from such news, or found a way to make light of it. Now Sybilla was expected to shoulder the burden and be the protector. That, as much as speculative talk of betrothal, told her that matters had indeed changed and that she was no longer considered a child, but a fully fledged adult.

19

Marlborough, Wiltshire, May 1140

His heart thundering, John withdrew from Aline and rolled on to his back. She closed her legs and eased her chemise and gown back down from where they were bunched at her waist. Little enough flesh had been exposed, although he knew the fact it was broad daylight had unsettled her, especially as he had dismissed the servants and everyone knew they were not together in the bedchamber to talk. But the obligation to produce more heirs meant they had to mate. He had seen to his part – coaxing and cajoling until she cried out and clutched him as her seed descended to mix with his. Now the rest was up to God and her body. Of love, he did not think; that estate was not part of their marriage and the potential for it to grow had long dwelt in barren soil. Duty was what held him; the need to secure the future for his sons – and perhaps one day his daughters.

He regained his breath, but lay still for a moment in the lassitude of aftermath. He said nothing to Aline, for there was nothing to say. It had come down to moments like this: the occasional obligatory act of procreation, taking meals before the company in his hall, attending church together. Otherwise their lives seldom touched.

A throat was loudly cleared outside the bedchamber door. 'My lord, I do not wish to disturb you,' his chamberlain, Osbert, announced, 'but the sons of the Earl of Gloucester are here with their troop requesting lodging and food.'

The news filled John with surprise and wariness. 'Admit them,' he said, 'and tell them I shall join them in a moment.' He left the bed and adjusted his clothing. 'I wonder what they want.' He spoke as much to himself as Aline. William of Gloucester was a pleasant young courtier, handsome, well mannered and a reasonable soldier, but without the authority and backbone his father possessed. Philip had a fine sense of his own worth but at sixteen was a rash youth. John turned to Aline, whose face was campion-coloured with chagrin at having been thus interrupted.

'When you are ready, you will need to organise the cooks to feed our guests. Tell Walchelin how many and he will do the rest. You'll need to arrange sleeping space for their men in the hall and give William and Philip the guest chamber.' It shouldn't have been necessary to explain such details, but she worked better if what was required of her was mapped out explicitly. 'If they decide to ride on and not accept a night's hospitality, I'll send word to you.'

She nodded and bit her lip.

Robert of Gloucester's sons had been furnished with wine and given seats before the fire while they waited. William was sitting down, drinking in fast swallows but Philip had risen to pace in agitation. John went forward to greet the young men, putting on a courtly smile, speaking solicitous words of welcome. William rose to his feet, his own smile no more than a token stretching of the lips. Philip gave John a swift bow, his mouth remaining straight and serious. Their greeting was so obviously the result of hard-won manners that John too dropped the courtesies.

'What's happened?' he demanded.

William thrust his cup at a nearby attendant and refused more. 'You must have heard what happened at Devizes, my lord?'

John gave him an astute look. 'I knew your father sent Robert FitzHubert to attempt the castle and FitzHubert succeeded. Daringly too, so I hear – by soft scaling ladders at night.' There was grudging admiration in John's expression. He disliked FitzHubert and wouldn't trust him out of his sight, but there was no denying the man's audacity.

William flushed. 'You have only heard the half of it. FitzHubert is now refusing to hand Devizes over to my father.' His voice bristled with anger. 'I arrived there to take command, and FitzHubert ordered his archers to shoot at my heralds! He's saying that Devizes is his and he'll answer to no man either as lord or paymaster.'

John swallowed a smile at the virulence of the young man's indignation, but swiftly sobered. The situation had the potential to be very dangerous indeed. If he were FitzHubert and had dared all to take such a powerful fortress and was then faced by a pair of beardless youngsters demanding he hand over control, he too might have closed his gates and, in a manner of speaking, waggled his backside at such dubious authority.

William and Philip were staring at him as if to ask what he was going to do about it. Almost like children complaining to a parent about having a toy taken away by a stronger child. Looking thoughtful, John folded his arms and sat down on the bench. Doublet, his adolescent

198

hound bitch, came to lie at his feet, nose on paws. 'No man can stand as an island.' He lowered his hand to stroke the dog's silky ears. 'It was one of the reasons I left King Stephen's court; I was too isolated. Sooner or later FitzHubert will have to seek alliances or sell Devizes to the highest bidder.'

'Hah, all my father will sell him is a noose!' Philip spat, his voice raw with adolescence.

'There are buyers in the market other than your father, remember that,' John said. 'Tell him I will keep an eye on the situation. FitzHubert may be strong of arm and quick to see and snatch opportunities, but it doesn't make him a great leader.' He gave both young men a piercing look. 'What you must do is learn from this and harden your steel.' William's fair skin reddened and John shook his head. 'I am not insulting you, just rendering some difficult-won advice. Back down if you must, but always do it facing your opponent. Never turn away.'

William of Gloucester compressed his lips and rested his left hand upon the pommel of his sword, thus informing John that he did believe himself insulted and not in need of instruction. Philip glowered. John supposed he had been the same at their age – considering himself a man and swift to take offence at anyone who questioned that manhood. 'If you and your troops desire a bed for the night you are welcome.'

William shook his head. 'Thank you, my lord, but no. The sooner we report this perfidy to my father the better.'

'As you wish. At least exchange the weariest horses and eat first. My wife' – and at this juncture he sent up a swift prayer – 'will already have told my cooks we have guests.'

*　　*　　*

199

Two days later, John was not surprised to receive envoys from the new lord of Devizes. He told his guards to admit the men; welcoming them into the solar, he gave them wine. Aline made to leave the chamber, but he bade her stay. He didn't expect her to be of use as an extra mind to analyse the meeting, but she was a witness, and it suited his purpose to have these men see a particular facet of his life. An anxious wife toiling over her needlework was excellent camouflage.

The men were affable in their manner and he had no doubt that they too were hiding their motives and intentions.

'My lord FitzHubert sends his greetings to an ally and fellow baron,' said the spokesman, whose name was Thomas de Cambrai. He rested his cup on his paunch and crossed his legs at the ankles. His companion, Serlo, kept darting glances at Aline, the way a hungry fox might watch a chicken in a coop.

John managed not to curl his lip at the way de Cambrai said 'my lord FitzHubert'. 'Yes, I heard about his success. In truth I was expecting a visit sooner or later.' He had not missed the detail that their scrutiny of his possessions was also incorporating the wall hangings and furnishings. Everything of value was being inventoried, and the strategic defences and weaknesses of the keep assessed. He had noticed them observing the guard posts on their way to the solar, and the position of the well.

De Cambrai smiled. 'You are shrewd, my lord.'

John waved a casual hand. 'I try to be.'

'Then to the matter. My lord desires a discussion with you, man to man, concerning Marlborough and Devizes and what can be done to strengthen your mutual hold on the region.'

'Ah, then your lord wants to make a pact to our joint advantage?'

'Just so, my lord.' Again the smile – the other side of which was a snarl. 'Why serve a master – or mistress – when we can serve ourselves?'

John rubbed his index finger slowly back and forth across his upper lip. 'I might be interested, depending on what he has to say.' He gestured. 'I am not averse to meeting with him.'

De Cambrai's eyes gleamed. 'An alliance will be to the advantage of both.'

'Perhaps. If your lord wishes to visit Marlborough in, say, three days' time for discussions I will be pleased to receive him.'

He registered the sly look exchanged between the men. They thought him the foolish farmer opening the hen-house door.

'I am certain he will be delighted to accept your invitation. He is keen to talk with you.'

'And I am keen to hear what he has to say.'

John saw FitzHubert's men to their horses, marking again how they stared at everything. His eldest son was in the stable yard exercising his pony and two-year-old Walter was watching, holding his nurse's hand and sucking his thumb. Seeing the way de Cambrai and Serlo eyed his children, John's gut somersaulted. He had a deal of swift thinking to do if he and his family were going to emerge from this intact.

'I want you and the boys to go to Hamstead,' he told Aline when he returned to the solar. 'At first light tomorrow. Pack what you need tonight.'

She gave him one of her frightened looks but he was so used to them by now that it was like water off waxed leather. 'Because of those men?' she asked.

201

'That's part of it. There may be trouble at Marlborough and I want you safe. I know what you were like at the siege. Even if there isn't any fighting, my guests are not the kind with whom you'd wish to associate.'

Aline stared at him anxiously. 'You're not really going to make a pact with them, are you?'

John snorted. 'I'd rather bed down with a host of demons.'

She shuddered. 'Then why invite FitzHubert here?'

'Because it's more than my life's worth to go to Devizes . . . and I mean that.' He narrowed his eyes. 'Let him come to me, and let it be the other way round.'

A cold rain-laden wind gusted fiercely across the Downs. John stood on the wall walk of the keep, protected from the elements by his fur-lined cloak. Robert FitzHubert and his troop were expected at any moment and he was poised, ready and waiting, having spent the last three days in detailed preparation for the event. His first move had been to send Aline and the boys to Hamstead, well out of the way. With them gone, he had bent his concentration to the matter in hand, knowing that he was taking a gamble and therefore had to load the odds in his favour as much as he could.

What did FitzHubert really want? What was the mercenary going to gain out of making a pact with him? John could see little sense in such a move from FitzHubert's point of view. He was almost certain that FitzHubert's approach was more about threat and domination than the cooperation of allies. The thought of being dictated to and threatened by a worm like FitzHubert brought a curl of disgust to John's lip. He had decided he would listen to what the mercenary had to say, but knew the upper hand had to be his from the start. His men all knew

202

their part – where they should be and what they should be doing. An hour since John had eaten a hearty dinner with his senior knights in his private chamber as they went over the plans for the last time.

'My lord, they're sighted!' came a cry from further along the battlements.

John hastened to the lookout's side and followed the pointing finger. He studied the glitter of armour and counted numbers. Not too many, but certainly enough if he had read FitzHubert's intentions correctly. 'Open the gate,' he commanded, and went down to greet them.

FitzHubert arrived at a pounding gallop and, mouth wide in a boisterous laugh, rode his stocky dun stallion straight at John, who calmly stood his ground, forcing the mercenary to rein back and haul the destrier aside.

'Welcome, my lord,' John said without a trace of sarcasm. 'You appear to be in a hurry.'

FitzHubert laughed again, although his eyes were calculating. 'The faster a man arrives, the more time he has for the important things. Besides, I like my horses the way I like my women – hot as hell and hard to stop. I'm sure you'd agree with that, my lord!' He dismounted and tossed the reins to the waiting groom.

'Certainly I agree with you about the women,' John replied amicably. 'Come within – your men too.' A gesture brought servants forward to lead the soldiers into the keep, and others to attend to the horses.

John had had the dining trestles set out in the hall with jugs of wine and baskets of bread for the men. But instead of ushering FitzHubert to the dais, John brought him to his private chamber on the floor above. FitzHubert followed him, gazing about covetously. John noted it and said nothing. However, he had to hide his satisfaction when FitzHubert glanced round as they reached the

203

chamber door and saw the two mail-clad knights following up the stairs.

'Ignore them,' John said with a dismissive wave. 'I like to keep them near, but you need pay them no more heed than you would a piece of furniture.'

FitzHubert rallied and squared his shoulders. John could almost see the cogs of his mind turning on the realisation that he had been isolated from his own men whilst John remained well guarded.

John ushered him into the room, closed the door, leaving his two knights menacing in the stairwell, and gestured FitzHubert to a seat on the hearth bench.

'Your wife not here?' FitzHubert stared round as if expecting Aline to pop out from behind the tied-back bed curtains beyond the seating area.

John heaved a regretful sigh. 'Sadly not. She and my sons are visiting their godmother.' He did not intend to tell FitzHubert where Aline really was. 'You will have to suffer my poor service, I am afraid, but since by its nature this must be a private conversation, it's all to the good.' John poured wine for them both, using the training he had received at court. No coarse tavern-sloshing into common earthenware, but an elegant red ripple from glazed flagon into cups of pale green Italian glass, worth a ransom in themselves.

FitzHubert's fat fist looked ridiculous closed around the delicate vessel, like a dung-shoveller holding a flower. John's own hand, slender and long-fingered, was a perfect foil. 'A gift – in a manner of speaking – from the Bishop of Salisbury and his kin,' John said.

'Hah, like Devizes then!' FitzHubert guffawed and spread his muscular thighs, affording John an astonished glimpse of purple silk braies above the hose. He had to choke down his laughter. Dear God, where on earth had he purloined them?' 'We have a great deal to be grateful for in the down-fall of Bishop Roger,' FitzHubert said, 'I heard he was a common peasant boy from Caen before he took the tonsure and that he owes his rise to his ability to say mass as quickly as a youth finishes with his first woman.'

John smiled. 'Being brief with the mass sounds as good a reason as any to me.' He sat on the fine chair he had had placed in the room for this meeting. Its size and ornate carving made the bench look plain and rustic. The space between the two seats was occupied by a coffer on which stood a dish of little rose-water tarts and another of deli-cate fried pastries – food of the court and the King's private chamber. Not the kind of morsels to satisfy the likes of FitzHubert, but pointedly displaying John's court-liness and sophistication.

John drank from his glass cup and leaned back in his chair. 'So,' he said affably, 'what is this pact of which your men spoke the other day? What do you want to talk to me about?'

FitzHubert took one of the pastries and devoured it in two bites. Crumbs flaked his upper lip and speckled his tunic. 'I thought since we were friends and neighbours, we might have things in common worth investigating – things we might do united that we might not have consid-ered on our own lest we bite off more than we can chew.' With a grin at his own weak pun, he gobbled down another pastry.

'United,' John repeated thoughtfully and sipped his wine.

FitzHubert hunched forward, an eager glint in his eyes. 'We could use each other's men, for instance. If you lend me soldiers when I need them, then in my turn I will lend you mine. We both have troops of trusted and proven ability. I'd not have taken Devizes Castle with a herd of sheep, and those lads of yours on the stairs look as if they can handle themselves in a fight.'

'They can.' John met FitzHubert's stare head on. 'But I wonder what advantage there is in this from my point of view?'

FitzHubert gave him a patronising, almost contemptuous look as if he was talking to someone he considered dull-witted or slow on the uptake. 'I am saying if you wanted to take on something bigger than you normally would, you'd be able if you had more men.'

'Yes, I understand that,' John said, 'but why should I want to do so?'

'Oh, come now.' Impatience glimmered in FitzHubert's expression. 'You're an ambitious man; don't tell me you haven't thought about expanding your territory. I know I have.'

John raised his eyebrows at his guest. 'Have you indeed?' His voice was courteous but glacial. 'And where would that be?'

FitzHubert dropped his gaze and withdrew a little. 'Who knows where ambition takes us?' he said with a vague wave of his hand. 'There are many opportunities we can both explore if you are agreeable.'

'Indeed,' John agreed, struggling not to let his revulsion show. 'It is true a man needs to be strong in himself and in his allies. I cannot ignore the fact that a new and powerful lord sits at Devizes with whom I should be better acquainted. I am glad to remedy that now.'

FitzHubert drained his wine and stood up, his impatience tangible. 'We should return to the men. If we are to make a pact, it should be done before all.'

John did not miss the sly flicker of his visitor's eyes and felt his belly tighten at the danger that still lurked.

The mercenary extended his hand. John took it, clasped

it and felt the bite of the fingers: fleshy, but hard as oak beneath. His own thinner, finer grip bore the tensile strength of good steel.

Opening the door, he gestured his knights on the stairs to escort them down to the hall and brought up the rear himself. He wouldn't have trusted FitzHubert at his back and besides, it was a courtesy to let the guest go first.

The hall was raucous with noise. FitzHubert's men raised a huge cheer and pounded the trestles when they saw their lord and John together. Most of them were already half inebriated. The sight of them at the judicial core of his keep sent a jolt of anger through John. His own soldiers, with the exception of a few deliberately placed to counter suspicion, were cold sober and waiting his command. Until he had spoken to FitzHubert, John had been hedging a decision, but now he was clear what he had to do.

John watched FitzHubert taking a mental inventory of all he hoped to gain. So be it. The dolt could start with the cells at the back of the undercroft and a pair of iron fetters. He made a sign to Benet, who in his turn signalled to the other, strategically placed men. The knights who had stood guard in the stairwell seized FitzHubert and John moved in to relieve the mercenary of his sword and dagger in a single smooth motion.

'You treacherous hellspawn whoreson!' FitzHubert roared. 'I am here in good faith as your guest. You can't do this to me!'

'Call me what you will, but never a fool,' John retorted coldly. 'I know why you are here and good faith has nothing to do with it.'

FitzHubert bellowed at his men to rise up, but they had been grabbed by John's prepared and sober soldiers

207

and most were in no fit state to fight back. 'Bastard!' he howled at John, struggling against his captors.

'Perhaps I am,' John said, 'but I know the meaning of integrity as you do not. You are right about ambition though. I will use you and your men to my own advantage, and I thank you for your earlier offer.' He gave a brusque nod to his knights. 'Take him away to the "guest chamber" and see him fêted with suitable hospitality.'

With grim pleasure, his men hauled the sputtering FitzHubert away to the cells. John sat down on the lord's chair at the dais trestle, FitzHubert's sword laid across the cloth before him. In the pose of a lord sitting in judgement, he waited until the last mercenary had been dragged away. Only then did he rise to his feet and return to his private chamber. On the way, he handed the sword to Benet who had just returned from supervising the incarceration.

'It's all done as you wished, my lord,' Benet said, 'although not without some resistance and rough handling – nothing the lads couldn't deal with.' He looked speculatively at John. 'What are you going to do with them, my lord?'

John pursed his lips. 'I'm not entirely certain yet, but I have a few ideas to mull over.' He handed the sword to Benet with a grimace of distaste. 'Here, take this and break it on the anvil.'

Benet's eyes widened with dismay. 'But it's a fine sword, my lord.' Without any of John's revulsion, he tested the balance and twirled it in his hand, describing fancy patterns in the air.

'Even so, break it. I want the pieces fastened to the castle door as a warning to anyone else who would try to take what is mine – by whatever means.'

* * *

Robert of Gloucester stared at John with eyes full of admiration and mirth. 'God's blood, I don't believe you've got FitzHubert in your gaol!'

They were sitting in John's chamber at Marlborough. This time the stairwell was empty of guards. Gloucester held his green glass cup with the appreciation of a courtier and a man of tasteful sensibilities. Although the son of a king, his braies were of plain but superb quality linen and he didn't sit in such a way as to expose his crotch to the view of all and sundry.

John gave a casual shrug. 'Believe it, my lord. He played me for a fool and whatever else I may be, I am not one, nor do I suffer them gladly, especially when they come intending me harm. Nor, with the greatest respect to your sons, am I twenty and wet behind the ears.'

Gloucester gave a wry laugh. 'Indeed not. I would caution any man to trifle with you. What are you going to do with FitzHubert now?'

John pretended to ponder the question, although he had already made up his mind. 'I have heard he was wont to smear his victims with honey and leave them out in the sun to be attacked by every stinging insect on God's earth,' he said. 'I thought about doing the same to him, but while it would be amusing for a while, it wouldn't be of lasting benefit.' He gave Robert a considering look. 'Perhaps you would like to buy him from me, being as he was in your pay when he turned traitor.'

Robert choked on his wine. 'Buy him from you!' he coughed.

John smiled. 'If you want my strength in the Kennet valley, I need to be able to pay my troops and provide them with good horses and equipment.' He studied his cup. 'I can hand him back to his own men at Devizes for a fee or give him into the custody of William D'Ypres,

209

since they're kin. Or you could have him from me for five hundred marks.'

'What?' Robert gasped, his throat still in semi-paroxysm. 'Five hund— You jest!'

John kept his own gaze steady. 'I don't think it too high a sum for what he has done to you. If you buy him from me, you can do as you please with him.'

Robert glared at John, but then he began to chuckle. 'You're a wily one, John FitzGilbert, you know that, don't you? Very well. For five hundred marks, I will have him from you, but I expect good value in return.'

'And you will receive it, my lord. I do what I must to survive – as do we all.' John inclined his head, restraining the urge to laugh and fist the air at how well everything had worked out. Five hundred marks was an appreciable sum and once FitzHubert was in Gloucester's custody, John was certain the mercenary would never trouble him again . . . and Devizes was now open to be taken on the Empress's behalf.

20

Bristol, February 1141

To a commanding royal fanfare, the Empress entered the great hall of Bristol Castle. She was clad in a crimson gown, the panels and gores embossed with twists of spiral silk thread in the same shade of red. As usual, a gem-set coronet adorned her brow – the least she would consider to wear when holding an audience.

With everyone else, John flourished a bow, knowing how much store she set by obeisance and protocol. Partly it was a result of her training at the German court, but it was her personality too. She saw her dignity upheld in the deference of others. With his years of experience as a courtier, the flourishes and rituals were second nature to John; but even so, he found it wearisome at times. Matilda seldom dropped her guard or smiled. Perhaps only with Brian FitzCount was she her true self and the rest of the court was never allowed a glimpse into that relationship.

John made his report to her. A baron had sent her two palfreys complete with saddle and harness as a measure of his goodwill. A merchant wanted to present her with a bolt of silk cloth in person. Matilda was gracious about the horses but less keen on accepting the cloth from the hands of the merchant, particularly when she learned he was from London. As far as she was concerned, the Londoners were one of the reasons she was not yet Queen of England. They had welcomed Stephen; they had turned their backs on her. She was of the opinion that the folk of the city should be given no privileges and visited with a rod of iron rather than wooed with gentle words.

John had bade his ushers keep the merchant in the antechamber ready to be summoned but Matilda made it clear that while she would accept his cloth, she did not want to see him. 'Thank him and send him away,' she commanded John with a lofty wave of her hand.

'Is that wise, sister?' Gloucester looked troubled. 'He may have wealth and influence we can use.'

Anger sparked in her fine dark eyes. 'Stephen may choose to water with the horses,' she said in a clipped voice, 'but I will not be bought by a London merchant for a bolt of silk.'

'But you could buy London for a smile and a word,' Gloucester said.

She looked irritated, then sighed. 'Oh, admit him,' she capitulated with obvious displeasure, making sure everyone knew she was just humouring her half-brother.

John fetched the merchant and cautioned him to bow low, say little and let his fabric do his talking. The man slipped John a bag of silver for his advice, which John stared at in disbelief. He was frequently offered bribes; sometimes he took them, but not from merchants touting bolts of cloth. He reckoned from the weight of the small leather purse to have been tipped about a day's wages and didn't know whether to be insulted or amused.

Matilda looked down her nose at the merchant, but deigned to accept both his cloth and his felicitations, with the kind of mien that revealed she thought him well beneath her and was tolerating him on sufferance.

'He was probably a spy,' she sniffed to Gloucester after he had been dismissed as swiftly as possible with a vague assurance that his business would prosper should she become Queen. She bade one of her women remove the fabric – beautiful red silk brocade – to the storage coffers.

'Doubtless he was, and he's learned very little here, except you are well guarded and have a court that would be the envy of any prince in Europe,' Gloucester said. 'Let him spy. He'll learn nothing of value . . .'

As John was seeing the merchant on his way, a messenger pounded in on a sweating courser. There was blood in the horse's nostrils and it was staggering, its wind broken. John left the merchant to the gatekeeper and conducted the messenger straight to the Empress – and although he bowed and flourished, he was peremptory now.

The messenger, swaying with exhaustion, blurted out the news that Earl Ranulf of Chester had seized the keep at Lincoln from Stephen's castellan. Chester had ridden to fetch reinforcements, leaving his wife, Gloucester's daughter, to defend the keep which was under siege from Stephen and in desperate need of aid. If it didn't come, she would have to surrender herself and the castle.

'I have to go to her,' Gloucester said. 'Even were she not my flesh and blood, this is a God-given opportunity. We cannot let Lincoln slip from our grasp. The Earl of Chester has long sat on the fence, but if we can win him over now, then we become twice as powerful.'

Matilda leaned forward, her gaze as fierce as a hawk's. 'I have no love for Ranulf of Chester,' she said, 'but you are right, we need him; his support will make all the difference. Go, my lord. Go as soon as you may.'

John felt the news surge through the court like a clean,

bright wind, blowing in change and a freshening of optimism. He wouldn't trust the Earl of Chester farther than he could throw a feather. He was fickle; an earl by birth and a mercenary at heart; but Lincoln was a strategic fortress and if he was prepared to hold it for the Empress, then he had to be helped.

Within the hour John was busy with lists and tallies, and orders for supplies and carts to take them up the Fosse Road to Lincoln.

In Marlborough, Aline stared at the cross on the altar of the Church of Saint Mary and prayed with intensity. Dear, sweet Virgin, let John be safe. Let him come home from Lincoln in one piece. What would happen to her if he was taken for ransom or killed? What would happen to their sons? She had nightmares that his absence would provoke an attack on their lands from their enemies. Sometimes she thought about going up on the battlements to look out for John's return but she never got that far because she was terrified she might see hostile troops instead. Even the Candlemas feast of the Purification of the Virgin, which was one of the high points between winter and spring, had been marred by the worry of what might be happening at Lincoln and she had not been able to give her full heart to the ritual.

When she had married John, she had thought he would protect and care for her, but life hadn't turned out like that. He spent all of his time on the Empress's business, or else patrolling his domain. He would sleep the occasional night at Marlborough, but he had his own chamber, and showed small inclination to share hers beyond the obligatory procreative duty. She craved the security of knowing he was near. She needed to feel he was looking after her, but that need was not being met. Her only security was the Church. When she prayed, she was in communication with God and His Holy Mother, as she was never in communication with her husband. It was the only straw she had left to grasp in a world otherwise bereft of comfort.

In Salisbury Sybilla too was praying – for her brothers who had ridden to join King Stephen and put an end to Ranulf of Chester's ambitious designs on Lincoln. For the soul of her mother also, who had been buried two days before her brothers rode out. A winter cold had thickened on her chest and then settled on her lungs. Sybire had died of the congestion, leaving the household bereft of its maternal rudder and Sybilla as sole chatelaine. She was accustomed to responsibility and had taken over the duties with efficiency and aplomb, but little joy. Nor was the season conducive to lifting the spirits. The wind was bitter; there had been snow showers last week. Today it was raining and the colours of the cathedral interior were muted. The reds were rust, the blues were charcoal and the yellow was the hue of weak urine.

She lit a candle for her mother who had been buried at the Augustinian priory at Bradenstoke. Sybilla's third brother Walter was a canon there, so at least their mother was resting close to her family and masses would be said for her soul on a regular basis.

Shivering despite her fur-lined cloak, Sybilla left the cathedral and made her way towards the castle. The wind was blowing hard across the plain, assaulting the bank and palisades in sweeping gusts. Eyes narrowed and tear-stung, her veil flapping about her face, she hurried towards the anticipated warmth of the solar fire.

Then she saw the troop riding up the track towards the gate, the foremost bearing the red and gold standard of Salisbury. The horses were plodding, heads down, legs heavy

215

from being hard-ridden, and the men astride were slumped like half-filled sacks. She saw her brothers, side by side. William had a long cut down one cheek. Patrick was unmarked, but his expression was bleaker than the rain-spattered February wind. Sybilla hurried to meet them.

She noticed quite a few wounded men, although no one needed a litter. But there were gaps in the line and several familiar faces were missing.

'What's happened?' she gasped.

William neither turned his head nor answered, but fixed a desperate gaze on the approaching stronghold.

Sybilla swallowed. 'Patrick?'

He looked at her. 'The King went down,' he said through stiff lips. 'He's Gloucester's prisoner. Lincoln was a disaster . . . a rout.'

'The King is a prisoner?' She stared at him in dismay.

He shook his head in grim reply and urged his horse up the hill and through the heavily guarded entrance.

Sybilla waited until the horses were through and into the courtyard, then pushed her way through the dismounting men, the bundles of baggage and gear, until she reached Patrick again.

She grasped his sleeve. 'What does this mean for us?'

'Well, it's hardly an opportunity on a golden platter, is it?' he snarled. 'We've to decide whether to hold for Stephen or bow our heads to the Empress.' He spat the last word as if it were a piece of gristle, making it abundantly clear what he thought of such a notion. 'The cowards broke and ran. The men he's made earls of the realm. Hah! About as much backbone as a bucket of boiled eels. Even William D'Ypres fled the field rather than stand.' He flicked a jaundiced glance towards his brother, who was staring straight ahead, his mouth as tight as a sealed coffin. Sybilla wasn't blind to the antagonism between the men.

216

'You didn't stand either?' she risked.

'There was no point,' William said wearily. 'What could we have done on our own except be captured like Stephen, and that would have left our lands unprotected and our father with a ransom to raise. When we saw how it was, we cut our cloth to suit . . . but we didn't quit when there was all still to fight for . . . unlike some.' Again, the brothers exchanged looks. 'There are wounded to be tended,' William said tersely to Sybilla. 'See to them.'

She bridled at his tone, but compressed her lips and, for the sake of the injured men, held her tongue and went to do his bidding.

For the next few hours she was kept busy binding, tending, overseeing the provision of washing water, food, beds and raiment for injured and uninjured alike. The story continued to emerge in fits and starts. Stephen had been in command of the town, but not the castle, which he was besieging. When Gloucester's force had arrived, bolstered by a host of Welsh mercenaries and dispossessed knights, Stephen had chosen to go out and give battle instead of staying behind the town walls. His lords had not been as keen on the prospect of embroiling themselves in vicious hand-to-hand fighting when the odds were evenly stacked. When it came to standing firm, their resolve had faltered and they had abandoned the field. Her brothers had not been in that first wave, but had fought on until they knew they must either flee or be captured. Now they were furious; both felt their manhood had been shamed because they were not the kind of men who ran away. And they could not agree what they should do next.

Stephen was being brought to Bristol under heavy guard and the way lay open for the Empress to make her bid for the throne. Sybilla's brothers had to choose whether to support Stephen's Queen, who was continuing to fight on her husband's behalf, or to give their allegiance to the Empress and hope for a good outcome. Patrick wanted to stay with Stephen and what they had always known. William was of the opinion they should go to the Empress.

'You want a woman to rule over us?' Patrick scoffed. 'You might as well ask our sister to don a hauberk and swing a sword.'

Sybilla gritted her teeth and suppressed the urge to tip the jug of wine she was holding over Patrick's head. There was more to governance than the ability to fight. Who did they think had organised the household in their absence and dealt with the estate? Or perhaps they preferred not to think about it. It was easier to pretend that their father was still capable of directing operations on a local level than accept that Sybilla might be the driving force behind everything.

'With Stephen in prison, his wife commands, so either way, we have to bow to a woman,' William retorted. 'You should be asking yourself which you would rather – de Beaumont or Gloucester? Gloucester's nearer. We can't afford to stand in the path of the storm.'

'Hah, so you'd desert at the first blow like all the others you called fickle?' Patrick sneered. 'I say it's too early to go to the Empress. She's not Queen yet.'

William clenched his fists. 'I'm the head of this household. Our father's not capable of making a decision like this. I say we go to the Empress.'

'You'll regret it,' Patrick said curtly.

'My mind is made up. Let that be an end to it.' Rising to his feet, William stalked from the room.

Patrick swore in his brother's wake. 'Men won't follow a woman who behaves like a man,' he growled. 'I'll not be governed by such a one. I don't know why Gloucester supports her.'

'He's her half-brother,' Sybilla said. 'Would you not support me?'

He coughed at the notion, but then conceded her the point with a raised forefinger. 'I suppose I'd have to, but Gloucester didn't do it for love, you know. He wasn't receiving the patronage he desired at Stephen's court, so he turned to the Empress instead. The same with John FitzGilbert. Brian FitzCount's another matter. He worships the ground she treads on, the fool. He could have gained plenty by being Stephen's man.'

'So it is better to betray those you love than to hold by them?' Sybilla said neutrally.

Patrick glowered at her. 'You prattle of things about which you know nothing. Love is a conceit of women encouraged by troubadours. A man's loyalty is to his family first, and then his lord. He cannot afford to be softened by devotion to a mistress – whether he beds her or not.' He gave an impatient wave of his hand. 'Enough of this fond talk. I have better things to do.' He strode out in William's wake.

Sybilla cast a fulminating glance at the door, but then the anger dropped from her face and she heaved a deep sigh. She should know by now that banging one's head against a stone wall only caused headaches. What Patrick said was partially true. She and her women did sometimes discuss FitzCount's devotion to the Empress and harbour secret longings that a man would one day show them the same chivalrous loyalty. To that extent, it was indeed a conceit of women. It was also true what Patrick had said about loyalty. Family and the ties of homage were of paramount importance – but surely there was a little room for the lightning jolt in the gut, for the moment when the room lit up because of one person's presence? Not that such had ever happened to her, but she lived in hope, and if it did, she intended to seize it in both hands and hold on for dear life.

219

21

Westminster, London, Summer 1141

Lying on his bed, her thick fair hair cloaking her naked body, the young woman regarded John out of wide blue eyes. Her lips were swollen and a pink flush was slowly receding from her throat and bosom. 'I would have sought among the Empress's lords earlier if I had known what I do now,' she purred.

John pillowed his head on his hands and studied her through heavy lids. The intensity of his release had momentarily drained him. It had been too long; too much tension, both physical and mental, kept on a tight rein. The girl had come to the gates, seeking employment, claiming experience. She had been the mistress of one of the town burghers until his sudden demise last month. The thorough interviewing of prospective new concubines for the court was one of the perquisites of John's position. The Empress pretended such women did not exist, even while she understood the need for their services. He gave a sardonic smile. 'Ah, sweetheart, but you have to be prepared to take the rough with the smooth.'

'And which are you?' She gave him a pert look.

He chuckled, liking her spirit. 'That depends on the

circumstances. Just remember that your first duty is to please your customers and be discreet.' He could apply that to his own position with the Empress, he thought wryly.

'And did I please you?'

'You shouldn't need to ask.' Making the effort, he rose from the bed. For once, he would like to have stayed there and closed his eyes, but knew he would be expected in the hall to keep order when the Empress sat down to dine.

Two days ago Stephen's brother, Henry, Bishop of Winchester, now in Matilda's camp, had requested of the Empress that Stephen's eldest son Eustace be allowed to inherit his father's county of Mortain. She had snapped an immediate refusal and the Bishop unsurprisingly had chosen to sulk about it, Eustace being his nephew, and a claimant to the throne.

'My name's Oswith,' the girl said, fiddling with a strand of her hair. 'I thought I might change it to Petronella.'

John rolled his eyes as he pulled on his shirt. 'Stay with Oswith if you want the custom,' he told her.

She pouted. 'Why?'

'Because your clients would rather have an English wench under them in the bed and play Hastings all over again than futter a substitute for their Norman wives. You'll be unusual too. If I had a shilling for every cour- tesan who goes by a fancy name, I could have bought London by now.'

He watched her frown and absorb the advice. Perhaps she'd last, perhaps she wouldn't, but the flaxen hair, deep blue eyes and ripe curves would ensure a steady stream of clients at the outset.

Once she was dressed, he gave her into the custody of the usher in charge of the concubines and bade him escort her to their lodgings.

William, eldest son of Walter of Salisbury, paused to watch the exchange on his way to dinner, and gave John a salacious grin, his tongue stuck in his cheek. 'Recommended?' he asked.

'Potential,' John answered with a laconic shrug. He was always civil to William of Salisbury when he saw him, but he was not a bosom friend. Salisbury had changed sides and bowed to the Empress following Stephen's defeat at Lincoln, but John was still wary. From what he had heard, the other brother, Patrick, had wanted to continue supporting Stephen. William was popular among the men, and a decent soldier. John afforded him respect, was civil, but never exchanged more than a few words with him. The matter of Ludgershall was still a bone of contention between them.

'At least she's got a smile on her face, which is more than you can say for the rest of them.'

'What – the whores?' John looked surprised.

'No, the Londoners.' Impatience swirled in William's voice. 'I thought we were going to have a riot yesterday when they came here and she said she would fine them for supporting Stephen and how dare they ask her for concessions.' He touched his sword hilt for reassurance and grimaced.

John said nothing. He would not discuss the Empress with Salisbury, who was not a familiar, even if the latter was soliciting reassurance. Matilda was preparing for her coronation and a grand entry into London complete with a magnificent procession, but at the same time was treating the citizens like dirt under her feet. He knew Matilda neither liked nor trusted them. Their support had given Stephen his crown. In their turn, the Londoners were tepid in their support of her and it was proving impossible to have the two sides meet halfway with Matilda in her current mood. It didn't help that Stephen's Queen had mustered an army and was ravaging the land south of the river dangerously close to the city.

Excusing himself, John went to speak with his other ushers, watchmen and serjeants, then took up his position in the hall. With a sinking feeling, he realised that Matilda's mood had not improved since yesterday. The vertical grooves between her brows were deep and her mouth had a sullen droop. She ignored the servants attending to her and paid scant attention to those seated at the board with her, including Robert of Gloucester and the Bishop of Winchester. Even Brian FitzCount didn't merit the lift of a smile.

Probably her time of the month, John decided. Policing the whores, one learned more about the affairs of women than most men did and it was worrying to think of the unevenness such a state of affairs might create in governance. For all that he had put Devizes in her hands, Matilda had rewarded him with little more than tepid courtesy, taking his efforts on her behalf as no more than her due and worthy of small comment and even less praise. Since there was no alternative, he had to dig in his heels and stand his ground.

Henry of Winchester seemed to be trying to persuade her of something. He was talking earnestly, opening and closing his hands, gesturing. Her expression carved in stone, Matilda was leaning slightly away from his movements. John was not close enough to hear, but he could guess the talk was of Eustace again and that the Bishop was receiving short shrift.

Becoming aware of urgent whispering behind him, John turned round and saw an Angevin merchant who lived in the city and who was one of Matilda's spies talking rapidly to an usher.

223

'What is it?' John demanded.

'My lord, the citizens are on their way to invade Westminster.' The merchant looked at him with panic-filled eyes. 'They are going to denounce the Empress and declare for the Queen. Her army is very close. If the people break into these precincts . . .' He licked his lips. 'It's a mob, my lord, a frightened, angry mob. There is no telling what they will do. I have brought my wife and babe and goods . . . I dare not stay.'

John hesitated for an instant then summoned a serjeant and told him to check the details. 'Go,' he said to the merchant and slapped him on the arm. 'If you have a woman and child with you, you need to be free and clear.' Without waiting to see if the merchant took his advice, he heeled about and strode to the dais.

'Domina, there is grave news.' He flourished her the deep bow she expected of her retainers, but without waiting on protocol for the rest, told her what he had just heard.

She drew herself up and gave him a scornful stare down her nose. 'You interrupt me for this? For a mob?'

John looked at her, then at Gloucester who at least seemed perturbed. 'A mob that will swarm over this place like a nest of ants and we will be unable to stop them. A mob that will open London to the forces of Stephen's Queen and William D'Ypres. We cannot hold Westminster; we are not prepared. Domina, with respect, you will be captured if we stay.'

Her lip curled. 'I will not flee.'

John mentally clenched his fists in exasperation. 'No, Domina, but a strategic withdrawal might be in order.'

Brian FitzCount leaned towards her. 'The marshal is right and he is not one to cry danger unnecessarily. It would be prudent to withdraw until we better know the situation.' Even as he spoke, they all heard the distant sound of church bells tolling from the direction of the city. A call to arms if ever John had heard one.

Henry of Winchester had risen to his feet; so had Robert of Gloucester. John bowed again. 'With your leave, Domina, I will have the horses brought.'

She gave him a stiff nod. 'Do so,' she said, her lips barely moving to articulate the words. John bowed again and hastened outside, snapping his fingers to his ushers and subordinates. In the hot, midsummer air, the sound of the bells tolling in the city was clear and loud. A rallying cry, a tocsin . . . a knell.

Salisbury Cathedral had been filled to capacity for the mass celebrating the Assumption of the Virgin. The day was fine and bright and sunlight streamed through the painted glass windows, creating a mosaic of coloured patterns on the nave floor. Folk stood in groups, talking, gossiping and catching up. Patrick of Salisbury had joined a handful of cronies and stood with arms folded, cloak thrown back from his shoulders, very much acting the lord in his brother's absence with the Empress.

Sybilla was preparing to follow the servants who were helping her father into the litter that would carry him back to the castle when she saw a small, slender woman sitting on the benches at the side with her maid and two young children. Sybilla bade the servants continue to the castle and went over to speak to them. Aline Marshal gave her a sweet smile, but her face was pinched with tension and Sybilla noticed how her delicate hands shook. Her right one clutched her prayer beads as if they were as important as her soul. She was wearing a blue robe and plain white wimple, the latter draining the colour from her complexion.

'You are well, my lady?' Sybilla asked politely.

'Indeed yes.' Aline's voice was a whisper.

'I was admiring your gown. What a beautiful shade of blue.'

Aline's uncertainty receded and a tinge of pink flushed her cheekbones. She released the beads to smooth her palm over the sky-coloured wool. 'I wore it to honour the Virgin, not out of vanity,' she said and looked down the nave towards the altar. 'It is a pity we have no bishop to celebrate the mass since Bishop Roger died.'

'No, but the Archdeacon was excellent, I thought, and in all likelihood he will be admitted to the see.' Sybilla smiled at the boys. 'Your sons are growing swiftly, and aren't they handsome?' The older one gave her a solemn stare from wide grey eyes. The youngest buried his face against his mother's skirts.

Aline murmured in the affirmative, but instead of embracing the boys, lowered her gaze to her beads and fiddled with them. Sybilla was tempted to make her excuses and leave, but it would have been rude and against her duty. 'You will join the feast in our hall?' she asked, and when Aline began to make her apologies, added, 'We should celebrate the Assumption of the Virgin fittingly. The Archdeacon is attending.'

'Then thank you, my lady.' Aline smiled again, but it was strained and without pleasure – the grimace of a cornered creature.

When the feast in the hall was over, Aline spent a while in the bower with the women of the castle – the wives of the knights, vassals and retainers pertaining to the sheriff and the Archdeacon. She settled herself on a bench near the embrasure, making herself as small and inconspicuous as a mouse. Her sons were playing with some children belonging to the other women and she could hear occasional shouts from the sward beyond the open shutters, bright with boisterous life. Watching the daughter of the house, Sybilla, oversee matters, Aline felt a twinge of wistful envy. The girl was no more than seventeen yet already displayed a capability far beyond anything Aline could manage after eight years of marriage. When to speak; when to hold silent. What to say to put folk at their ease. What to offer to guests and all in a natural, smiling manner. The room was clean and bright with fresh green rushes strewing the floor and a jug of herbs and flowers standing on the embrasure ledge. How did one accomplish such things and remain unflustered when surrounded by such a gathering? The girl herself was stylishly dressed in a gown laced tightly at the sides, enhancing her figure. The sleeves were fashionably long and lined with yellow silk. When Sybilla spoke and gestured, those linings flashed their colour and drew attention to the line of the arm within the tight-sleeved pale undergown. Aline would never have dreamed of arraying herself like that – would not have had the confidence or daring; indeed, she would have felt brazen.

From general gossip about clothes and jewels, children and alliances, the talk inevitably turned to the situation in Winchester, where many of the women had husbands, sons and relatives involved in the contention. Aline clenched her fists in her lap and gripped the security of her prayer beads. She didn't want to listen to such talk but was constrained by propriety to stay where she was. The less she knew the better she was able to cope. Ignoring it didn't make it go away, but at least she could pretend it wasn't there. They were talking about the quarrel between the Empress and the Bishop of Winchester, which was the reason John was currently away from home. The

227

Empress was besieging the Bishop in his palace at Wolvesey.

John had returned briefly to Marlborough following the debacle in London when the court had had to abandon its dinner and leave the city to Stephen's forces, led by William of Ypres and Stephen's Queen. Then he had gone to Oxford for a court gathering. The Bishop of Winchester had failed to appear and it became clear he had deserted the Empress for his former allegiance, hence her descent upon his palace at Winchester. John had been growling something about people who couldn't organise an orgy in a whorehouse, but at that juncture, she had shut out the rest of what he had been saying and taken herself off to church.

'I always said Winchester couldn't be trusted,' opined a florid older woman. 'He only joined the Empress in a fit of pique because his brother didn't get him elected Archbishop of Canterbury. That's what he really wanted, and instead he was pushed out by de Beaumont's candidate.'

'After what the Beaumonts did to Roger of Salisbury, he couldn't be blamed,' a knight's wife said.

'It must have been a shock to find his nest's no more silk-lined on the other side. Who'll give him their trust now? It'll be bloody though. He won't surrender his palace to the Empress without a hard fight. I hope she doesn't send my Ranulf up a siege ladder. My children need their father.'

Aline must have made a sound, for the woman turned to her, eyes avid with curiosity. 'Your husband is in Winchester too, Lady Marshal.'

Aline swallowed. There was a lump in her throat and suddenly it was hard to breathe. 'Yes,' she whispered.

'You must worry for him when he's the Empress's marshal. Bound to be in the forefront.'

228

Aline nodded and compressed her lips. Her ears were ringing and she thought she might faint.

'You must be so proud of him.'

She heard herself agree that she was. Knowing she had to leave the room before she made a fool of herself, she muttered an excuse concerning her sons, and hurried out. Ignoring the boys, who were playing a noisy game of chase, she leaned against the cool, pale stone wall of the guest hall and prayed to the Virgin. Holy Mary, let this conflict be at an end. Let there be peace and let it not be the peace of the grave. She was unravelling like a frayed edge of cloth and soon there would be nothing left but a few bare windblown threads.

229

22

Abbey of Wherwell, Hampshire, August 1141

The woman's assumption that John was in Winchester was wrong. He was nine miles away at the Benedictine nunnery of Wherwell. The convent stood at a crossing of the river Test on a major supply route to Winchester and John had been sent to guard that crossing and make sure provisions got through to the Empress's troops in the city. There had been too many raids on supplies and shortages were beginning to bite.

At dawn, he had received reports from his scouts that didn't bode well. Royalist troops had sacked Andover and were headed straight for Winchester via the ford at Wherwell.

The Abbess was livid that her convent had been invaded and taken over by a band of armed men. Standing before him as the morning brightened with heat, she lashed him with her tongue.

'God will punish you for this!' she warned, eyes blazing.

'Doubtless he will,' John said grimly, 'but I must take that chance. You and your sisters in Christ must leave these precincts.' He looked up as another scout arrived on a lathered horse.

'I refuse to be driven out of God's house by a horde of . . . of routiers!'

John clung to patience by the skin of his teeth. 'For your own sake, you must. Sooner or later there will be hard fighting here and you do not want to be caught up in it.'

'If you leave there will not be a fight.'

He gave her a barren smile. 'I cannot do that, Mother Abbess. I pray you, withdraw your nuns.'

She glared at him for a moment longer then pivoted on her heel and marched off. John turned to his scout.

The man bared his teeth. 'William D'Ypres is coming up fast, my lord, from the Andover road with all his Flemings.' The hollow of his throat shone with grimy sweat. 'You are badly outnumbered; you will not hold him.'

The news created a void in John's gut, but he maintained a composed expression. 'His men will be tired, mine are not,' he said. 'I do not fear the odds. Get yourself a fresh horse and be ready to ride for Winchester on the moment.'

'My lord.'

John tightened his jaw. From small boyhood, he had been taught to stand his ground. Never give in. Never. It was a sign of weakness and a reason for shame. He had sometimes wanted to run away, especially when he was taking a drubbing from an older, more experienced opponent; but as he matured he had learned to hold fast and, like a horse trained for war, had transmuted the desire to flee into battleground aggression.

Another rider pounded in, this time from Winchester with the news that a division of royalist troops under the Earl of Surrey had hit the city from the east and the Empress was retreating to safety. 'Winchester's in flames, my lord, it's hell in there,' he gasped. 'The Earl of

231

Gloucester is fighting a rearguard to hold off the Queen's troops while he gets the Empress away. He's sent her before him with my lords of Wallingford and Cornwall. They're taking the west road through Le Strete to Ludgershall and Devizes. My lord Gloucester bids you do what you must to stay D'Ypres and prevent him from closing the trap. If he gains the Stockbridge road before the Empress has had a chance to make good her escape . . .' He let his words trail off.

John gave a brusque nod. So there was no point sending his messenger on to Winchester. Stephen's Queen with all the Londoners behind her and the Kentish militia would overrun the Empress's positions like a high spring tide. If D'Ypres took this crossing at Wherwell, he would be able to race up the river road to the next bridge at Le Strete and cut off the Empress's escape, trapping her like a grain between two millstones.

He looked at the sun glittering on the ribbon of the river, at the trees, still green with summer, but showing a little tired and dusty now. The thatched and shingled roofs of the nunnery buildings. A herd of red cows drinking at the riverbank, their hocks caked in drying mud. He felt the ground under his feet, hard after the heat of a long, dry August. Such weather was perfect for harvest. Cutting the wheat, scything it down. He was six and thirty. Better to die now than live down the years to become a dribbling wreck like Walter of Salisbury.

'My lord?'

He turned to look at Benet, seeing with a sudden sharp clarity the lugubrious features and steady brown eyes. Through thick and thin. 'We're going into the jaws of hell,' he said to the knight. 'Find the nuns' priest and get him to shrive the men. The quicker the better because William D'Ypres is going to be on us very soon.'

'That bad?'

John found a smile. 'Close enough.'

The unspoken message passed between them. 'Good thing my sword's sharp and my horse fresh,' Benet said, bowed deeply and departed on his errand, striding swiftly but without alarm.

John called for his stallion, organised the men and spoke with the other senior knights. His company had the support of Geoffrey Boterel, brother to the Earl of Richmond, and Robert of Okehampton, both steady, seasoned men, strong in the saddle and impervious to panic. They all knew what they were being asked to do and what it meant. John sent the youngest squires and the grooms to escort the nuns away from their abbey. The villagers had already fled into the woods taking their goods and livestock with them. The news of what had happened to Andover had spread as swiftly as the fire that had consumed the town.

They heard them first – the clatter of hooves, the jingle of harness and weapons, the intimidating clamour of spears beating on shields. The sound grew louder, like an approaching storm on the verge of flattening the wheat in the field. Then they saw them, the Flemish mercenaries of William D'Ypres – hardened veterans of skirmishes and battles throughout Flanders, Normandy and England. Their armour was dirty from the fighting at Andover, but it was a veneer to encourage fear. John watched them come but refused to allow himself to think of defeat. These men had destroyed Andover and had marched all the way from there. Burning a town took effort, as did looting. Then a four-mile ride to Wherwell on top of earlier, strenuous effort. Enough to make the odds a little less overwhelming. He'd settle for that.

*   *   *

233

John had been in battles before, both skirmishes and heavy fighting, but never anything as hard and desperate as the attack launched on him by William D'Ypres as his Flemings strove to punch their way through. He slashed and cut with his sword, swung his shield, pivoted his stallion and redoubled his efforts. A mercenary went down. Two came at him at once. He spurred his horse, then reined hard and came across the front of the men. A swift hack of his blade brought one horse down and fouled the path of the other. The rider of the fallen horse screamed once as his mount crushed him. John took the other mercenary and spurred forward into the storm. *'Dex ai le Maréchal! Dex ai l'Empresse!'*

William D'Ypres struggled to think as he turned a blow on his shield and manoeuvred his stallion. He was sweltering inside his armour and his breath was rattling badly in his chest, courtesy of the cold that had been doing the rounds of his men and had now visited itself upon him. He needed to breathe; he had to have a respite from this punishment in order to collect his thoughts. He was losing too much time and too many men. The Empress's troop was much smaller than his own, but the enemy were fighting out of their skins – like madmen. He struck again, and his vision darkened at the edges. He couldn't draw breath fast enough, was suffocating inside his mail shirt and gambeson. Someone else came at him. He saw the raised arm, the sword preparing to strike, and then he noticed the blood. The man was wounded. Gritting his teeth, D'Ypres put his last effort into striking back and, with a gasp of relief, felt his opponent shudder and saw him fall. D'Ypres pulled his horse back, withdrawing up the hill a little, to the shade offered by a lime tree, and sucked air into his mucus-raw lungs. As he struggled for

234

breath, he cursed. John FitzGilbert's aggression and skill were daunting. His fire was cold and he always knew precisely what he was doing and where his men were. This was proving no easy battle, especially not after the push through Andover, and he couldn't afford a delay.

He needed to splinter the opposition – drive a wedge through their middle. If he could do that ... He summoned up an adjutant and, between gasps for breath, relayed instructions. The man galloped off. Moments later a group of Flemings sheered off the left flank where the fighting was less severe and arrowed into the centre of the mêlée like a spear driving through soft wood. The fighting group split apart and the Empress's soldiers on the left were gradually encircled and killed or captured, while those on the right were held at bay by the troops already in situ. As his breathing eased and his heart ceased pounding as if it would leave his chest, D'Ypres watched the battle begin to turn his way. The banner of Geoffrey Boterel went down. He reached for the water costrel slung around his saddle bow and started to raise it to his lips. Then lowered it again and used obscene words as John Marshal broke away from the centre of the mêlée and in his turn threatened to loop round and join up the fighting again. God on the Cross, didn't the bastard know when he was beaten? In a moment, the captured men, including Boterel, were going to rally and it would be mayhem again. A small troop of his foragers had arrived from the Andover road and he committed them to the fray too. *God, if I ever did anything to please you, let the tide turn. Let them break*, he prayed.

At first, he thought God had heard, for he saw FitzGilbert's green and gold banner waver and turn. Saw FitzGilbert himself hack twice at an opponent, forcing him to back off before turning tail and spurring his horse towards the abbey gates, signalling his men to follow. Even as D'Ypres coughed to clear his lungs and thank God, he realised it wasn't over. FitzGilbert wasn't retreating in order to save his skin. The abbey was a sanctuary from which he would be able to sally out and attack from the rear . . . and D'Ypres had no doubt that attack he would if left to recuperate and regroup.

Grim-mouthed, he summoned his senior adjutants. 'Bring torches,' he said. Some of them looked at him askance, but knew him too well to question his orders.

D'Ypres bared his teeth at them. 'How else do you purge a devil from the house of God?' he asked before coughing into his sleeve.

After the heat of the morning and the desperate fray, the church was a cool sanctuary, silent but for the harsh breathing of the men and the snort and clatter of the horses they had brought inside with them. Robert of Okehampton directed two of his knights to bar the door with vestment coffers. John swiftly assessed their numbers and situation. No one was badly wounded but there were a lot of superficial cuts and bruises. They had a moment's sanctuary and respite, but he did not delude himself that their hides were safe. William D'Ypres was no fool. He would balance his need to be on his way with his need not to have John on his heels, and act accordingly.

'At least we're in the right place to pray,' someone said nervously.

No one answered. They were fighting men who had put out the nuns and violated the house of God – and for that, a price would be exacted on their souls.

John cleaned his sword on his surcoat. The edge was pitted and nicked from numerous contacts with mail, wood and flesh. His shield was battered and scratched.

236

But he remained alive and still had the ability and will to fight on. His standard-bearer Jaston was crouched, one hand covering his eyes, the other gripping John's banner with white knuckles, but whether he was protecting it or using it as a crutch was uncertain. John went to him and laid his hand to his shoulder in a firm, steadying grip.

The young knight swept fingertips and palms across his lids to meet and pinch at the bridge of his nose. 'I am all right, my lord,' he said and, with a loud sniff, rose to his feet. Sweat and the momentary release of tears had created grimy streaks down his face.

There was a sudden heavy bang on the church door as if a large man had set his shoulder to it; then the sound of axes chopping at the wood.

'It'll hold,' John said. 'And even if they break it down, they can't come through more than two at a time. We'll take them.'

The banging ceased and silence fell again. John felt the hair rise and prickle at his nape. The windows were too high to see out of, but there was a squint in the stairwell of the bell tower. He strode down the nave to the internal door, shouldered it open and climbed the twisting staircase. The rectangle of light set into the thickness of the wall gave him an imperfect view over woods and fields but there was no sign of D'Ypres's troops.

He ran back down and, as he strode into the church, heard a swishing sound, accompanied by loud shouts and jeering, and then, after a pause, the ominous crackle of flame. Suddenly there was smoke above them, wispy like the layers that formed in the hall on a draughty night, but strengthening, materialising, growing acrid shape and form.

'Christ,' said Okehampton. 'The bastards have fired the church. What are we going to do?'

The horses began to stamp and snort with fear as they drank in the scent of the smoke. The sound of incendiary bombardment from outside continued and smuts of burning debris began to fall from the roof and sting the men like wasps. John ran to the holy water stoup, hacked the lid off it with his sword, soaked a torn strip of altar cloth in it and bound it around his mouth and nose. Men began to cough and choke as the smoke intensified. The occasional spark stings became a burning rain. One of the horses was singed on the rump and went wild, kicking its owner in the belly. He went down with a surprised look on his face and didn't get up again.

Okehampton sprinted to the back of the church, to the door where the nuns' priest entered to conduct services. 'Here!' he shouted. 'We have to get out!'

John opened his mouth to bellow no, that D'Ypres would have men waiting too, but it was too late. Okehampton was already ramming back the draw bar and others were racing to help him.

The world dissolved and hell came in its stead. Those who ran from the church had to fight D'Ypres's men in the midst of a firestorm. All the outbuildings were ablaze too. There was no escape. Men either died from fire or sword, or threw themselves upon their enemy's mercy and hoped to be ransomed. John knew it was over, that D'Ypres had outmanoeuvred him, but still he would not give in. If he was captured, they would hang him and he'd be damned if he'd swing for their pleasure. He retreated further into the church, backing to the bell tower as shards of burning roof crashed into the nave, sending up clouds of smoke and starbursts of sparks. Jaston remained with him, still clinging grimly to the banner, choking into his sleeve. John seized his arm and dragged him into the tower and slammed the door.

238

Jaston stared at him, his eyes showing white around the iris. 'Holy Christ, we will roast in here!'

John snarled a grin. 'How far do you think we'll get if we take the door? They're waiting outside with their swords and they'll stick them in anything that comes out. John FitzGilbert and his standard-bearer . . . what chance do you think we have? I'd rather take the fire!' He gestured around. 'Stone stairs and stone walls. We can hold out.'

'It'll be like sitting in a chimney!'

John snorted at the analogy. 'I've been more comfortable. Take off your surcoat.'

'What?'

'And give me the banner.'

When Jaston continued to look dazed, John snatched the banner out of his hands, yanked it off the spear pole and, wrapping it into a cylinder, stuffed it against the foot of the door. Then he used his own surcoat in a similar manner. Belatedly understanding, Jaston did the same.

Some of the arrows and torches had reached the wooden shingles on the belfry roof and that too was now ablaze. John sat down on the stairs. Muffled through the stone and roar of the flames, they could hear the shouts of D'Ypres's men as gleeful as children round a bonfire, taunting those still inside the church to come out.

Jaston gave a convulsive swallow. 'Perhaps we should take our chance, my lord. I am no coward but surely it is better to surrender than die in here. At least we stand a chance of living . . .'

John looked at him through the barely lit darkness of the stairwell. 'You make a move towards that door and I will kill you myself,' he said softly.

'Holy God,' Jaston whispered. 'Is she really worth it? Is your honour worth this death?'

Sardonic mirth squeezed John's chest. 'She is not worth

239

a bean,' he replied, 'and I'm not doing this for my honour. Those men outside need to be gone. D'Ypres won't stand much longer. He'll assume we're all dead and ride on.' He heard rather than saw Jaston slump on the stairs and knew the young man had put his head in his hands. 'We'll survive this,' he said. 'Just a while longer, just a few moments and they'll be gone.'

'But that'll mean they'll be on the Empress's tail.'

'I've given her a chance. If she can reach the Downs, then she'll disappear and they won't know which road she took. Nor will they want to string themselves out too far after the mauling they've taken. The garrison at Ludgershall will greet them fittingly if they do.'

Outside there was more noise. Shouts, the thud of hooves, the neigh of a horse. John listened as intently as a cat and breathed shallowly. The taste of smoke filled his throat. Jaston was coughing. Burning debris and cinders were flickering down from the belfry roof like hellish snow. They couldn't stay much longer. If the beams collapsed or there was a heavy fall of shingle and roofing, they would certainly die. Just a few more heartbeats, John thought. Just long enough to let D'Ypres see nothing but a burning church should he look over his shoulder on the way out.

He grasped his sword hilt and, easing himself off the step, touched Jaston's shoulder. Something dripped on his sleeve, gleaming in the darkness like heavy water. He glanced at it, looked up in an instinctive reaction and was struck on the left side of his face by another molten drip. The world dissolved in a white burn of agony and he staggered. 'Ah God, ah Christ!' He blundered against the door; reeled; went down.

Jaston leaped to his feet. 'My lord, my lord, what is it?'

John swallowed bile. He couldn't see, couldn't think for

240

the blinding pain. All logic and reason were gone, eaten up in searing agony. Yet some final thread of instinct remained and forced him back to his feet. 'The door,' he gasped. 'Open the door!'

Jaston scrabbled at the latch. 'It's jammed!' he panicked, then realised the wedged surcoats were causing the problem. Frantically he tugged them out of the way and yanked the door open. The interior of the church was a mass of flaming debris from the roof. The priest's doorway was an arch of fire and the heat flared at him like the blast from a bread oven. Facing into the tower, Jaston drew a deep breath, then seized John's arm and dragged him through the fiery aperture and into the abbey compound, not caring whether they ran on to enemy swords or not.

There was nothing but a waste of burning buildings, dead men, slaughtered horses. God's house had become an antechamber of hell. Jaston kept hold of John and half dragged, half carried him away from the burning buildings and down to the bank of the tree-shaded river.

'Here my lord, here, we're safe. They've gone.' Jaston dropped to his knees, retching and coughing.

John curled up in a foetal ball. The pain was excruciating. He whined through gritted teeth.

'My lord, what is it, are you burned?'

John tried to push his will through the pain. He was nauseous, sweating. He felt Jaston's hand on his sleeve, turning him. And then heard the young man's breath suck sharply over his larynx. 'Water,' John gasped. 'Put water on the wound.'

Jaston scrabbled the banner from beneath his belt and soaked it in the river. Then he wrung it out over John's face. The cold trickle gave momentary relief but John couldn't see out of his left eye. His ear was stinging too.

'Lead, my lord . . . from the roof. It's melted lead,' Jaston said. 'Your face . . .' He compressed his lips.

John didn't want to know. He gave the banner back to the young knight. 'Soak it again.'

With the cold wet silk pressed to the burn, John staggered to his feet. The vision in his good eye blurred and then steadied. He wove erratically back to the abbey grounds, making himself put one foot in front of the other. The pain was still verging on the unbearable, but had receded enough to allow him a modicum of thought. A white numbness was taking over. He didn't know if it would last. He had been told that badly and mortally injured men didn't feel the same pain as those with superficial wounds – that it was a blessing in disguise – but he knew he was cursed.

The only horses were dead ones and they had had their harness taken. The men who had fallen in battle had been divested of their hauberks and gambesons. Fighting nausea, John stooped, stripped the shirt from a dead serjeant and with shaking hands, tore off a sleeve to use as binding for his wound.

He turned to Jaston who was seeking among the dead. 'They must have taken Benet prisoner,' the young knight said with relief in his voice. 'He's not here.'

John said nothing. He couldn't deal with an exchange of conversation just now. He had to save his resources. They had no horses and knew none would be found after D'Ypres's army had ridden through like a plague. He was aware of Jaston watching him with expectation in his eyes, awaiting orders. Think, Christ on the Cross. Think! They dared not head for Ludgershall for that was the Empress's road and they would endanger her if the enemy saw them. The nearest safety was Marlborough – twenty-five miles away. Fluid filled his mouth. Do or die. He turned his

242

head, spat and looked at Jaston out of his good right eye. 'Help me take off my hauberk,' he said. 'We've a long way to go, and we'll not do it in our mail.'

'Madam, my lady, come quickly, come quickly!'

Aline had been leaning over a coffer in the clothing store, searching for a square of embroidery linen, but the fear and urgency in the maid's voice caused her to spin round, eyes widening. 'What is it?'

The woman shook her head. 'Madam, Lord John has returned. You had better come.'

Aline's stomach twisted. 'Why, what's wrong?'

'That I don't know, my lady. Jaston de Camville is with him. They arrived without horses and staggering like drunkards. They look as if they've been rolling in a hearth. They stink of smoke too . . .'

Aline swallowed. It was bad, it must be bad. Something had happened in Winchester. The woman was watching her with a mingling of pity and contempt. She rose to her feet, closed the lid of the chest and somehow brought herself to go to the door. 'Where is he?' she heard herself ask in a faint voice.

'The bedchamber, madam.'

She wanted to run away but knew she couldn't. It was her God-ordained duty to tend to him. At least he was home, she told herself. She wouldn't have to weep about that any more.

He was lying on the great bed in their chamber, surrounded by a flurry of anxious attendants. Even from the doorway, she could see that he was covered in blood and streaked with horrible black grime. The smell of charred wood was like a vile thread twisting around everything. Jaston de Camville sat on a bench, his hands constantly raking through his dark hair in a distraught

243

manner. He too was filthy, and there was what looked like a raw red burn on one of his hands. Aline raised her index finger to her mouth and bit upon it.

John made a sound from between clenched teeth: a sound she had never heard before, but it knifed through her. Then someone stood aside and Aline saw the appalling damage to the left side of his face, the redness, the blistering. Her knees buckled. Her maid, who had been standing close in anticipation, grabbed Aline's arm and steered her to the bench on which Jaston was sitting.

Aline's breath shuddered in and out of her lungs. Dear God, dear God . . .

Jaston raised his head. 'Molten lead from the church roof,' he said. 'It dripped on his face . . .'

'The church roof?' Aline said faintly.

'Wherwell Abbey. We took refuge there and William D'Ypres set fire to it . . . burned it down round our ears.' He clamped his lips as he realised what he had said.

She knew Wherwell, had been there sometimes – had even toyed with the notion of taking vows there one day. 'Oh, sweet Virgin, Mother of God, is he going to die? What's to become of us?'

He shook his head and said nothing. Aline rose to her feet. She felt as if she was standing in a great, echoing space that was expanding by the moment and she was growing smaller and smaller, soon to disappear.

'Madam . . .' said her maid. 'Madam?'

John cried out again – the sort of scream that gave her nightmares during the November slaughter month when the animals were held down and butchered. Uttering a gasp, her hand clapped to her mouth, Aline fled the room, reached the haven of her own chamber and retched and retched until her stomach was raw. She couldn't cope – she didn't want to know. The dreadful thought blossomed that it was all her fault. She had sinned by admiring his beauty and now God had punished her by taking it away.

Sybilla gazed at the silver piled on the trestle. Patrick was counting it into leather pouches and muttering to himself. Two rich wall hangings were folded near his elbow and a box full of assorted gold rings and brooches. This was her brother William's ransom. The sooner his release was agreed the better. He had been captured during the retreat from Winchester whilst fighting a rearguard action at Stockbridge with Robert of Gloucester. Gloucester was a prisoner too, but it was going to take more than a trestle full of coins and baubles to ransom him.

'It's a disaster,' Patrick growled. 'William should never have sworn us to the Empress. If we'd stayed with Stephen, we wouldn't be beggaring ourselves now.'

'Is it truly a disaster?' Sybilla envisaged a hungry tide of enemy troops surging around their walls, and then valiantly quashed the thought. Stephen was still under guard and the Empress free. In all likelihood, Gloucester would be exchanged for Stephen and nothing much would change.

'It'll leave us poorer by the price of a year's wool clip,' he snapped. 'William's a fool.' He compressed his lips and counted in silence. Sybilla was turning to go about her duties when he added, 'I don't suppose John FitzGilbert is counting his blessings either.'

'Was he captured too?'

'No; the whoreson won free, but it's done him no good. He was defending the crossing at Wherwell and when he retreated into the abbey, William D'Ypres burned it down round him. From what I've heard, he's lost the sight of an eye and he's not expected to live.' He scooped another mound of silver into a pouch. 'Even if God does spare him, he has no future. He's finished.'

Sybilla caught her underlip in her teeth. 'Poor man,' she said with appalled compassion.

Patrick's lip curled. 'Save your sympathy, sister. You wouldn't give it to a wolf intent on raiding our sheep, would you? It's a good thing for us he's gone down.'

Sybilla felt a sudden sting of tears. Patrick was probably right, but it was still a harsh thing to say. She wondered how a man renowned for his looks, and who enjoyed using them to good effect, was going to cope with being disfigured – if he survived. And what of his wife; how would she manage? Aline Marshal was already of fragile mind and totally squeamish. Sybilla still remembered that day at Salisbury when Aline had fainted at the sight of the man with the broken arm. Perhaps widowhood would be a blessing for her.

'Still,' Patrick said with reluctant admiration, 'you have to respect the will of the man. To have walked twenty-five miles with an injury like that is no mean feat.'

Sybilla stared at him. 'Twenty-five miles?'

Patrick nodded. 'From Wherwell to Marlborough. No horses. D'Ypres took them. Won't have done FitzGilbert any good walking all that way with such a wound. Bound to die.' He returned to counting the money. 'I suppose it might be of some benefit to us if he does. We can take Ludgershall because there's nothing to stop us. That milk-and-water wife of his won't put up any resistance. Marlborough too, if we're fortunate.' He pulled the draw-string tight on the money pouch. 'But first we need to get this ransom sorted and paid. All else will follow in time.'

Unsettled by the conversation, Sybilla went to her chamber and brought out the enamelled jewellery box that had been her mother's. After a final, longing look at the contents, and a little weep, she kept back only one ring and a brooch and put the rest for her brother's ransom. Patrick said all else would follow and she shivered with trepidation at just what that might mean. And although her brother had called John FitzGilbert a wolf and he was probably right to do so, she still added him to her prayers when she went to light a candle in the cathedral later that day.

At Marlborough, despite Patrick's prediction, John was far from dead – although much of the time he wished he were. The pain was excruciating and blotted out all reason, all cogent ability. They gave him poppy syrup in wine to dull the agony but it brought little relief and burdened him with vile dreams, ablaze with images of fire and scalding, glutinous metal that dripped on to his face and melted long silver tear tracks into his flesh, eating inwards, exposing him to the bone until he was picked as bare as a corpse at the crossroads. He would drag himself out of such dreams with his heart pounding with terror, and because he was ashamed of that terror, it made him angry too.

The left side of his face was bandaged at first, but when the linens and unguents were removed to be changed, he had no vision on that side either and could tell from the looks on the faces of the servants and retainers that it was bad. They tried not to expose their feelings, but, like his burned, raw flesh, they were obvious, whether they willed it or not.

Aline had not been near him, although he had heard her twittery voice in the antechamber several times enquiring how he was and saying that she had been praying for him – as if that was going to make a difference. She should have prayed for him to die. He was glad

247

her courage had failed before she reached his bedside, because he could not have stood her presence, or the look of frightened revulsion he knew would cross her face if she gazed upon him.

Once the bandaging was off and the damage exposed to heal in the air, he had the shutters opened on daylight and called for a mirror. Jaston brought it to him. His own abrasions and burns were healing well, although his expression bore the imprint of haunted, sleepless nights.

'My lord, I don't think you should . . .'

'Christ, give it to me. I will know the worst!' John had to turn his head to snatch the small, round mirror case from the knight. He snapped the catch and as he stared into the tinned glass at his reflection, a bolt of shock tore through him. He had once seen a leper in Winchester with a face like this: distorted, eaten. The right side of his face still possessed its elegant symmetry; the high cheek-bone, fine, straight nose, deep socket and clear eye. The other, across browbone, orbit and ear, looked as if the hand of death had passed over and wrought violence with a casual swipe. In a way, it had. His hair was flat and lank with sweat and grime and his jaw was stubbled with the beard of a five-day corpse. A man half-dead. How easy it would be to take a knife and kill the rest. He closed his fist around the mirror and hurled it at the wall. The glass within the case smashed into myriad dagger-bright shards and the reflection was gone. 'Get out,' he snarled to Jaston, who was staring at him with anxiety.

'My lord . . .'

'Out!' John spat.

Jaston bowed and left. An older man, more experienced in the ways of the world, might have stayed, but Jaston, although a skilled warrior and strong in his art, was young and lacked the knowledge to deal with this.

248

John cursed and sat on the edge of the bed. Pain throbbed across his left socket and cheek. He had seen the way Jaston's glance had slid over him and away. No one could bear to look at him and he didn't blame them. He didn't want to look at himself either and see the face of a gargoyle. There was nothing left. His best men were dead or taken for ransom; the Empress's army had scattered in disarray. There had been no word from Matilda, no offers of succour, no gratitude for his stand at Wherwell. Silence. But whether it was the silence of a woman who thought his sacrifice no more than her due as his duty, or the silence of a cause on the bitter edge of defeat, he did not know.

He left the bed and went to the bright splinters of glass lying on the floor. The mirror was one he had bought for Aline before their wedding. It was more than appropriate it should lie in pieces now. She never used it, and he had seen enough. He picked up one of the glittering fragments in his right hand and turned the wrist of his left, exposing the strong tendons, the blue veins still pulsing with his lifeblood. He had always said he would fight to the last drop, never guessing what that might mean. He swallowed, closed his good eye and tightened his jaw. Coward.

'Papa?'

He spun round, staggering slightly because of the difficulty in orientating himself. Gilbert was looking at him with the same, steady stare that until recently had been his own.

'What?' He fought for the control to answer in a level voice.

'The horse-coper has arrived with some destriers. Do you want to look? Jaston says he can do it, but he wondered if you wanted to come out.'

249

'And why should I want to do that?'

'For when you're better and can lead the men again. Shall I tell him no?' The steadiness was replaced with trepidation.

It was as hard looking at his son as it had been to stare into the mirror. The side of his face was pounding like a fist on a drum. Hot pain was building in his ruined socket. There was rage and grief and hurting. From the open shutters the whinny of a horse floated up and the sound of men shouting – splinters of life being lived beyond the walls of this stuffy chamber. He clenched his jaw. 'No, I'll come. Give me a moment. Find your mother's women and tell them to sweep this up before one of the dogs cuts its paws.'

Gilbert nodded and dashed out. John dropped the sliver of glass and turned away. He would never look in a mirror again. With grim determination, he went to lift his tunic off the clothing pole. Donning it over his head was agony, but he steeled himself to absorb the pain.

Outside the strong September sunlight dazzled his good eye. The left side of his vision didn't exist and the warmth of the sun was like someone raking their nails in his flesh. He was aware of the men of the garrison looking at him and looking away, not knowing what to say or do. He would have to do it for them.

He gave a brusque nod in their direction to indicate he was out of his sickbed and in command, no matter his private thoughts on the state of his mind, and went up to the horse-coper.

The man bowed to him a tad too obsequiously and his gaze shifted and darted over John's face, unable to fix.

'I am told you have some beasts for sale,' John said curtly.

'Yes, my lord; fine destriers. I'm on my way to Salisbury

to sell them, but I thought you might want a look first. I reckoned you'd be in need after . . .' He broke off and cleared his throat, indicating he was too tactful to say the rest.

John raised his right eyebrow. The left tried to follow and the pain sharpened. He looked at the string of horses tethered near the trough in the stable yard. They were a motley collection, some no more than spavined pack beasts, or long in the tooth and hollow-backed. Others bore evidence of hard riding and many had superficial cuts and abrasions. A few were glossy and in good condition. Then John saw a chestnut stallion that had belonged to one of his knights who had fallen at Wherwell. There was no mistaking the rosette of white hair between its eyes and a jagged pink strip on its otherwise dark muzzle.

He looked at the coper with revulsion. 'You are trying to sell me dead men's horses,' he said in a husky voice.

The trader gave a shrug. 'Dead men have no need for mounts and living ones do. I came by these animals honestly. If you don't want them, I'll take them on to Salisbury.'

John swallowed on rage. He was tempted to seize the man and string him up but instead forced himself to be as pragmatic as the coper. His men did need horses and he would have to recruit more of both to replace the missing ones. He didn't know what the situation was at Salisbury just now, but it would be foolish to let them have the pick of the animals rather than the cast-offs. Plus, if he treated the horse-trader well, he would return and might prove a useful recruit into John's network of informants throughout Wiltshire and the south. 'I will take the chestnut, those two browns and the grey if you name the right price,' he said, and settled down to haggle.

He knew horses; he knew what they were worth and

251

how to drive a hard bargain, and while doing so, the pain and anger became less vivid. By the time the deal was completed and a sum agreed, John was sore, exhausted, but felt better. Nor, now that he had been outside and reattached himself to life, could he just reel back to his bed and shut everything out. He had been doing that for too long already.

He told the servants he would dine in the hall that night at the dais table. Then he called a meeting of his knights and conferred about what was to be done concerning those who were prisoners. He discussed the situation they were in and made plans to deal with it. He would tighten his grip on the Kennet valley, lock down and hold fast against all comers while playing a waiting game.

John bade Aline come to the hall and eat with him, and in deference to her squeamishness, had her sit at his right hand. He also had his physician bind clean bandages over the damaged left side. Even so, she perched on the edge of the bench as if about to take terrified flight, picked at her food like a bird and avoided looking at him. There was no conversation. As soon as the meal was over, she begged leave to retire to her own chamber.

John granted it with a wave of his hand and was relieved. He had no intention of seeking her chamber later either. His inclination to render his debt to their marriage bed was dead. Procreating with her had been a sporadic chore since long before Wherwell and he had no desire to resume relations. He knew she would lie with him if bidden because it was her God-ordained duty to do so, but he also knew she would be thankful to be spared the obligation. They had two sons; it was enough. Let it rest.

When he retired it was to the solitude of his own

chamber. Doublet padded after him and, heaving a sigh, flopped down at the side of the bed, occupying the same position she had taken up during his recuperation. The end of her tail thumped on the floor rushes. John smiled wryly. Aline had opted to absent herself in prayer and the dog had chosen to stay in devotion.

He spoke softly to her and sat on his bed to remove his shoes, but had gone no further than unfastening the first toggle when Jaston banged on the door and burst into the room. Doublet sprang to her feet with a startled bark of alarm, then wagged her tail harder.

'Sir, great news!' Jaston's eyes glowed with excitement. 'Benet has returned, and Hubert and Alain. They're alive, sir, they're alive!'

John looked at the dazzle of excitement on the young knight's face. It took a moment for him to digest the words, and then suddenly he was refastening his shoe, rising to his feet, striding from the room with Jaston and Doublet hard on his heels. He shouldered his way through the group surrounding the three knights and stared.

'Dear Christ.' His voice was as raw as it had been on the day after Wherwell for suddenly there were tears at the back of his throat. 'You took your time getting here!'

Benet rose to his feet, looking gaunt and exhausted. A healing but ugly red burn marred one cheek, another had made a raw mess of the back of his left hand. The others too bore various bruises and mending superficial wounds.

Benet looked John straight in the face. 'I am sorry, my lord. It was a small matter of breaking free from our captors. We didn't want to hang and we wanted to spare you the expense of the ransoms.'

'What makes you think I'd have paid them?' John asked. His throat had almost closed by now and the words emerged as a dry whisper.

Benet shrugged. 'We knew you'd have to be dead not to. They said you were, but we didn't believe it.'

'Hah!' John turned away. There was a blur of moisture in his right eye, a dreadful dry burning in the place where his left one had been. He tightened his fists, controlled himself, and turned round again, his jaw set like stone.

'You'll have to take your ease tonight while you can. There are new mounts for you all in the stables and you'll be out on them tomorrow at dawn.'

Benet gave him a bleak smile. 'You fall off, you climb back on,' he said. 'I trust you'll be leading us, my lord.'

'Who else?' John answered, and wondered whether, when it came to the crux, it would be a case of the blind leading the blind, or an eye for an eye.

23

Salisbury Castle, July 1143

Sybilla bent over Patrick's hand in consternation. While out on patrol, he had been involved in a bloody skirmish with John Marshal's men not far from Ludgershall and had taken a wound to the fleshy pad running from the base of his thumb into the palm. 'It needs stitches,' she said and sent one of her women to fetch Ralf the physician from his house outside the walls.

'Was FitzGilbert with them?' William demanded, pacing the room like a restless lion. His cheekbones were gaunt and flushed. He had been unwell for several days with a low fever and lack of appetite – ever since his return from the latest skirmish in the campaign between Stephen and Matilda. Another abbey had burned to the ground: Wilton this time. William hadn't wanted to talk about the atrocities committed but Sybilla knew about them anyway. Gytha had told her what had happened to the men who had taken refuge in the church and to the nuns who had been caught between the armies. She also knew more than usual because Wilton was on their doorstep and William had woken up screaming every night since his return from the battle.

Grimacing in pain, Patrick looked up. 'No . . . it was Benet de Tidworth.'

'God's blood, I don't know why you went there!' William growled. 'You're like a little boy, Patrick. You just have to poke your stick into a nest of ants, don't you?'

'They attacked me, not I them!' Patrick gasped and went rigid as Sybilla washed out the wound with hot water.

'Yes, but knowing you, you rode too close and provoked them.'

'Do you know how hard it is to get hold of a good horse these days?' Patrick snapped. 'FitzGilbert has got the supplies stitched up to Sodom and back and he's not for sharing!'

'Christ, Patrick, yes I do know!' William retorted. 'But I'm not idiot enough to go and beat down a castle wall with my head.'

'No, you'd rather be ravishing nuns!'

William's complexion whitened and he clenched his fists. 'You'll take that back,' he said hoarsely. 'I touched not one of them! If we hadn't cleared Stephen out of Wilton, Salisbury would now be under siege. If you weren't my brother I'd—'

'You'd what, swing me on a gibbet and let the crows pick out my eyes?'

'Given enough rope, you'd hang yourself! Take it back now!' A muscle twitched in William's cheek and his eyes glittered with unspilled tears.

Patrick reddened. 'Very well, brother.' He scowled. 'I retract my words. If you say so, you were the flower of chivalry at Wilton.'

'Stop it!' Sybilla cried. 'You are brothers. If you tear each other apart, what will be left if we do have to face the wolves!'

256

There was a brief silence. Then Patrick grimaced and offered a more sincere apology, albeit mumbled, and William sat down on the bench nearby and, groaning, put his head in his hands.

Sybilla's stomach swirled with anxiety. Her brothers were constantly sniping at each other. Ever since being ransomed from the debacle at Winchester, William had been on edge, as if being captured in the first place had devalued or unmanned him in his own eyes. What had happened at Wilton had only served to compound his edginess and increase Patrick's needling.

'We have to do something about FitzGilbert,' Patrick muttered. 'He's a scourge – robs from the church, takes from the merchant trains. He's got a grip on everything that moves between Marlborough and Newbury. Last week the Abbot of Gloucester complained about him stealing grain out of one of his tithe barns. Root and branch of hell, he calls him, and I agree.' He exhaled down his nose. 'Like to die from that injury at Wherwell, my arse. He's ten times worse one-eyed than he ever was with two, and you let him get away with it!'

'I'll speak with him when he returns from court,' William said stiffly. 'I'm sure he's amenable to negotiation.'

'Don't be so certain. That stunt at Wherwell means he can do no wrong in the Empress's opinion and look what happened to Robert FitzHubert when he tangled with the bastard. He needs putting in his place.'

'He did us a service with FitzHubert. There are ways and means of getting around obstacles other than butting them down with your head. FitzGilbert knows it; so do I. Leave it with me . . . that's an order.' William rubbed his hand across his forehead.

Patrick made chewing motions with his jaw. 'If we had

been allied with Stephen, we could have asked him for mercenaries and taken the Kennet piecemeal, starting with Ludgershall. Wilton wouldn't have happened either.'

'Leave it, Patrick. I'm in no mood.' Making a weary gesture, William headed to the door and Sybilla frowned to see how leaden his tread was. She decided that when Ralf had finished with Patrick, she would have him look at William too.

'He's right,' she said to Patrick. 'It will be better if we can negotiate a truce.'

'Mind your distaff,' Patrick snapped. 'You're a woman and this is men's business. What do you know of such things?'

Sybilla bit her tongue on a facetious retort and, murmuring that she had affairs to see to in dairy and kitchen, left the room as Ralf entered with his phial of leeches and his satchel of nostrums.

Prince Henry rode his sorrel pony with aplomb, his spine straight and his hands relaxed on the reins. At ten years old, he was a sturdy boy, stocky and robust, although not tall and showing none of his father's long-limbed grace. Indeed, John thought as he rode a little behind him, apart from his auburn colouring, he most resembled his grand-father King Henry. If he was going to develop similar capabilities, then all to the good. The child's precocious-ness amused John. Henry could converse in Latin as easily as in French and knew how to swear in a multitude of languages – courtesy of the mercenaries swarming over his mother's court.

After the rout at Winchester, Gloucester had been exchanged for Stephen and everything had returned to what it was before Lincoln, with neither party holding the advantage. There had been continuing defeats and successes on both sides. The Empress had almost been caught at Oxford and had had to escape across the frozen river in the snow. Stephen had nearly been taken again during hard fighting at Wilton. Currently the scales were evenly balanced. The Empress kept court in Devizes and to boost the morale of her supporters and remind them why they were fighting, had had ten-year-old Henry brought from Normandy to join her for a season. Now he was being escorted back to Bristol to embark for the safer shores of Normandy and his father's custody.

The boy had not been in the least fazed by John's disfigurement; indeed was inquisitive and forthright about it, asking detailed questions. John found his curiosity refreshing. Generally people acted as if they didn't see that side of his face, or looked away in embarrassment or distaste. It was the pity he hated most though and it curdled his stomach. Henry, however, reacted in none of these ways and appeared to see the whole man, not the external trappings. All unformed and malleable as the child was, John could see the potential.

'Now you understand what this struggle is all about,' Gloucester said, joining John. 'Stephen's son will be no match for this child when he becomes a man.'

John bowed his head in acknowledgement, for what Gloucester said was true. Young Henry had the common touch his mother lacked, but still possessed the air of a king-in-the-making.

'Our task is to build him the time he needs to grow up,' Robert added.

'Oh, that's easy then.'

Robert looked uncomfortable. 'I know the Empress does not say a great deal, but she is grateful for all you have done for her.'

John felt bitterness well up inside him. What good was

gratitude when weighed against what he had permanently lost? Matilda had few resources out of which to reward her followers for their loyal service. Remuneration was almost non-existent and funds were short unless one took them from an enemy or someone weaker than oneself. One had to be permanently on one's guard – witness that incursion by Patrick of Salisbury that Benet had fought off. John knew if he didn't maintain an iron control on his territory, then order would shatter apart and anarchy rule. If he showed one moment of weakness he would be torn down by the pack. He was also enough of a realist to know that even if Matilda won through and her eldest son survived to become King, personal reward might not be forthcoming. The young man would have his own circle of friends and men he wanted to promote. 'Let us hope she has a good memory,' he said.

Robert was silent for a while, clearly giving time for the moment's tension to dissipate. Then he changed the subject. 'I am glad you have made your peace with William of Salisbury,' he said.

'I never had a quarrel with him,' John answered. 'It was his brother Patrick who overstepped the mark. He has a flea in his breeches about Ludgershall. William's more intelligent about the realities.'

Robert grunted. 'How did William seem to you at court?'

'In what way?'

'The state of his health. I've been told he's ailing.'

John made a considering face. 'I thought he was thinner than when last I saw him and he looked as if he needed to lie down and sleep, but his speech and reasoning seemed sound enough.'

'The battle at Wilton affected him badly.'

'We all have our nightmares to fight,' John said curtly.

260

'Mine happen every time I dream I have two eyes and wake up with one. You learn to carry the burden and live with it.'

Robert cleared his throat. 'Indeed, indeed,' he said, his tone over-hearty. 'The point I was making is that if William fails, we will have to deal with Patrick, and he's of a different nature – and perhaps a different allegiance too.'

'But he can be handled. There is always a way around for the sake of some thought on the matter.'

'Yes,' said Gloucester. 'And it might be wise to start pondering now.'

It was quiet in the hall at Salisbury. Most folk had gone to their beds and only a few candles still burned in isolated corners and crevices to light the darkest watches of the night. One such illuminated the dais and the figure of Patrick, sitting in the chair from which his father in his prime and then William had dispensed justice and presided over the affairs of the sheriff.

Quietly Sybilla joined him, setting a fresh cup of wine at his right elbow and lighting a new candle from the drip-festooned remnants of the old. At first, because he was gripping his head in his hands, she thought he was mourning for their brother. William had been buried yesterday before the altar at Bradenstoke Priory following his painful death from some internal malady that had wasted his body to skin and bone.

Patrick's eyes, however, were dry and his mouth was set in a hard line that spoke of deep thought and resolution rather than grief. Sybilla poured wine for herself and sat down beside him. Her own eyes were burning and heavy. She felt wrung out. She had loved William because he was her brother, but they had not otherwise

261

been close; however, no one should have to die like that in such pain and terror, convinced he was damned.

Patrick sighed and, straightening up, looked at her. 'I am sorry William is dead. We did not always see eye to eye, but I would rather he had lived to share disagreements than lie in cold ground . . . But now I am master of Salisbury, there are going to be changes.'

Sybilla's stomach leaped with alarm. 'What kind of changes?'

'If I swear my allegiance to King Stephen, he will give me mercenaries with which to rule Wiltshire and keep our lands safe. I'll be able to clear the Kennet of FitzGilbert's scourge and regain Ludgershall for us.'

'But William had made peace with him . . .'

'Because he didn't have the resources to take him on. He's a wolf, Sybilla, and I won't have him on our borders if I can fashion it otherwise. I followed William's way for long enough. Now it's my turn to rule.'

'Then be careful,' she said. 'I cannot afford to keep losing brothers.'

He gave a taut smile. 'I am not William and I won't be led into the same kinds of traps. Don't fret your head about it. Leave the business to me.' He pressed his palms flat on the board and eased to his feet. 'I'm for my bed. It's going to be a long day tomorrow.'

Sybilla too rose. She supposed if you had a thorn in your flesh, it would fester until you were rid of it, but what if it got rid of you instead by working its way in until eventually it killed you? She knew Patrick wouldn't listen to her. If she tried to say something now, he would only grow more stubborn in his resolution. He would have to be tackled from the side with gentle nudges, hints and soft words.

Feeling sad and pensive, she made her way to bed. Her father's door was open, but showed only an empty space.

262

He had chosen to remain at Bradenstoke in the care of the monks. Her youngest brother Walter was a canon there, her mother and now William were buried within the church, which was endowed by their family's money. Why should her father not be happier there at the end of his days than here in the midst of war and uncertainty?

Dismissing her maids, Sybilla undressed to her chemise and lay down on her bed in a corner of the women's chamber. She had thought herself wept dry for William and the entire miserable situation, but hot new tears tracked down her face and seeped into her pillow.

24

Ludgershall, Wiltshire, April 1144

John sat at a trestle in Ludgershall's bailey, eating bread and cheese with his men and taking a moment's ease. The sun was warm on his spine without being hot, and the early April was glorious. A wine pitcher had done the rounds several times and although no one was drunk, the conversation was mellow and the jests raised swift laughter. Today John found he could smile a little too. The grass was lush; there was grain in his barns and silver in his coffers to pay the men. That some of it had been obtained by less than legitimate means, he acknowledged with a pragmatic shrug. You did what you must to survive in times like these. The Bishop of Hereford, the Church, and certain of his neighbours called him a scourge and a plague, and it gave him dark satisfaction to hear it. Let them fear him and his reputation if it kept him safe. He would build an edifice of military prowess on the scars of Wherwell and emerge stronger than before.

His men were discussing women they had had, or would like to have. John cut another sliver of cheese and listened with dark amusement. Someone jokingly mentioned the

Empress and there was speculation about whether she'd be a cold fish on a mattress, or as hot as pepper.

'What do you say, my lord?' asked Benet with a grin.

John ate the cheese and pretended to think. 'It would depend on the man – how she felt about him and how good he was.'

His comment elicited more laughter and several risqué jests at the expense of Brian FitzCount.

'Has anyone seen Patrick of Salisbury's sister lately?' blurted a young knight, his face wine-flushed. 'She's a real beauty.'

He was immediately engulfed in a cloud of good-natured jeers, back-slapping and innuendo. John slowed his chewing. He remembered a coltish girl dwelling in the space between child and woman. Slender and supple as a willow wand, burnish-haired, hazel-eyed and energetic. She'd be older now, of course, and by rights probably should have been wed a couple of years since. 'Is she betrothed?' he asked casually.

The young man shook his head and reddened further. 'No, my lord, not that I'm aware.'

'Hah!' declared Benet, raising his own cup in toast to the young man. 'You're dreaming if you think she's for the likes of you. Her brother will have someone sorted out for her – doubtless of Stephen's faction.' He sneered on the last word.

John glanced across as one of the gate guards came towards the group clutching a rolled-up parchment.

'What's this?' He took the document from the soldier and eyed the attached seal. Stephen. What did he want? He cleaned his knife on a chunk of bread, slit the tags and studied the parchment. The writing was the neat, competent hand of an exchequer scribe. John read it, reached for his wine, drank nonchalantly, and then looked at the expectant men. 'It seems that the King intends paying us a visit on the morrow and bids me open my gates to his army.'

Benet spluttered over his wine. There was uneasy laughter and exchanged glances. John tossed the parchment across the trestle and folded his arms. 'Well, much as I'd like to accommodate him here, I have other matters to attend to.'

Still coughing, Benet wiped a dribble from his chin. 'This means the King is sending his army to take us?'

John shook his head. 'Stephen's got greater business in hand than Ludgershall. I doubt it's his notion at all.'

'Then who . . . ?'

'Patrick of Salisbury, who do you think! He's been feeling his feet ever since his brother died. He wants to be lord of all Wiltshire, and I'm the fly in his dinner. I'll warrant the King has lent him men and supplies to attack me and gain Ludgershall for himself.' John's gaze roved the defences.

'What do we do?'

John pursed his lips. Ludgershall wasn't as strong as Marlborough and if they stayed to fight it out, they risked being destroyed. But if they pulled back to Marlborough, their grip on the vale of the Kennet would weaken and their enemy, biting piecemeal, would make either Marlborough or Hamstead their next target. 'They're not going to get anywhere near Ludgershall,' he said with quiet decision, 'because I won't let them.' He shifted on the bench so that he had Benet in full vision. 'We're going to take the fight to them.'

Glancing through the open shutters at the luminous disc of the moon, John thanked God for its fortuitous light as he donned his gambeson over his tunic and shirt. Riding

266

at night was always perilous and he was going to need all the luck that came his way.

'Be careful,' Aline said, her eyes filled with worry. She had come from her chamber to bid him farewell. These days, to all intents and purposes, they lived apart even while they lived together. She had her rooms, he had his and their paths only crossed formally in the hall and at church.

'I'll do what I must. If an army turns up at these walls before dawn, you'll know I've failed.' He felt a brief surge of dark triumph as he saw the horrified look on her face, and then was disgusted with himself. It was like striking a three-year-old for not understanding. 'If that happens, yield to them,' he said in a gentler voice. 'They'll be generous to an innocent and you'll have the mercy of widowhood.'

'John, don't.' Her voice was stricken.

'In the circumstances, you might want to withdraw to Clyffe, or Woodhill, out of the way,' he said. 'You have my leave.'

She continued to chew her lip. Turning from her, fastening his cloak, he strode outside, already putting her from his mind. In the bailey his men were waiting, some of them bearing torches to light their way, although much of their road would be moonlit. John set his foot in the stirrup and swung to the saddle. He felt a surge in his gut – anticipation that almost bordered on pleasure. Glancing round, he saw the same expressions in the shadowed faces of his men, particularly those who had been at Wherwell. They had all been through the fire that day, one way or another. By contrast, this journey through cold, lucid moonlight had the potential to quench, heal and restore.

They rode through the night, making their way cautiously in the direction of Winchester, an army of shadows and wraiths. John sent scouts ahead and had them report to him at regular intervals to ensure their enemy knew nothing of their movements. As the light began to pale on the horizon but before the first streaks of dawn, John brought his troop into a narrow valley and bade them hide among the trees to wait. He dismounted from his stallion to rest it for the work to come and ate and drank to give himself strength. Some of the soldiers fidgeted with the crosses they wore around their necks and muttered prayers. Others fussed their horses or whispered between each other, but their movements were small and all were at pains to be quiet. The dawn chorus started in the trees and swelled around them. John was pleased, for had the birds been alarmed into silence, it would have given away his position to the enemy.

As a band of gold parted night from day on the eastern horizon, the scouts returned and came quietly to John. 'They're on the move, my lord, and led by Patrick of Salisbury. They are twice our number, but not wearing armour. It's all in the baggage carts or strapped to their saddles. It'll be like sticking our spears in fresh dung.'

John smiled at the analogy. 'More fool them,' he said, 'but all to the good for us.' Remounting his stallion, he signalled to his men.

They heard the troop before they saw them, processing in the loose order and carefree manner of men setting out on a jaunt. As the scouts had said, the majority were not armed. Here and there was a cautious glint of mail, or gleam of leather padding, but nothing that would protect the bulk of the troop from the havoc about to be loosed on them.

John let them come almost abreast, then spurred his stallion, Jaston riding at his blind left side with the banner unfurled. *'Maréchal! A Maréchal! Dex ai!'*

268

Amid disbelief and consternation, the Winchester troop scrabbled for their weapons as John's knights hit them in a surge from either side of the road. After the initial charge, John discarded his spear, drew his sword and went for the throat. He had spent long hours on the tilt ground, sparring with Benet and others, learning how to fight one-eyed, and now that retraining reaped dividends. The difference in his level of skill was negligible and it was bolstered by the knowledge that he had nothing to lose. Patrick did.

The air filled with the screams of injured and unhorsed men, bellows of rage and effort, the clash of meeting swords, the hammer of blade on shields. Loose mounts and pack beasts ran amok. The ground reddened with blood as if someone had tipped over a cartload of wine. In the centre of the vicious onslaught, John came face to face with Patrick of Salisbury. The latter had managed to don his helm in the middle of the fray but only had a leather gambeson for protection. He was bigger and stronger than John and he had two good eyes, but John was swift, muscular whipcord. Their swords clashed once and then again, striking sparks off the steel. John hammered home his assault and Patrick held him off, struggling frantically to keep the honed sword from his flesh. Then Patrick's horse stumbled on a corpse and Patrick was thrown. For an instant the loose destrier was between them, hampering John's assault, and it gave Patrick's knights time to close around him. Patrick bellowed at them to sound the retreat. His expression ablaze with triumph, John signalled to Benet, who raised a horn to his lips and blew the hunting halloo.

Sybilla washed her hands in a bowl of clean water and directed her maid, Gundred, to remove the reddened one next to it and tip it down the latrine shaft. She wiped a weary forearm across her brow. The last of the wounded had been seen to, and a sorry tally it was. Cuts, bruises, broken bones . . . and they were the fortunate ones. Patrick was drinking wine as if his right arm was attached to a pulley, swearing about John FitzGilbert and making plans to retaliate and finish the bastard once and for all.

Sybilla clenched her jaw and said nothing. Patrick's mood was beyond volatile; it would take just one comment to send him over the edge. Her brother had underestimated his opponent and paid for it. It was no use saying he should not have sent John Marshal word of his intention. Patrick had thought that at best, the marshal would retreat from Ludgershall, leaving it as easy pickings, and at worst, he would stand and fight, but since Ludgershall's ability to resist a siege was in doubt, Patrick hadn't anticipated trouble either way. But instead, FitzGilbert had added a third strand to the strategy and brought the fight to Patrick, taking him off his guard and wreaking havoc. Her brother kept calling John a wolf, but such a comparison was foolish. John was a clever, accomplished, experienced soldier whose job was assessing men and situations and dealing with them rapidly and efficiently.

Patrick took a final gulp of wine and banged the cup down on the trestle. 'I won't underestimate FitzGilbert again,' he growled. 'He may have won this time, but we'll see who has the final victory.'

25

Marlborough Castle, Wiltshire, May 1144

John gestured and a servant poured wine for his guest. Robert of Gloucester lifted the cup, tasted, and raised an eyebrow at John. 'I won't ask where this came from because I'm not sure I want to know.'

'Bristol,' John answered promptly. 'And paid for.'

'By Patrick of Salisbury?'

John twitched his shoulders. He didn't want to talk about Patrick of Salisbury, for he had been kept busy fending off assaults from his stronger neighbour. His territory wasn't shrinking yet, but he knew the danger. If this inexorable pressure kept up, he was going to go down. He just had to hope Patrick was growing weary of the constant sparring. The latter had not had it all his own way. Following that first massive success, John had scored several lesser victories too, but had suffered drubbings and setbacks himself.

'I heard you've recently had another run-in with him.'

John's expression closed. 'What of it? If he leaves me alone, I'll extend him the same courtesy.'

'You should know that the Empress and I are disturbed by this feuding.'

'You think I am not?' John stretched out his hand and Doublet came to have her ears fondled. 'I'm willing to make my peace with him. All he has to do is abandon his claim to Ludgershall.'

'And all you have to do is cease raiding his supplies and running off his flocks and herds,' Robert answered, looking stern.

'And all Stephen has to do is agree to give the Empress England and everything will be right in God's heaven,' John retorted.

'That may take a little more arranging than what I've come to talk to you about.' Robert glanced round the hall. 'Is Aline here?'

John shook his head. 'I sent her to Clyffe for her own good. She doesn't cope well in a keep on a battle footing – she faints if she pricks her finger with a needle. I sent the boys with her.'

'Good,' Robert said. 'It's better to talk about this without them overhearing. I have a proposition for you.'

John eyed him warily. 'What kind of proposition?'

'The kind to put a stop to this fighting between you and Patrick of Salisbury. I know he is a sharp thorn in your side.'

'I thought I was one in his.'

'There is no need to pretend with me. I know you can hold your own and that you'll fight to the death, but I am offering you a way out before it comes to that – for both of you.'

John leaned back and looked interested but not eager. One of the few advantages of his disfigurement was that it made it harder for men to read his expression. 'I am listening.' He continued to stroke the dog.

'The Empress is going to offer Patrick the title of Earl of Salisbury if he will bring his allegiance back to us. He'll

272

accept; his family has always sought that recognition. If you and he will end this fighting and make an alliance, then all of Wiltshire will be secure for the Empress.'

Grim laughter welled up inside John. 'She didn't feel inclined to grace me with the title instead?' he asked. 'Then again perhaps I'm too dangerous, or perhaps she wants to forget I exist . . .'

'Now you're being totally blind, man,' Robert snapped. 'The Empress esteems you well.'

'Does she? Well, that's more than I know. I won't give an inch of what I hold. Does Patrick know of his potential great good fortune yet?'

Robert shook his head. 'No; I came to you first to find out if you were amenable to peace.'

'And if I'm not?'

The Earl perused the hall. 'I don't need to tell you.'

John leaned forward, hands clasped between his knees, his right side turned fully towards Robert so that he could see him clearly. 'So what's your proposition? I tell you now, I won't surrender Ludgershall.'

'You won't have to.'

'Then what's the catch?'

Robert crossed one leg across the knee of the other and examined the fastening on his boot. 'He has a sister unwed . . .'

'Aah.' John began to understand. Suddenly he was more than curious. Suddenly he was very interested.

'If you are willing to marry the girl, it will cement a bond between you and the Salisbury family. If there are children born of the match, then Ludgershall will be appropriated back into the Salisbury bloodline whilst still remaining in yours.'

John nodded slowly. 'There would have to be an annulment.'

273

Robert toyed with his boot fastening for a moment longer, then looked at John. 'I understand your father and Aline's were third cousins on the distaff side,' he said nonchalantly. 'It should be easy enough to arrange on the grounds of consanguinity. That way the sons of your union remain legitimate in law.'

John opened his mouth to speak then changed his mind and compressed his lips.

Robert snorted. 'You're not telling me you object to being rid of Aline. She's a millstone round your neck, man. Patrick's sister will do you well indeed. She's young – but she's old enough too.'

'What makes you think I want a girl in my bed, especially Salisbury's sister?'

Robert's eyes gleamed with humour. 'Because she *is* his sister. You'll have her under you in the marriage bed, so you'll be subjugating Salisbury by proxy. She's a lively young thing, too.'

John quirked a brow. A reluctant laugh was forced out of him.

Robert responded with a laugh of his own. 'I know you, John. You may have changed, but not that much. I still remember that day at Winchester when you were late to court because you'd been entertaining three at once – and don't tell me you were indulging in polite conversation. I'm sure you'll manage.'

'I don't need to tell you anything because plainly you know it all,' John retorted. 'You are wreaking revenge for those five hundred marks you paid for FitzHubert, aren't you?'

Robert chuckled. 'Perhaps I am, but even so, you were a legend at court, even if you didn't acknowledge it.' He sobered. 'If you agree to do this and cement a peace between you, I'll act as go-between. I should be able to negotiate a reasonable dowry out of Patrick. It goes without saying that any children born of the marriage will do well from the association. They'll be nieces and nephews not only of the Earl of Salisbury, but the Counts of Perche too.'

'You'd make a good horse-coper,' John said drily.

Robert waved his hand. 'I have sometimes thought that selling horses would be a useful occupation – and not so different.'

The proposal was as heady as strong wine, but John was too cautious just to plunge in and get drunk. 'What of Aline? What am I to do about her? The cloister is too dangerous. I wouldn't put it beyond some enterprising mercenary of FitzHubert's ilk to seize her out of a convent, force a marriage and claim her lands for himself.'

Robert gave a purposeful nod. 'You are right, it does to be cautious and I had already given it some thought. You know my mother's brother, my uncle Stephen? He's a widower and would welcome gentle company. Nor would he expect too much of a new wife . . . in all senses of the word.'

'You have spoken to him about it?'

'In passing.'

'God's blood, you have been busy!'

'Look, I need Patrick of Salisbury committed to my sister's cause, and I need you too. We have little room for manoeuvre. This arrangement can be of nothing but benefit to you. You keep Ludgershall and the fighting between you and Salisbury ceases. You get a pretty young virgin in your bed . . .'

'It's a fine deal for an old warhorse with half a face, you are saying.'

'Christ, it's a fine deal for any man, John; stop being contrary!' Robert finished his wine and stood up. 'I'll give

275

you a few days to think about it, but I want to know within a week.'

John curbed the impulse to say he would accept the terms there and then. It wasn't good policy to seem too eager. Instead, promising to send a messenger, he saw the Earl on his way, then retired to his chamber to think. Lying on his bed, he stared at the rafters. Doublet joined him and for once, he didn't order her down, but absently stroked her flanks. What should he do? Robert's suggestion was eminently sensible. The war between Stephen and Matilda was at a stalemate, neither side able to overcome the other. Uniting with Salisbury would give him security; despite the current friction between him and Patrick, he knew they could be allies. Did he want to start again? Another wife, a girl half his age. He'd had nigh on eleven years of Aline's whining, instability and incompetence. Would this be a fresh start, or was he courting more of the same? He supposed in the balance it didn't matter. When weighed in the scales a powerful alliance, a nubile young wife and relative peace were a more than fair exchange for what he had at the moment.

26

Clyffe Pipard, Wiltshire, May 1144

Aline was content at Clyffe. She had been born and raised here, and its solid, squat timber walls were a comforting bulwark against the world. Few demands were made on her; John seldom visited; and she could forget that she was the wife of a royal marshal and that warfare was endemic. Clyffe was off the beaten track and plodded along to its own local rhythm. The most exciting thing to have happened in a year was when the village bull became stuck in a mud wallow and the entire village had turned out to drag him free. The ungrateful beast had then charged his rescuers, resulting in two gorings and some broken ribs. Fortunately, Aline had not had to deal with those.

She was busy with her spinning when she heard the creak of wheels and the shout of men. Looking out of the window, she saw that a small covered wain had drawn up in the yard, accompanied by several well-dressed attendants. Her stomach fluttered. She wasn't expecting visitors and the manor was in no fit state to receive them.

She sent her maid to find out what was happening, and the woman returned almost immediately with a sealed scroll and a small pouch of embroidered silk. 'From my lord FitzGilbert,' she said.

'Has he summoned me?' Aline shivered, hoping not, but why else the covered wain? Her heart sank. She was happy here – didn't want to leave and return to dwelling in the anxiety of a castle under constant threat.

'I think so, my lady. The men didn't say – only that they were here to fetch you.'

She opened the pouch and a ring dropped into her hand, set with a gleaming dark green stone. Aline admired it, turning it this way and that. It was one that she knew John had in his jewel coffer and she had long had her eye on it as a gift for the church. She put it down on the trestle and focused on the letter, expecting it to be a summons. It was in John's own hand, neat, swift, slightly more right-slanted than a professional scribe's. For a moment the words lay upon the surface of her mind, making no impression; then gradually they gained weight and began to sink in, and as they did, she gasped and pressed her hand to her mouth. He spoke of remorse and regret. He said that their marriage was unlawful because their fathers were related and that therefore it was null and void and he had embarked upon a series of penances. He had sent a wain and servants to bear her in safety to the protection of the Bishop of Exeter with whom he knew she had an affinity. The Bishop was to act as a substitute for her father until arrangements could be made for her permanent future.

'Madam?' Her maid hastened over to her, but Aline neither saw nor responded. She was stunned, disbelieving. 'No,' she whispered, 'no,' and clutched her prayer beads. 'It's a mistake. It's not true.' It was as if a part of her had been ripped out and the pain was excruciating. People married and they stayed married – surely that was God's ordained law? She had done her duty to their union, had given him sons and been good and compliant. A lump of panic tightened in her throat. She thought about flinging herself out of the window into the arms of God, but taking one's own life was a mortal sin and the Devil would come cackling for her soul if she did that. And then she didn't think at all, but sat down abruptly and stared at the wall, while her being wisped out of the hole torn in her world and dissipated like wind-blown smoke. Time ceased to exist. People spoke to her and she didn't hear them. Someone gave her sugared wine and had to hold the cup because she refused to relinquish her grip on her prayer beads. They were her lifeline. Let go of them and it would be as if she had never existed. When someone tried to prise her hands off them, she started to scream.

Around her, the servants packed her travelling chest and the chaplain was fetched. She was vaguely aware of Father Thomas reading the letter, of him murmuring reassurances that all would be well, but it would be best if she went to the Bishop of Exeter. He patted her shoulder as he would pat an infant's.

'It's not true,' she whispered. 'It's not true. I made my vows in good faith.'

'As did he, my lady, but the marriage is discovered to be consanguineous. It is unlawful in the eyes of God. For the good of your soul, you must do this. The Bishop will look after you.'

Aline tried to focus, tried to make her mind work, but it wouldn't. It was as if it had been slowly grinding to a halt for a long time, and this letter was the final jam in its workings. 'My sons . . .' she said. 'What of my sons?'

'Their inheritance is untouched and they are not disparaged,' the chaplain said. 'And neither are you, my lady.

The law is clear on that point for such annulments. You will be well taken care of and honourably provided for.'

Aline said nothing more because speech too had fled through the rent in the fabric of her being. *Sancta Maria, Mater Dei, salve, salve Regina.* The words tumbled over and over in her head like pebbles rattling against each other in a heavy tidal wash. A prayer to the Mother of God not to desert her when everyone and everything else had. Over and over. Prayer beads clicking one on the other, the only solid objects in a world of shifting quicksand.

It was cool in the dairy, something Sybilla appreciated given the burning summer heat outside. She had slipped off her shoes just to feel the icy stone floor against the soles of her feet. Apron tucked at her waist, she was making cheese and supervising a maid who was paddling butter in a churn. The girl was new and had yet to develop the muscles required for such a task, and the rhythm. Sybilla suppressed the urge to snatch the handle out of her hands and do it herself. The girl had to learn. Besides, Sybilla needed to give her attention to the cutting of the cheese curds. She had developed something of a reputation for her cheeses. They were served to guests at the high table and the Bishop always requested a wheel for himself and his visitors. Sybilla enjoyed dairying and didn't consider it beneath her. An ability to turn her hand to most domestic tasks meant that she knew when the servants were working well and when they were slacking. She was also a firm believer that people should do what they had a talent for, and since her cheese was sublime and her stitchery the opposite, she preferred to spend time in the dairy when possible.

'Madam, is this—' The maid started to speak, then broke off with a curtsey.

Sybilla looked up as Patrick arrived and stopped in the doorway, blocking the light. She made a face at him, but he was impervious.

'You need to come to my chamber,' he said. 'I've some important news.'

'Now?' Sybilla shook her head at him. 'I'm busy; the cheese . . .'

'The cheese can wait.'

Sybilla rolled her eyes and puffed out her cheeks. However, she knew when Patrick was in this sort of mood there was no arguing with him. She checked on the butter, told the girl to keep churning for at least as long as it took to say two paternosters slowly, then followed her brother.

Father Geoffrey, one of their chaplains, already occupied the chamber, sitting at a trestle table, positioned so that the light from the high windows shone down on several parchments arranged on top of it. Neatly assembled by his right elbow were his quill, trimming pen, ink horn and the box containing her brother's seal.

'What's this?' Sybilla asked, mystified, as she untied her apron and draped it over a coffer.

Patrick sat down on his chair and gestured her to take the carved stool at his side. 'I've had an offer for you and I've agreed to the terms. I need you to put your seal to these contracts – there's a messenger waiting.'

Sybilla blinked at him in shocked astonishment. 'What do you mean: you've had an offer for me?' Her voice rose a notch. 'When? Why have I heard nothing of this?' Her heart began to bang against her rib cage.

Patrick glowered. 'It's my business to sort out your future, not yours. There was no point in telling you before because it might have come to naught.'

'No point!' Rage percolated through the other emotions

and she drew herself up. 'With whom have you arranged this?'

Patrick heaved a sigh and waved his hand. 'I have made a truce with John FitzGilbert and his union with you is part of the bargain.'

Hot and cold chills ran down Sybilla's spine. 'But he's already married! If you think to sell me off as a concubine, you may think again!' Suddenly she was trembling. She thought about seizing the priest's quill pen and sticking it under her brother's ribs. How dare he! She leaned to the table and dashed the parchments to the floor. 'Amputate my right hand, but I will not put my seal to this . . . this document of whoredom. I am no man's slut!'

Patrick began to flush. 'Then I will do it for you,' he snarled. 'You will obey me!'

She stared at him, her eyes ablaze with tears. All she could think of was that John FitzGilbert had custody of the court prostitutes and her brother had sold her to him for that eventual purpose. She thought she was going to be sick.

The chaplain gently cleared his throat. 'My lady, you have not given your brother time to say that John FitzGilbert is no longer married to the lady Aline.'

Sybilla whipped round to face him. 'What?'

'The marriage has never existed in the eyes of God. They are related within the forbidden degree through their fathers and they have been living in sin. The lord Marshal has asked forgiveness and done due penance, and is now free to take another wife.'

Sybilla stared at the chaplain. She was so stunned and enraged that it was difficult to assimilate this new piece of information. Shaking, she sat down on the stool and cast a fulminating look at her brother.

Father Geoffrey poured her a cup of wine from the jug

on the trestle and picked up the scattered pieces of parchment. Sybilla took several short sips and tried to calm herself. Patrick said nothing; he just tapped the trestle with an impatient forefinger, but Father Geoffrey gently began to explain the legal details of the proposed contract – what would be hers in dower, what she would gain from the match. 'Should you choose to consent to the marriage, it would be of enormous strategic value to your family,' the chaplain said with a glance at Patrick. 'Moreover, John FitzGilbert is a fine man with a well-earned reputation for courage and valour. You will be well settled with him.'

Sybilla shook her head, neither impressed nor convinced. 'He has turned out one wife,' she pointed out. 'What stops him casting off another as it suits his purpose?'

'I've already considered that point,' Patrick said smugly. 'The contracts declare that there is no known impediment to the match on either side and FitzGilbert has already agreed to the terms. All you need do is agree and seal.'

Sybilla glowered at him, not prepared to yield so easily after the shock he had given her. 'It is not a matter entered into lightly,' she said. 'I need time to consider.'

Patrick opened his mouth, caught the priest's eye, and changed what he had been going to say. 'You have until nones. The messenger needs to be on his way before the light goes.'

Sybilla gave a stiff nod. She took the contracts from the table where the chaplain had just neatly replaced them. For a moment, Patrick looked as if he was going to protest, but then he shrugged and gestured her away. 'Nones,' he repeated.

Sybilla gave him a hard look and, without replying, went from the room to her chamber. Dismissing her women, she entered the small embrasure space containing her bed. She lay down on the coverlet and propped the bolsters against her spine. She was still trembling and a headache throbbed at her temples. Just now, she hated Patrick with a vengeance. With a determined effort, she made herself read and absorb the details of the contract. The act of doing so demanded cooler thought patterns and gradually calmed her anger. She pursed her lips and pondered the issue. It certainly wasn't what she had expected, nor the kind of match she had envisaged for herself. A second wife, the match made so that her brother and John FitzGilbert could honourably cease battling each other to fragments over the matter of Ludgershall and allied territory. And yet it wasn't so bad and there were many advantages. John FitzGilbert was certainly a better prospect than some of the oafs who had been sniffing around Salisbury of late, dropping hints to Patrick and giving her the eye.

She was sorry for Aline, of course she was, but in truth perhaps the annulment had happened for the best. From what Sybilla had seen, Aline was a fish out of water in her role of wife to England's marshal, without the abilities to cope with what was required of her. Sybilla considered the contract again. Did she herself have those abilities, and could she deal with John FitzGilbert the man, who she suspected was no easy prospect? She thought about what she knew of him and what she had heard. She hadn't seen him since long before the incident at Wherwell, which she knew had scarred him badly, but his injury didn't seem to have held him back.

She remembered the way he moved – the straight spine, the fluid coordination and grace. She thought about the quiet intensity of his glance and pictured him sitting at ease in Ludgershall's bailey, a wine jug at his elbow and his sleeves pushed back to reveal strong forearms dusted with fine gilt hair. Suddenly her mouth was dry and her loins moist. Dear Jesu! She laughed at herself and hastily left her bed. Hot with embarrassment, she went to look out of the narrow arch of window at the bustling bailey below. Those feelings had probably always been there but unacknowledged until today, because she hadn't allowed herself to think that way about a man with a wife. But now . . . Her breathing calmed again and she began to smile with wry humour. All unwittingly, her brother had just done her the best turn of her life, but she wasn't going to tell him that. Let him stew awhile!

'My lady . . .' One of her women tentatively parted the curtain she had drawn to have privacy and poked her head round. 'Lord Patrick is asking if you have come to a decision.'

Sybilla shook her head and knitted her brows. 'Tell him I'm not ready,' she said. 'Tell him it's too important; I need more time. And when you've done that, go to the dairy and fetch me a cup of buttermilk and some bread. I can't think on an empty stomach.' She had to compress her lips to stop herself from giggling, but when the woman had gone, she doubled up. Part of it was nervous reaction. Sybilla was more inclined to laugh than weep in times of stress.

By the time the woman returned with a cup and platter, Sybilla had regained her composure. She sat in the window, looking out, and made a slow pleasure of her meal. The buttermilk was fresh from the churn and the bread was fluffy and just a little moist, the way she liked it. She savoured each mouthful as if was years since she had eaten anything this good.

The maid returned. 'Mistress, Lord Patrick asks if you are ready.'

'I haven't finished eating,' Sybilla said, although in truth there was only a swallow of buttermilk and a morsel of bread remaining.

'He says you have to come now. The messenger has to leave.' There was a worried note in the woman's voice.

Sybilla sighed and rose to her feet. 'If I must,' she said. She ate the bread, drank the last mouthful of buttermilk, fetched her seal from its casket and, documents in hand, returned to her brother who was pacing the room like an agitated hound.

Sybilla scowled at him. 'You are forcing me to make a decision without due time for consideration,' she told him with her head held high. 'Furthermore, you are forcing me to marry a man who turned over his first wife. But for the good of our family and your honour, I agree.' From the corner of her eye, she was aware of Patrick closing his eyes and swallowing with relief. Once she had pressed her seal into the hot wax, Father Geoffrey took the document and hurried from the room.

'It'll be for the best, you'll see,' Patrick said, trying to be conciliatory.

'That remains to be seen.' She went to the door.

'You've forgotten your apron.' He pointed to the garment draped over a coffer.

Sybilla gave him a strong look. 'I'm not going back to the dairy,' she said loftily. 'If I'm to be married as hastily as I've been betrothed, I've a wedding gown to make. Let others see to the cheese.'

27

Salisbury Castle, Wiltshire, May 1144

Sybilla's wedding gown was cut from a bolt of shimmering red silk damask, purchased in Winchester by one of Patrick's merchant contacts. There was also a bolt of teal-blue wool. Although both colours suited Sybilla's rich dark hair and hazel eyes, the red was stunning and she had chosen it for her wedding. She suspected Patrick had offered her the fabric as a sweetener after springing the marriage contract on her; he wasn't usually so generous and there had still been some good pink twill in the cloth cupboard that would have sufficed. Whatever the reason, she was delighted. She would go to her new husband with garments suitable for the wife of the Empress's marshal. Two of her women were accomplished seamstresses and they had been charged with making the gowns and putting the stitches in the crucial parts of the garments. Sybilla's task was hemming since she was competent enough at plain sewing. The wedding day had been set for the feast of Saint John the Baptist, a month hence, and the celebrations were to be held at Ludgershall in token of the new alliance between Salisbury and Marshal. Sybilla felt excited and apprehensive as she worked. Very soon, her life was going to change for ever, and she didn't know what to expect. All she could do was imagine and that was by turns delicious and terrifying. Sometimes, she would think of Aline Marshal, and the brightness of her feelings would be dulled by guilt and pity.

Leaving her sewing for a moment, she went to the trestle where her maid Lecia was cutting out the blue gown.

'The red will contrast well in the sleeve linings, my lady,' Lecia said, indicating a length of spare cloth from the wedding dress. 'Or do you want it all blue?'

'No, use the red. Then there'll be enough blue for—' She stopped and looked round as her brother's chamberlain entered the room. 'Hubert?'

He bowed. 'The lord Marshal is here and wishes a word, my lady.'

Sybilla's stomach plummeted. 'What, here and now?'

'Yes, my lady. He specifically requested to see you. Lord Patrick desires you to come down.'

Sybilla swallowed her panic. This, she hadn't expected. Not with the suddenness of the nuptial agreement. She had thought he would wait. 'Tell him I am coming,' she answered in a tight voice.

When he had bowed from her presence, she summoned Lecia and Gundred from their tasks to attend her. In her private domain she was wearing a working gown of unembellished grey wool and no head covering. 'The brown dress, quickly,' she said and immediately changed her mind. 'No, the green . . . and the veil with the yellow stars.' She felt dithery, scared and embarrassed. The young women helped her into the gown. She folded back the hanging sleeves, double-looped a braid belt at her waist and tried not to fidget while the maids pinned the veil to her hair.

'Oh, it'll have to do,' she said, suddenly impatient with

herself. 'If he wanted more, he should have given me fair warning.' Before her courage could desert her, she took a deep breath and sallied from her chamber.

The men were seated before the hearth in conversation, but as she approached, they looked up, and John FitzGilbert rose to his feet. Sybilla hesitated for a step, then went forward, forcing a smile on to her face.

'My lord, welcome.' She made herself look at him rather than at the safer option of the floor. The scarring across the upper left quadrant of his face was worse than she had expected in her naivety and for a moment, her gaze faltered over the livid red tissue. Then she pushed herself through the initial recoil. The rest was still as she remembered: the firm mouth, straight nose and strong, clean jaw. He was of a height with Patrick and straight as a lance. His tunic was of the finest, softest blue wool with not a speck of dust or drip of candle grease. 'Had I known you were coming, I would have made better provision.'

'I am sorry,' he said. 'I would usually have sent word ahead, but I didn't want to trouble you . . . I do not usually act on sudden impulse, which is what today's visit is.'

His voice was cultured and quiet but, despite the latter, each word was enunciated clearly and she had no difficulty hearing him. She did not doubt it could bite when its owner wished it to, or soften like honey. She murmured a platitude and lowered her gaze.

'I wanted to say that you do me great honour, my lady, in accepting my proposal of marriage, and I will endeavour to live up to the duties of a groom.'

A note that might have been amusement entered his voice and Sybilla, looking up again, saw she had not mistaken it. There was a definite gleam of humour, perhaps even challenge. Her breath shortened. 'I am sure

289

you will, my lord,' she answered, 'as I will endeavour not to disappoint as your bride.'

'I doubt that . . .' Softer now. Sybilla almost shivered.

'You'll have no reason to complain, my lord, I can assure you,' Patrick interrupted heartily, speaking about her as if she wasn't in the room. 'She's been well trained.' He grinned. 'She's very good with the dairy; she'll put meat on your bones, even as you're putting a belly underneath her girdle.' He spoke in proprietorial fashion, but Sybilla was mortified and could have slapped him.

John Marshal said nothing but the glance he cast her was wry and his half-smile apologetic.

'Of course, you may find that she talks too much for your taste, especially after the lady Aline,' Patrick continued. 'If Sybilla has a fault it's that she's inquisitive and wants to poke her nose into men's business. You might have to bridle her tongue, but otherwise she'll do very well.'

'I am sure we will get along in fine fettle,' John murmured.

'Aye, well, she's easy on the eye and she sings very prettily if you've a mind to music. Good dancer too. Her sewing's not up to much, but she has other women to do it for her and she's good with the servants. She knows how to make them work for her. Show her what you want of her and she'll do it.'

By now, Sybilla was fuming, almost tearful. She wanted to smack Patrick and shout that she was not a brood mare to be paraded in the ring before the man who had just bought her. A glance under her lashes showed her that John's face was impassive, but she could sense his internal laughter.

'Then I am indeed to be blessed,' he said. 'A month will seem a long time to wait.'

Sybilla inclined her head to his statement. 'And not

long enough, my lord, if my women are to accomplish all the sewing and duties without me by to "make them work".' She cast a fulminating look in her brother's direction. 'You will excuse me to my tasks.'

John took her hand and bowed over it. 'Thank you for coming down, my lady. I appreciate you have much to accomplish between now and the feast of Saint John. Now I know what to expect, the time cannot pass quickly enough for me.' He gave her a slow smile and a look that in less fraught circumstances would have melted her bones.

Sybilla curtseyed to him, ignoring her brother, and went from the hall. Halfway back up the stairs, the awfulness and the humour of the situation struck her like a delayed blow and she began to laugh.

'My lady?' Gundred touched her arm. 'Have a care, you will fall.'

Sybilla compressed her lips, swallowed, got herself under control and, with brimming eyes, climbed the rest of the way to her chamber. When asked by her worried ladies if she was all right, she laughed some more, and wept a little too, but finally composed herself and retired to the window-seat to continue with her sewing. Her hands were trembling and she almost started laughing again. God, he would think her as much of a milk custard as his first wife! The scarring was bad but, once over her initial shock, she had felt no revulsion. Beyond it lay John FitzGilbert the man, and she still found him very attractive. The voice, the dry humour, the courtliness, the firm touch of his hand. That playful, mischievous gleam from his good side. Her hands steadied. The urge to laugh became a smile instead. She took several stitches, then paused to look out of the window. So short and long a time, a month. She already felt as if she had lived a lifetime in less than an hour.

28

Ludgershall, Wiltshire, June 1144

The sun was setting in a basin of liquid gold when Sybilla arrived at Ludgershall on the eve of her wedding. They had covered the eighteen miles from Salisbury in good time, using pack ponies rather than a baggage cart to bear Sybilla's possessions and trousseau.

They had been sighted and the word given, for the gates were wide to admit them and they were ushered within the compound by John's porter who was spruce in a russet tunic and cap. As they were dismounting, John himself emerged to greet them. He saluted Patrick with a warm handclasp and a polished smile, then turned to her. This time Sybilla was more prepared for the juxtaposition of beauty and ruin on his face and didn't recoil. She gave him her hand and curtseyed demurely.

'Welcome to Ludgershall, my lady.'

'Thank you.' She looked around. 'It's different from last time I was here.'

He laughed. 'I should hope so, since it was little but rubble and timber then. I have allotted you a chamber above the hall for tonight. I hope it meets with your approval.'

'I am sure it will, my lord.' Sybilla felt herself growing tongue-tied under the stilted formality. That too was different from her last visit when Patrick had lost his hawk; but back then she had been a child and not about to give herself in marriage to this man.

John was clearly perceptive of her mood, for he had an attendant show her and her maids to the chamber and left her in peace to unpack her baggage, bidding her come to the great hall when she was ready.

The room smelled musty and stale, although someone had opened the shutters to let in air and daylight, of which there was still sufficient left to show cobwebs clinging to the shutter edges. The bed was sturdy and of a decent size with two mattresses – a lower one of straw topped by another of down – but there were no hangings and there was evidence of moths in the coverlet. Dust motes hovered in the air, speaking of recent attention, and there was a ewer and a jug of fresh water for washing. The general air was one of a room little used and even less considered. Sybilla wondered about Aline. Had she not taken an interest or chivvied the servants? Perhaps she hadn't been here in a while. One thing was certain, this room was crying out for a woman's touch.

In thoughtful mood, she washed her hands and face, changed her travelling gown for the one of green wool she had worn when John came to Salisbury, and returned to join the men.

Dinner was served later than usual to accommodate their arrival. The shutters had been closed, the candles lit and the atmosphere was convivial, the tables in the well of the hall crowded with guests and retainers. The dais was reserved for immediate family, worthies and clergy, including the new Bishop of Salisbury, Joscelin de Bohun, wearing dark colours tonight, although on the morrow

293

Sybilla knew he would blaze like a peacock. She had seen his official robes of office on several occasions now.

John had seated Patrick on his left, Sybilla on his right – which she found interesting since it defied convention and he should have put Patrick to his right. She wondered if he had placed her thus out of deference to her feminine sensibilities or because he was being defensive and wanted her to see his good side. Perhaps he was doing it to unsettle Patrick, or it might be all three. John Marshal had a reputation as a cunning and subtle tactician.

Was this where his wife had sat when she was at Ludgershall? Doing the same as she was now doing? Sybilla pushed the thought away with an inward grimace.

The main dish was beef in a spicy sauce, served with fresh white bread and side dishes of mushroom frumenty. There were small fried pastries and platters of roasted songbirds. She and John shared a trencher and he served her with dexterity despite his blind eye. He was attentive, enquiring of her what she liked, giving her the choicest morsels, behaving with the suave polish of an accomplished courtier. He had better manners than Patrick. He didn't loudly suck his fingers and he had the knack of being able to eat without dripping sauce all over his clothes or the napery. Fastidious without being finicky, she thought with approval, and hoped he was viewing her with similar appreciation. Although she hadn't caught him looking yet, she suspected he had been giving her a thorough scrutiny.

He had employed some musicians, including a troubadour from Aquitaine who possessed the rarity of a lute. Multicoloured ribbons dangled from the instrument's neck, their hues repeated in the man's striped hose. Sybilla's face lit up for she adored music and novelty. She forgot to be restrained and demure, and clapped her hands with delight.

Sybilla's assumption concerning John's scrutiny was correct. He had indeed been studying her and was intensely aware of her presence beside him – as if her body warmth was giving off an extra glow. Her hair was decently braided and half hidden by her veil, but he could imagine how it would look, spread like burnished wood upon a white linen pillow when released from its pins. He had been a trifle disturbed by her silence, her downcast eyes and the way she toyed with her food, for such behaviour reminded him of Aline and he didn't want more of the same in his life. He hoped it was nothing more than tiredness or natural apprehension. However, when the musicians arrived to perform, her expression blazed to life, as if a candle had suddenly illuminated a darkened room.

'You enjoy music?' he asked.

'Yes, my lord.' She turned to him, lips parted in an enthusiastic smile. 'Do you?'

'It has its place. It's useful for occasions like this . . . and of course musicians make excellent messengers and spies, depending on who's paying them to sing the tune.'

Her gaze widened. She picked up a pastry and took a bite. Her lips were full. She had even, white teeth. He imagined kissing her and felt a pleasant jolt of anticipation. 'But beyond that, my lord?'

John tilted his head and pondered. 'Yes,' he said. 'I suppose it can be an entertaining diversion.'

'I like to sing,' she said. 'I love all music. It's more than entertainment, don't you think? It can lighten or darken a mood. It creates atmosphere . . . and it's good for dancing.'

'Ah, you have a fondness for dancing then?' He was pleased that she conversed in more than monosyllables and had opinions.

'When I have the opportunity – which hasn't been often of late.'

295

He grimaced. 'That's true.' Except for the death dance of the warrior with sword and lance. He had forgotten what it was like to dance as a courtier. 'I might be persuaded to remember the steps on the morrow though,' he added with a slow smile.

She blushed and grew a little flustered, but then forgot to be embarrassed as she listened to the troubadour and continued to eat. Jesu, she was a beauty, John thought and felt his gut tighten with apprehension. His luck had turned around so completely: it couldn't be this good.

'What was life like at court?' she asked him after a while.

'Was, or is?' He raised an eyebrow.

'In the days when my father went there to render his account. Before the fighting.'

John leaned back and folded his arms to consider. 'I could tell you about the exchequer and bore you to tears,' he said, 'but I'm not sure that other stories are for the ears of unwed virgins.'

She flashed him a look and wrinkled her nose. 'Then tell me those tomorrow.'

John grinned. 'They wouldn't be for my wife either.'

She laughed. 'Oh, that isn't fair!' She folded her elbows on the table and leaned towards him. A faint, spicy scent wafted from her garments. The beaded embroidery at her neckline winked softly with the pulse in her throat. Her expression was genuine and a little flirtatious. 'I suppose you'll just have to bore me with tales of the exchequer then. Did you ever have to arrest anyone for not paying their debts?'

'From time to time . . . the occasional sheriff, several barons. We usually managed to come to some sort of agreement without anyone becoming too uncomfortable. I've only committed murder once.' He looked at her straight-faced.

296

She parted her lips and stared at him, briefly taken in, but then she laughed and shook her head. 'I don't believe you.'

'It's true. A rat got into one of the forel cases and made itself a nest out of a page of fees owed by the Bishop of Winchester. Then it bit an usher and ran amok across the tables spilling ink and scattering parchments. It's my duty to keep order, so I had to do something . . .' He shrugged. 'Made a mess of the chancellor's table, but I had no choice. There's a permanent knife mark in it now. After that I went out into the market and bought a cat and gave it the forel box to sleep in instead.' He smiled at her again, enjoying himself enormously.

The meal continued and so did the conversation. He found he could tell her about more serious parts of the exchequer duties without her eyes glazing over and her attention wandering. Some of it she understood; he could see that a lot went over her head, but she had a sharp mind, a keen wit and a genuine interest . . . and whether consciously or not, she knew how to use the language of her body to convey subtle, unspoken meaning.

When she rose to retire, leaving him and Patrick to talk by the fire, he was reluctant to see her go.

'Well,' said Patrick with a knowing smile and a cup raised in toast, 'you seem satisfied enough with your part of the bargain.'

John returned the toast in laconic fashion. 'I'll tell you whether or not I'm satisfied on the day after tomorrow, but I am not displeased thus far.'

Patrick gave him a haughty stare. 'I would take my sword to you if you were. I expect you to treat her with the respect due to a lady of her rank.'

Even though you didn't when she was under your roof at Salisbury, John thought. 'Due to the sister of an earl,' he said, his

297

expression as solemn as when he had been telling Sybilla about the rat in the exchequer forel. 'I suspect though, I am going to cherish her more than I cherish you . . . with all due respect.'

The next morning, Sybilla was married to John and their wedding mass celebrated in the church of Saint Mary in Ludgershall village. Robed in her gown of red silk damask, Sybilla knelt beside John to receive the Bishop's blessing. A light veil pinned in place by a chaplet of roses covered her hair, but beneath it her tresses were unbound and had been combed until they shone like brunette silk. John stood with the handsome side of his face on view to her. He was wearing a tunic of night-blue wool that enhanced his colouring. He wore his sword too as a symbol of his knighthood and a reminder that he was well able to protect everything that came to him. After the mass, as they left the church, he kissed her, but it was a formal gesture, performed before all, and Sybilla responded in a similar manner. She had become the wife of the Empress's marshal, but for the moment that title and responsibility seemed a distant whimsy and nothing to do with her.

Once more, she sat in the hall to eat and listen to music, but it was different this time – formal, of course, because of the ceremony that had gone before, but encompassing many more guests than there had been the previous evening. The food was more elaborate and the best wine had been brought from the undercroft, including some from France that sparkled and bubbled on the tongue. All the shutters were thrown wide to admit streamers of sunlight and the wall above the dais was decorated with tendrils of evergreen and wild flowers. Arranged on the white table napery were dishes and cellars of enamelled silver, delicate green glass and more robust glazed ware.

John paid his new wife compliments and attention, but had perforce to spread the latter over a broad field. A marriage wasn't just about the binding together of a man and a woman. It was about allegiance and prestige, about making bonds and social connections with others who might have similar interests and persuasions. Sybilla found herself having to talk to the sons of Robert of Gloucester, then a senior knight belonging to the household of Brian FitzCount. Then vassals and the wives of vassals. Her father had been too frail to travel from Bradenstoke, but the Prior was here, and her brother Walter. She was kept almost too busy to eat or drink, and certainly had no time to be nervous about the other duties soon to be required of her.

Between courses, the musicians entertained the company. A troupe of players tumbled and juggled for their supper. The Bishop gave a long speech about the duties of marriage and Patrick a rambling incoherent one as he was in his cups, declaring he was glad for the new accord between the houses of Marshal and Salisbury – which would bring Ludgershall back into his family where it should always have been. John's own speech was sober and brief. He too was glad of the new accord and the opportunity he had been given to direct his attentions elsewhere than war against his neighbour. Here he smiled at Sybilla, and received laughter and approbation. 'And, of course,' he added with a bow in Patrick's direction, 'any sons that come of the match will be Salisbury by half their birth, but all Marshal by name.' And before Patrick could bridle at the remark, he gestured to the musicians and called for the dancing to begin. Holding out his hand to Sybilla, he bade her rise from the trestle and join him. She left her seat in a rustle of red brocade and let him lead her to the floor.

'You're still fighting him though, aren't you?' she murmured as they took their places.

John shook his head. 'No, he's still fighting me, and I am no one's floor straw to be trampled upon.' He bowed to her, stood straight and pressed his palm to hers on the diagonal, turned, changed palms. 'I don't want to talk about him. I'd far rather dance with my wife.'

She smiled. 'I don't want to talk about him either.'

Sybilla discovered that John was an excellent dancer. He had the lithe coordination of a cat and a sense of rhythm that made it a joy to partner him. Most men, Patrick included, could perform the moves, but were as wooden as planks. John was as fluid as water. Enticed, she moved and flowed with him, and it was as if they were two currents winding through the same stream. She flashed him a look through her lashes as their hands touched and their hipbones brushed edge to edge. He gave her a slow smile that made her quiver as much with anticipation as fear. The music coursed through her blood and sang in her loins as she matched him move for move. Oh, this was heady. Her breath grew short but not owing to exertion.

It was almost midnight when she and John finally retired to their marriage bed. He had chosen to dispense with the bedding ceremony, declaring it was not that kind of occasion. If he was satisfied with his bride and she with him, there was no need for a host of witnesses crowding into the chamber. Patrick had not protested as she thought he might. Thinking about it, Sybilla suspected he didn't want to see his sister naked in a bed with John FitzGilbert, even if he acknowledged the fact of the marriage. She too was relieved, for she hadn't been looking forward to everyone squeezing into the bedchamber and making bawdy jests as she disrobed. As it was, she blushed at the

300

barrage of well-wishing that followed them out of the hall and up the stairs to the room above.

Holding her hand, John pushed open the door, then stopped on the threshold and stared. Sybilla gasped. A shower of pink rose petals strewed the marriage bed while garlands of flowers decorated the tied-back hangings. Sybilla's two women waited demurely near the door, hands folded, but with coy smiles on their faces. John's chamberlain, Osbert, was standing to one side looking both sheepish and disgruntled.

Sybilla laughed and clapped her hands. 'Oh, how lovely – and how thoughtful!'

'I knew you would like it, my lady,' smiled one of the women.

'I do, oh I do! Thank you!'

John went to the bed and looked down at the petals. 'At least they're not dried herbs,' he said with a straight expression. 'That's like lying in a bed of crumbs.' He turned to the maids. 'You obviously care about your mistress.'

'Indeed, my lord,' said the taller one, who had freckles and bright brown eyes with a mischievous glint. 'I love her dearly.'

'Gundred is my milk sister,' Sybilla said with a gesture at the maid. 'Her mother was my wet nurse. Lecia is my chaplain's cousin.' She indicated the other, slightly younger girl, who was red-cheeked and round-chinned. The latter gave him a pert curtsey and a dimple appeared beside her mouth. John flicked a glance at Osbert who was looking as ruffled as a cat chased up a tree by two lively young dogs.

'Then it seems you are in good hands.' John inclined his head to the women in acknowledgement. 'Osbert, you have my leave to retire until summoned. The guests

301

shouldn't have eaten all the almond cakes yet if you want to avail yourself, and I ordered a tun of good wine left in the kitchens for those on duty.'

Osbert flicked a jaundiced glance at the maids. 'Yes, my lord. This wasn't my idea.' He pointed indignantly to the scattered rose petals.

John bit the inside of his mouth. 'I know it wasn't. I couldn't imagine such a thing would enter your head. Go to. Lady Marshal and I can manage.' He gave a prompting glance over his right shoulder at Sybilla.

For the briefest instant, she hesitated, but then she caught on and gestured a dismissal to the women. 'Thank you again,' she said.

They curtseyed and followed Osbert out of the door. 'I wish you good rest, my lord, my lady,' said Gundred, the twinkle in her eye irrepressible, before she whisked out and pulled the door shut. There came the sound of a soft giggle from the other side.

'I am sorry, my lord,' Sybilla said. 'Gundred has a heart of gold and she means well.'

John shook his head and allowed his smile to show. 'It's a long time since I heard laughter in the domestic chambers. I do not mind.'

Sybilla removed the chaplet of flowers and plucked out the gold pins securing her veil to her hair. John sat down on the coffer at the foot of the bed, unfastened his sword belt and took off his tunic. Sybilla's breathing quickened. Now that the moment was approaching, she was apprehensive and uncertain. She had imagined it so many times, but imagination would only take her so far, and anticipation warred with a fear of the unknown.

She took her comb from her trinket box and began drawing it through her hair, and because being afraid always caused her to talk too much, she spoke to fill the

302

silence. 'I was surprised at how well you dance, my lord. Patrick has two left feet, especially when he's drunk.'

He gave an amused grunt. 'But I am not drunk. It is true that some men need to be in their cups to dance, but I have always thought a man should have all his faculties intact for any physical activity.' There was a slight emphasis on the 'any' that made Sybilla flush.

'Perhaps *you* ought to be drunk,' he added and suddenly the humour was gone, 'although it is said that all cats are grey at night.'

Sybilla frowned. 'I do not understand your meaning, my lord?'

'Ah, no matter. I know you have been gently raised, but even so, I assume you know your duty.'

'Yes, my lord.' She steadied herself. 'I am not afraid.'

'Are you not?'

Sybilla shook her head. 'No, my lord, or no more than is natural on such an occasion. I know you will treat me in a proper manner, because if you do not, my brother will kill you.'

John gave a sour smile. 'He might die trying, I grant you.'

She paused in her combing. 'Also you seem to be an honourable man.'

'Hah, that's useful for a new wife to think. Not many believe it of me these days, including your brother. Without the Earl of Gloucester's intervention, I doubt this marriage would have happened.'

'No, but it has – and I am not my brother.'

His smile remained. 'Sweetheart, if you were, I'd not be contemplating getting into a bed with you. Don't imbue me with the qualities the knights have in those songs, because you'll be disappointed.'

Sybilla tightened her lips and turned away to clean

303

the comb of stray hair before replacing it in its coffer. She didn't hear John move, but suddenly she felt his closeness. Fear jolted through her, but so did expectancy. She turned round quickly and, in so doing, caught a flicker of trepidation in his expression. With sudden insight she realised she was not the only one concerned about tonight, although he was better at concealing it. The knowledge lessened her anxiety. Stepping into his guard-space, she reached up and with gentle fingers traced the line of the burn scar. She felt him stiffen and knew he was holding himself rigid because otherwise he would have flinched. In the last few years, she had become accustomed to tending wounds and healing battered pride. 'You say I should not imbue you with the qualities knights have in songs, but you have honour and steadfastness, my lord.'

'Is that what you think?'

'Yes, it is. Would you gainsay your wife on her wedding day?' She stroked the ridge of red, angry flesh on the side of his face. Her voice dropped to a whisper. 'On her wedding night?'

She saw the apple in his throat move as he swallowed. At the same time her gaze absorbed the strong column of his neck, the unlaced ties on his shirt, moved up again to his face, to that straight, firm mouth. She raised her head invitingly.

He looked wry. 'You are an innocent,' he said.

'Not for much longer.'

For an instant, he hesitated, but no more than that. Then he kissed her and Sybilla did what she had wanted to do all along: she ran her fingers through his hair.

Sybilla gazed up at the embroidered canopy above the bed. She felt wrung out and blissful; a little sore, but less

304

so than she had expected. It had been a revelation on both physical and emotional levels. She felt she had learned a great deal about her new husband during these past moments of intimacy, and even more about herself.

She rolled over on to her stomach and felt the cool clamminess of crushed rose petals under her body. He was lying with his good side towards her, his features softened into lines of contentment. The sheet covered him to his waist, but his arms and chest were exposed, showing smooth, firm muscles, long with relaxation.

She met his heavy glance, smiled and stretched languorously. 'Oh, that was nice,' she purred.

He arched his brow, then laughed low in his throat. Turning towards her, he wound a thick strand of her hair around his palm and knuckles. 'Nice? Is that all you can say?'

Sybilla giggled and moved closer to him. 'It was beyond me to say anything at all a few moments ago.' She ran her hand up his arm, enjoying the feel of his bare skin under her fingertips. It was a complete novelty to her, this sensuous touching and stroking. Her life had not been sheltered; she knew what happened in the bedchamber and her nature was such that she was happy to embrace that duty, but she had never imagined anything like this. 'And you, my lord. Did I please you?'

He gave a lazy smile. 'It was nice,' he retorted in kind, then took her hand from his arm to kiss the fingertips and palm. 'Very nice indeed.'

He left the bed to pour them both wine and, while admiring his body, she wondered about Aline. She must have lain here in this same place, borne his weight in the act of procreation, conceived his children – perhaps the first on her own wedding night. It was a disturbing, slightly uncomfortable thought – like seeing a ghost in the periphery of one's vision – and she pushed it aside and sat up to take the cup he offered her. Looking at his hand, touching his fingers in the exchange, she remembered their alchemy on her body and gave a small, pleasurable shiver.

'You must have had many women,' she said.

He rearranged the covers and adjusted the bolster until his shoulders were comfortably positioned. 'My share, but not of late, it has to be said.'

'Because of what happened at Wherwell?' she dared. 'Or because you are no longer the King's marshal, but the Empress's?'

The way his expression closed showed her that she had struck beneath his shield. 'Does it matter why not?' His voice was still quiet, but devoid now of the melting timbre it had held before.

'Not to me, but perhaps to you, my lord.'

He was silent for a while, and she didn't interrupt him. Her brother had said she would talk the hindquarters off her new husband and it was true that anxiety made her loquacious, but she had an innate sense of when not to speak.

At last, he sighed, set his cup on the floor at the bedside and turned to her again. 'When I married you all that mattered was that you were Patrick of Salisbury's sister and that the match would end the bloodshed between him and me. You could have been a toothless hag and I wouldn't have cared. The bargain with Patrick was the important part.'

Sybilla gave a brusque nod but was not offended. The subject matter might not be romantic but he was talking to her on the kind of level which Patrick had seldom done, and this she relished. 'My brother ordered me to agree to the marriage because he could see the advan-

306

tages and he wanted to be an earl. I understand my worth very well indeed.' She gave him an impish smile. 'He doesn't realise the good he did me though. He still thinks I consented under duress and because of his authority, but I agreed because I wanted this match and it suited my desires as much as his.'

John threw back his head and laughed, but for all the vigour of his response, it had a bitter edge. 'So you desired a battle-scarred man who was ridding himself of his first wife in order to make a treaty with his neighbour.'

'I admit I was bothered about you giving up Aline – until I read the clause about no impediment – and I am sorry for her, but as to the rest . . .' She stroked his arm again, drawn to the supple curve of muscle. 'Your scars show me that I have a strong and formidable husband who is not afraid to be a man and who will stand his ground. I will be proud to care for every part of you – the scarred and the unscarred – for it will bring me great honour too.' She put her own goblet down and faced him, a possessive glint in her eyes. 'At Salisbury I was just Patrick's sister and put upon. Now I am the marshal's wife and I have a household and a husband that will be mine to me – mine! Why should I not desire such things?'

He said nothing for a moment, opened his mouth as if to speak, then swallowed, shook his head and took her in his arms instead. He meshed his fingers through her masses of burnished hair, kissing her and kissing her again until she was breathless. His fingertips wrote intimate patterns over her body with the weightless strength of a pinion feather and the sensations made her arch towards him and gasp. Sybilla reasoned that if she derived pleasure from his touch, then surely he must do so from hers. She kissed him back and her own fingers were greedy on his skin, exploring the hard, supple muscles of arms and torso,

307

the lean flanks and firm buttocks. His locked breath, his hiss of pleasure in response told her all that she needed to know and she gave a soft laugh compounded of lust and delight.

He kissed her again and thrust into her full measure. Sybilla was sore, but the pain was overridden by other congested sensations. For a long time he lay within her, his weight braced on his forearms while he continued to nibble and kiss her lips. He kept up a steady, barely moving friction on her pubic bone and Sybilla felt the pressure gathering in her loins, stronger and stronger like an approaching thunderstorm. His kiss deepened, the infinitesimal movements continued. She wanted to cry out, to release the tension but couldn't because his mouth was over hers. She shuddered and pressed her hand to the hollow of his spine and felt the slickness of sweat; she clung to him. And then the storm was over her and breaking. Her fingers clawed, her body jolted against his and she tore her mouth free to sob aloud. 'Holy God!'

She was barely aware of him tensing above her, his head going back, the throb of his release and the sound of his own voice muted in his throat as he swallowed.

As she slowly orientated herself, he withdrew from her and lay down again at her side. 'Enough,' he laughed. 'You and your "desires" are going to kill me.'

'I am sorry, my lord. I was only following your lead.'

He made an amused sound. 'I'm not sorry, but I am tired.'

Sybilla drew breath to answer him, but then changed her mind. There was a note of finality in his voice suggesting he would not welcome further conversation, and besides, she was weary too, and even more sore. She wondered as she closed her eyes if she had conceived and laid her hand lightly over her belly. So much the better

308

if she had because it would give her position in the house-hold added lustre, Patrick would be delighted at the notion of an heir of Salisbury blood for Ludgershall, and she suspected her new husband would not be displeased either.

Awake in the early morning, John glanced at Sybilla who was still fast asleep, curled round the bedclothes like a squirrel in a drey. Her hair spilled around her shoulders in a rich brown tangle and her face was flushed in slumber. She had dense, dark eyelashes, a sweetly curved mouth and beautiful skin. She was gorgeous. Remembering her explosive howl of 'Holy God!' and knowing there was no artifice involved, that it was entirely spontaneous, he was filled with a mixture of tenderness and lust. Once she was more experienced, he suspected that the fillip of her innocence would be replaced by a natural talent and curiosity that would keep him up to the mark for a long time. He had kept the light too and she hadn't been embarrassed about uncovering herself or worried that taking pleasure was sinning.

Smiling, he moved quietly from the bed to the chamber-pot to relieve himself. It was also refreshing that he could talk to her on the same level that he would talk to Benet or Jaston and not have her look as blank as a sheep or wring her hands in fear. Not since Damette had he encoun-tered the enticing combination of femininity and mascu-line forthrightness in a woman. But she was younger than Damette and less marked by the world. She still had it in her to be moulded, and he was the one who would do that moulding. Glancing over his shoulder again, through the parted bed curtains, he thought that this just might be the marriage he should have had in the first place.

29

Hamstead, Berkshire, Autumn 1144

John and Sybilla moved from Ludgershall to Hamstead, and over the ensuing weeks, as the summer advanced into autumn, she was kept very busy about her new domain. She ripped down the moth-chewed hangings in the bedchamber, replacing them with good ones of heavy wool that would give privacy and keep out the cold. She had fresh plaster applied to the walls and employed an artist from Winchester to paint a frieze of green scrolls and delicate spring flowers. Beneath the frieze, she put up her own hangings, brought as part of her trousseau. A brightly painted marriage coffer went under the window. An ivory chess set that had been a marriage gift from a vassal was placed on a table under the light from a candle sconce, together with a merels board and dice. She had the floors scrubbed and swept. Everywhere was purged, scoured and renewed until she felt that it belonged to her and not Aline.

The servants grumbled at first. Under Aline's regime, they had been accustomed to do as they wished and had neglected their duties. Sybilla discovered petty stealing in the kitchens and dismissed the culprits forthwith. She spoke sternly to the steward and made it clear that as a new brush, she was sweeping clean, and it was going to stay that way. The dairy horrified her. Aline, apparently, had never set foot in it since the day she became mistress and the place was almost a hovel. The senior dairy maid was decrepit and no longer up to the task, and her subordinates had not received the proper training, nor been inclined to do the work. Sybilla dismissed the elderly woman to a place by the hearth in the kitchen to watch the fire and undertake general stirring and simmering duties. Then she rolled up her sleeves, directed the other women, and set to work.

Yet she was no termagant, nor did she hold grudges. Yesterday was done and today was new. Once everyone realised that young and pretty did not equate to feather-headed and gullible and that the new mistress had a ready smile, an impish sense of humour, and was prepared to work as hard as she expected everyone else to, they settled to the yoke and began pulling together instead of bulking in the stall.

Despite being busy about her duties, Sybilla took the time to pay attention to her new husband. She quietly got to know his preferences and dislikes – when it was best to leave him alone and when he was likely to be receptive; when he wanted to talk and when he didn't. She strove to please him, but not slavishly. She would have the respect that was her due and not be taken for granted and she would be mistress in her own domain. John had seemed amused by her air of propriety, but he had neither belittled nor patronised her. He had upheld her rule and let her deal with matters domestic as she saw fit.

On the morning after their wedding, he had presented her with a key to the strongbox. When she had looked at him askance, he had shrugged and smiled. 'Now's your

311

chance to run away,' he had said. Sensing the tension beneath his flippancy, she had taken the key and threaded it around her neck on the same cord as her cross.

'Why should I do that, when I know where I'm well off!' she had answered with a mischievous gleam. Her gaze on his, she had slowly tucked the cross and key down inside her gown, the obvious inference being that they would lie between her breasts.

Patrick, entering the chamber looking rather the worse for wear after a long night's carousing, had stared at the pair of them with bleary eyes. John's smile had become a conspiratorial laugh. 'Strangely enough, I believe you!' he had said.

The marriage bed was a joy to Sybilla for John aroused a hunger within her that had been so long suppressed it was ravenous. She would watch his hands at practical tasks – reining his horse, wielding his sword, holding his knife to cut food – and would think of their tactile eloquence on her body. She would stare at his wonderful hard mouth that could be as subtle as silk, think of the knowing point of his tongue, and shiver with lust. She was also learning what he liked in the bedchamber and suspected that poor Aline must have been completely out of her depth when faced with such sensual intensity. His appetite was carnal but so was Sybilla's and she found it pure pleasure to dine.

If the memory of Aline's presence was no more than a wispy ghost that Sybilla sought determinedly to expunge from hall and bower as efficiently as she removed the strands of cobwebs from corner and rafter, then the sons of that first marriage were a different matter. Her heart had gone out to them – lost little boys of ten and six, as wary as two starving stray dogs cowering near the kitchen door and hoping for scraps. She could sense their frightened hostility at having to accept their father's new wife as their stepmother and was not surprised. Having witnessed their mother being bundled off into the custody of the Church and being told that she and their father had never been married in the eyes of that Church was bound to have repercussions. Their stability had been shattered.

John, she saw, was uneasy around his sons, and obviously felt guilty about the effect the annulment had had upon them. However, he was determined to do the best he could for them and was looking to engage tutors and bring their education up to scratch. 'I have neglected their instruction for far too long,' he had confided in her. 'I should never have left them in their mother's keeping, knowing what she was like. I can only hope there's still time to rectify the damage.'

A great deal had gone unsaid and Sybilla had chosen not to probe, sensing that she wouldn't get very far. She had noticed how his horses, his men, his equipment were of the best and how he demanded the full effort from everyone – as he demanded it of himself. His sons were an extension of him – the future – and she suspected he was troubled at their lack of spark.

In between all the bustle of cleaning and sprucing at Hamstead, Sybilla brought the boys into the bower to sort out some fabric to make them new tunics. The cloth had come with her from Salisbury with her trousseau. She had quietly raided one of the livery cupboards before she left, reasoning that the end bolts of green and rust-red twill had been there long enough and she had more need of them than Patrick did.

Her women spread the fabrics across a trestle and she set about measuring her stepsons. Gilbert eyed her warily from under his fringe and the younger one kept thinking about sucking his thumb, then remembering he wasn't supposed to.

313

'I hope you will learn to trust me and know you can come to me if you need anything,' Sybilla said as she worked, making knots in the cord to mark arm length and neck-to-hem dimensions. 'I may not be your mother, but your father is now my husband and you are his boys; therefore you are my boys too, and I will care for you as best I can.' Finished, she handed the cords to Gundred, then beckoned Gilbert and Walter to follow her to the marriage coffer. 'I have something for you.' She produced a couple of leather slings and some smooth polished white stones with which to practise.

'I have no doubt your father can use one because he knows every weapon skill back to front, but I warrant I could still show him a trick or two . . . and so could you if you train.'

Gilbert's eyes widened. 'You can use a slingshot?'

She smiled. 'Why shouldn't I? When I was a little girl it was my task to keep the birds off the tender plants in my mother's garden with one of these and I always had it with me when I walked the dogs.' The smile became a laugh at their faces, which could not have worn more astonishment had she suddenly grown two heads. 'I can use a bow too; I'm quite good at archery.'

The boys exchanged glances. 'What about a sword?' Gilbert challenged.

She shook her head. 'Oh, not one of them. I leave that to you men.' She spoke in a tone designed to salve and flatter their masculine pride. 'Go and practise now in the ward while I see to the cutting of your tunics. I'll join you in a while.'

Heads together, whispering, they left the room. Still smiling, but with pensive eyes, Sybilla turned to her task. Moments later John arrived, munching on an apple he had purloined from one of the orchard baskets in the

314

ward. 'Eating out of your hands,' he said with a glance back over his shoulder towards the stairway.

She pursed her lips. 'Not quite, but getting there . . . although in a moment I am going to have to prove that I can use a slingshot.'

'And can you?' His good eye gleamed.

She nodded. 'My father taught me when I was little. I used to be good, but I haven't practised in a while.' She stuck her tongue in the side of her cheek. 'Of course trebuchets are much more interesting.'

John started to grin. 'Trebuchets?'

'I was older then of course. We didn't have much recourse to those sorts of weapons when old King Henry was alive – although perhaps you did.'

'Not that much, but I've had plenty of experience since,' he said drily. 'It's useful to know my wife can man one though, should it ever come to a siege.'

She made a small sound of amusement and turned back to the sewing trestle.

'There's news arrived from court,' he said after a moment.

Sybilla inserted a pin into the cloth and faced him again.

'The Norman lords have bowed to the Empress's husband and offered him Normandy. Whatever Stephen does he cannot get it back; it's too great an undertaking.'

He was watching her with that same cautious look she had just seen in his eldest son's gaze. Sybilla felt as if she was being tested and that her reply was somehow important. 'So Stephen won't be able to call on Normandy for resources,' she said, 'but he'll be able to put what he has into holding England. Should we brace ourselves for assaults on our castles?'

She must have said the right thing, because his tension

eased. 'I think we should, although they're all primed anyway. Stephen will constantly be looking to the coast for the threat of an invasion.'

'So my trebuchet skills may be invaluable.'

He gave a soft laugh. 'Ah Sybilla, you are priceless.'

She narrowed her eyes.

He sobered. 'Oh, I mean it. You are beyond rubies, believe me.'

Comprehension dawned. He had been waiting to see if she showed interest or understanding and had been preparing for her to look at him with the vapid stare of a sheep, or start twittering with fear. 'I do believe you,' she said with a mischievous smile. 'So you might as well tell me the rest.'

'How do you know there is more?'

'I'm guessing ahead with loaded dice.'

He looked both amused and wry. 'Then you have two sixes. I've to go to court. Things change quickly. Even with word from my deputies, I have to see for myself from time to time.'

She nodded briskly and again saw him react with relief. Aline, she remembered, had always feared his absences. Sybilla didn't particularly desire to see him gone, but she wasn't afraid. She was accustomed to running a household and could find plenty to keep her occupied while she waited for his return. With that in mind, she asked his leave to visit Salisbury.

'Are you pining for your brother already? Is life here so bad?' His tone held a sudden sharp undercurrent.

She made a face at him. 'It would serve you right if I said yes to both, but the truth is I need more needles and thread. All this sewing is eating up supplies. There's almost no linen either.' She didn't add that the fabric she had brought with her was almost all gone and that there had

316

been virtually nothing in store, with what there was being of poor quality. She would not denigrate Aline aloud, no matter her private thoughts on the matter.

'I will begin to think you profligate,' he said with a straight face.

She made an indifferent gesture. 'It is up to you if you desire yourself and your retainers to walk around in rags. Once the initial sewing has been done, there will be less outlay. I know the men have to be paid first and your castles kept in good repair.' She came to him, removed the apple from his hands and took a juicy bite from the other side. 'My lord,' she added pertly.

John pulled her against him. Ignoring the presence of her women, he nuzzled her throat. 'If I didn't have matters to attend to . . .'

She swallowed, laughed and set her arms around his neck. 'You would do what?'

'Put you on that table and swive you until you screamed,' he growled against her earlobe.

Sybilla rubbed playfully against him, fully aware of the effect she was having on him, before pulling reluctantly away. 'Entertaining,' she said, 'especially if your sons should return – and my women would never be able to look me in the face again or cut cloth on that table without smirking . . . although if you wish to render your debt then it is my duty to comply.' She gave him a coquettish look through her lashes as she handed the apple back to him. She was as aroused as he was, but knew it would go no further than teasing. They both had duties more pressing, if less pleasurable. 'Besides, I'm expecting a visit from my chaplain, and it would make confession interesting, don't you think? It is one thing to confess to the sins of lust and fornication, quite another for your priest to have witnessed you indulging in those sins.'

317

'It's not a sin if one is intent on procreation.'

Sybilla smiled and put her hand to her flat belly. 'What if the intent has already been fulfilled?'

His gaze quickened. 'Are you telling me that you are with child?'

'I don't know, but perhaps. I should have had my flux by now and I haven't.'

'Are you sick?'

She shook her head. 'No, but my mother never was with any of us.'

John gave her a considering look. 'Then while you are uncertain, it is not a sin.' He glanced round as one of his knights entered the chamber in search of him, followed by the chaplain. 'Still, it's a moot point for the moment.' He gave her a laconic half-smile. 'Patrick said you were good breeding stock.'

Sybilla made a face at him. 'I was an innocent virgin. He didn't tell me what you were.'

He laughed softly.

The priest was almost upon them and Sybilla moderated the exchange before she caused the poor man embarrassment. 'So, do I have your leave to go to Salisbury to buy what I need?'

'As you wish.' He kissed the back of her hand in formal fashion, placed another kiss on the tender inside of her wrist, and took his leave with a pointed glance at the trestle as he did so.

Sybilla swallowed a giggle and, touching the imprint of the second kiss, tried to give her attention to Father Geoffrey and a discussion about the distribution of alms at the castle gate.

30

Devizes, Wiltshire, Autumn 1144

Robert of Gloucester looked at John from eyes pouched with weariness – formed not just of the moment, but the result of the drag of a war that had been burning for five long years. 'Ah God, I'm getting old and tired,' he said.

John didn't think it diplomatic to agree. He had been through his own darkness three years ago, but currently felt as if he were in the springtime of his life rather than the autumn . . . but then Sybilla had a lot to do with that. He only had to imagine her waiting in his bed, smiling at him, her rich hair spilling around her shoulders, and all was well with the world – even if outside his jurisdiction it patently wasn't.

'We have Normandy,' he said, 'and Normandy is the key. Without it, Stephen is cut off from support and resources.'

'That means he is free to concentrate his efforts on England – pull back the mercenary companies he had over there and make fresh assaults on us here.'

John had seldom heard Robert sound so depressed. Perhaps it was the result of the rain slamming against the shutters and the damp day aggravating his joints. But then ever since his capture at Stockbridge he had been more reticent and circumspect. Although he had continued to fight, something had gone out of him on that day and his flame no longer burned with the same zeal. 'Yes, he can concentrate his efforts here, but we can now harry him from Normandy and plan an invasion unhampered by his presence there.'

Robert gave a drained smile. 'Ah, you are right, John. Pay no heed to me. I didn't sleep well. My head is filled with wool when I need it to be clear. If we can only hang on a few years more, Henry will be ready for kingship. He's eleven now – past halfway, and has brothers following close in his wake should it be necessary.'

'Stephen has sons too,' John pointed out.

'They won't be a match for Henry. I tell you, that boy is formidable.'

John received the impression Robert didn't want to imagine the war continuing in the next generation. He didn't either. Putting himself in jeopardy was one thing. Imagining Gilbert and Walter in the thick of some of the fighting he had seen froze his marrow. They would not survive. Robert's own sons, of fighting age, were already deeply committed, Philip in particular. He had been at the forefront in the now notorious battle of Wilton and was currently involved in harrying the garrison at Oxford from the new keep of Faringdon of which he was constable.

John considered it interesting that Robert was thinking in terms of Henry rather than the Empress. Of late, there was a tacit understanding, even among the men most loyal to her, that she would not become Queen. No one dared speak such blasphemy aloud though. It was all clandestine.

Leaving Robert to his business, he set about his own

duties, but was accosted by another lord – Stephen de Gai, Robert's uncle. He was an accomplished warrior, taciturn, but courteous enough when he chose to speak. His first wife had died over a year ago, and his sons were grown.

'My lord?' John said politely.

De Gai studied him from beneath craggy silver brows 'My nephew must have spoken to you at the time of your ... ah ... annulment concerning my interest in your former wife.'

'He mentioned it in passing.' John eyed him slightly askance. 'Forgive me; have you ever seen or spoken to Aline before?'

'Not often, but on occasion, my lord. I have always thought her a charming, dutiful lady.'

'Indeed, duty means much to her,' John said, cultivating a bland expression.

'Do you have objections?'

'Why should I? She is no longer married to me and the Church has responsibility for her now.'

'But you still have an interest through your sons. I suppose it will matter to them who their mother remarries.'

'I foresee no trouble in that area,' John replied. 'You are uncle to the Earl of Gloucester and that is a fine kinship bond that will stand them in good stead in the future. Were I to make any caveats, I would ask you if you were certain you desired this match?'

De Gai gave John a shrewd look. 'I am not looking for a mettlesome young thing or for good bed sport and a bevy of heirs. I already have my children. Naturally if sons and daughters should come of the match, I will be pleased to provide for them, but what I mainly desire is companionship at my hearth.'

321

John was torn between being thoroughly candid and holding back. Perhaps de Gai and Aline were ideally suited. Who was he to say? An older man would indulge her, and not expect of her what she could not perform.

'Then I wish you well,' he said, 'but make sure she has women around her who are honest and competent in household matters. Aline was never one to bother about moths in the clothing chests or seasoning in the food. But if you want a wife who is dutiful, loyal and devout, she will serve you well.'

De Gai smiled. 'I see your reservations, my lord. If I were a younger man, I might heed them, but at my age, my needs are different; nor am I the active warrior I used to be. I hazard she will be more settled with me than she ever was with you.'

John stiffened for an instant, but then the humour of the situation struck him and he swallowed a smile 'I think she probably will,' he said. 'And I wish you well of your courtship.'

Aline had returned to Clyffe. Bishop Robert had deemed it better for her to dwell on her own lands where she had been born and raised than be held among strangers at Exeter. She had not protested, for it seemed a sensible move and, besides, she felt as helpless as a straw in the wind. She had neither the energy nor the will to fight what was set upon her.

She was still struggling to come to terms with the shocking detail that her marriage had been a lie – that it had never existed in the eyes of God. She still found it hard to believe even though she had seen the documents confirming she and John were related within the prohibited degree. She felt as if she had been punished and pulverised for a sin she was unaware of having committed

322

until now, and it hurt. If she thought about it for too long, her stomach would begin to ache, the tears would come and she would make herself ill.

She hadn't spoken to John – their last communication had been his letter concerning the annulment – but she had heard about his swift remarriage to Sybilla of Salisbury. During her less charitable moments, she thought of the girl as a brazen slut, but that was just the anger and hurt surfacing. Doubtless Sybilla had had no say in the matter and was as much a straw in the wind as herself. The notion of Sybilla sharing John's life, however, when she had been shut out of it, was painful. Not that she had ever done much sharing with John. They had lived separate lives side by side. But she still missed the sight of him in her peripheral vision. Sometimes she thought it was her own fault she had lost him. She had admired his beauty and God had punished her shallowness by marring it for ever. She had loved him and been proud to be his wife, and now God had taken that too, leaving only the raw ache where her life had been torn out and discarded like old straw on a midden heap.

She was feeding grain to the pigeons outside the turreted loft beyond the stables when the visitors clopped into the ward. Her first instinct was to hide in the loft until they had gone, but someone was bound to come looking for her, and what excuse could she make? Besides, it might be word from John. The empty grain bowl clasped to her breast like a shield, she crept up the path to the stable yard.

Amid an entourage of servants and clerics, she saw the Bishop himself. Beside him, a big man wearing spurs and sword was dismounting from a chunky roan cob. His white hair and beard stood out against a face brown from the summer sun and his gaze was shrewd as he swept it around

323

the stable yard and handed the reins to his squire. He looked vaguely familiar. Timidly, Aline went forward to greet them and knelt to kiss Bishop Robert's ring. He had been a rock of support during the early days of the annulment and she was pleased to see him – if anxious at the same time.

He raised her to her feet and presented her to his companion. 'Daughter, this is Stephen de Gai, uncle to the Earl of Gloucester.'

She curtseyed to him and gestured to the empty bowl. 'Forgive me, I was feeding the pigeons.'

'To make them plump for the table?' de Gai asked with a smile.

She shook her head and looked down. 'Not really. I like doing it. I don't eat much meat. Will you come within?' She made a flustered gesture in the direction of the hall, hoping the wine was up to scratch, knowing it probably wasn't.

The Bishop didn't say why he had come to Clyffe, but accepted her halting offer of dinner. He prayed with her and spoke comforting words, while de Gai wandered round the hall, looking in the corners, speaking to the servants, and accustoming himself to his surroundings. She saw him remove his swordbelt and lay it across the dais table. There was an echo of John in the movement and it tumbled her stomach. Belatedly she sent for water so the men could wash their hands and faces.

She thought once they had dined they would be on their way, but they displayed little inclination to leave. Aline began dreading that they might want to stay for the night, which would mean airing bed linen and stuffing mattresses and she didn't know where to start. Plus she would have to provide them with another meal and that would take thinking about as well.

324

While the Bishop was busy talking to one of his clerks, de Gai drew Aline aside to a bench before the hearth. 'My lady, you probably realise there is a purpose in our visit here to you, beyond the social.'

Aline gave a small, anxious nod. 'Yes, but I cannot imagine what you want – unless it is Church business?' She fiddled with her prayer beads.

'In a way it is, since Bishop Robert is officially your guardian. My lady . . . I wish to make you an offer of marriage.'

Whatever Aline had been expecting, it wasn't this and she gasped aloud.

'I know it is sudden, but these are harsh times for an unmarried woman. If you are willing to accept my protection, I would be honoured.'

She felt the world start to wobble and lose its focus. She didn't know what to say or do.

'My wife died a year ago,' said de Gai. 'I would welcome a companion at my hearth. You are still young and it would be a pity to think your life is over for the sake of what has gone before. The Bishop has no objections and when I spoke to your former husband, he seemed pleased.'

She swallowed. 'You . . . you have talked to John?' A pang shot through her stomach and loins.

'I saw him at court at Devizes. He spoke of your loyalty and duty.'

She bit her lip. The words were like thorns. 'It was all in vain though,' she said. 'It didn't stop him from casting me off, or our marriage being a sin against God.'

'There are no ties of consanguinity between us,' de Gai said gently. 'And his loss will be my gain.'

Aline looked down and tried to think. What choice did she have? If she refused him, other suitors would come sniffing around. He seemed decent enough, and if he was the Bishop's first choice, then she ought to take him. She had been lonely and frightened for a long time – even before the dissolution of her marriage to John. She didn't have the courage to ride the whirlwind even while she admired its fierce, elemental beauty. Dear Virgin, what should she do? Her voice stuck in her throat. She couldn't say yes, she couldn't say no. She tugged on her prayer beads, willing an answer. *Maria Regina . . . salve . . . salve . . .* The string suddenly snapped in a shower of golden bees. Aline stared at the dangling mouse tail of waxed string in her hands, and then at the beads strewn far and wide, no longer in order but scattered, reflecting the chaos of her mind. One had landed in de Gai's lap. He brushed it off on to the floor, his expression impassive.

'Leave them,' he said when she reached to pick them up. 'I will buy you new ones as a marriage gift.' He held out his hand.

With trembling fingers, Aline slowly passed him the cord and the few remaining beads still strung on it. Her prayer, it seemed, had received a reply.

Sybilla moved among the booths and stalls of Salisbury Fair, surveying the goods on offer with a critical eye and enjoying herself. There was money in her pouch, for John, despite some pithy remarks about the ruinous spending abilities of frivolous young wives, had spoken with actions rather than words and endowed her with a generous purse. As an exchequer official with a shrewd fiscal brain, he was good at balancing what came into his coffers against what went out and, unlike some of his colleagues, was not in dire financial straits.

Sybilla was now certain of her pregnancy. She had been married for ten weeks and there had been no sign of her flux. She felt queasy on rising, although nothing that debilitated her, and her breasts were swollen and tender. Uncertain if she would come to Salisbury again before the birth, she was making the most of what the stalls had to offer. She had bought fine linen chansil to make chemises, shirts, braies and swaddling bands. Silver needles in different sizes; skeins of thread. Ribbons and braid; bolts of woollen twill in forest green and the night-sky blue that so suited her husband. She had visited a wood carver to commission a cradle. Gilbert and Walter had accompanied her around the booths, their eyes growing wider with each successive sight and stall. Her gentle questions brought forth the detail that they had seldom left the family castles or manors. Salisbury was not large when compared with Winchester, but even so, the thriving stalls and urban atmosphere were a novelty to them for although they had visited the city on occasion with their mother, their destination had always been the cathedral, never the traders' quarter.

Sybilla bought them each a knife with a fine leather scabbard to go with the new shoes and tunics they were wearing, and pieces of jaw-gluing gingerbread from a cookstall – something they had never sampled before. Remembering her own childhood pleasure in the confection, Sybilla smiled at their delight and wondered anew and a little sadly at their lack of awareness of the world around them. It was almost as if they had spent their days asleep and had only just awoken.

At midday, she brought her spruced-up stepsons to the cathedral: another reason for their presence with her in Salisbury today. She had considered sending the boys to this appointment with a serjeant and retiring to wait for them at the castle, but it would have been unfair to them and cowardly on her part. Better to face the moment, get it over with, and go forward from here.

A small wedding party had assembled in the cathedral porch. The groom was a wide-shouldered portly knight of about three-score years, with silver hair and beard. A younger man who bore him a strong resemblance stood at his right shoulder. Facing him was Aline, wearing her customary blue dress and white wimple. A plain cross on a leather cord hung around her neck. She was accompanied by the Bishop of Exeter and the ceremony was about to be conducted by Joscelin de Bohun, Bishop of Salisbury. A deacon, two clerks and two chaplains were also present, plus a scattering of passers-by, drawn to the sight of a wedding. Quietly Sybilla joined the party, ushering Gilbert and Walter before her.

Aline raised her head from contemplation of the ground and saw her sons. She gave a small indrawn gasp and her gaze widened. Then it fixed on Sybilla and a flush mounted her previously pallid cheeks. Sybilla said nothing. Lowering her own gaze, she stepped back, feeling awkward. The bridegroom nodded brusquely to Gilbert and Walter and, giving them a half-smile of welcome, directed them to stand at their mother's side.

The wedding ceremony was brief. De Gai placed a ring on her finger, gave her the traditional gold coin and they spoke their vows. There followed a mass inside the church before the altar where Sybilla saw de Gai glancing at his new wife indulgently, as a parent might at a favoured child.

Emerging from the church afterwards, Sybilla curtseyed to Aline and de Gai. 'My lord, Lady Aline, I am pleased for you both.'

Aline looked at the ground and murmured something indistinct.

De Gai inclined his head to Sybilla. 'You received my message then.'

'Yes, and I thank you,' she replied. 'As the Empress's marshal, my lord has duties in the field and at court, but he desired his sons to be present as witnesses to your marriage.'

Visibly struggling with the social awkwardness of the situation, Aline made an effort and turned to the boys. She reached out, stroked their hair, embraced them, but Sybilla saw that it was superficial. Aline's concern was with her own emotion, not theirs. Gilbert endured it. Walter did too, but returned to Sybilla's side as quickly as he could and slipped his hand through hers, seeking reassurance.

Sybilla felt pity for Aline, but tempered with irritation. She would not have been so meek and biddable had the circumstances been reversed. Indeed, she would have fought every step of the way, but then Aline did not have that kind of fire in her nature. Sybilla could understand how a man of John's strong personality would find marriage to Aline like being shackled to a sack of wet sand, and how Aline, timid and God-fearing, would find John with his high standards, his pragmatism and his vital masculinity an equally difficult prospect.

Saddened, Sybilla turned away, determined that if she bore daughters, she would raise them to be confident and aware of their worth. She would fight tooth and nail to secure them well-suited marriage partners. If her womb brought forth sons, she would find them compatible wives in more than just terms of landed wealth. She squeezed Walter's hand in hers and gave him a reassuring smile. The future had to be made better than the past – for the sake of everyone concerned.

329

31

Hamstead, Berkshire, March 1145

John's third son entered the world on a wet, windy morning at the end of Lent. The labour was hard work, but progressed smoothly throughout the night and Sybilla delivered the baby without difficulty an hour after dawn. He cried the moment he emerged from the womb and he was a good healthy colour and size.

'A son for Ludgershall,' Sybilla said to John with proud delight when he came to view the baby. 'He has your nose.'

John studied his third heir. Babies always resembled skinned rabbits and this one was no different. He had the sense not to say so to his wife, who was looking immensely pleased with herself, and radiant to say she'd been in labour for twelve hours. Her rich hair lay in a loose braid spilling over one shoulder and her eyes were aglow. Indeed, it was an auspicious occasion: the birth of a son to crown this second marriage. 'He's a fine lad,' he said dutifully.

'How do you wish him named?'

He shrugged. 'I have no preference ... except not Patrick. I have no quarrel with your brother at present, but I'd rather not see a lord of that name at Ludgershall when I am gone.'

She gave him a thoughtful look. 'Then he must be named John, because when you are gone, and pray God it is not for a long time to come and this little one grown to manhood, there will still be a John Marshal at Ludgershall.'

He gave a delighted laugh at her comment and came around the bed to kiss her.

'I know,' she said, sensing his pleasure as well as seeing it. 'I am priceless!'

Sybilla did not remain in her chamber for long after childbirth. She was young, strong and impatient to be about the manor and outside as the days lengthened and the spring took hold. The baby was thriving and plumping out, becoming less of a rabbit and more of a pink silk cushion. John said little enough about his new son and didn't pay that much attention to the infant, preferring to leave him to the women, but she did notice him casting proprietorial glances into the cradle when passing, and if he was around when his namesake was being bathed in the large latten basin in the bedchamber, or nursed, he would often pause to watch.

In May, Sybilla's churching took place at Ludgershall. The ceremony was held to give thanks for her survival of the ordeal of childbirth. It was a recognition of her motherhood, and a cleansing ritual to welcome her back into society. She came to Saint Mary's wearing a new gown of dark-red wool embellished with seed pearls. She also wore a belt that John had given her. Set with twelve rubies in token of the private jest between them, it emphasised her narrow waistline. Six weeks of feeding a hungry baby had almost restored her figure to its previous proportions and she carried her candle of thanksgiving to the altar with the grace of a young queen. Patrick attended

331

the ceremony and briefly held his new nephew along one broad forearm.

'John,' he said with a look between his sister and the baby. 'I should have expected no less.' He looked both annoyed and amused.

Sybilla smiled. 'It was my choice,' she said. 'My husband gave me the naming.'

'You are content with him then – after all your fuss before the deed.'

She gave him a severe look. 'If I made a fuss it was because of the way you presented the matter. And yes, I am very content.' She glanced across as John arrived and deliberately gave him a long, melting smile.

She saw the quirk of his mouth corner, the lift of one eyebrow and no longer had to contrive her expression. He slipped his arm around her waist, and the pressure of his fingers over the ruby belt in a private sign of affection and knowing sent a jolt through her compounded of desire and affection.

'You make a good nursemaid, Patrick,' John said with a lazy smile.

'I have every reason to,' Patrick retorted. 'Should anything happen to you, this is the heir to Ludgershall and all my sister's property. As her brother and his uncle, I'll be responsible for their welfare.'

'Fortunate I trust you then,' John replied straight-faced. 'You should beget some sons of your own, or you might find yourself holding your heir as of this moment.'

Patrick's eyes narrowed and he handed his nephew back to John with an abrupt gesture that made the baby squeak. 'Keep him; I intend to,' he snapped, and stalked off to speak with some of the knights.

'Neither of you will ever give in, will you?' Sybilla sighed.

332

The suspicion of a smile still hovered at John's mouth corners. 'We understand each other and that's what matters. We might spar, but the opposition we face is mutual. If it came to the crux, we'd stand side by side.' He regarded the baby in his arms with a thoughtful look. 'It's an interesting notion though . . . a son with the potential to become an earl.'

John walked quietly across the courtyard of Wallingford Castle. It had rained earlier, but now the stars were out between ragged patches of cloud. The downpour had freshened the air and filled it with the green scent of summer. Many folk were abed but he was restless; old habits dying hard. He didn't need the sleep and these quiet times were always good for setting one's mind in order.

He had been reporting to Robert of Gloucester and Brian FitzCount on the number of knights owing service to the Empress and giving them a tally of the wages owed to her mercenaries. Since John was owed two pence on every shilling granted to men in the field, he was keen to keep those tallies up to date. On the morrow he would ride home to see Sybilla and his three sons, then set about finding more men, more horses, more supplies at the best price he could. If making a little stretch to the horizon was a virtue, then his standing was of the highest, but at some point he knew he would reach the end of his resources and his pedestal would topple.

He had already been threatened with excommunication by the Bishops of Salisbury and Hereford for appropriating men and supplies from their demesne lands. As far as he was concerned, that particular sanction had been used so often to belabour 'sinners' that it was more like a smack in the face from a bundle of wet laundry than a clout to bring him to his knees bursting with terrified repentance. It was true the Earl of Essex had been refused burial in sacred ground because of his crimes against the Church, and was currently waiting Judgement Day in a lead coffin up a tree in the grounds of the Temple Church, but John had been in worse places and did not fear such a fate. Besides, there were churchmen other than the Bishops of Hereford, Bath and Salisbury with whom he was on better terms and trusted to intercede for his soul – including the Templars. At least being warriors and protectors of the pilgrim routes, they had a use other than tittle-tattle.

He was near the gate and about to speak to the watchman when he heard the sound of horses approaching. Immediately he was alert. Casual visitors never craved admittance after dusk and those arriving were making too much noise to be sneaking up on the keep. A guard called down from the top of the tower. A reply was shouted up, and an instant later two burly serjeants were pulling the draw bars and opening the gate.

John stared as Robert's youngest son Philip rode into the bailey on a sweating, lathered horse. Stubble rimmed his jaw, his surcoat was torn, his bridle hand was bandaged . . . and his eyes were dead. So were those of the soldiers who rode in after him. Slumped, dejected, exhausted, battle-mauled. There were bodies too, and empty saddles.

Someone went running for the Earl and others hastened to help the wounded down from their mounts. The priest was sent for. A woman jostled through the throng, saw one of the corpses and began to wail. Philip dismounted from his horse and staggered as his feet touched the ground. John caught his arm and steadied him.

'My father . . .' Philip said and swallowed. His brown

hair hung in lank rats' tails around his face and he stank of sweat. 'I don't . . .' Then his lips compressed. John looked round and saw Gloucester pushing his way through the gathering. His tunic was unbelted and his hair stuck up at one side where he had been lying on it.

'Christ, boy, what's all this?' Robert demanded, looking round at the torchlit chaos of men and horses. 'Is there trouble?'

Philip's throat worked.

'Is Stephen close by? Do we need to prepare for siege?'

Philip shook his head. 'It's nothing like that, Father, I wish it was.' He swallowed. 'I . . . Is there some wine?'

Robert narrowed his eyes at his son, looked around at the men, exchanged glances with John, then, with a brusque nod, brought Philip to the private apartment beyond the hall. When John made to take his leave, Robert bade him remain. 'You're the Empress's marshal,' he said. 'When my son arrives in the middle of the night with wounded and dead men in his tail, these are matters that may concern you.'

John nodded and sat down before the hearth. Philip, despite the fact he was almost ready to fall down, remained standing. Robert handed him a cup of wine. 'Tell me,' he said. 'What has happened?'

Philip took a drink, but his swallow was forced. 'There wasn't anything we could have done,' he said in a rusty voice that didn't belong to a youngster of one and twenty. 'They were all over us. Rather than lose all the men, I decided it was best to withdraw and replenish while I still had the option.'

Robert's expression hardened. 'I take it you were routed by Stephen's men.'

Philip lowered his voice. 'We received a drubbing,' he said.

335

'And why did you come here to lick your wounds and not to Faringdon?' Robert's voice was soft and dangerous now. John's nape prickled.

'Because . . .' Philip raised the hand not holding the cup and rubbed his face, 'because it was at Faringdon they took us. We couldn't sustain the onslaught. We had no choice but to surrender to them.'

John hissed softly through his teeth. Faringdon had cost a great deal of money to build and was strategic to Robert's campaign in the Thames valley. The Earl said nothing, although his cheeks and jaw tightened to show taut grooves of muscle. The silence from him filled the room like air inflating a bladder balloon to bursting point.

'You whore!' Robert exploded at his son. 'Do you know what you have done in selling it to Stephen?' He took a step forward, fists clenched, and struck at the young man.

Philip blocked the descending blow on his raised forearm. 'I had no choice. There were too many of them. Would you rather we had all died?'

'At least I would have been proud!' Robert snarled, braced against his son. 'What use are you to me when I lean on you and you break in two?' He pushed himself away and turned his back, his chest heaving.

Philip was white with shock. 'You don't understand.'

Robert whipped round. 'I understand that you relinquished your charge of Faringdon without so much as an appeal for aid. You were in a strong position. You had the security of a stout palisade around you. You could have withstood a siege for at least two months; you had the supplies. I understand all that. What I do not understand is why you left it?'

'We had to,' Philip said in a voice that shook. 'They were coming at us from all sides and over the top. We

336

couldn't hope to hold them. It was either surrender or death.'

'Then death should have been your choice. You should have stood! I never thought I would have a coward for a son!'

'I am no coward, as well you know, and I will not have you call me one.' The young man jutted his jaw.

'What I see standing before me is a coward,' Robert said through bared teeth. 'Get out of my sight.'

Trembling, Philip drank up, slammed his goblet down on the board and strode out without looking back.

Robert stared at the door as it banged shut behind the young man. Cursing, he strode back and forth across the room like a caged lion. 'Christ, how could he lose Faringdon? How?'

John looked at him sombrely. He was shocked by what he had just witnessed. Robert's troubles were mountainous and a new range of them had just surged out of the ground with Philip's failure to hold Faringdon, but to react thus showed how close to the edge Robert was. 'Inexperience,' he said flatly.

'He's a fledged soldier; he's been in the thick of battle before.'

'But not commanding a keep against a determined foe without senior commanders backing him up. He's only one and twenty.'

'Would you have yielded? I doubt it.'

'At that age I can't say what I would have done. Made mistakes, certainly.'

Robert flashed John a belligerent look. 'You think I was too hard on him?'

'I wouldn't interfere between you and him. He lost Faringdon and he's let you down but he feels he has let himself down even more.'

337

Robert tightened his jaw. 'That is no mitigation. I can't trust him ever again; I can't rely on him.' He let out a hard sigh. 'It's late and I'd rather have my own company to think about this. I'll see you in the morning. We're going to have to sort out what to do next with Faringdon gone.'

John rose to his feet. He said nothing because there was nothing to say that would help the situation. He briefly gripped Gloucester's shoulder and left in silence.

Outside, he discovered that Philip had not just removed himself from his father's sight, but from Wallingford itself, taking his sound knights with him and heading for his other keep at Cricklade. Brian FitzCount had appeared, belatedly summoned from his bed and looking bleary and rumpled.

'What's been happening?' he asked

John gave him a succinct résumé. 'Faringdon lost and the Earl and his son estranged. It's not a good night's news.'

FitzCount looked morose. 'And Faringdon's only thirty miles from here,' he said. 'I had better look to my own walls.'

338

32

Devizes, Christmas 1145

Across the room, John watched Sybilla talking to the
Empress. The latter's smile was unaccustomedly warm as
she listened to what Sybilla was saying.

'I swear that wife of yours could charm the birds out
of the trees,' remarked Gloucester, joining him.

'More than that, she could charm the feathers off them
too,' John answered, quietly proud.

'You sound like a man besotted.'

John waved the comment aside as if it were nothing,
but in fact it struck close to the truth.

Sybilla had wanted to come to the Empress's court at
Devizes for the Christmas season. Their son at nine
months old was now being suckled by a wet nurse and
taking weaning foods, so was not dependent on her. John
had been unsure about bringing her into his domain, but
she had had ways of persuasion that were below the belt
in all senses of the word. Now he was glad he'd capitulated for she was proving an asset. She knew how to handle
people and possessed a natural warmth that put folk at
their ease. She was skilled at drawing smiles and confi-
dences from the reluctant and taciturn and moved through

the world of the court with the glide of an accomplished veteran, rather than a stumbling newcomer. Even the Empress, who was hard to please and not always fond of other women, had warmed to her.

With Matilda, Sybilla had been deferential but not obsequious, adopting a grave air that had almost made John splutter because of the incongruity. Then the smile had left his face as he was struck by an epiphanic moment of deeper emotion that had lodged like a soft ball of light at his core. He suddenly realised that what he had on his hands was not just a delightful, sunny-natured girl who was as keen to be tumbled as he was to tumble her, but a fiercely intelligent woman, subtle and complex. Still innocent, still open-hearted, but no one's fool and equally not one to suffer fools gladly.

'There has been no word from my son,' Gloucester said abruptly, breaking into John's fond contemplation. 'Cricklade might as well be on the other side of the world.'

Making an effort, John gathered his wits and faced the Earl. New lines of worry dragged at the latter's mouth corners and his eyes were sad and tired. 'Can you not send word to him?'

Robert sighed and looked older than ever. 'Many times I have sat down to write to him and just as many have I risen again. I will not beg his forgiveness because he should have held, but I put more on him than he was capable of achieving and that is my fault. I shouldn't have listened to him at the outset but trusted to my own judgement and not given him command of the place. If I was harsh, it was out of my own disappointment that my flesh and blood had failed.'

'If you want to see him, one of you must build a bridge. Perhaps he too has sat down to write and then abandoned the issue.'

340

Robert nodded and agreed, but John sensed a withdrawal in him. He knew the answer but he didn't want to accept it. 'But is it the coward who breaks first, or the strong? Ah John, I tell you I am weary of this. I have a campaign to plan, and my heart sinks at the thought. But if I don't, who will? Too many give me the support they would not give to my sister.'

Later, John strolled back to his lodging house with Sybilla. The air was sharp with frost and the night aglitter with stars. Across the ward, the porter was sitting in his shelter, warming his hands and feet at his brazier.

'The Empress told me you are a fine man,' Sybilla said with a sidelong smile.

John snorted. 'Words are all very well, but I do not suppose she offered you lands and riches to go with them?'

Sybilla nudged his ribs. 'Don't be so sour,' she reprimanded. 'Talking to her now will reap future reward, and why should one not converse for the pleasure of doing so? She gave me a brooch and a silk veil which she need not have done. And she asked after our boys.' She gave a thoughtful frown. 'I think she finds it difficult to show her gentler side lest folk take it for weakness, but she does have one. When she looks at Brian FitzCount she softens like kindled wax.'

'It's an affair of long standing,' he said.

Her eyes widened.

'Ah no, not like that. If they ever took each other to bed, they'd set the sheets afire, but they're both careful of status and propriety; they know what's at stake. The closest they come to adultery is what you have seen and remarked upon.'

'I pity them,' she murmured.

'Don't,' he said. 'They don't pity themselves any more than I pity myself for my blind eye and scarring.'

341

Their conversation was stopped by a pounding on the gate. The porter left his brazier and, with cloak bundled about his body, went to enquire and then pull the bolt. A messenger rode through the postern opening and dismounted from his tired courser. On seeing John and recognising him as a royal official, he came to him and bowed. 'My lord, I have messages for the Empress and the Earl of Gloucester.'

'Urgent news?' John held out his hand for the letters.

The messenger nodded. 'Earl Robert's son, the lord Philip, has given his oath to King Stephen and handed him the keep at Cricklade ... He is ravaging the lands he had a remit to protect.'

John looked down at the packets he was holding and a blank look settled over his face. He dismissed the messenger to the stables and turned back to face the keep. Sybilla laid her hand on his sleeve. 'Oh John.' She caught her lower lip in her teeth.

'Go to bed,' he told her. 'Don't wait up on me; I may be a while ... If you want to spare pity for anyone, then do it for Robert of Gloucester and his son.'

33

Salisbury, July 1146

In response to the fall of Edessa, a new crusade had been called. King Louis of France had announced he would join its ranks and take an army to the Holy Land, together with his young Queen, the vivacious Eleanor, Duchess of Aquitaine. The news had reached England's shores and in every church, cathedral, manor and castle, at every market cross, the word was proclaimed and the cry went out for soldiers to cease fighting their fellow Christians, abandon their petty warring, renounce their sins and head for the Holy Land.

Bishop Joscelin preached a stirring sermon in Salisbury Cathedral, hands outspread and palmed with light from the great painted window at his back. Standing beside John in the nave, Sybilla could feel the tension rippling through her husband. He was like a mettlesome horse just waiting the prick of the spur. She was concerned about how strongly the crusading ideal might strike into a warrior's heart. It wasn't just the absolution from sin that mattered, or the ideal of fighting for one's faith; it was the notion of adventure and pastures new. By his very nature, John was bound to be attracted. Patrick had a gleam in his eye too. He stood with arms folded, head thrown back, listening attentively. Several Templar knights populated the congregation – austere, hard-jawed warrior monks. She had noticed the men giving them admiring glances. It was one thing to be exhorted to join the crusade by a village priest; quite another to be harangued by a bishop and seasoned knights bearing a fierce glamour about their persons. She could see Gilbert and Walter drinking it in too and thanked God they were still children. Women exchanged rueful, worried glances with each other. The Queen of France might be bound Amazon-like on the expedition, but few women present in Salisbury Cathedral were eager to follow her lead or relinquish their men.

Other than the sermon, part of the day's business was the churching of several recent mothers. Sybilla started in surprise as Aline walked up the nave to the altar, bearing her candle of thanksgiving for the safe deliverance of a baby girl. Her expression was quiet and set, like a small wooden mask. Beside her, Sybilla felt John stiffen. Gilbert and Walter looked round at her and their father, the significance not escaping them. They had a half-sister.

Aline knelt, was received and blessed, before returning to her husband who stood at the back of the nave. As she walked, her glance stumbled over John, Sybilla and her sons. Immediately she quickened her pace and looked away.

Following the mass, Patrick wanted to talk to John about the crusade and they were joined by Stephen de Gai, broad, smiling, very much the doting father of the baby girl held in the arms of a maidservant. 'Never had a lass the first time around,' he said smugly, folding his hands around his belt and pushing one foot forward.

At his side, Aline said nothing. She kept her head down

and stood back, a quiet, drab little mouse. Adorning her plain charcoal-grey gown, though, was a magnificent string of rock-crystal prayer beads with a tassel of silver thread and ornate belt hangers. Sybilla ushered the boys forward to greet and kiss their mother and inspect the baby, who was pink, rosy and enchanting. Sybilla admired her. 'Your lord is very proud.'

Aline glanced towards the men. 'He is good to me,' she said in her high-pitched voice, then added with stiff politeness, 'I hear you have a thriving son.'

'I left him at the castle with his nurse,' Sybilla said, 'although perhaps I should have brought him and prayed for his wails to drown out the Bishop's sermon.'

Aline looked shocked, as if Sybilla had uttered blasphemy.

'Bishop Joscelin's far too persuasive. By all means let men take the Cross if they must, but by no means let it be John and Patrick!'

Aline recoiled at the vibrancy in Sybilla's tone, but then inched out of her shell again. 'Stephen won't go.' She cast her husband a relieved look. 'He says his fighting days are over, and he wants to stay at home and protect me and our daughter.'

'Sensible man,' Sybilla said with a rueful glance in the direction of her husband and brother.

'His great-nephew's taking the Cross though. He came to visit the other day and said so.'

Sybilla raised her brows in question and her interest quickened.

'Philip,' Aline said. 'The Earl of Gloucester's son.'

That was very interesting indeed. Sybilla stowed the information in her mind like a bright coin in a purse. With gentle persuasion, she drew other details from Aline until she had the full tale, by which time John and the

345

others had finished their conversation and were ready to leave.

John took Sybilla's arm. 'Aline,' he said, inclining his head towards his former wife in courteous but distant greeting.

'My lord,' Aline answered, dipping him a curtsey in return. Her gaze anxiously sought her husband's and when he came to stand beside her, she leaned on him with obvious relief. Whereas John would have been irritated by such a move, Stephen de Gai merely looked indulgent and smug.

Sybilla waited her moment with John until the evening when they were alone in their private chamber back at Ludgershall. His sons were asleep in the anteroom and the nurse had taken the baby off to his cradle in the women's chamber where she could tend him if he cried.

Having removed her veil, Sybilla sat down beside John on the fleece-covered bench and turned towards him. 'Do you think many will take the Cross?'

'Quite a few, I suspect. Baldwin de Redvers and Waleran of Meulan have already done so, I hear.'

'So has Philip of Gloucester . . .'

He gave her a keen look. 'Indeed?'

'Aline told me. Philip came to visit them and said he was weary of England and heartsick at having to oppose his father all the time. She said he wasn't well either – coughing blood and thin as a lath. De Gai offered to intercede with the Earl, but Philip wouldn't hear of it. He said he had to make peace with his own soul first before he could make it with his father.'

'I am sorry for both of them,' John said with a sad shake of his head. 'They are each ploughing a barren

346

furrow.' He sipped his wine in thoughtful silence and fondled Doublet's silky black ears.

'What about you?' she asked at length. 'The way you and Patrick were talking earlier, I thought you might be lured by the Bishop's words too.'

His lips twitched. 'Aha, so that is what all this is about?'

'All what?'

'You looking at me like that and leaning forward with the neck of your gown unfastened and your veil removed. I know what I have at home, sweetheart, without you having to put your wares on show.' Mischief glinted in his expression. 'I also know what a crusader's vow will offer me.'

Sybilla unfastened a second brooch, lower down on her neck opening, and pulled the confining under-net from her hair. Her braids tumbled down, glossy as polished oak. 'More war,' she said. 'More killing and plundering.'

'Yes, but in the name of God and I receive absolution for my sins.' He pulled her against him and slipped his hand inside her gown, cupping her breast. 'And let's not forget the Saracen women. Henry had a Saracen woman among the court whores at one time.' His voice had fallen to a whisper against her ear and his breath upon her skin made her shiver with arousal. 'Hair as black as a raven's wing and perfumed like roses.'

'And you think all Saracen women are like that?' she rallied and her own hand was suddenly investigative too. 'Jerusalem's a long way to go for exotic futtering. You once told me that all cats were grey at night.'

John gave a congested laugh. 'Ah, sweetheart, they might be, but you're not a cat, unless it be a lioness . . . come to bed and devour me.'

'Well,' Sybilla purred, rising on one elbow to look down at him. 'Are you still as eager to go on crusade?' The fire

347

in the hearth had settled to a soft red glow and the candle was guttering. She traced a lazy forefinger over his chest. Their lovemaking had been fierce, intense and deeply satisfying. He had given her the image with which to fuel her lust and she had used it with abandon, pinning him as if he were indeed her prey, play-biting and teasing him until he was gasping and rigid with the effort of holding on to his control. The knowledge that she could bring him to this had enhanced her own desire, making of it a voracious, carnal thing. She had wrapped herself around him and urged his body into hers, and they had taken each other with leonine ferocity and feline grace.

John chuckled. 'I had no intention of going in the first place, my love. Do you think if I took the Cross there would be anything left for my sons to inherit in the time it took for me to reach Jerusalem and return – even assuming I survived?' He ran his fingers lazily through her hair. 'No, let others go. I will remain a scourge of the Church and take my chance here with you. It can't be any less dangerous . . .'

She bit him again.

34

Bradenstoke Priory, Wiltshire, March 1147

Tears running down her face, Sybilla kissed her father's cold hand, mottled with age spots, shiny with the years of his living. She remembered his warm grip, hard and firm around her small child's fingers, and the way he had held his cup or gestured to make a point. Vigorous, always in motion . . . until he had taken ill. Even after his seizure, his hands had still moved, sometimes with languor, at other times trembling and not in his control, but always in motion. Now they were still and would not move again except by God's command on Judgement Day. At least he had still been alive when she reached Bradenstoke; at least he had been able to see his small grandson and know of the new life she carried in her womb and would bear, God willing, by the time the May blossom budded the trees. She had seen the gleam in his eyes, even if the most he could achieve was to blink one eyelid.

Her tears now were as much for herself as for her father. This passing was a blessed release to him. She knew he had hated the debilitating loss of power, control and esteem. No longer had he been Walter of Salisbury, respected sheriff and castellan, proud of his English blood, but Walter the infirm, Walter the waiting-to-die. He would join her mother and her brother at rest under the chapel floor. One day she would lie here too, and John and their children, down all the years of men to Judgement Day.

The baby kicked vigorously in her womb, speaking of new life. At almost eight months pregnant and soon to retire to her confinement, she was as large as she had been at full term with young John. The child, whether boy or girl, was robust and energetic. Her belly was a constant flourish of movement. With an effort she rose to her feet and immediately John's hand was beneath her elbow, gently assisting her. She put her chin up and wiped her eyes on the heel of her hand. 'He would disdain my tears,' she sniffed, forcing a smile. 'He wasn't like that, and he is in heaven now.' Diffidently she embraced Patrick, who was also at the bedside. The title Earl of Salisbury was now well and truly settled upon his shoulders and already she thought she perceived a new gravitas about him.

Moving with ponderous care, she went outside to the waiting litter which would bear her back to Hamstead. An early March gale tossed the trees which had not yet begun to bud with spring, but remained as stark black branches mossed with green.

Jaston had arrived while they were within the priory and was waiting for them by the litter. She felt John tense at her side. Being within a priory he wasn't wearing his sword, but his hand reached for the non-existent hilt all the same. Sybilla prepared to hear the worst. If Benet had felt the need to send Jaston here from Hamstead, rather than waiting for their return, it must be urgent and something Benet was unable to deal with.

'My lord, there is news. Prince Henry has landed with

a force of mercenaries from Normandy and he's gone to lay siege to Cricklade and Purton.'

'What?' John's brows rose in astonishment. 'Impossible! Where's he got the mercenaries from? His father wouldn't give them to him. Christ's blood, he's fourteen! That's only a year older than Gilbert, and I wouldn't trust him to head a hunting party, let alone cross the sea and lay siege to a castle.'

Jaston's brown gaze filled with anxiety. 'It's true, my lord. The Prince brought them to Marlborough and demanded food and supplies.'

Sybilla felt John begin to vibrate. 'I hope Benet refused,' he said icily.

The knight looked uncomfortable. 'Messire Benet felt it prudent to give him some flour and salt pork . . . and they . . .' Jaston swallowed. 'They took the trebuchet and ten horses.'

John said nothing, but his silence was more telling than a flurry of rage. Then he carefully unclenched his fists. 'The trebuchet and ten horses,' he repeated in a soft voice with a hoarse catch.

'The Prince said he was entitled and Benet thought better to humour him and send to you immediately. He would have taken soldiers and money too, but Benet refused him. He said he had already done enough to get himself hanged on your order.'

'More than enough,' John said. For another instant he remained still, then he shook himself and swung to one of his serjeants. 'Go and fetch Earl Patrick. Sybilla, I'll have an escort bring you home, but I must deal with this now. You will be all right?'

His question demanded only one answer and she gave it with a courageous nod. 'Have a care, my lord,' she said.

He took her face between his hands and kissed her, but

351

although the embrace was genuine, it was that of a man preoccupied with other business. His wife might matter, but so too did a trebuchet and ten horses. Sybilla allowed herself to be helped into the litter with her maids and settled herself against the cushions. The baby continued to kick and surge. So much, she thought, for the midwife's dictum that she ought to think placid thoughts throughout her pregnancy and suffer no undue disturbances. As the litter moved off, she saw Patrick emerge from the church, speak briefly to her husband, and then stride for his horse. John gained the saddle, reined about, and spurred towards the priory gates at a clod-showering canter.

Two hours of hard riding brought John to Marlborough, although his courser almost foundered at the pace he set. Benet was prepared for a verbal flogging, but John had held his temper and was able to see matters from his constable's viewpoint. If the heir to England suddenly arrived on the threshold demanding succour it was foolish to turn him away empty-handed. He was not, however, overjoyed to discover that one of the ten horses was the destrier born of the Spanish mare the Empress had given him. Now a powerful eight-year-old, Aranais was John's favourite stallion. To pursue Henry he had to settle for his second-string grey.

'I did my best to limit the damage, my lord,' Benet apologised as John snatched a cup of wine and chewed down bread and cheese whilst donning his padded tunic, hauberk and sword.

'No, I would have done the same,' John growled. 'Then again, I might just have tied the young idiot across his mount and taken him to his mother and uncle in Devizes to see what they make of this prank. I warrant he doesn't have the funds to pay for a band of mercenaries either.

352

They'll be serving him on high hopes of plunder and that's not good. Men need wages, food and shelter to keep them loyal. The kind that are prepared to follow a youth of fourteen into battle are scarcely going to be reliable, are they?' He made an impatient gesture as he headed for the stairs. 'Send word to Ludgershall and Hamstead. Have all the surrounding farms and villages put on watch. In circumstances like these, friendly foragers are just as likely to drive off the pigs as foes.'

'My lord.'

John strode into the courtyard, set his foot to the stirrup and swung to horse. 'Gentlemen, we have some property to retrieve,' he said, and gave his stallion the spur.

John rode hard for Cricklade, which lay nineteen miles to the north-east of Marlborough, but broke off to camp for the night and rest the horses when he was within striking distance. He discussed the situation with the men and ordered everyone to check their equipment. Around the camp fires, his troop sharpened their swords and axes, inspected shield straps and talked with desultory cama-raderie. John was still astonished that Henry was here at all. Fourteen years old – barely of squiring age. He kept trying to imagine his son Gilbert in a similar position and failing. Either Henry was entirely precocious for his age, or they were all in deep water.

By dawn, John had the camp fire doused and once more set out at a brisk pace. As they approached Cricklade, the scent of smoke veered in the wind and they heard shouts and the clash of fighting. At the roadside, the skeletal remains of a dwelling thrust charred wooden bones towards the sky. A bucket lay on its side beside the well and the ground was trampled and reddened. Too much blood for a human, probably cow, John thought, absorbing the detail with one part of his mind, while the other focused on the sounds ahead of them. He thrust his left hand through his shield grip and braced his lance. God knew what they would find, but the chances were they were going to have to fight.

They came upon the castle and the sight of soldiers battling on the open ground before its gates, or rather, John discerned, men being routed and giving battle as they tried to grab their baggage and flee. His trebuchet was there and John noticed a particularly vicious swirl of combat around it. A slight figure, waving a sword, was trying to control John's Spanish stallion. He was yelling something in a cracked, adolescent bellow – attempting to rally his troops, who were ignoring him. John fastened his aventail across his jaw, signalled to Jaston at his left shoulder, levelled his lance and spurred the grey.

Prince Henry turned at the thunder of hooves, fear leaping in his eyes. He had been so busy doing one thing that he hadn't noticed the approach of the new force. Had John been the enemy, he could have taken the lad on the point of his lance and ended everything there and then with a single thrust. Instead he pounded past Henry with a bellow of *'Maréchal, Maréchal, Dex ai le Maréchal!'* and brought down a serjeant who was chasing one of the fleeing men.

'Maréchal!' Jaston howled in response as he smashed aside another serjeant with his mace and ploughed after John. The fighting renewed around the trebuchet as John's troop engaged hard and took command of the situation. John threw down his lance and took up his own mace for close-in work. The aim was to crush, to disable, to over-power. Trusting Jaston to stay on his blind left side and deal with any assault from that periphery, he attacked hard. Knowing that attitude was as important as ability

354

at a moment like this, he used himself and the snapping, kicking horse to instil fear in his opponents. As he roared his battle cry again, pricked his grey into a rear and struck with the mace, they broke. A horn sounded the retreat and the knights of Cricklade's garrison disengaged and ran for the safety of the keep.

'Hold!' John roared as a couple of over-eager men gave chase. 'Hold, you dolts. Ware their archers!'

Even as the men pulled back, a sally of arrows hissed overhead, plummeting short by a whisker.

John reined the grey around and rallied his men. 'Get this dismantled – fast as you can,' he snapped, gesturing to the trebuchet, and trotted over to Henry, who had removed his helm and coif and was staring at John with flushed face and bright eyes. His red hair stood up in flaming tufts and an embryo copper moustache fuzzed his upper lip. Beneath him, John's stallion Aranais sidled and stamped.

'You should have arrived earlier, my lord,' Henry said with a defiant thrust of his chin. 'We might have taken the castle then.'

John could feel his temper hammering in his skull with each stroke of his heart. He had never been so furious in his life. 'With what, sire?' he snarled. 'The men defending it are seasoned troops, battle-hardened in the forge of war. Do you think a single trebuchet, a straggle of mercenaries led by a stripling and my personal conroi are going to unseat them? God's cock, you're lucky they didn't take you prisoner and hang you in chains from the keep walls. It's what I'd have done were I their commander. Nor am I at your beck and call. I'm here to retrieve my trebuchet and my horses, including my destrier.' He gestured to Aranais. 'Are these all your men . . . including the ones I saw running into the forest?' Behind him, the

355

rapid chunk of mallets on wood told him his soldiers were dismantling the trebuchet.

Henry glowered at him. 'I sent a detail to Purton.' His jaw worked. 'Someone has to do something,' he burst out. 'You all need stirring up.'

'Well, you've certainly poked your stick into an ants' nest, sire. What your mother and uncle are going to say, I don't know, but I can guess.'

To his credit, Henry dismounted from Aranais and held out the reins. Not that John felt like giving him credit at the moment. A good thrashing was the mildest of his notions. 'How much are you paying this rabble?' he asked as he made the exchange, settled himself in the saddle and ran his hand down Aranais's powerful silver shoulder.

Henry compressed his lips and said nothing. 'I thought so.' John nodded. 'Unless you keep them happy, they'll evaporate like autumn mist in sunshine. If you ask men to give their lives, then you pay them well and you attend to their welfare.'

'They're promised their wages,' Henry said sulkily.

'Out of what, sire? Your gains?' John gave him a scathing look. He glanced over his shoulder at the castle. Jeers and insults were being hurled at them from the ramparts. 'Come. I'll escort you to your mother's court at Devizes.'

Henry gave a stubborn shake of his head. 'My troops at Purton could have taken the victory.'

John took up the reins. 'We'll soon find out, won't we?' he said with heavy scepticism.

35

Hamstead Marshal, Berkshire, April 1147

Sybilla clenched her teeth, gathered her strength and bore down. The contraction was extremely painful and progress slow. She knew the child was large and that the midwives were anxious – although not yet panicking. She had been pushing since the hour of terce and it wasn't yet sext.

Her women had opened the shutters to let the bright, late April morning stream into the room, bringing with it a blessing of cool fresh air and even a scatter of blossom from the apple trees in the garth. Sybilla strained and bore down, determined that this wasn't going to be her dying day. God grant her and her as-yet-unborn child their lives.

Another contraction swept over her. Supported by her women she heaved and struggled. Planting the seed was one thing. Harvesting it quite another. Gundred bathed her brow with rose water and gave her a cup of honey and warm water to sip. 'It'll be all right, my lady,' she said, her voice warm with the kind of reassurance Sybilla herself used to those in extremity.

Sybilla closed her eyes. 'Yes,' she panted. 'One way or another it will. Either I'll give birth or I'll die. I . . . ah!'

She broke off to strive and push again . . . and push . . . and push. The midwives urged, and Sybilla wept and screamed and swore. And at last the baby's head crowned at the end of the birth canal and the midwives busied themselves, bringing warm towels, a basin of water, swaddling bands, a knife.

John stood out on the sward beyond the manor and watched the villagers of Hamstead preparing for their May Day celebrations. The great pole had been erected in the meadow near the river and decorated with braids of red and white. A crown of May blossom would adorn it on the feast day, but this morning was by way of a rehearsal for the children and youngsters. He folded his arms and watched the dancing, heard the bright laughter, the giggles, and felt a little detached from it all. If only his cares could be as easily dispelled by the grabbing of a coloured streamer.

The shepherd had brought his bagpipes to make music and his son had joined him with a bone whistle. A village woman was jogging a baby in her arms and watching two older children binding the streamers around the maypole. John glanced briefly at the infant, then looked away.

They had told him the child in Sybilla's womb was big and strong – which was all to the good, but he wasn't a fool and knew the other side of the coin. Not in so many words, they were warning him Sybilla might struggle to give birth. He remembered the time on the battlements in Rouen, awaiting news of the Empress when she sickened after bearing her second son. At the time, he had not fully comprehended the anxiety of those who cared about her, but he well understood it now. If he lost Sybilla, he would be like a boat with a hole torn in its keel and the sea bleeding in to sink it. He'd still exist, but not as he was now. He had even been to church to pray for them, although he despised men who made bargains with God because of their own dire needs. Why should God listen? Such pleading reminded him too much of Aline.

He had been home for most of Sybilla's ninth month of pregnancy. Prince Henry's attempts to seize castles in the keeping of Stephen's men had proved a debacle. By the time he and Henry had reached Purton, the Prince's rabble was fleeing from it in disorder and demanding pay for risking their lives. John had escorted the youth to his mother's court at Devizes and left him there to face the consequences. Thus far, from what he had heard, the Empress and the Earl of Gloucester were refusing to pay for the expedition out of their own funds and had given Henry short shrift for his folly – which was as it should be. You had to discipline an unruly pup to get the best from it. Henry's coming to England with a small band of mercenaries was seen in a few quarters as a courageous gesture, but most folk thought it the act of a foolhardy young idiot. Certainly it had made the opposition shake with hilarity rather than terror. However, he supposed it had also made men aware of Henry. He was no longer some unseen whelp, coddled in Normandy, but a young prince, pulling on the reins and eager for his opportunity.

He noticed his chamberlain coming round him in a wide loop so as not to approach on his blind side. The consideration irritated him while he acknowledged its necessity.

Osbert bowed. 'Glad tidings, my lord. Your lady has been safely delivered of a strong, healthy son.' He straightened, a smile beaming across his face.

John's gut churned with relief. He thanked Osbert with a more restrained smile, although inside he was bursting. 'My lady is well, you say?'

Osbert nodded. 'So Mistress Gundred said when she gave me the news. She said my lady was in good spirits.'

John thanked and dismissed Osbert and turned to make his way back to the manor. He wanted to run but, conscious of his dignity as lord, he walked with a measured stride. He was aware of the villagers whispering between each other and knew that in the way of things, the entire population would know the news in minutes – and expect free ale to toast the event, and bread to soak it up. He paused at the kitchens to give that order before entering the hall. Servants and retainers smiled at him. Benet and Jaston were familiar enough to clasp his hand and slap his back. Others bowed and murmured congratulations, which he accepted with preoccupation.

Lecia was waiting at the foot of the stairs and curtseyed. 'My lord, your lady asks that you will come to her chamber and see your new son.' She spoke formally, but her eyes were glowing with emotion – much of it relief.

'Willingly,' John replied and followed her from the hall to the long chamber above.

Sybilla was sitting up in bed, the covers tidy around her and the sheet folded back over the top quilt. Her hair spilled over her shoulders in a rich brunette skein, glossy from recent combing. The scent of rose water filled the air from the basin used to bathe the baby. Snuffling, squeaking sounds came from the direction of the cradle.

John went to Sybilla, stooped over to kiss her, but was careful of touching her body lest she was in pain. Emotion welled within him at the sight of her strong colour and the life dancing in her eyes. 'You had a difficult time,' he said.

Sybilla made a face. 'It was like birthing a baby whale,' she admitted, but then her expression grew proud. 'He's going to be tall and strong – a fine knight. He's already

360

fed once – as if he was starving. He has a strong appetite for life!' She smiled. 'Are you not going to look at him?' she prompted gently.

John glanced towards the cradle, then back at her, most of his being caught up in the concern that she was safe after the ordeal. However, to please her, and out of mild curiosity, he went to look at what the sowing of nine months earlier had wrought.

The baby lay on a soft lambskin fleece and was as yet unswaddled so that his father could examine him, and the sight suddenly made him smile. Sybilla was right; he was indeed a fine little man. His new son had dark hair, still damp from his first bath, and good, long limbs. Once they had muscle on them and adult strength, he'd be an excellent warrior.

'I thought to name him William,' Sybilla said, 'for my brother – if that meets with your approval.'

'Name him as you will,' John said. 'It's small enough reward for your ordeal.'

She thanked him.

Gundred said, 'Four sons you have now, my lord. You are blessed.'

John gave the maid a wry look. 'Finding them occupations will be interesting.' He turned to Sybilla. 'It's useful nonetheless to have a few arrows in the quiver. King Henry had no shortage of bolts, but none of them counted at the target. It's a pity he didn't marry Gloucester's mother.'

'Perhaps he should have stayed longer in his wife's bed than the begetting of a son and a daughter,' Sybilla said waspishly.

'Indeed he should,' John replied and gave her a mischievous smile. 'How many do you think is a good number?'

The baby started to cry and it wasn't a fractious wail, but a full indignant bawl like a young bull. John winced.

361

'Fine lungs on him too for bellowing commands,' he said, aware that his previous remark had caused Sybilla to regard him with amused irritation. Now probably wasn't the time for such teasing. The howls were deafening. He abandoned his stance by the cradle to let the midwives pick up and swaddle the yelling, red-faced baby. Returning to the bed, he kissed his wife again. 'I'll come back later,' he said. 'I can see your women still have things to do.'

Sybilla gave him a tired smile. 'It has nothing to do with noise,' she said. John laughed and acknowledged her perception with a salute. Before he reached the door, he paused by two of her women. 'Tend your mistress well,' he said in a tone that carried a warning. 'She means the world to me.'

Hearing his words, Sybilla gave a small shake of her head and indulged in a little weep. She knew he valued her, but to hear him say so meant the world to her too.

John propped his bare feet upon a stool and sat before the fire, cup in hand. Doublet had settled on the bench beside him and was resting her head in his lap, eyes half closed but watchfully adoring.

He gently fussed her silky ears in an absent manner that filled Sybilla with a stirring of affection that would in other circumstances have held a surge of lust. Being only a week out of childbed, such an appetite was not to the front of her mind. If it was to John's, he was either controlling it or making discreet arrangements elsewhere, and she was pragmatic enough not to go poking around to find out.

She sat down at his side, as content as he was to be still for a while as the spring dusk gathered outside. She could hear the soft chatter of her women in the inner chamber as they changed the bed from day couch to

362

sleeping space. Gilbert and Walter were playing chess in the embrasure and John's namesake had just been carried off to bed by his nurse, having fallen asleep at his father's feet like one of Doublet's pups. The baby slept in the cradle, his breathing catching quietly. John gazed into the flames, something he often did when he was thoughtful. It had disturbed her at first and she had harboured a concern that perhaps he still felt he was trapped inside the inferno of Wherwell Abbey, but she had come to realise that her fears were ungrounded. The random patterns of the flames helped him to think, sending him into a half-trance and shutting out the world. He would go to the riverside to ponder too, the fluid patterns on the water having the same effect on him as the fire.

Sybilla reached in her sewing basket and took out the soft fabric ball she was making for William. Fashioned from leftover scraps of material and stuffed with wool, it would be perfect for when he started to reach out and grasp things – although that wouldn't be for a while yet. He had a rattle too, with a pea in the middle, and a small silver bell dangled and shone at the side of the cradle, tinkling when she or the nurse rocked it.

John took another drink of wine. 'Newbury,' he said thoughtfully. Sybilla raised an eyebrow at him. He obviously wasn't referring to anything to do with her sewing. 'Newbury, my lord?'

'It's one of your family's manors. Your sister took it with her to her marriage to the Count of Perche, God rest his soul.'

Sybilla stitched quickly at one of the segments, winding her needle in and out like a dance. Hawise had been widowed, but still dwelt in France where she had recently made a second marriage with King Louis's brother, Robert. 'Indeed, what of it?'

363

John stroked the dog's glossy black head. 'I was thinking that if Newbury was fortified, it would give the Empress another stronghold in the vicinity.'

'Ah,' said Sybilla. 'And who would fortify it, or need I ask?'

'It would give us a strategic advantage. It would guard the place where the Reading road crosses towards Oxford. I'll speak to Patrick, of course.'

'After all, with Ludgershall and Mildenhall under your belt, you don't want him thinking you're taking over Salisbury lands piecemeal,' she said with a sharp look.

John was insouciant. 'It would be to his advantage as well as ours. It will tighten our control over the river valley and give us a further layer of protection.'

'And be an outpost,' Sybilla said.

John resumed fire-staring. 'That's how it begins,' he said softly. 'With outposts and daring. I have four sons to provide for, and perhaps more in the fullness of time.' He met her troubled stare. "Do you have objections?"

'I have worries,' she temporised. 'You will be courting trouble from King Stephen; you will have to find the resources to build at Newbury as well as maintaining our other holdings; and our sons are only babies. There is time. But I know you are not the kind to sit with your feet in the hearth except by way of novelty. Your ambition is restless.'

'Not as restless as some.' His expression grew harsh. 'I've seen murder and foul play committed aplenty by those who would have all. Little good it has done them – or those of us who didn't cry hold when we should have done.'

Sybilla opened her mouth to ask him what he meant, but was forestalled by Osbert's arrival. 'Sire, my lady, Henry, FitzEmpress, is here requesting a night's lodging for himself and his retinue. Messire Benet asks what he should do.'

Sybilla hastily set her sewing aside. John ceased fondling the dog and sat up, already reaching for his boots. 'How large a retinue?'

'Just his personal guard, I think.'

Irritably John stamped into his footwear and lifted his folded tunic from the back of the settle. 'Yes, admit him. Put his men in the hall and escort him up here. He can have my chamber for tonight. Go and tell Walchelin to provide food and drink. The grooms should use the back stable. It was swept out yesterday and there's room for the horses and tack.'

Osbert bowed and departed.

John rubbed his forehead. 'God's teeth, why me? What does he want now?'

'A night's lodging apparently.' Sybilla moved to the sideboard to find a cup suitable for England's heir to drink from. Not delicate glass, but the silver gilt one set with gems that John told her had belonged to the Bishop of Ely.

'Hah, and I believe in talking donkeys and flying pigs too.' John donned his tunic and pulled it straight.

'Do you want me to retire?' She gestured towards the bed which her women had finished preparing. She knew that some folk – usually purse-lipped clerics – considered a woman who had not been churched after childbed unclean.

John shook his head. 'Henry's not the kind to be sensitive about fraternising with a woman recently out of childbed and it's my chamber and my rules apply.' His mouth curved in a dry smile. 'Besides, you'd only eavesdrop behind the curtains. If I'd wanted to keep things private from you, I'd not have directed the chamberlain to bring him here.'

She made a playful face at him and swiftly directed her women to help her don a loose gown over her chemise and cover her hair with a wimple. She had a stool brought and set a little apart from the bench and close to William's cradle so that she could hear what was said without seeming to intrude and also so that she could watch the baby.

Having never seen Henry FitzEmpress before, Sybilla was surprised at the stocky youth whom Osbert ushered into the room. Had he been with others, she would have mistaken him for someone's groom or lackey. His red hair stood up in tufts where he had removed his cap and not smoothed it down and his clothes were well lived in and a little faded, although a closer look revealed that the embroidery on his tunic was exquisite. Swiftly she curtseyed to him. John had already knelt. Doublet, completely ignoring propriety, wagged up to Henry and licked his hand. The Prince laughed and patted her, while gesturing his hosts to rise. His complexion was slightly flushed, which might have been the exertion of clambering the stairs, but Sybilla suspected might also be a touch of discomfort. He was only fourteen years old and had arrived on the verge of nightfall at the keep of his mother's marshal. John had given him short shrift over the affair at Cricklade and, from what they had been hearing, Henry's mother and uncle had been no less angry.

'Sire, you do us great honour,' John said. He gestured to the settle. 'Will you be seated?'

Henry glanced at the cushioned bench and shook his head. 'I've been riding all day. I'd rather stand.' He took the wine Sybilla poured for him and went to glance into the cradle at the sleeping baby.

'My new son, William – a week old as of this morning,' John said.

Henry raised the cup in toast. 'God grant him a long and prosperous life.'

'Amen to that.'

Silence fell. Henry contemplated the baby, then his cup. Finally, ending the procrastination, he fixed John with a bright, pale grey stare. 'I'm returning to Normandy,' he announced.

John tried to look grave rather than utterly relieved. 'I think it a wise decision, sire.'

'You want rid of me too?'

'Normandy would seem safer for you at the moment, sire. You have shown your face and reminded your followers why they should hold true. You have proved you are no coward and willing to lead men, but the time is not ripe. That is why I say I consider it wise.'

Henry flushed. 'I would stay if I could. I promised my soldiers reward and booty if they followed me to England, but now I can't fulfil that promise.'

Now they came to the crux, John thought. 'With respect, sire, I know your lady mother cannot fund you. I am her marshal; I know the state of her finances. She and your uncle barely have two pennies to rub together this side of the Narrow Sea. I certainly cannot support you.'

'But you are a good and feared soldier,' Henry said with a calculating look in his eyes.

John was having none of it. 'Yes, and a tactician, which is why I say you must return to Normandy for a while longer, unless you have your own resources and a strong body of loyal men rather than the rabble of adventurers you have brought with you. You are welcome to my hospitality on your way to your ship, and I acknowledge your right to be King, but I must go by the advice of your mother and the Earl of Gloucester.'

Henry's colour remained high. 'I don't have the silver

367

to pay off my men, nor even the fee for taking ship back to Normandy.'

John's expression remained impassive. If the Empress was teaching her son a harsh lesson about the consequences of rash unthinking behaviour, John wasn't going to undermine her. 'I am prepared to account for the wages of two of your soldiers and take them into my garrison, but I can do no more for you than that.'

'Thank you, my lord, but it is a drop in the ocean.' A spark of defiance edged Henry's chagrin. 'I will have to send to my father for funds and hope he provides them. Without them I'm stranded here.'

John inwardly grimaced. He didn't want Henry on his hands for days on end, draining his resources and attracting enemies. But he certainly didn't have the finances to bale him out.

The baby woke and began to cry. Sybilla scooped him up and cradled him in the crook of her arm. His wails quieted for a moment, then were renewed with a hungry, fractious edge. 'Who else has the funds to pay off a troop of mercenaries and would be interested in seeing my lord Henry leave the country?' Sybilla asked as she turned towards her women.

Henry swung to stare at her. So did John. 'You mean Stephen?' John's voice rose a notch on the last word.

'He is known to be chivalrous, is he not?' she asked dulcetly and, bowing her head, retired behind the bed curtains to feed William, who was now bawling in earnest.

Henry stared after her, his lips slightly parted. With difficulty, John swallowed his pride and amusement. 'She does have a notion,' he said. 'What would Stephen give to have you safely out of the country? He'd be rid of you, he'd be showing others he makes nothing of the threat you pose, and he'd be making your mother and uncle look miserly for refusing you – while he'd be cast in the role of benevolent lord.'

From behind the bed curtains, the sound of the baby's wailing was replaced by choking splutters, the soothing tones of Sybilla's voice and then small, gratified sounds as William settled to feed. 'I knew Stephen before he was King,' John continued, 'and I served as his marshal for several years afterwards. Go to him with open boldness in the same wise that you came to England and ask him. He can only refuse you.'

The servants arrived with trenchers of bread, smoked sausage and some of Sybilla's famous cheese. Henry set to the meal with a voracious adolescent appetite and a new gleam in his eyes.

'If you want me to accompany you and add my word to yours, I will do so,' John said.

Henry ceased chewing and pondered for a moment, then shook his head. 'Thank you, my lord, but the impact will be greater upon Stephen if I go alone and am seen to be acting of my own will and not under instruction.'

John nodded and felt relieved. He would have gone, but knew there would be consequences, as much from the Empress and Gloucester as from Stephen. Mountains would be made of molehills and loyalty put in question. 'As you wish, sire,' he said gracefully.

Meal finished, Henry went off to consult with his men and John went to the bed, drew back the hangings and sat down beside his wife. Hunger briefly sated, William drowsed in her arms. 'You would make a fine general, my love.' John handed her his cup to take a drink.

'I was trying to think of ways of escaping an impossible corner. I remember you saying Stephen was easily swayed by brave gestures and that he could be manipulated. It seemed to me the Prince would have an easier time getting around him than he would the Empress and the Earl of Gloucester.' She looked at him. 'Why are you smiling?'

'Nothing. I was remembering what your brother said about you – that you had a tendency to meddle and that I should nip such behaviour in the bud.'

She put her chin up and John immediately pinched it between forefinger and thumb and kissed her hard on the mouth. 'I pay little heed to what your brother says. His notions of meddling and mine are somewhat different.' He rose to his feet and sighed. 'I suppose I'd better go and talk to Henry's men and sort out which two I'm going to keep.'

36

Gloucester, October 1147

Robert of Gloucester massaged his temples and frowned at the parchments laid out on the trestle in his chamber as if he was suddenly unsure what they were.

John eyed him and them. He was gathered with other commanders, senior barons and court officials to discuss the latest campaign against Stephen. Robert had led a disappointing sally into Hampshire earlier in the year and was now regrouping for another effort. The general mood was one of grim weariness – not quite exhaustion, but coming close. John could see it in the lined faces, the tight mouths. Humour was absent and tempers short.

'There are more horses due to arrive,' John said, indicating a tally stick at Gloucester's right hand. 'Thirty from Ireland and a hundred mercenaries. I've managed to find stabling and fodder for the horses and a hall for the men, but when they arrive and what condition all are in will depend on the weather in the Hibernian Sea.'

Gloucester nodded and swallowed with difficulty. He had been sneezing for two days and was suffering from a heavy chill. 'I trust to your efficiency, John.' His voice was hoarse. 'Is there any other business? Does anyone wish to speak?' He glanced around at the others, but matters, it seemed, were finished for the day. Everyone knew their role and had given an accounting of the resources they had and how they were going to deploy them.

Gloucester retired to his chamber with his eldest son. Watching him go, John noticed the heavy step, the pause to gather himself, and thought that the man looked at the end of his tether. He was carrying a weighty burden. They all were, but Gloucester's load was the greatest.

Patrick slapped John's arm. 'A drink before retiring?' He gestured to a cushioned alcove.

John had a deal to do, but since he functioned on less sleep than most men he was still alert and restless. A woman might have settled him down, but he was not going to conduct business with one of the castle whores under the gaze of his brother-in-law and there were other ways of scratching an itch. 'Why not?' he said.

Stephen de Gai was on his way to bed, but paused to speak. 'I hear you've added another son to your tally, FitzGilbert,' he said. 'Four boys is a fine number to have, but finding employment for them all is going to be a trial, eh?'

'Good education and training should see to most of that,' John replied. 'Skilled men are always in demand, be it in castle or church. I do not doubt William will make his way in the world as surely as any of the other three.' He looked wry. 'If his ability to crawl is any indication, he's already halfway there.'

De Gai grunted and smiled.

'Your daughter is well?'

'Flourishing,' de Gai replied, 'and bidding fair to be a beauty. You must send your older boys to visit. Their mother misses them.'

372

John murmured that he would and the men parted. He would indeed send Gilbert and Walter, but he doubted Aline's maternal needs were gut-wrenching. They never had been when she had the boys with her all the time. She had shown them affection because they were her gift to the marriage; loved them as symbols of duty fulfilled rather than for themselves. She had never cooed over their cradles, given them suck or dandled them the way Sybilla did with little John and William.

Patrick poured wine. His hair was Sybilla's colour but with more red in it and his beard, which he had let grow, was a startling shade of auburn. John thought he looked rather like an English peasant but kept it to himself. His brother by marriage was touchily proud on the matter of his native ancestry.

'So,' Patrick said as he slid John's cup across. 'I've been considering what you said about Newbury.'

John drank and waited. He had put the facts before Patrick but not made a great thing of the matter. Patrick was much more receptive to ideas if he believed they were his in the first place.

'I have no objections,' Patrick went on. 'If we have thought about it, then doubtless Stephen will have considered the notion too and rather we should control that road than him.' He gave John a hard look. 'Just so that you understand Newbury is a Salisbury manor and not a Marshal one.'

John raised an eyebrow at him. 'Yes, brother,' he replied, 'I understand it clearly.' It amused him to see how Patrick winced at being called 'brother'. The feeling was mutual, only he was better at concealing it. He intended remaining on the best terms he could with Patrick, but for the sake of his sons rather than himself. The Salisbury connection would be useful when planning their careers. To be polite

373

he drank a couple of measures with Patrick; he even enjoyed some of the conversation, since the discussion ran to horses, armour and battle tactics, subjects on which they had much in common. Patrick was also curious about the visit John and Sybilla had received from the young Prince Henry in the spring.

'You wouldn't have had anything to do with his going to Stephen for succour, would you?' Patrick enquired as he divided the dregs of the flagon between their two cups.

John shook his head. 'Nothing whatsoever,' he said, telling the literal truth. 'He came to me for lodging and I took on two of his best men who were content to remain in my garrison for regular food and pay. What happened afterwards was none of my doing.'

'I just wondered. You think I don't notice, but I know how devious you can be.'

John drank down his wine. 'Patrick, you only know what I want you to know – and you certainly don't know your sister at all. I'm going for a piss.' He rose to his feet, clapped the puzzled younger man on the shoulder and took himself off to the garderobe.

The latrine was already occupied by Robert of Gloucester. He was slumped on the far seat, his body at an angle and his head tilted back. By the flare of the latrine torch, John could see the sweat glistening in the hollow of his throat. His eyes were closed and his breathing stertorous. A smell of vomit hung in the air despite the cold draught from the squint window. John attended to the need of his bladder, readjusted his braies, then went to the Earl. Leaning over him, he felt the heat rising from his skin as if from the coals of a brazier. 'My lord, you should not be here, you should be abed.'

Gloucester opened his eyes and stared at John blankly out of glazed eyes, then he rallied and struggled to his feet. 'I can't take sick now,' he croaked. 'Too much to do. I'll be all right in the morning. The breeze in here . . . it's cool. Servants fuss too much.'

'Have you ever known me to fuss?'

'No. I don't expect you to start now.' Gloucester started towards the entrance, staggered and almost collapsed.

John grabbed him and braced him up. 'Nor will I, my lord.' He helped him out of the garderobe and to his chamber. As they approached the door, Gloucester insisted he was all right and shrugged John off. 'Sleep, all I need is sleep,' he said, 'but thank you. Don't let me keep you from your own bed.'

John hesitated, then bowed, turned round and came face to face with a guard and a dusty, mud-spattered monk. Gloucester narrowed his eyes in their direction as if struggling to focus.

'My lord Earl,' said the monk, 'there is news . . . grave news.'

Robert backed and leaned against the wall. 'Not Stephen . . .' he rasped. 'Stephen hasn't taken . . .'

'No, my lord – it's your son . . . Philip. He took sick on the way through Hungary and died at the roadside. I bring you his effects and his request for your blessing and forgiveness.' The priest held out a ring on the palm of his hand, the shank set with a ruby that gleamed like a dark eye in the torchlight.

Gloucester stared at the ring and then took it with a trembling hand. His throat worked and twitches ran across his face like raindrops striking a pool. 'No.' He shook his head. 'Ah, dear Christ, no!' His knees buckled. John grabbed him and the guard hastened to his other side. Together they brought him into his chamber, the monk following behind. Gloucester was making crowing noises in his throat that might have been grief, or just the struggle

375

to breathe. His eldest son, who had been asleep, roused from his pallet and came in his chemise and braies to see his father helped into bed. Gloucester's fist remained tightly clenched around his son's ring. 'Philip,' he gasped. 'Philip, God forgive me, child.'

'Send for a physician,' John snapped at Gloucester's usher of the chamber. 'God's life, he's burning up.'

William leaned over his father. 'Sire?'

Gloucester opened hazy eyes. 'Your brother is dead,' he said. 'Philip is dead . . . and I never told him that it wasn't his fault but mine . . .'

The physician arrived and John left the room. The wine he had drunk had turned to lead in his stomach. Everyone was exhausted, hurting, but if Robert died, it would be a cut so deep that it might prove mortal to the Empress's entire cause.

37

Hamstead, Berkshire, February 1148

'Dog,' William said. For some time he had been trying out different sounds in a babble meaningless to anyone but himself, but on this occasion the word was emphatic, intentional and directed at Doublet who was sitting by the chamber door, pawing it and whining.

Sybilla stared at her son, who was contained in a walking frame, then at Gundred. 'Did he just say . . .'

'Dog . . .' William said again and began scrabbling the frame towards Doublet. 'Dog . . . Dub . . .' The rest of the word failed him. 'Dog!' he said again, louder, arm outstretched, finger pointing.

Sybilla laughed and clapped her hands. 'Oh, aren't you a clever boy!' She went to lift him from the frame and into her arms. 'Yes, dog!' He was almost ten months old, a sunny, sturdy infant, good-natured but determined and fiercely energetic. She and her women dared not turn their backs for a moment or he would be into mischief. He would soon be walking, and was a swift, adept crawler, covering the length of the bower at an unbelievable speed. Yesterday she had had to stop him from eating the charcoal in the brazier basket, unravel him from the tangle he had made of a skein of wool, and had been just in time to prevent him from pulling a dangling cloth off a trestle and braining himself with the ewer standing on it. His older brother had added the word 'pest' to his own vocabulary and used it frequently with reference to William. Young John was currently sitting on his mother's bed, well out of William's reach, playing with his wooden animals.

Sybilla opened the door for Doublet, thinking the bitch wanted to relieve herself, although she had already had a walk around Hamstead's slushy, freezing yard once that morning. The hound clattered down the steps and began to bark, her tail wagging furiously and her eyes fixed on the gate as the guards slid back the draw bar. Sybilla's heart began to pound. 'Your papa's home,' she said to William and felt a jolt of mingled excitement and apprehension.

John and his troop clattered into the yard in a mist of white vapour from breath and hard-ridden horses. 'Dog!' William declared, excitedly opening and closing his hand in a gesture towards his father's stallion. Doublet had flung across the ward to greet her master and, as John dismounted, she threw herself at him, twisting and wriggling, frantic to lick him while John laughed at her efforts and fended her off.

'I don't know what it is about you and women,' Sybilla said with a shake of her head as she joined him. 'They all turn to wantons in your presence!'

He smiled at her and removing his helm, pushed down his coif and arming cap. He had grown his hair longer over the bitter winter season and it curled around his ears, darker than its bleached summer gold. A tawny hint of beard gleamed along his jawline. He looked her slowly up and down. 'Is that so?'

378

'Dog!' William exclaimed again, pointing at Aranais as the groom led the stallion off towards the stables. 'Dog!'

John grinned. 'Let's hope he learns the difference before he grows up, although to look at him he's halfway there already.' He set his arm around Sybilla's waist and kissed her, then his son's cheek.

The men were trooping into the hall or heading for lodging and guardroom. Sybilla climbed the stairs back to the domestic chamber. John had been gone since January and it was now almost the feast of Candles. Six weeks in the darkest days of winter. She was aware of him close behind her and it wasn't just the return up the stairs carrying a hefty infant that made her breathing grow short. Doublet pushed past her into the room and flopped down in front of the brazier, pink tongue lolling. Sybilla put William in the frame and directed one of her women to keep an eye on him.

'Have you eaten?' she asked her husband. 'How far have you ridden?'

'From Devizes across the Downs,' he said, extending cold-reddened hands towards the brazier. 'The men won't turn down bread and hot broth, I'm sure.'

'And you?'

'I had something less commonplace in mind . . .' He gave a suggestive glance towards the bed.

Sybilla bit her lip, torn between her duties as chatelaine and her duties as a wife, not to say her desires.

'. . . but it can wait a while at least,' he added after a teasing pause. 'Hot wine will have to suffice.' He went to the bed but only to ruffle young John's hair and sit down to unfasten his swordbelt. Sybilla gave brisk orders to her women regarding the provision of food and made haste to help him unarm. In the background William continued to try out his newfound word in a series of vocalisations.

John took his scabbard from her and hung it on a wrought-iron stand near the bed. 'The Empress is on her way to Bristol to take ship for Normandy,' he said.

Sybilla remained calm because John did not appear agitated or unsettled. His air, as far as she could tell, was one of being glad to be home – perhaps even relief. It might be the still before the storm, but on balance she thought not. John was always still when he was *in* the storm, never before it: then he would be a blur of sharp-tongued activity. She thought that was why he was so gifted a warrior. His organisation was meticulous; his courage indomitable. 'What does that mean for us?'

He shrugged. 'I do not know yet. I suspected she would not stay when Gloucester died, and I knew for certain at the Christmas feast. It was only a matter of when.'

Ah, she thought. So he had been preparing since October. That's why he was quiescent now. 'Has she said when she will return?'

He shook his head. 'My love, she is not returning.'

Her gaze widened.

'I am certain when she arrives in Normandy she will do what she can to further her cause, but here, without Gloucester to lead the campaigns, we can do nothing but hold fast until Henry is of age to rule. There is no one else – or no one whom everyone will follow. William of Gloucester is not made in the same mould as his father.'

'What about Brian FitzCount?'

'He has enough ado to hold Wallingford. Even as Matilda's champion, he will not take on the responsibility for all else.' He stood up and she helped him shed his mail shirt and then his gambeson. 'We all swore an oath to her that we would give our allegiance to Henry,' he added. 'She would not have demanded such a thing of

380

us if she intended to return.' The hot wine arrived and John took his cup with alacrity. 'If we don't hold on for Henry, we might as well walk into the sea and let the waves close over our heads now. I admit I thought him a foolish boy after what happened at Cricklade, but the young grow up and he has fire and courage.'

Sybilla wondered if he was putting a brave face on matters. It didn't sound like good news to her. 'Stephen will think he has won when he hears of this.'

He shrugged his shoulders as if limbering up for a fight and did nothing for Sybilla's peace of mind. 'He won't have won until he has this part of the south under his control and to do that he's got to come through me and Patrick. He's not as strong as you think. Men are coming to their own compromises the way Patrick and I did over Ludgershall. Robert of Leicester and Ranulf of Chester have been discussing peace settlements between themselves, for a start. Stephen doesn't have the grip he would like.' He sat down on the bed again and stretched out his legs. 'Nor will the Church acknowledge Stephen's son as the heir to England, and that is a major obstacle for him and an advantage for us. The Empress has the support of the Pope. As long as Eugenius rules in Rome, Stephen hasn't a chance of naming Eustace the heir to England's crown.'

'So it is not a setback that the Empress has gone then?' Sybilla sat down beside him and took his free hand in hers. It was still cold from his ride across the Downs. She ran her thumb over his palm.

'Only in that a few lily-livered men will panic, but no, it is not a setback. Indeed,' he said thoughtfully, 'it might even play to our advantage. Some who disliked her ways, or refused to be ruled by a woman, will gladly swear for Henry. Nor will we have to hem her around with guards

381

and protect her everywhere she goes. In a way it's a release.' He lifted her hand to his lips and kissed it, then looked across the room at his youngest offspring. 'Let's hope by the time he's old enough to ride a horse unaided, this conflict will be over.'

'Amen to that,' Sybilla said in a heartfelt voice.

'Dog,' said William cheerfully.

38

Bradenstoke Priory, Wiltshire, Summer 1149

John had brought Sybilla to Bradenstoke to visit the tombs of her family and give alms for their souls. She had knelt with her sons at the graves of her parents and her brother. At four years old, little John was old enough to under-stand and be solemn and silent – a trifle wide-eyed too in the presence of his ancestors, the Prior, and his living uncle, Walter, who was cowled in a brown Augustinian robe. He knew what was expected of him and behaved beautifully, much to the pride of his mother and father.

Two-year-old William, however, was a raucous bundle of energy and had to be carried outside by his nurse because keeping him still and quiet was impossible, and while shouting in the crypt for the joy of hearing his voice echoing off the walls was delightful to him, the adults were less enamoured.

William's personality was emerging as that of a strong-willed individual, constantly exploring his surroundings and testing the boundaries with insatiable vigour and curiosity. He exhausted everyone and the only time there was any peace was when he himself was exhausted, or when he paused to eat. However, since food went straight to his feet, he'd soon be flying around again like a whirl-wind. The only things that did quiet him down and some-times even lull him to sleep were music and stories. He would sit still for them and was already memorising tunes and words beyond his routine vocabulary.

John emerged from the church to find William tearing about on his toy hobby horse and laughing. Despite himself, John's lips twitched. It was very hard not to find William endearing even when he was being a nuisance. You couldn't ignore him, and he was such an affectionate child, brimming over with good nature, that being cross with him was nigh on impossible. With his other sons, there was a restraint and a distance that John felt appro-priate, but William ignored such rules. He would throw his arms around his father's legs, would demand to sit on his shoulders, would scramble into John's lap the moment he sat down and want to play with the hilt of his dagger or the cross around his neck. Or he would want to ride on John's knee as he rode on his nurse's. Somehow John found himself being drawn into the games. He was enter-tained, amused . . . rewarded. The child's fearlessness was a joy and his constant chatter comical. John had always considered that the best place for infants and small chil-dren was with their mothers and the women of the house-hold, but William had made a nonsense of the boundaries and found a seam of indulgent tolerance in his father's nature that, until now, John had not realised he possessed.

Sybilla came from the church, their eldest son walking very properly at her side. Young John gave William a look that would have been more appropriate on the face of a long-suffering adult and it became a scowl as William galloped towards him at full charge. John, who was nearer to his youngest than the nurse, took a side-stride and grabbed William, tucking him under one arm and the hobby horse under the other. William wriggled and shrieked.

'Next time we'll leave him at home,' Sybilla said with wry apology.

'Next time he'll be older and he'll either be silent or whipped,' John responded. 'Unless he's already been sold in Devizes in mistake for a piglet.' He set William on the ground and beckoned to the grooms. 'I'll take him up with me a while on the ride home. That should keep him out of mischief. You want to ride with me on Pegasus?' He ruffled William's hair.

William nodded vigorously. He might not be able to say 'Pegasus' yet, but being allowed up on his father's fast silver courser was an enormous treat.

Sybilla gave her husband a smiling look. 'He binds you as fast as the rest of us.'

John shook his head. 'He'll sit still with me, and he'll be learning more about riding than he will with Alfled.' He glanced briefly at the nurse. 'He's like a puppy. You can only train them so far until they've grown enough to understand.'

'I can ride my own horse,' young John said, jutting his chin. Sybilla suspected he was a little put out at the privilege being vouchsafed to his naughty little brother.

'And very well too,' his father answered. 'Without a leading rein. You'll be squiring for me soon.'

The child puffed out his chest and gave his brother a smug look, which was totally lost on William's infant comprehension.

John gained the grey's saddle and Sybilla lifted William up to him. The latter settled in his father's grip and, as John made a seat for him out of a fold of his cloak, looked around, bright as a squirrel. The grooms helped Sybilla to her side-saddle, and young John to his small bay pony

– a sedate little mare that had been the training mount of his older half-brothers by turns until they had outgrown her.

Leaving the priory, John and Sybilla took the road home to Marlborough, heading along the ancient trackways in a general south-easterly direction towards the herepath at Avebury and the way over the Downs.

William stared round from the courser's back at the passing countryside, his finger and voice in constant use, pointing out what he saw and telling John about it. A chatter of goldfinches in a thicket; a hare on a slope which the dogs chased but were too slow to catch. Sometimes he pointed to things on John's blind side, and John had to guess since he couldn't fully turn his body to look. Finally though, the steady plod of the courser, the warm sunshine, the security of his father's arm and the earlier vigorous expending of energy took their toll and William grew drowsy.

Holding his son's warm, vulnerable weight, John felt a painful lurch in his solar plexus.

'Quiet at last,' Sybilla said with a smile.

'Patrick would say he inherited it from you.'

She made a face at him and he laughed softly. It was pleasant to be riding out like this. While he had to be constantly on his guard, there were still occasional days to be snatched, like stealing rare golden apples from God's orchard. Sybilla liked to make a pilgrimage to Bradenstoke at least once a year, and he was happy to oblige her, especially in good weather. He had left his two older sons at Marlborough and intended taking them hunting when he returned, so that they too should have some of his attention. At fifteen and eleven they were old enough to benefit from such masculine expeditions.

'I wonder how Henry is faring in the North,' Sybilla mused.

'Let us hope he makes a better showing than he did on the previous occasion,' John said.

'He's two years older now.'

John gave a non-committal grunt. Henry had returned to England in April and before travelling north, had held court at Devizes. Despite his reservations, John had been impressed by the youth's development during those two years. He was still an adolescent with much to learn, but there had been signs of maturity and he had handled men with a sure and natural hand. Already he was better than his mother at setting his courtiers at ease whilst still maintaining his authority. John suspected that given manhood, he would be everything that his grandfather had been . . . and perhaps more. But there was many a slip and sixteen was perilously young.

Currently Henry was campaigning in the North with York as his objective. He had claimed that it was his right to be knighted by a senior male member of his family, in this case, his great-uncle, King David of Scotland. Numerous barons and magnates, including the Earls of Chester and Norfolk, had gone to attend the ceremony, which was a thinly disguised excuse to raise an army and rally men to his cause.

'He will be King though,' Sybilla said.

'God willing.'

'Yes, God willing.' She gave a little sigh and he saw her gaze towards a skylark. He could hear its throaty warble but not see it without swivelling in the saddle and disturbing both the horse and the sleeping child. Then the bird ceased singing and plummeted to the fields and it was as if it had never existed.

Clouds had been gathering during the morning and the first flurry of rain hit them as they crossed the Devizes road at Avebury and took the track over the top to

Marlborough. Here, rows of strange standing stones pushed up through the sheep-cropped grass like grey giant's teeth, and John shivered. The rain itself was as sharp as needles of stone, prickling his skin, hurting his scar. His left arm was numb from William's weight. The child stirred within the folds of cloak and rubbed his eyes, his little face flushed with sleep.

Suddenly from the rear of the column, one of his men shouted a warning. 'Soldiers, my lord. Soldiers on the road!'

John cursed. There shouldn't be soldiers in this vicinity lest they be from the garrisons at Marlborough or Devizes and, since he commanded those, he knew full well they wouldn't be here. He bundled William across to Sybilla and pointed to the herepath. 'Go!' he commanded. 'Ride for Marlborough and don't look back! Hugh, take John on your saddle, you'll cover the ground faster that way. Benet, escort my lady.' He drew the sword from the scabbard at the side of the saddle. There wasn't time to don his gambeson but the packhorse was carrying his shield and he was able to reach that and slide his left arm through the grips

A part of him heard Sybilla urging the mare; young John's protests; William crying; the nurse screaming. It was Wherwell all over again. Putting himself across the road; making a stand to hold while others made their escape . . . only this time the stakes were ten times as high.

As Sybilla rode, she heard the first shouts, the clash and scrape of meeting weapons and forced herself not to look round, to keep riding. Every time her mare tried to slow, she pricked her with the spur. Not that a flat-out gallop was feasible or sensible with an infant in her arms, and the horses needed to be conserved for the miles over the

388

Downs. After the initial spurt, she reined the mare to a swift trot. The pace jarred her spine. Her heart was pounding. Whose soldiers were they? What were they doing in the heart of John's territory?

William had ceased crying and was looking around, wide-eyed and interested anew, delighted at the mare's swift pace. 'Faster?' he said hopefully to Sybilla.

She felt laughter welling up inside her as it always did when she was agitated. Jesu, Jesu! William giggled with her, thinking it all a great game.

The rain arrived with a vengeance, lashing down on the party in vicious silver arrows. She put her head down and protected William within the folds of her cloak. The horses baulked and had to be forced into the wind. A flock of sheep sheltering in the lee of some standing stones scattered, their light footfalls swallowed in the heavier pounding of the horses' hooves. They would belong to the manor at Rockley, she thought, less than a mile to the north. There were no defences there. Just farms and shepherds.

Horses were thundering up behind them at a hard canter. Benet shouted something to her that the wind snatched from her hearing. She dared a look over her shoulder, almost fearing that what she saw, like Lot's wife, would turn her to a pillar of salt. Horsemen and a silver courser leading.

'John!' she gasped. She eased up on the reins to give her blowing mare a respite and allow the followers to catch up.

He reached her and she saw blood running from a nick along his jawline. A serjeant clung one-handed to his mount, teeth gritted in pain at what was obviously a broken arm. They had a prisoner with them, his hands lashed to his mount's saddle.

'Foragers,' John panted, riding up alongside her. 'Eustace's men and fortunately for us no more than a scouting party.'

Sybilla stared at him through the lashing rain. Eustace was Stephen's eldest son and while the father had gone north to try to contain Henry, Eustace had been left in command of London and the south . . . so what was he doing in Wiltshire?

'Don't stop. The rest of them could be anywhere. I need to return to Marlborough, liaise with Devizes and Wallingford and get the patrols out.' His expression twisted. 'Henry is headed south; the northern alliance has splintered, and Eustace is out to trap himself a prince . . . and where else to lay his ambushes except where he knows Henry will be headed?'

'When you say "splintered", do you mean . . .'

'I don't know yet, until the captive bird has sung some more.' He glanced over his shoulder at the hostage. 'I dare say he'll be keener than a skylark when it comes to the test.'

Sybilla swallowed bile. She had been sick every morning for a week and a deep lethargy had engulfed her so that everything beyond sleeping was an effort. Her boast to John that she was barely touched by the early months of pregnancy now seemed hollow. The midwife who had come yesterday to look at her opined that it was probably going to be a girl since Sybilla had not been visited by the sickness when carrying her sons. A daughter. She wondered what John would say. She hadn't yet told him she was with child. Indeed, she had barely seen him in a month . . . a month in which the world had turned to fire as Stephen and his son Eustace ravaged Wiltshire, particularly targeting Devizes, Marlborough and Salisbury. John's manors at Rockley and Woodhill had been burned to the ground. Winterbourne had suffered an attack; so had Nettlecombe and Tidworth. Sheep, cattle and pigs had been slaughtered or driven off . . . and where fat grain sheaves had been stacked to dry in the fields, now there were only charred wastes and the threat of famine. They couldn't go on. The people couldn't go on. Henry's attempt to seize York had been thwarted by a combination of bad timing, over-ambition and Stephen's speed in bringing an army to the city's defence. Henry had had to turn south and Stephen and Eustace had chased him, bringing fire, sword and devastation in their wake. Henry was dodging from pillar to post without the resources to do anything but fight on the back foot.

To combat her lethargy and nausea, she chewed on a piece of candied ginger root. Her sons were tumbling like puppies on the bed, play-wrestling, testing their muscles, their strength and each other. Already. And if they didn't, they wouldn't survive. Sybilla castigated herself for her mood. This wouldn't do at all. It was the way of the world and unless she intended retiring to the cloister, she would have to cope with it.

The ginger made her feel a little less queasy and she summoned her women, donned her cloak and took the dogs and children to walk the bailey grounds. William ran ahead, waving his toy sword, chasing the yard hens with ferocious yells. His limbs were lengthening as he made the transition from infancy to childhood. She noticed absently that his tunic, one that had fitted John until he was almost four, was only just long enough at the sleeve and could do with an extra band of fabric adding to the hem.

A guard shouted from the watchtower and the soldiers on the ground moved to slot back the great timber draw bar on the gate. With thumping heart and renewed queasiness, Sybilla watched her husband ride in with the troop. He swung down from Aranais and handed the reins to the groom. William ran to him and in customary greeting, tackled his father's knees. John grabbed his youngest son by the scruff of his tunic and swung him into his arms. He tousled the older one's hair and kissed Sybilla.

'We were walking the dogs when the guard called out.' She strove to sound calm. Knowing what he had endured with Aline she would not cry . . . she would not! She studied him for signs of injury or morose humour, but he moved easily enough despite the weight of his mail. Before he had left for Henry's court at Devizes he had been nursing a bruised shoulder and cracked ribs from yet another skirmish with Stephen's soldiers.

She busied herself directing the hall chamberlain to see that the men were attended to, and had her women prepare John a tub in the private chamber, knowing he would want to bathe.

The sight of him naked confirmed to her that he had no new wounds to add to his tally. He endured her scrutiny with composure and a touch of bleak amusement. 'It's a trifle late in the day to be eyeing up the goods and deciding whether or not they were really a bargain after all,' he said.

Sybilla flushed. 'I was doing no such thing!'

'No?' He stepped into the tub. 'Perhaps you'd like to make a closer inspection to be sure.'

She laughed. 'I can see you quite well from where I am.'

John gave her one of his long looks and Sybilla decided that either the news must be terrible and he wanted to escape from it, or it was good enough for a celebration. With sudden decision, she dismissed her women and had

392

the nurses take her sons to finish walking the dogs. Then, with slow deliberation, her eyes on him, she reached to the laces of her gown.

Clean, warm, sated and still a little damp around the edges, John poured them both wine. 'Ranulf of Chester and Hugh Bigod are going to rise up in Lincolnshire and Norfolk,' he told her. 'Stephen and Eustace will have no choice but to respond. It'll take the pressure off us and let us gather in what we can for the winter.'

Sybilla combed the tangles from her wet hair. Nausea threatened the periphery of her awareness, but she managed to keep it confined there. The pleasure of coupling lingered in dissipating flickers through her loins. 'Thank Christ for that, but God help those they go to burn,' she said with a small shudder. 'What of Henry?'

'He's going into Devon. He'll try to take Bridport and see if he can salt Henry de Tracy's tail at the same time.' Sitting down on the bed, John gave a deep sigh. 'Henry doesn't have enough men or resources. It's like David fighting Goliath, but we don't have the benefit of a slingshot. What we do need is help from Normandy in sufficient numbers to stop Stephen and that means Henry will have to go back across the Narrow Sea and garner it.'

Sybilla sat down beside him. 'Will it ever end?' She worked at a particularly difficult knot.

'It must,' he said grimly. 'The Church refuses to crown Eustace heir to England and with each month that passes Henry grows in stature.' He drew her against him. 'Tomorrow I'll start work on increasing our defences. I have to believe that before our sons are old enough to wield swords, there will be peace and order in the land again.'

'And before our daughter picks up her first spindle.'

His breathing caught and he gazed at her.

She laid her hand to her womb. 'I believe I am with child again. The midwife says so, and that it will be a girl.'

His expression softened but was tinged with concern too. 'When?'

'Spring . . . like the others.' She set her arms around his neck and kissed him. 'How would you have her named?'

He lifted his hand to tuck a damp strand of hair behind her ear in a tender, intimate gesture. 'Assuming the midwife is right and it is indeed a girl, I would have Margaret for my mother. Besides, such flowers always grace the spring with their beauty.'

39

Salisbury Castle, Summer 1150

'Look, Mama!' Standing in front of his mother, William twisted his head to gaze up at her as he pointed. His voice was filled with such awed, astonished delight that Sybilla laughed and squeezed his shoulders. They were standing in the courtyard outside the hall at Salisbury Castle. A balmy June day was gracing the marriage of her brother Patrick to the lady Ella Talvas and the celebrations were going forward apace.

Sybilla had brought her sons and stepsons into the courtyard, away from the drinking in the hall, to watch the entertainment outside, including the antics of this performing horse. Its hide was a buttery gold and its mane and tail a silver cascade. Little bells tinkled on its red leather bridle and saddle cloth. Using his voice and finger commands, its owner made it kneel before God, count by pawing a forehoof and bang on a drum with back-kicks. For a grand finale, he made it lie down and 'play dead'. Just when William was becoming agitated and thinking the horse might really be dead, the man touched it with his stick and made it rise to its feet again and do a dance to the music of a bone whistle.

Sybilla gave her sons silver to throw into the man's hat and, with a smile, he put a crust of bread in the palm of William's small hand and bade him feed the horse. William was entranced and Sybilla asked the player to bring his miraculous horse to Marlborough. She had already invited a troop of musicians and some mummers and realised she had better stop. It was like gorging oneself at a feast and stuffing as much as one could in a basket to save for later too. Merriment and pleasure had been so fleeting of late that occasions like this were to be seized upon and wrung dry.

Prince Henry had sailed for Normandy in January to raise an army and bring more support to England. In March he had been created Duke of Normandy, his father handing the Duchy over to him on the occasion of Henry's seventeenth birthday. He was no longer a magnate in waiting, but one in his own right, and with all the revenues of Normandy behind him, a fact which hadn't escaped Stephen's son, Eustace, who had crossed the Narrow Sea to continue his pursuit of an inheritance on Norman soil. But at least while Eustace was fighting across the Narrow Sea, he wasn't burning Wiltshire to a cinder and folk could snatch moments like this to marry and celebrate amid the ruins.

Her stepsons wanted to watch a wrestling contest between two of Patrick's knights who were grappling bare-chested in a roped-off arena in the corner of the ward. Predictably young John and William didn't want to be left out. Entrusting the older boys with the care of their half-brothers, Sybilla went to check on her baby daughter.

The bride was in the women's quarters changing her gown, a drunken lord having spilled a cup of wine in her lap. She was rueful about the incident, but still smiling, which boded well. With Patrick for a husband, she was going to need every iota of her patience and good nature. However, since this was her second marriage, her first having been to William de Warenne, Earl of Surrey, she was no frightened virgin and well able to hold her own. She joined Sybilla at the cradle to admire little Margaret.

'She's as sweet as a sugar comfit,' she said.

'Her father dotes on her,' Sybilla said with a proud smile. 'I . . .' She fell silent as another woman joined them before the cradle. Maude of Wallingford was wife to Brian FitzCount. She was past child-bearing age, but by few enough years to mean that although hope had died, its ghost remained.

Maude took a long look at the sleeping baby. 'You are fortunate, Lady Marshal,' she said. 'Were I offered the riches of the world on a golden salver I would trade them all for a fruitful womb. God intended it should be otherwise and I must accept His will. I wish you joy in the blessing of your children.'

'Thank you, my lady,' Sybilla said and curtseyed deeply as the woman moved off, the rich silk of her gown rustling over the floor.

'Poor lady,' said Ella Talvas. 'I have heard it said that they have no children out of God's displeasure for his sin of loving another woman, but I do not believe it.'

'Neither do I,' Sybilla said, but she knew the harvest the gossipmongers had reaped out of Brian FitzCount's devotion to the Empress. Bending over the cradle, she gently touched her daughter's sleep-flushed cheek. Margaret. Sometimes Alfled, the English nurse, would call her Daisy, translating it into the flower-name the English used. John absolutely doted on her. Sybilla suspected it was rather a novelty to him to have fathered a daughter, and to have a female sprung from his own flesh. He was almost more proprietorial about Margaret than he was about his four robust sons.

Outside in the ward, John had joined the crowd watching the wrestling; Brian FitzCount stood with him. Neither man had wanted to take part in another round of toasts in the hall. Indeed, John suspected that the bridegroom was going to have trouble finding his bride in the bed, let alone consummating the marriage.

William had found another child of about his own age and they were play-wrestling in earnest imitation of the knights competing in the makeshift arena. John watched with a grin for a moment before returning his attention to the real contest. He had been a good wrestler in his youth, lithe and supple. He could probably still have taken part now and not disgraced himself, but he was content to let the bachelors test each other's strength and flex their muscles for the women.

Brian FitzCount stared at the fighters, but his gaze was preoccupied and it was plain he wasn't really seeing them. 'There is something I have to tell you,' he said. 'I have been trying to find my moment, but no time has ever seemed right, and I doubt it will, so I might as well do it now.'

'My lord?' John looked at him.

'I have written to Prince Henry, and the Empress,' FitzCount said in a flat voice. 'I am to take the cowl and retire from the world. My wife intends doing the same. All that remains to be done is tie up the business of my life before I leave it behind.'

John knew he shouldn't have been surprised but still the news came like a movement to his blind left side: there all the time, but unseen until put in front of his right eye. 'God's blood, my lord, there are few enough of us remaining. What about Wallingford?'

'William Boterel, my constable, will take over. He's as experienced as I am. These past few months he has had the command anyway.' He looked at John. 'It has been in my mind for some time now. If I have held on it is to give Henry time, but now he is knighted and Duke of Normandy, he no longer needs me for a prop.'

'And since his mother has retired to the cloister herself, perhaps it is the closest you can come to her in affinity,' John snapped, anger making him blunt and incautious.

FitzCount narrowed his gaze. 'Be careful what you say, my lord. I haven't yet taken vows.'

'You were only holding on for her though, weren't you? Not for Henry.'

'If my lady the Empress saw fit to retire in favour of her son when she had fought for so long, then I respect her judgement. Henry is ready to take on the mantle of government and men cleave to him.' His mouth twisted. 'Do not glare at me like that, FitzGilbert. Given other circumstances, he might have been my son. Do you think I do not care?' Suddenly there was a raw edge to his voice. He gestured to William who was now playing an energetic game of tag with his newfound friend amid laughter and squeals. Their heels flashed as they ran; their faces were flushed and alight with life. 'Do you know how it has cut me not to beget children and see them quicken like that little lad of yours? To know that when I depart this world there will be nothing of me left in it? I have defended Wallingford for more than ten years in bitter circumstances, knowing it will never be my lot to see a son of mine inherit those walls. But Henry will, and I . . . ah . . .' He pressed his hand to his abdomen and his complexion greyed. He staggered and John grabbed his arm to steady him.

Gasping, FitzCount recovered and threw him off.

'Besides, I don't think a dying man consumed by pain is going to be of much use in the field, do you?'

'I am sorry, my lord, I did not realise you were sick.' John was shaken despite himself. 'Have you seen a physician?'

'Several.' FitzCount gingerly straightened up but kept his hand pressed to his side. 'The ones who hold out hope are either fools or treasure-hunters. The truth-tellers have taken their fee and informed me I will not have to suffer another winter's snow.'

FitzCount's tunic had come unpinned at the throat and John caught a glimpse of what looked like a hair shirt. FitzCount glanced downwards, saw the direction of John's stare and secured his throat clasp. 'I trust you to keep a closed mouth on the matter . . . and that is not an insult or a warning. We may not be bosom friends but we know and trust each other. Without your grip on the Kennet valley, Wallingford would have been subject to far greater depredation. Oft-times you have borne the brunt and kept the wolves from my door – I acknowledge my debt to you.'

'I have no choice, my lord.'

'Even so, you have stood firm.'

'Does the Empress know?'

FitzCount shook his head. 'And I will not tell her because there is no point. You are one of the few who does. Let Henry have Wallingford with my blessing. You've had a second chance at life, Marshal. Take it in both hands and live it to the full like your son.' He looked at William, inclined his head to John and walked away, limping slightly. John stared after him and, although the June day was as warm as new milk, he shivered.

400

40

Newbury Castle, June 1152

Clutching a small loaf still warm from the bakery, Benet mounted the timber stairs to the walkway along Newbury's battlements. Soft dew greyed the sward and dawn bird-song drenched air still scented and green from the rain that had fallen the previous evening. Benet always enjoyed this part of the day. Everything was peaceful and the promise of a new morning lay ahead. As yet the only bustle was in bakehouse and dairy, and he had room to spread his thoughts abroad and ponder without being interrupted every few minutes by queries and demands.

John had appointed him constable of Newbury with a brief to watch the Oxford and Reading roads and deal as necessary with what came along them. The castle also performed the function of buffering Hamstead from sudden assault and did the same for Wallingford, now commanded by William Boterel. Thus far nothing had disturbed the tranquillity beyond a few minor skirmishes – the usual detritus of a war that had gone on for so long that everyone was exhausted and could only manage the occasional wild swipe. Coffers and barns were empty and endurance a habit that men wore like lead shackles.

Benet bit into the bread and then cursed as he encountered grit. They needed a new millstone over at Hamstead where the flour had been ground otherwise no one would have any teeth left with which to chew. 'Anything?' he asked the guard on duty.

'No, sir. Been as quiet as a crypt all night.'

Benet cracked a morbid smile. 'Just the dead turning in their graves then.' He broke off a chunk of bread and handed it to the soldier. The man rested his spear against the timbered palisade. 'God knows, there must be more of them than the living, I sometimes think.'

A rooster crowed from the midden pit near the stables and the sky showed a pale band of oyster shell in the east. Colours began creeping back into the world: green first; then red and blue, muted and soft.

The guard's jaw abruptly ceased rotation as he too crunched on grit, then swore.

'Bad millstone,' Benet said. 'I'll have a word with my lord when he rides over on the morrow.'

The young guard masticated more gingerly and swallowed. 'One of the lads was saying in the guardroom last night he'd heard Prince Henry was gathering an army across the sea. Said he'd heard Barfleur was awash in men and supplies.'

Benet contemplated his loaf. 'How often have we heard such things before and they've come to naught? It's like finding a piece of gold in this bread. Believe it when you see it.'

'You don't think it's true then?' The young man looked disappointed.

'Oh, there's probably an element in it. I have no doubt there are men and supplies in Barfleur, but while they're there, they're not here, are they?' He stepped up on to an upper platform and gazed out over the walls, sniffing the air like a hound. It was going to be a glorious day.

Then he heard it, faintly on the breeze, a jingle of harness, the sound of a voice. His head came up.

'What is it?' The guard reached for his spear.

'Do you not hear it?'

The young man looked baffled. For a moment, Benet thought he must be going mad, then realised his companion was wearing arming cap, coif and helm, whereas his own ears were uncovered. 'Listen.'

The guard screwed up his face as if doing so would aid his hearing. He started to shake his head, but then his face changed. The noises were louder now. The unmistakable thud of horse hooves, the rumble of wheels and clink of harness.

'God on the Cross,' Benet said hoarsely. He knew what the noise presaged. He'd heard it often enough on both sides of the barrier. 'Sound the alarm,' he snapped. 'Summon the men to the battlements!'

Ashen-faced, the young guard fumbled with the horn at his belt, then raising it to his lips blew three long notes, sundering the air. Again he blew and soldiers began spilling out of the guardroom, buckling on their weapons as they ran. Now there was noise everywhere and Benet had to focus his mind. His belly was churning with shock as the sound of approaching troops continued. No casual patrol this. His hope that it might be William of Gloucester on the move or men belonging to William Boterel at Wallingford died as the banners came into sight and the troops began to spread out before the keep. There were baggage wains piled with tents, armour and disassembled siege machines including trebuchets and perriers.

Benet looked round as Roland, his deputy, joined him

403

on the wall walk, attaching his sword to his belt. 'It's the King,' Benet said hoarsely. 'God help us, it's Stephen himself.' He pointed towards a broad man with greying fair hair astride a black stallion with a saddle cloth of dark blue and gold. A cloak of blood-red wool blew at his shoulders and a fine battle-axe occupied a ring grip at the side of the saddle.

Roland completed the final tie on his belt. 'What are we going to do? We can't withstand this. The keep isn't stocked for it. We don't have the men or the supplies.'

There was a sour taste in Benet's throat and cold sweat in his armpits. He knew the odds. 'We fight,' he said, 'and we hope Stephen doesn't have the stomach for it. He's backed down before. If he takes us, then he's free to move on either Hamstead or Wallingford.'

Roland looked out over the mass of troops, for the most part Flemish mercenaries. 'He doesn't look as if he's preparing to back down,' he said.

Benet grimaced. It was little more than a month since Stephen's wife had died. She had been his helpmate and backbone, and a lady who had commanded great respect from everyone, whatever side they fought upon. Some said that without her Stephen was finished, but, if this was any indication, he certainly seemed to be channelling his grief into aggressive action. 'He may be trying to intimidate us into surrender,' Benet said. 'With Henry in Barfleur, Stephen has to destroy his bridgehead into England, and that includes us and Wallingford.'

'They're sending a herald.'

Benet gazed briefly, then, hand on sword hilt, turned to the wall-walk stair. 'They'll demand formal surrender first, just in case we might be willing to yield the place without a fight. We'll formally deny them . . .' He hesitated, then clenched his fists, the gesture both resolute and resigned. 'Then we'll start wishing that all we have to worry about is grit in the bread.'

At Ludgershall, the sun had begun to dip towards the horizon, but its rays still swathed the bailey in summer gold. William loved the long evenings when he could play outside until the swallows returned to their roosts and were replaced by bats, diving and flitting through a twilit sky the dusky colour of lavender flowers.

A group of squires and young garrison knights had been practising their sword strokes and now stood around talking, wiping themselves down with their balled-up shirts and drinking ale from the jug on the nearby trestle. One of them grabbed his crotch and made a jest – something to do with pushing a sword into a scabbard – and the others laughed and jostled him.

Behind them stood a circular straw targe of the kind used to shelter behind in siege warfare. Someone had thrust his sword into the centre and had yet to retrieve it. William eyed the weapon and then the group. Sometimes they let him join them, treating him with the easy tolerance they would afford a stray pup. He reasoned that if he could show them how good he was with a sword, they might take more notice of him and make him one of their brotherhood rather than just an indulged tag-along. William knew he wasn't supposed to touch real swords because of their sharp edges and because the imprint of his sweat or whatever stickiness might be on his fingers would rust the steel. However, he wasn't as obedient as his brother in that area. Told not to do something, John would obey, but William always had to question and test the boundaries.

Confidently he strode up to the targe, reached up and set both hands around the sword's handgrip of tawny

405

buckskin. A firm tug yielded no result for the blade was deeply embedded and refused to budge. William tried again, harder, but the weapon remained firm. One of the squires facing the targe noticed his efforts and alerted his companions.

'Go on, pull!' yelled his father's knight Baldwin de Stowell, whose sword it was. 'Let's see how strong your muscles are! I'll give you a penny if you can shift it!'

The others whistled and laughed. Silver changed hands as good-natured wagers were made on the likelihood of William freeing the sword. When William set one foot on the targe to aid his leverage, then the other, several of the knights doubled over with laughter. Those who could speak through their mirth bellowed encouragement.

Determined not to be bested, William grunted and heaved. Exerting every last ounce of his strength, he felt the sword begin to give; next moment he was lying on the ground, holding the weapon in his hands, free and clear. The soldiers were cheering him, some laughing so hard they were crying. William grinned at them and, clambering to his feet, danced and feinted with the sword. It was larger and less balanced than his father's blade and it was a struggle to control it.

Baldwin strode forward, palm extended to show a shining silver penny. 'Well done, lad. I didn't think you had it in you, but you're strong, I'll give you that.'

William narrowed his eyes. He had worked hard for the sword and wasn't ready to give it up just yet. His father said that things worth fighting for were worth keeping . . . or was it the other way round? He wanted to savour his victory and have a practice, the way the grown knights did. Ignoring the outstretched hand, he ran behind the targe, waving the sword around his head. The knights and squires clung to each other, roaring, as

406

Baldwin pursued William and William led him a merry dance, ducking round the shield, capering off, yelling because having a real sword in his hand made him feel all tingly with excitement and he just had to shout at the top of his lungs. He'd give it back in a minute, just another minute. Swoosh, parry, cut.

Baldwin lunged, missed and swore. Taking pity on their comrade, a couple of the others joined in, but still it took all three of them to avoid the sword, bring William down and finally, after a struggle, disarm him. He lay on the grass, panting hard, sore from where they had twisted his arm. Tears prickled his lids. He dashed one sleeve across his eyes and gulped hard. He wouldn't cry; he was a warrior.

'Hup, lad.' Baldwin stooped to haul William to his feet and then dusted him off. 'It's no dishonour to be brought down three against one . . .' Having run an oiled rag over the sword blade, he sheathed it in his scabbard, which was now buckled at his hip. A gleam in his eyes, he handed William his cup of ale. 'Here, take the dust out of your mouth,' he said.

William drank, his equanimity restored by the privilege of being invited to share with the men. Baldwin crouched to William's eye level and gave him a serious look. 'You shouldn't have taken the sword from the targe, you know that.'

William lifted his chin. 'No one said I couldn't.'

Two lines appeared in Baldwin's cheeks as if he were trying not to laugh. 'No one said you could, either. Next time, ask.'

William nodded, knowing there probably wouldn't be a next time, and even if he did ask, the answer would be no. It usually was to those kinds of questions. Baldwin retrieved his ale and finished it in three swift gulps, then rose and hefted William on to his shoulders. 'You're being sought,' he said. 'Time to go in.'

William grimaced at the sight of a beckoning Gundred at the entrance to the hall, but knew from experience it wasn't worth being difficult. Baldwin strode over to her and swung William down at her feet. 'By the faith I owe my lord' – he grinned at her – 'this boy will grow up to be one of the greatest knights the world has seen – providing he learns to leave my sword alone.' The last words were spoken playfully but nevertheless held a warning.

Gundred gave William a severe look. 'What have you been doing this time?'

'Nothing,' William replied with wounded innocence. This morning he had been reprimanded for recklessly racing his pony bareback and jumping a row of upturned buckets. His brother John had told on him, indignant because he himself had been doing as bidden during their riding lesson, not misbehaving and going his own way. And then William had torn a hole in his chausses climbing a tree beyond the palisade when he shouldn't have been outside the castle defences in the first place.

'He pulled my sword out of a targe and it was buried almost hilt-deep. God knows where he found the strength. Then he wouldn't give it up, but we've settled the matter man to man, haven't we?' Baldwin ruffled William's hair.

William nodded. Gundred clucked her tongue, but her hand at his shoulder was affectionate as she turned to take him in. 'I don't know,' she said, 'what are we going to do with you?'

Sybilla parted the curtain and glanced at her sons in the bed they shared. Both were sleeping – turned away from each other rather than huddled together like puppies.

408

William as usual was spread out like a starfish, taking up far more room than John. He expended so much vigour during the day that when it came time to sleep, he was guaranteed to be deep in slumber within moments of his head striking the pillow. Beside the boys' bed two-year-old Margaret slept at one end of the big cradle, and Sybilla, born in early March, occupied the other. Sybilla's heart filled with love and fierce pride. They would all make something of their lives, on that she was determined.

She returned to the main chamber and by the light from the fire and well-placed candles picked up her sewing, heaving a small sigh as she contemplated William's chausses and the three-cornered tear in them. He was a hellion, always into scrapes, usually of the kind caused by his enormous physical energy and wild appetite for adventure. Young John was far more responsible: his clothes lasted twice as long and were generally in a fit state to hand down. There was very little of William's that would be fit to pass on. Shaking her head, smiling through her exasperation, she threaded her needle and summoned Gundred and Lecia to play the harp and citole while she worked.

The door opened and John came into the chamber from the guardroom where he had been spending time with his knights. Doublet plodded at his side and went to flop down under the bench. She was getting old, Sybilla thought. He no longer took her out hunting for she couldn't keep up with the pack.

He sat down beside Sybilla on the bench and glanced at her mending.

'William,' she said succinctly. 'Tree-climbing.'

He gave an amused grunt. 'They've just been telling me in the guardroom about his escapade with Baldwin's sword. I don't think William's bound for the priesthood.'

'No,' she agreed. Gundred had given her the bald details. The notion of a five-year-old running amok with a sharp sword was one she had deliberately avoided dwelling upon.

'A messenger rode in just as the gates were closing,' he said.

She stopped sewing and studied him. His expression was ambiguous – irritation and reluctant humour, she decided. 'And was his news good or bad?'

'Awkward for us. Henry's not going to be returning to England just yet.'

She knew he had been hoping for Henry's return this summer – or autumn at the latest. The Prince had already been gone two and a half years, and although supplies were fed into Bristol from Normandy, she and John had been living a perilous existence, always fighting on the defensive and struggling to keep their lands intact and their people fed. 'Why not?'

He leaned the back of his hand along the bench and stroked her hair which she had unveiled and loosened in the privacy of their chamber. 'Because he has married the former Queen of France.'

Sybilla slewed to stare at him with widening eyes. 'He's done what?'

'Married Eleanor, Duchess of Aquitaine. Louis cast her off because she has only borne him two daughters – although how you expect a crop to grow if you won't plough the furrow and sow the seed is beyond my simple wit to understand. Henry's taken advantage. Married her in Poitiers at Pentecost.' John gave a rueful grin. 'He's nineteen years old and Duke of Normandy, Count of Anjou and Maine, and lord of Aquitaine and Poitou. All he needs now is a crown.' He thought of the bawling red-haired baby in his cradle at Rouen, of the belligerent

410

youth trying to lay siege to Cricklade and failing miserably. One thing that could be said about Henry, he learned from his mistakes and he learned swiftly. He matured swiftly too. Nineteen years old with the former Queen of France in his bed, and John had no doubt that Henry, unlike King Louis, would be delighted to play the diligent ploughman.

'So why can't he come to England?' Sybilla asked. 'Surely getting married won't prevent him?'

'Because Louis of France didn't set his wife free to marry the presumptuous young Duke of Normandy,' John replied. 'He's refusing to recognise Henry's claim. If Henry sails for England, he can bid farewell to his duchy. Before he can secure England, he must make his other domains safe.'

'So we live on promises for another year.' She tried not to sound petulant.

'At most. One way or another it will be finished because we cannot hold out beyond another winter.'

Sybilla bent her head to her sewing once more. John had contingency plans for most eventualities, but she wondered if enduring for a final year was that plan. He was pragmatic and always spoke the truth to her, for which she was grateful. He wouldn't tell her it was going to be all right if it wasn't. She remembered the stories she had heard about Exeter Castle at the start of this war, and how its lady had gone out to Stephen with her hair unbound and wept at his feet for the lives of the people in the garrison. She could do the same if necessary. Indeed, she could probably make a better scene of it than Baldwin de Redvers's wife. She had kin in France; they could go there as a last resort if John was dispossessed. And if he was killed . . . well then, she would be a widow still of child-bearing age and able

411

by remarriage to do something for her children and stepchildren even if her heart was dead. Her vision blurred and a sudden tear darkened the fabric of her son's chausses.

'Sybilla?' John stroked the back of her neck beneath her hair and looked at her with concern.

She bit her lip. She would not cry. She would be strong and pragmatic. 'They say the Queen of France is a beauty.' Her voice cracked around the edges despite her efforts to keep it light and blithe. 'Have you ever seen her?'

'I haven't,' he said, and a quirk of disbelieving amusement entered his voice. 'Surely you are not driven to tears of jealousy?'

She sniffed and raised her head. 'No, because even if you are led by your pintle, you're unlikely to receive an invite to her bedchamber.'

John gave a delighted grin at her use of such a vulgar English word. It always surprised and amused him when she came out with scraps and phrases in her grandfather's native tongue.

'I spoke of Eleanor as a distraction,' she said. 'She has gone from one husband to another. I was trying to imagine myself doing the same.'

'Oh yes?' John caressed her cheek with the side of his thumb. 'And how far did you get?'

'Enough to know I could manage if I had to and that I would make the best of it.' She swallowed and leaned into his touch. 'But it would be like dining at a rough trestle on savourless fare when I have grown accustomed to fine napery and salt and spices.'

'Ah, Sybilla,' he said softly and kissed the corner of her mouth, her jaw, the tender spot on her neck behind her earlobe. He gathered her in his arms, and with a flick of his fingers dismissed her women. 'It's a hunger

412

that never goes away. I know. I've been there . . .' He did not have to add Aline's name. They both knew.

A while later they lay in bed, limbs entwined. He was still within her, his lips moving softly over her throat and collar bone. She set her fingers in his hair and tugged it gently. She loved his hair, had done so long before carnality and notions of bedding him had entered her head. He never let it get lank or greasy like some of the soldiers. If he suffered an infestation of lice, he did something about it. It always smelled clean and made her want to touch it. He was right about the hunger not going away. The appetite was more than a blending of healthy lust and platonic companionship. It was a need that hurt if it wasn't fed. He must feel the same, she knew, even if most of the time he guarded his thoughts and emotions in a typically masculine way. Otherwise he wouldn't have kept her at his side through thick and thin – and sometimes their circumstances had been so thin they were threadbare. When he took her to bed, as now, he was driven by more than the desire to procreate heirs and satisfy lust – although both those aspects were involved. When he was with her, she knew she was Sybilla to him, not just another body to ease a basic need. He would gasp her name in a way that melted her bones, and she well knew how to set a fire in his.

As they kissed and touched, the sound of voices carried to them from outside their chamber – Gundred saying the lord and lady were busy and a man's agitated response that they would not be too busy to hear the news he brought.

'No peace for the damned,' John muttered against her throat. Lifting himself off her, he sought his braies and shirt. Sybilla hastily donned her chemise and closed the bed hangings as he went to the chamber entrance. The rail clattered as he drew back the curtain and she heard

413

him speak to the messenger, but then they moved out of her hearing and all she could make out was the indistinct rumble of male voices and the occasional word. She heard 'Newbury', and 'the King' and 'hard fight', and suddenly her stomach was queasy.

By the time John returned she was dressed again, her hair braided, and she had lit fresh candles in the sconces and poured wine. 'What's happened to Newbury?' she demanded.

He headed back to the bed, sat on it and began dressing. 'Stephen's brought up his mercenaries and laid siege,' he said grimly. 'They fought him off and bloodied him badly enough for him to be willing to negotiate their surrender. He's given Benet a day's grace to ask my permission to hand over the keep and then he'll assault again.' He fastened his hose, tugged on his tunic and fetched ink, parchment and quills from the shelf above his coffer. 'My messenger's to be back at Newbury by dawn.' His voice was hard and swift, all trace of honeyed warmth gone from its timbre.

'What's to be done?' Sybilla brought another candle, knowing he would need the extra light if he was going to write. She sat down close to him, but made sure her shadow did not impede his work area.

'If Newbury falls, then Stephen will be able to isolate Wallingford and take me apart piecemeal. And if Wallingford falls . . .' He sighed and, sitting down, drew the first sheet of parchment towards him, weighing it down with a heavy glass smoother. 'I cannot surrender. I have no choice but to hold out.'

Sybilla sifted her memory for what she knew about the situation at Newbury. 'Are there sufficient men and supplies to withstand Stephen? Is the castle strong enough?'

'The answer is no, and no,' he said without looking up.

414

'Newbury isn't Marlborough, and Stephen will be determined because he knows he can win – and win against me.'

Sybilla pressed her lips together and watched him trim a quill and remove the lid from the ink horn. However, he didn't begin writing, but sighed again and looked at her. 'I can authorise Benet to sue for terms, but that means surrendering Newbury and leaving Wallingford and Hamstead exposed. I can don my mail and go out to do battle, but if Stephen has his host there, I would go down in an open fight. A one-day truce is useless. I need to buy as much time as I can, because each day we delay and hold out is a day more for Wallingford.'

Sybilla's brow furrowed. 'If Benet needs your permission to yield the keep, do you not also need the Empress's permission to do such a thing . . . or Henry's? That will take a least a fortnight. Can you not ask Stephen for an extension of the truce?'

He nodded slowly. 'That is the only option – although if Stephen agrees, I suspect he will demand a price.'

She tried to keep her voice level. 'What kind of price?'

He stood and, leaving the trestle, went to the partition behind which their four children were asleep. 'Manors,' he said. 'Herds.' He gently parted the curtain to look within. 'Hostages.' His voice barely stirred the air, but Sybilla heard it well enough and it sent a cold shudder down her spine. He clenched the fist not holding the curtain, then he released the fabric and, rubbing his hand across his jaw, returned to the trestle.

'Holy God,' she said. Time and again when she thought it could not get worse for them it did. 'He won't . . .' She closed her mouth. Of course Stephen would ask, and he would be within his rights. John said nothing. Picking up the quill again, he swiftly, unthinkingly, pricked out the

415

lines and began to write as neatly as any scribe. He had told her once that his father had recognised there would be a need for lettered men who were more than just clerks and had seen to it that John was educated to competence with both pen and sword. He finished writing and passed her the hawthorn-wood box containing his seal and a stick of hard green wax so that she could finish for him while he started on another letter.

Sybilla scanned the drying words on the first parchment and saw that it was a letter to Stephen requesting him to grant a longer truce until John had been able to inform his overlord, namely Henry, to whom he was sworn, of his predicament. Should no help come of that word, he was prepared to sue for terms. The tone was formal and contained the customary flourishes but it also stated the position clearly. Sybilla heated the wax in the candle flame and dripped it on to the folded parchment, then pressed the silver seal firmly into the cooling puddle. She needed a steady hand and she made it so, even if inside she felt as if she were dissolving. John's second letter was to Henry, informing him of the assault and requesting assistance. A third letter was for Patrick and was couched in language more terse than the previous two. Then there were more for the castellans at Marlborough and Ludgershall, for the bailiff at Mildenhall and the stewards of John's scattered manners and serjeantries.

Once the letters had been sealed, he took them and went to the door.

Sybilla bit her lip. She felt as if they were standing on the edge of a precipice and the stones crumbling away beneath their feet. There had to be a way over, around or back. She dared not allow herself to believe otherwise.

41

Hamstead, Berkshire, June 1152

'My lord, the King's messengers have arrived. There's a knight and three men-at-arms.' Panting hard, the sentry poked his head round the guardroom door.

John ceased his conversation with Jaston. He had been anticipating and dreading this moment for two days, but he allowed neither emotion to show on his face. 'Admit them,' he said. 'And bring them to the hall.'

'Sir.'

Rising to his feet, John pulled his tunic straight and hitched his belt. His sword was propped against the trestle and he picked it up and girded it on – not because he was expecting trouble, but because it was a mark of rank and masculine pride. He knew the latter was about to face a bitter assault. 'Carry on with this business,' he told Jaston with a wave at the tally sticks arranged on the trestle where they had been talking. 'And don't forget to add in those barrels of arrows from Marlborough.'

He took a deep breath and leaving the guardroom, crossed the sward at a steady pace, schooling himself to cold detachment. He was prepared to bargain if there was room, and to be civil, but he would show no weakness. His shield was up; no one was going to get past it.

In the hall Sybilla had already welcomed the visitors and furnished them with cups of wine and seats on the benches gathered near the hearth. She met John's gaze as he entered the room and, for an instant, he saw naked fear in her eyes, but then she mastered it and he was proud of her. Aline would have been a hysterical wreck by now.

The knight was one of Stephen's household – a Flemish veteran by the name of Hugo de Wartenbeke and a soldier as battle-hardened as John himself. The serjeants with him were seasoned men too.

John greeted them with formal courtesy and de Wartenbeke handed over the sealed letter that had been tucked into his belt. 'I know the contents, my lord,' he said to John. 'The King is expecting our return before nightfall with the fulfilment of our office. Any delay or refusal on your part and we will resume the siege.'

'And receive a drubbing for your pains or you would not be so willing to negotiate for a bloodless surrender,' John answered sharply. 'I doubt the King's willingness to parley is down to any compassion or goodwill towards me.' He slit the seal tags and opened out the document.

Stephen wasted few lines on effusive greetings but John had not expected them. The list of demands was harsh, but not impossible. He was to yield his manor of Cherhill for a year and the income from it. He was to hand over the wool clips from his manors at Nettlecombe and Tidworth and provide women to spin the wool into yarn. He was to swear not to raise arms against Stephen and the surety for such was to be the life of his son who was to go with de Wartenbeke and his escort as a hostage. In return, Stephen granted John two weeks in which to gain honourable permission from Henry FitzEmpress for the surrender of Newbury, which would then be occupied by Stephen's garrison.

John compressed his lips and gave the letter to Sybilla. 'The King makes harsh demands,' he said. 'I do not know how quickly I will be able to find the women he asks for and the sheep are not yet shorn.'

De Wartenbeke narrowed his gaze at John. 'You were the old King's marshal and you have served both our King and the Empress in that capacity. Your powers must have grown feeble indeed if you cannot arrange something as simple as a wool clip and some spinsters . . . or perhaps you are trying to pull the wool over our eyes.' It was an intentional jest but there was little humour in de Wartenbeke's greenish stare.

John shook his head. 'That is not my intention. I will do what I can.' He glanced at Sybilla, who had now read the letter. Her face was set and pale. 'I will have word sent out to my stewards at my manors and I will make every effort to do as the King requests.'

'Commands,' contradicted the Fleming.

John let it rest. 'I assume you will give me some time for a word with my son before you leave. He will have to pack his coffer and have his horse readied.'

De Wartenbeke nodded. 'His mother will want to bid him farewell too,' he said, watching Sybilla.

John shook his head. 'My wife is Gilbert's stepmother. His own mother is married elsewhere now.'

The knight wrapped his hands around his ornate leather belt. 'You misunderstand which of your sons the King requires. The oldest may be your heir, but the younger ones are nephew to Patrick of Salisbury and as such are of greater value. The King desires one of them. The choice is yours, my lord. I leave it up to you, but do not take too long to decide.'

419

Sybilla made a sound in her throat and immediately stifled it against the back of her hand. John felt his body tighten as if he were turning to stone. He had been prepared for them to demand Gilbert of him and had spent much of yesterday bracing himself and his heir for that likelihood. Gilbert's quiet resolution in response to the news had made him proud of the way his son was growing up. To have Stephen demand one of the little ones was a shock. Nor had Sybilla bargained for it. She had blenched and was fighting for composure.

'I am surprised the King requires a babe of me rather than a youth who could be useful around the court,' John answered impassively, 'but if such is his wish, let him have my fourth child, William.'

'As you choose, my lord,' replied de Wartenbeke, 'but know that if you raise your hand against the King, his life is forfeit.'

John gave a terse nod. 'I think we are clear on the terms.' He turned to his wife. 'Sybilla, make William ready and assemble whatever baggage he needs.'

She curtseyed to him, her face like ice, and left the hall.

'You're backed into a corner this time, my lord,' said de Wartenbeke, holding out his hand in the gesture of a man being conciliatory and reasonable. 'Why wait? Why not surrender now?'

John looked steadily at the mercenary. 'Would you?'

De Wartenbeke returned his look. 'I was at Wherwell when you fought us to the bone and then barricaded yourself in that burning church rather than yield. You tell me, was it worth it?'

John held his breathing steady even though he felt as if he had been punched in the solar plexus. 'If I had yielded, do you think I would be here talking to you now? I'd have ended my life riding a gallows tree. The only difference between dross and gold is in the perception. You will excuse me. I have letters to write and spinsters to find. My steward will see to your needs.' With a snap of his fingers at the servant, he left the hall at a rapid walk and headed to the stables.

'My lord?' The groom looked at him askance as he entered the servants' quarters.

'Saddle up Aranais,' John commanded stiffly.

The man touched his forelock and went to fetch the harness. Alone, John leaned against the wall, head thrown back, jaw clenched so tightly that he could feel the strain begin a throbbing headache. He was nauseous, sick to the stomach at what was coming, but there was no other way. Damn Stephen; damn Henry. And damn his own soul to hell for what he was about to do.

Feeling numb, Sybilla entered the domestic chamber above the hall. Under the watchful gaze of her women, William and John were playing with an orange tabby kitten from a litter produced by one of Hamstead's several mousers. William was trailing a piece of string on the floor and the kitten was wriggling its small rump and pouncing, before springing away with its tail high and one-sided. William giggled and Sybilla's heart contracted. She could not bear this.

'My turn now,' his brother said. Somewhat reluctantly, but with a sense of what was fair, William handed over the string.

The two older boys had been playing chess in the embrasure. Gilbert left the board and came across to her, his grey eyes filled with apprehension. 'Madam?' he said. He was fine-featured and slightly built like his mother, and until adolescence had possessed a thin, almost whiny voice, but the changes of manhood had deepened,

421

broadened and enriched it to produce a pleasing timbre that was all John's. 'Have they come for me?' He laid a nervous hand to the knife sheath at his waist.

She shook her head. 'No, Gilbert. It's not you they want, nor Walter. You are not blood kin to Patrick of Salisbury.'

His eyes widened and he stared at his small half-brothers.

Sybilla swallowed the painful lump in her throat and steeled herself. 'William,' she said, 'come here.'

'William? They want him?'

'Your father had to choose.'

'Dear sweet Christ.' Gilbert's mouth twisted.

'Go back to your game . . . don't . . .' Sybilla clenched her fists. 'Don't make this more difficult than it is going to be.'

Gilbert gave her a long stare but did as she bade, pausing to ruffle William's fair-brown hair as the lad came to her side. Removing the cross on a leather cord he wore around his neck, he placed it around William's instead. 'For Christ's protection,' he said.

William touched the cord, still warm and a little damp from Gilbert's skin, and admired the incised silver gilt and the garnet stone at its centre.

Sybilla drew him to the bench near the hearth and sat him down beside her. He swung his legs and fidgeted. It was the start of the day and his energy levels were prodigious. With gentle fingers she smoothed the hair that Gilbert had just ruffled. 'William, I want you to listen to me carefully.'

Behind them, John yelped as the kitten pounced and caught him with its tiny needle claws. William looked round, then grinned.

'Carefully,' Sybilla repeated with emphasis and tapped

422

his arm. 'Never mind your brother for now. You have a task to perform for your family. For your father . . . for me. A task that I would usually ask of a squire or a knight, but the King says he will only have you.'

'What kind of task?' William ceased wriggling and sat up, his eyes suddenly full of curiosity and interest.

'One that will take you away from home. The King . . .' she swallowed. 'The King desires you to keep him company for a while. It's a very important duty.'

She watched him absorb the details as she told him. He was good at listening when he wanted to and had a phenomenal memory. He looked again towards his big brother, but this time with a smug glint in his eyes. 'Is John going too?'

'No, just you. Your father chose you.' She smoothed his hair again and felt the betrayal enter her vitals like a knife as his look of pleasure increased. 'Some of the King's knights are waiting in the hall to take you to the King's camp.'

'Where's that?'

'Not far from Newbury.'

William looked thoughtful, then nodded. He knew where Newbury was. Less than half a day's ride. 'Can I take Lion?' He looked towards the kitten.

'It's not the sort of journey for him. I'll look after him until you . . . until you come home.'

William gave a trusting nod. 'Am I going to be a squire?'

'A squire in training,' she said. 'You might be tested, so you'll have to remember everything we've taught you. Remember you are the son of the Empress's marshal and the grandson of the lord of Salisbury.'

He lifted his chin at that and thrust out his jaw. Sybilla put a smile on her face and went to pack his baggage in a large travelling satchel. When the maids came to help her she waved them away. It was something she wanted to do

423

for him herself because she might never have the opportunity again. His best blue chausses. The other pair she had so recently mended with a sigh at his escapades. Two tunics, two shirts. His green cloak and the woollen hood with the squirrel-fur lining. His spare shoes with antlerwork toggles and plaited red vamp strips. Their small size and the slight wear that showed evidence of running and vigorous play made her throat ache with dammed-up grief. Dear Holy Virgin, she could not bear this, and yet she must, and for William's sake not show how much it was costing her.

In her cradle, the baby began to wail, and the wet nurse went to tend her, already unpinning the neck of her gown. Sybilla's own breasts ached, but not for her infant daughter.

William skipped over to Sybilla with his toy hobby horse and the wooden sword and shield his father had made for him. A red lion snarled across the centre just like John's own. Through her pain, laughter tugged at Sybilla's mouth corners. Masculine priorities were always the same when it came to loading the packhorse. Before the laughter could take hold and become hysteria, she agreed that he could take his accoutrements; they were the necessities of a knight. She turned aside to her own coffer and brought out the new hair ribbons of blue silk brocade that John had given her at the May feast. 'Here,' she said. 'Wear these and be my champion.'

William's eyes shone with pleasure as she knelt and tied the ribbons to his wrists, just like the knights wore when they were in their feast-day finery.

Young John came over to see what they were doing, the kitten following him and pouncing at the string still dangling from his fingers.

'I'm going away to be a knight,' William declared. 'I've been chosen.'

424

John gave his brother a narrow look. 'You're not old enough. I'm older than you.'

'It's true, isn't it, Mama?'

Sybilla felt like an animal caught in a trap. Now she had to somehow gnaw herself free, then crawl off and bleed to death somewhere quiet and out of sight. 'Yes, it is true,' she said and looked at John. 'William is to go to King Stephen, but your father made that decision because he needs you here. You are older and better suited to protecting those within. If your father chose William to go, then he equally chose you to stay.'

John's stiff stance relaxed and Sybilla breathed an internal sigh of relief. Going to the fabric cupboard she brought out a bolt of charcoal-grey wool she had been saving to make winter tunics for the boys, and another of madder-red for chausses. William was growing faster than wheat in May. At least if he had cloth in his baggage, someone might have the charity to make new garments for him. She didn't know how long he was going to be gone. She packed the fabric in his baggage roll, her whole body rigid with pain. When she turned round, William was crouching to stroke the kitten in farewell and his father was standing in the doorway, his expression carved from granite.

A wave of panic washed over her. She wanted to seize William in her arms and scream that no one was going to take him away – that she would fight like a lioness to protect her cub. She knelt to William's level and embraced him, holding him tightly as if she could absorb him back into herself. 'Remember that I love you, William,' she said in a choked voice, then held him slightly away and looked into his face. Sudden apprehension glimmered in his eyes. Tears blurred her own vision. 'Kiss me and go with your father.'

She felt his lips on her cheek and his arms suddenly tight around her neck, clinging.

'Stop weeping, woman,' John growled, 'you're unsettling him.'

Still clutching William, Sybilla slanted him a furious look, but the set of his jaw and the compressed line of his mouth told his story as completely as her own.

'Are you ready, son?' John asked gruffly.

William turned and looked up at his father. 'Yes, sir,' he said. His hand came up for a very swift swipe across his eyes and then he jutted his chin and stood up as straight as the soldiers did when the master-at-arms had them at their drill.

'Brave lad.' John squeezed his shoulder and, with a brusque man-to-man nod, picked up his baggage roll. 'You'll carry your own weapons, hmm?'

William nodded stoutly and in direct imitation of the household knights, pushed his miniature shield round on to his back by its long strap.

Sybilla wanted to howl, but forced a smile on to her face. She could feel her mouth corners straining with the effort and concentrated upon how proud she was of William, rather than the terror that this was the last she was ever going to see of him.

The King's men were waiting in the courtyard and they had brought a brown pony for William, but then Sybilla saw that John had had Aranais saddled up in full barding with the red and green pendants on his breast-band and the decorated saddle cloth.

'Is Papa going too?' young John wanted to know. His eyes were huge as he tried to take in what was happening.

'I don't know.' She wondered what John was doing. He wasn't armed apart from his sword and she certainly couldn't see him taking William all the way to the King. She watched him swing into the saddle, bend down, then draw William up before him on the stallion. He leaned

426

towards William, spoke, and was answered with a solemn nod. Sybilla bit her lip and hugged her older son to her side.

The party rode out of Hamstead at a trot and the last she saw of William was a flutter of blue ribbon, for the rest was concealed by his father's body. Although the morning was warm and bright, Sybilla's teeth chattered as if it were the middle of winter.

John returned within the hour, striding hard, slamming and cursing. The servants scuttled for cover; his men kept out of his way. He blew into the domestic chamber, threw himself down at the trestle and stared with loathing at the parchments and tallies, still there from two days before. Then, with an oath, he stood up again and went to look out of the window, bracing his arms on the walls either side of the embrasure.

With a gesture, Sybilla dismissed her women and bade Walter and Gilbert take young John out to practise his riding. Then she went to her husband and tentatively laid the palm of her hand to the middle of his spine.

'I went a little way with them in order to say farewell,' he said in a choked voice. 'They gave him a beast he had never ridden before and he took to it as if he'd known it all his life. Already he rides with a spine like a lance. I could not have asked more of him than I received. God help me, Sybilla, he thinks it all a great adventure.'

'Did you tell him why he was going to the King?'

'I said that I had made a promise and that he was to stay with the King until I had kept that promise. He accepted it . . . smiled at me and waved. I . . .' He pushed away from the wall and past her into the room. Picking up the flagon on the trestle, he sloshed wine into his cup, spilling almost as much as he poured, and this from a man who despite the loss of an eye had a feline accuracy

427

of coordination. He cursed and Sybilla hastened with a length of the baby's swaddling to blot the spillage. John drank hard, slammed the cup down and then once more sat at the trestle. 'Ah, God,' he said. 'I would rather walk through the fire at Wherwell again than do what I have just done.'

Sybilla laid the wet swaddling aside and, kneeling before the bench, reached for his hands. She hadn't cried properly yet, although she knew when the tears did come, they would wash her away. There had to be a path round this for all their sakes.

'Can you not negotiate with Stephen?'

John looked at their joined hands. 'That is what I have been doing. I've earned us two weeks. He'll leave a token force and withdraw.' He pulled away from her and, facing the trestle, picked up and examined a tally stick.

'And then what?'

'And then I restock the keep with men and supplies,' he said and now his voice was hard and devoid of emotion.

She rose to her feet, her stomach quailing. 'You have written to Henry though.'

John snorted. 'He is hardly going to cross the Narrow Sea in that time to save Newbury from Stephen, and I already know his reply. I didn't ask him for permission to yield. I told him Wallingford was in great peril and that I would hold out and delay for as long as I could, but he should not expect miracles. I have ordered up supplies to take into Newbury – it'll probably have to be done at night once Stephen's men have drawn back.'

'What about William?' Her words emerged in a thready whisper.

'He'll have to take his chance.' He avoided her gaze. 'Stephen doesn't have the stomach for violence against women and children. Time and again I've seen him back

428

down and William has a way with him that could charm a smile from the sourest curmudgeon. Stephen's wife is dead. He's in mourning for her; he won't kill a small child.'

'He killed the garrison at Shrewsbury,' she said, feeling nauseous. 'Hanged them all. Are you prepared to take that risk with our son?'

'The garrison at Shrewsbury were grown men, not infants,' he said curtly. 'I promise you, Stephen won't do it.'

She blinked and shook her head, tears welling, and turned away to compose herself. If she started screaming and weeping she was lost. Drawing a deep breath she turned round again. 'Perhaps you could swear to Stephen in order to save Newbury and get William back, but quietly bide your time.'

'Give my oath without giving it, you mean?' His tone was dangerously flat.

'No,' she retorted with exasperation, 'give your oath and keep your head down. You don't have to go out on a limb all the time.'

Colour flooded into his face, matching the hue of his scar. 'For all your cleverness, wife, you haven't dwelt at court beyond a single Christmas gathering with the Empress. Believe me, if I yield to Stephen, you'll be a widow before the autumn winds strip the leaves from the trees. Those around Stephen would cut me down and spit upon my corpse.'

'Holy Virgin, you are ten times worse than Patrick!' She stamped her foot. 'There are more moves in a game of chess than two – as you should know if you are the great courtier you claim to be! Others have played the game to their own advantage by balancing a line between Stephen and Henry. Why can't we do the same?'

429

'Because it is too late for that and we are not strong enough on our own. It'd be safer to walk along the edge of a cliff with a gale at my back. Don't you see, there is no place for me at Stephen's side, whether I feign or not. Stephen owes me nothing but his resentment. I would have to bend myself backwards to do his smallest bidding, whereas Henry will owe me more than he can repay.'

'And will he not resent it?'

'No, because Henry is like his mother – he uses men to the best of their abilities and he will reward loyalty into the next generation. I am certain of that in the same way I am certain that Stephen will not. Our only chance is buying Henry time and we have to buy it now, not bide it.'

'Even if it costs us a son?'

His jaw muscles were as tight as iron, carving deep grooves down his cheeks. 'It won't cost us a son.'

'You cannot be certain of that.'

He drew forward a sheet of parchment and trimmed a quill. 'You either trust my judgement, or you don't, Sybilla.'

She stared at him. That was it: the end of the matter; and he had put it with unembellished clarity. A matter of trust. She had wanted him because he was the best, his reputation as a soldier legendary. She could think of no other man she would desire as her life-mate. But the very strength of the qualities she admired in him gave her a difficult field to hoe and never more so than now. She could strike the trestle with her clenched fist, ask him if he trusted *her* judgement on the matter, but it would be fruitless and damaging. If she didn't believe in him and that they would come through, what was left except threadbare rags? Whatever else, Sybilla was not prepared to be a beggar.

430

He said, without looking up from his work, 'I've sent Tamkin to keep an eye on William from a subtle distance. You don't think I'd leave him unwatched, do you?'

Sybilla swallowed deep in her throat, too overcome to speak. She should have known he would have some kind of contingency plan to hand, although what Tamkin could do should it come to the crux, she didn't know.

William's kitten suddenly leaped on to the trestle and paraded itself in front of John on tiptoe, purring fit to explode. John wasn't that enamoured of cats. As far as he was concerned they existed to rid the keep of small vermin and provide soft fur for lining cloaks and hoods. Essential but only tolerated, unlike his dogs, which could be depended on for loyalty and unswerving affection on his terms, not theirs. However, instead of swiping the little creature off the trestle, he put out his hand and gently scratched the top of its head.

'He called it Lion,' Sybilla said in an emotion-cracked voice.

'Ridiculous name,' John scoffed, but when it curled up in his hat and went to sleep, he left it there.

Sybilla set her arms around his neck and laid her cheek against the top of his spine. 'I do trust you,' she said, 'but I still fear for our son . . .'

John said nothing, but he put up the hand not holding the quill and squeezed her fingers.

The night was moonless but the stars shed a weak glimmer of light and John knew the trackways well. He was accustomed by now to moving troops quietly in the dark. Often it was the only way to gain an advantage over the enemy. Stealing a march; the element of surprise. He had left Aranais in the stable and was riding his black courser, Serjean. The men who were mounted

431

all had dark horses too and no man wore pale clothing. As well as a dozen archers, twelve footsoldiers, eight serjeants and two knights, a string of supply-laden pack ponies followed in procession. All the archers carried full quivers and more arrows were loaded on the ponies. There were pots of powdered lime, spears, axes, ropes, barrels of pitch and various other paraphernalia of siege warfare. Some of the pack beasts were laden with sacks of oats and flour, bladders of lard, flitches of bacon and barrels of salted cod. John had promised Benet the men and supplies to hold out and intended giving them full measure.

The air was scented with the green aromas of earlier rainfall and the trees and hedgerows dripped with dark jewels as the troop wound its way through the night on narrow pathways and came to the keep at Newbury. His scouts had reported that the King had taken his army and retreated a short distance, but a force remained outside the walls and would do so throughout the truce, observing but making no hostile moves. John had expected this. He knew that even with his plans laid for stealth, a report would go to Stephen that he had brought supplies into the keep; but since it had been under cover of night, it would be difficult for Stephen's scouts to report just how much had been restocked and of what nature. Tomorrow night was set to be moonless too, and the one after. By the time the truce officially ended, John intended Newbury to be stuffed so full with troops and supplies that men would have to squeeze sideways into the latrines to piss.

Most of the enemy's camp fires were banked low, showing little more than a glow of lazy red like a half-sleeping dragon's eye. There was little sound from the direction of their tents and just the occasional stamp and snort of a mount at the horse lines. Nevertheless a couple of watch fires still blazed on alert and some soldiers were gathered around them in conversation.

John sent three men forward to give the signal for those within to let down the leather scaling ladders and open the postern gate in the palisade. From the direction of the fires, John could hear Stephen's men laughing over a jest one of them had made. They were toasting bread on sticks and enjoying each other's conversation rather than watching the keep. John would have kept his own men on a much tighter rein and was glad that Stephen's captain was not as diligent.

The pack ponies were unloaded by the men-at-arms and the goods hauled in by grapnel and basket. Then the burden-free ponies were turned around by their drover and led back to Hamstead to collect another load. John supervised, then spurred Serjean up the steep incline. He felt the stallion's hindquarters bunch and strain with effort. Then they were at the top and squeezing in through the postern.

John dismounted and flung the reins to a groom. Benet shouldered his way forward, started to bow, but John caught and clasped him hard instead.

Benet gave him a mirthless, torchlit smile. 'I was beginning to wonder if you were coming,' he said.

'It's taken some organising. There's more on the way.' John's reply was terse as he strode towards the gatehouse.

'I've shored up and repaired where possible and the men are in good heart, but we could not have held them against another determined assault without the aid you have sent.'

'We have to stave them off for as long as we can.' John glanced over his right shoulder at Benet. 'That is not negotiable. We fight until we have nothing left.' He mounted the stairs to the gatehouse tower that looked out on Stephen's skeleton camp.

'And when that happens?'

'We cross that bridge when we come to it . . . and then we burn it.' John stopped short as he saw the fair-haired musician sitting at one of the trestles, his bright tunic and striped hose looking incongruous amid the leather and mail of the fighting men. 'Well?' John said and suddenly he was breathing hard.

Tamkin had risen to his feet at John's entrance. Now he bowed. 'I have seen him, my lord. A Fleming and his woman are looking after him and they are treating him well. He seems in fine fettle. There have been no tears. Indeed, he has been allowed to ride his pony around the camp and he talks to the men about their weapons and what they do as soldiers.' Tamkin's lips quirked. 'He also keeps asking when he's going to see the King.'

John found himself smiling too and although he felt pain somewhere at his core, there was a lessening of anxiety. If they were treating William well, it was a good sign. 'I would not expect him to cry or make a fuss,' he said proudly. 'He will hold his head up whatever happens.' *And so will I.*

'They seem much taken with him,' the musician added. 'If he keeps that charm into manhood then his future's assured. He'll have patrons vying with each other for his services.'

John looked rueful. 'He's got to live to manhood first,' he said, but he was not displeased by the musician's assessment of William's character. The child had little else to protect him just now except that sunny, endearing nature and the King's weakness. If John had misjudged the latter, he would have to live with the consequences for eternity.

434

42

King Stephen's Siege Camp, Newbury, Berkshire, July 1152

William sat at the trestle in Henk's tent, swinging his legs and breaking his fast on the bowl of oat frumenty that Henk's wife Mariette had set before him. She had sweetened it with honey and a scattering of raisins and William was savouring it to make it last. There wouldn't be anything else to eat until late in the afternoon when Henk returned from his duty. Apparently their dinner today was duck. A brace of mallards dangled from a pole at the tent entrance, feathers ruffling in the morning breeze.

Mariette was busy with her laundry, slamming Henk's shirts and braies in a large wooden tub of lye soap, along with the garments of soldiers from neighbouring tents, from whom she earned a coin or two. She was a buxom, florid-faced woman with a gap-toothed smile and twinkling brown eyes. Unlike his mother, who always smelled of rose water and cinnamon, Mariette carried with her a pervasive odour of lye soap and earth and there was a pungent smell from her armpits when she had been pummelling her washing. He couldn't understand a lot of what she said because her French had a heavy Flemish accent, but she was kind to him and seemed to think he needed feeding up – which he didn't. He was still delighted to eat whatever she put in front of him, for which he received much hair-tousling and praise and even the occasional odoriferous embrace. Henk called her a foolish woman and told her not to get fond, but he had allowed William to look at his weapons, touch his mail shirt and burnish his helm and shield boss, which William had thought very exciting.

He had a small bed a bit like his one at home, boxed in and stuffed with straw. A sheepskin cover went on top and his mother had sent his favourite quilt with his baggage roll – the one with the red whorls of embroidery. He quite liked living in a tent, although it was not what he had expected. He had thought he would be lodging with the King in a luxurious chamber – bigger than the one at home, with fine hangings and goblets of silver and gold. But when he had arrived at the camp, the King wasn't there and his army hadn't been very big. They had told him the King had gone somewhere else and that he would have to stay here until he returned. Then the mercenary captain had given him into Henk's charge and he had been brought to this tent. Every day he asked when the King was coming back, but it had been ages and still no sign of him.

William scraped his bowl clean, resisting the urge to pick it up and lick it out because such behaviour was appalling manners and not tolerated at home, even if he'd seen some of his father's soldiers doing it. Suitably fuelled he was now ready to leave the tent and go out and about the camp. He liked to gallop the big brown pony they had given him, talk to the men and play-fight with the youngest squires. Being in the company of the soldiers all the time made him feel like a real soldier too, especially

436

when they sparred with him or let him join them in contests of throwing the stone, at which he was good.

Mariette was singing a washing song as she pounded and scrubbed, but on seeing William emerge from the tent, she dried her hands on a cloth and set them to his shoulders. 'Don't wander too far,' she told him, 'and don't dirty your clothes. Your father's going to be coming for you today when he gives his castle to the King.'

William wasn't quite sure he had understood her. 'I am going home?'

'God willing, *mijn kleine*.' She smoothed his hair with her rough red hands.

'But I haven't seen the King yet.'

'You will today. He will be here soon. Mind what I say, don't go far now.'

William was excited at the thought of seeing the King at last – and his father too. 'How soon?'

'Am I an oracle to know? Heavens, *jongen*, go and play.'

'What's an oracle?'

'Someone who knows everything. Now go on and stop bedevilling me!'

William started to dash off, then ran back into the tent for his wooden sword and shield. The King might want to see them and he wanted to show his father that he had practised with them every day. If his father was coming to fetch him, he would soon be home again. He could play with Lion and show his mother the bone whistle given to him by one of the soldiers. He would surprise his older brother with the wrestling move Henk had taught him, and he would be able to teach little Margaret one of Mariette's laundry songs.

He was watching the knights practising at the quintain and imagining himself as big as they were, clad in mail and riding a destrier like his father's magnificent Aranais, when the King arrived. There was a flurry of trumpets and the knights charged off from their practice to go and greet their sovereign lord. William dashed after them but the King's men were arriving in such numbers that he couldn't tell who was who and there was no one who wore a crown or looked much like his notion of royalty. He saw many fine warhorses and knights in full mail. Some wore surcoats of bright silk over their hauberks and one lord even had a pack of hounds running beside his stallion. When William tried to squeeze forward for a better look, he was shouted at by a scowling arbalester and told not to be a nuisance. He had just decided to climb to the top of one of the trebuchets facing the castle walls for a better view when Henk scooped him up by the scruff and bore him back to Mariette. 'Stay put,' he commanded. 'They'll be coming for you in a little while.'

Having finished her laundry and draped it on a rope slung between two spears to dry, Mariette made William wash his face and hands again even though he protested they weren't dirty. Then she clucked at a mark on his tunic and made him change it for his best blue one. She tweaked the folds straight and combed his hair, lamenting a particular tuft that refused to lie flat.

'God's blood, woman, he's the whelp of a thrice-dyed treacherous rebel whoremonger, not your son!' Henk snapped.

She glared at him. 'He's a child!'

'He is at the moment,' Henk said darkly, then switched to Flemish to growl something that made Mariette gasp and then launch a tirade at him. William looked from one to the other, interested rather than alarmed. They were always squabbling. He noticed a youth wearing a fine scarlet tunic standing in the tent entrance. Henk turned to leave and saw him too.

438

'You're to bring the boy to the Earl of Arundel,' the youth said. 'Now.'

Mariette gave William's hair another stroke and then let him go. Her eyes looked all watery and William wondered if she was crying. His mother's eyes had gone like that when he left to come here. Henk nodded acknowledgement to the youth and taking William's arm drew him from the tent.

As they emerged from the camp on to the open ground before the castle, William saw several riders clattering over the lowered drawbridge. He recognised his father on Aranais, and Benet and Jaston, the latter on Ronsorel, his mottled red-chestnut. William thought about leaping up and down and waving and shouting to attract their attention but, knowing that such behaviour was discouraged at home, held himself back. However, he stared at his father as hard as he could, trying to make him glance in his direction. Even with only one eye, his father seemed to notice most things around him, but today, for whatever reason, William couldn't make him turn his head.

Henk gave him a sharp tug. 'Come, boy,' he growled. 'You'll see your father soon enough.'

The mercenary brought William to a group of lords and knights who were standing on the open ground waiting for the riders to reach them. William didn't know any of them and there was still no one who looked like a king, although one lord had a magnificent golden brooch pinning the throat of his cloak which was trimmed with ermine tails. No crown though. Henk muttered to him as an aside that it was William Martel, one of King Stephen's senior men, and that William should bow to him and stay quiet.

William did as he was told. He liked Martel's big gold brooch and he had a beautiful scabbard at his hip, but

439

the man himself exuded menace. William sensed he was being studied with disapproval, although he didn't know what he'd done wrong.

'Come here, boy,' said Martel and, before William could comply, seized him by the neck of his tunic and dragged him to stand in front of him. He had thick, strong fingers smothered in gold rings. William could sense the anger in him. It was like the surface of a cauldron of water when it was simmering up to the boil. He wriggled in discomfort, and Martel immediately increased his grip, pinching William's shoulder bone between fingers and thumb until William had to swallow a yelp of pain. He wasn't going to cry out in front of all these soldiers, and especially not in front of his father who had arrived to face Stephen's men. He was holding Aranais on a tight rein and showed no intention of dismounting. William looked up at him but still his father wouldn't engage his glance. His jaw was clenched as if there was a bunched fist inside his cheek. Aranais sidled and snorted, hind-quarters swinging and tail swishing.

William felt Martel's chest expand as he drew a deep breath. 'FitzGilbert, I do not know why you have bothered to come to the meet,' he sneered, 'unless it be to bid farewell to your son. We know you have fortified the keep with men and supplies and it's hardly for our benefit, is it?'

His father was silent for a long time. When he spoke, his voice was straight and cold. 'Where is the King?'

'Waiting in his tent for your surrender, my lord, and he will not speak with you unless you swear now to yield.'

'Then perhaps, knowing what you do, you might think it prudent to return my son to me and depart with your lives.'

William felt Martel's belly shake as he laughed. 'A fine

try, FitzGilbert. You have audacity, I'll grant you that, but it won't save you or the boy. Hand over the castle to us now – or his life is forfeit.'

William looked at his father, not certain what the words meant, but not liking the sound of them, or the bruising weight of Martel's hand still gripping his shoulder. His father's face was set like stone and the expression on it was the one he wore when he was furious about something – not just annoyed, but truly angry, beyond stamping or shouting. He'd gone white too so that his scar stood out in scarlet relief.

'Then it is forfeit,' his father said with a wave of his hand. 'I have three other sons at home and, as the King well knows, the anvils and hammers to forge better than this one. Do as you will.' He tugged on the rein, drawing Aranais around, pricked him with his spurs and cantered back to the castle without a backward glance, his two subalterns accompanying him. William stared after him, his tummy swooping with shocked surprise. Something was wrong. He didn't understand. His eyes stung, but he dug his fingers into the palm of his hand, held himself straight and didn't cry. His mother had said he was her champion and his father had told him that he had to be a good soldier and do his best.

'Bastard,' muttered one of the men, his voice filled with revulsion.

'He's bluffing,' someone else said. 'The brat's Patrick of Salisbury's nephew. He'll back down. He must.'

Martel gave a short bark of laughter. 'You don't know John Marshal.' They started talking about his father's fight at Wherwell Abbey when he lost his eye, a tale William had occasionally heard before from his father's knights and guards, then Martel went off, saying he was going to talk to the King, and Henk took William back to his tent.

441

Mariette left off plucking the mallards and squeezed William in a tight embrace. She gave him a cup of goat's milk to drink and fussed over him so much that he wriggled to get away. All he wanted to do was leap on his pony and ride after his father at full gallop. Failing that, around the camp would do. He felt as if he was going to burst with all the pent-up energy that being made to sit and stand and be still had built up inside him. All the fear as well.

Henk and Mariette started talking rapidly to each other in Flemish. He knew it was about him because he heard his name and he could recognise some other words too. Mariette started getting upset and buried her face in her apron to sob. Then a different messenger arrived with a summons.

Henk grabbed William's arm and bundled him out of the tent, dragging him swiftly away from the soldiers' bivouacs and towards another group of noblemen standing in contemplation of the castle. As well as the baron called William Martel, there was a lord carrying a beautiful silk banner wafting on a long, painted lance. He had been present before when his father had come out of the castle, but he hadn't said anything. With them was a third man: tall and broad-set with greying fair hair and vein-reddened cheeks. He looked sad, William thought.

Henk pushed William to his knees in front of him. 'Kneel to your King, child,' he said.

William was astonished. *This* man was King Stephen? All the same, he bowed his head like he was supposed to do before God in church.

He was bidden to rise and as he stood, looked up into the care-worn features of an old, tired man. 'Are you the King?' he asked to satisfy his own curiosity.

'I am, although your father seems not to think so,' the man said dourly, and glanced round at his advisers. 'So this is the boy whose only value to his father has been the buying of time.'

'My lord, he says you may do as you like with the child; he cares not,' said Martel with a sinister glare in William's direction. 'I say put him to the test. If he opens the gates we have won. If he doesn't, then he'll bear the guilt for this death – and there'll be one less flea to suck our blood.'

The King rubbed his beard and drew Martel and a couple of his captains aside to discuss what they should do. William turned to the man with the silk banner and asked if he could hold it. The man looked surprised, then amused and let him, warning him to be careful. 'You're as bold as your father, aren't you?'

William twirled the spear, making the banner ripple in the breeze. 'He has a red lion on his shield,' he said, pointing to the design on the rippling silk. 'My kitten's called Lion too.'

For some reason the lord bit his lip. Then he looked at the discussion going on between the King and the others and his eyelids tightened.

Martel broke from the group and strode to William. He snatched the spear out of his hand and thrust it back into its owner's. Then he hauled William across the sward to a timber frame that had been set up beside one of the trebuchets in full view of the castle. A rope had been thrown over the beam and one of its ends tied into a loop that swung gently back and forth, reminding William of the swing in the orchard at Hamstead, except the one at Hamstead had a seat to straddle made of a timber plank.

William looked round. His hand was burning because of the way Martel had snatched the lance from him. The lord who owned it was talking rapidly to the King and gesticulating.

Releasing William's arm, Martel reached for the rope and held the loop with a hand on either side. 'How would you like to swing on this, lad?' he asked.

William nodded, but then thought he had better be polite, since the man seemed so cross about something. 'You can have first turn,' he said.

Behind him, someone spluttered and William looked round to find that several of the men were laughing, and that made him laugh too. Furiously Martel grabbed William and set the noose around his neck. 'No,' he growled. 'Let's see how well you kick first.'

Standing on the wall walk between the two towers flanking the gatehouse, John watched them bring William out and then take him to the makeshift gibbet.

'Dear God in heaven,' Benet muttered. He looked at John, saying nothing, but with an appalled question in his eyes.

John raised his hand and felt the rough scarring under his fingertips and said nothing because he had to stand firm. He saw William grabbed, saw the noose go over his head and braced himself against the palisade. It was one thing to say it didn't matter, another to stand and watch it happen. He had gambled that Stephen's nature was too soft to hang a five-year-old boy, no matter his parentage. But he had also gambled that Stephen would be strong enough to gainsay the intention of harder men such as William Martel.

'Should we loose some arrows?'

'No, save them. They're out of range and we'll need them later. If they see we are moved by any of this, it will only prolong matters.'

There was an altercation at the gibbet. Martel was

444

gesturing, someone else gesturing back, and Stephen standing a little away, looking from one to the other. Suddenly William was hoisted up with a rapid jerk on the rope. John stared, straight-faced, one hand on his sword hilt, the other pressed to the palisade, knuckles showing white. Pain and shock ripped through him. His stomach muscles were so taut that he felt as if they were fusing to his spine. He daren't loosen any part of himself, daren't let anything through or he would shatter into a hundred irreparable shards, and he couldn't do that, because he had to command the defence of this place.

There was silence along the battlements. John swallowed hard and sought his voice. 'Tell the men to give my battle cry,' he commanded hoarsely. 'Tell them to beat their spears on the ground and shout. Loud as they can – do it now!'

'My lord!' Benet turned on his heel.

John let out his breath and stared across the open ground to the gibbet, not knowing whether to weep or exult. They hadn't strung the noose around William's delicate neck. They had hauled him up by the chest instead, taunting those in the keep.

'*Dex ai! Dex ai le Maréchal!*' He heard the first cry go up, then another, and another, ragged at first, but gaining momentum. The thud of the spears on the wall-walk planks set up a hard reverberation like a strong, steady heartbeat.

Christ, boy, Christ, boy, listen to this. It's all I can send you. His good eye was suddenly blind and stinging. '*Dex ai! Dex ai le Maréchal!*' He took up the cry himself and sent it full-throated across the space between them.

A herald rode out from the royal camp waving a flag of parley and John signalled for silence. It fell in ragged increments as the command was relayed.

445

'That was but a warning!' the herald bellowed up. 'Unless you surrender, John FitzGilbert, know that your son will die before your eyes!'

'You had your answer this morning!' John roared back. 'Do as you will with him, you will not move me.' He gestured and the chanting recommenced with vigour.

The herald hesitated, then wrenched his horse round and galloped back across the camp to relay the response.

'My lord.' Benet handed him a cup of wine.

John drank. The taste was heavy and sour, or perhaps that taste had been in his mouth already.

'What happens now?'

'They'll up the stakes to prove they're in earnest.'

'You mean they'll kill him?'

'I would not put it past Martel, but Arundel is a force for reason and, as I said before, the King has a tender spot for women and children.'

Benet looked sick. 'You meant it about the anvils and hammers, didn't you?'

John felt the wine strike his belly like a hot lead fist. 'You've known me all my life,' he said impassively. 'You shouldn't have to ask.' He glanced from the battlements to the small figure of his son, bound with rope, dangling aloft, and had to fight his gorge. 'Keep the spears beating. I don't want them to stop until it's over – however it ends.'

The herald returned to Stephen and his courtiers and relayed John's message.

Martel nodded with anger in which there was a seasoning of relish. Rubbing his hands, he turned to two serjeants standing nearby. 'Bring kindling,' he said. 'If John Marshal understands nothing else, he knows what fire can do.' He glanced up at William. 'Let's see, shall we?'

* * *

446

After the shock of suddenly being hoisted into the air, William had quite enjoyed the experience. It was like being up in a tree at home, except that there were no branches under him. He could almost imagine that he was a bird and that this was like flying. The baron called Martel said he expected him to kick a lot, so he did at first, but then he had stopped the better to watch the castle. A forest of spears lined the walls and a thundering noise began. Then his father's soldiers began to chant in time with the rhythmic thunder of their spear butts on the palisade walkway. It was very exciting and William shouted and waved. He couldn't see his father, but knew he must be there somewhere. It was too far away to tell, but he thought he heard him call something down to the herald. The latter returned at a hard gallop, relayed his message and Martel called for firewood to be brought. William watched them piling the faggots beneath his swing. Martel went away and then returned with a blazing torch. A gesture lowered William until he could almost touch the topmost pieces of firewood with his toes.

'Now then, lad, do you like bonfires?' Martel asked.

William nodded. He did, it was true.

Martel grinned up at him. 'Let's see how you and your father enjoy this one.'

He thrust the torch into the faggots. Almost immediately, flames caught amongst the smaller twigs and licked through the mesh of branches. Smoke rose in thin serpentine streamers and red tongues of heat flickered towards William's shoe soles.

'Are you watching this, John FitzGilbert?' bellowed Martel towards the keep walls. 'He'll roast like a coney!'

The chanting from the castle walls changed quality, becoming louder and stronger.

William began to cough as the smoke reached his lungs.

447

The heat was fierce and it frightened him, but he knew he mustn't cry because it would be breaking his promise. He bent his knees and tried to twist his body away from the blaze. A woman was screaming and a glance across the field showed him Mariette on her knees, wailing and pounding the ground with her fists.

'Enough!' the King roared and gestured the men to hoist William up away from the flames. 'Put this out!' He pointed to the fire.

'Sire, the child's life is forfeit,' Martel said. 'FitzGilbert needs to be taught a lesson.'

'Mayhap he does, but I will not do it with the life of an innocent child. Look at him. Look at what you are doing. I will not imperil my soul with a deed such as this. If the Queen were still alive, she would not forgive me, let alone God in his heaven.'

'You are making a mistake, sire,' said Martel, tight-lipped.

'That is nothing new in my life,' Stephen retorted. 'Whether the child dies or not, it is plain FitzGilbert is not going to yield unless we batter him into submission. Let the boy live another day. It may be that we can still use him.'

William watched the soldiers throw buckets of water on to the fire. He had been raised above the heat, but the residual smoke still stung his eyes and made him cough. He was hungry, thirsty, chafed and tired. The game had lost its appeal. Once the fire was doused sufficiently for it to be safe, they lowered him to the ground and the King himself pulled off the rope around his chest.

'Child, your father may not care if you live or die, but I have more concern for my soul and for yours. Are you hurt?'

William looked up into the faded blue eyes with their

448

inflamed red rims. 'I'm hungry,' he said. 'Is there anything to eat . . . sire?'

A smile parted the King's lips, and he chuckled. 'No matter how busy your father is with those anvils and hammers of his, I doubt he will ever get braver than you,' he said. 'Come with me and I'll find you something to eat and drink in my pavilion.'

In the silence of aftermath, the door bolted, John lay on his pallet and stared at the rafters, although he didn't see the roughly hewn wooden beams. Scenes from the happenings of the afternoon haunted his vision – riding out to parley and deliberately ignoring his son, who was looking at him, desperate to be noticed, a world of innocent bewilderment in his eyes. The small body swinging on the gibbet. The building of the fire and the moment – almost too late – when they had hoisted William out of harm's reach and doused the flames.

'Ah, God!' he groaned and rolling on to his stomach buried his face within his folded arms. His guilt and his grief were tearing him to shreds, but he knew he had to show an impassive face in public. Tears and recriminations were for women, not a battle-hardened commander with three other sons vouchsafed and a fecund young wife. But still the spasms wrenched through his chest like dry lightning and, finally, he let the storm have its way with him.

The dusk had seeped away into full darkness when at last he roused and stumbled from the bed to light the lantern on the coffer with a trembling hand. He splashed water on his face and felt the burn scar prickle like a severe nettle sting. He was ripped open, empty, but knew he had to go out and deal with matters. William had survived today, but there was still tomorrow and tomorrow

449

and tomorrow. Stephen might withdraw, but John knew in his gut he would not. For the King it was now or never to crush Henry's bases in England. Besides, Newbury had become personal.

John dried his face on a linen towel and drank down a cup of wine. He couldn't remember anyone leaving him food but obviously they had for there was a cloth on the coffer and when he lifted it, he found half a simnel loaf and some of Sybilla's cheese. He sat on his campstool and ate and drank with stoical deliberation, scarcely tasting the food but knowing he had to sustain himself if he was going to lead the men.

Arriving on the battlements a short while later, the trauma of the last few hours was concealed behind an impassive mask. He moved with his customary assurance and gave orders with unruffled certainty. He knew his men were eyeing him sidelong, admiring his 'anvils and hammers' and probably thinking him an unfeeling bastard. He knew he was a legend to them and he sought to keep their regard at that level, but it had its price.

'They'll attack at first light,' he told Benet as he halted on the same spot where he had stood that afternoon. 'Stand as many men down as you can tonight. Let them be well fed and rested, ready for the dawn.' He looked out over the dotted fires of the siege camp. Somewhere among those tents his small son still lived and breathed. Still a hostage, still a plaything and a pawn. A spoil of war, a sacrifice. He wondered if William understood anything of what had happened today – and if so, would the child hate him for it? Even if he did, it wouldn't be as much as John hated himself.

450

43

Newbury, July 1152

The floor of the King's tent had been strewn with fresh meadow grasses that morning to replace the trampled ones of the previous day. William inhaled the strong green scent, intensified by the enclosing canvas. It was a nice smell, he thought – better than smoke. He didn't much like that one at the moment.

He had recovered swiftly from his ordeal of two days since. After he had been freed from the rope halter, the King had taken him under his wing and brought him to his own tent where he had given him proper wine to drink and a whole platter of almond wafers. William had been excited to see the King's armour and weapons. He had loved the rich hangings and the silk coverlet on the bed. The King said that William should stay with him, enter his service and become his page. He said that he was giving him an opportunity to grow up and show what a loyal knight he was. William liked the idea of becoming a page and then a knight. None of his brothers had been granted such a privilege and he was to train with the King himself. He had decided that what had happened two days ago had been a kind of test. In the stories his mother told and the songs Tamkin sang in the hall at night, the heroes always had to undertake quests. It was a pity he wasn't being allowed to go home though. In the darkest part of the night he had almost cried when he thought about not seeing his mother and siblings again for a long time, but daylight had brought acceptance of what was going to be – and anticipation.

The tent entrance darkened as King Stephen stepped within and gestured his attendants to leave him in peace. He looked a trifle startled when he saw William, but stepped around him and sat down heavily in his barrel chair with its red embroidered cushion.

'You're like a little ghost,' he said, rubbing his hand over his face. 'It's as if I see my own sons playing where you now play.'

William wasn't sure he liked being compared to a ghost. 'Where are your sons?' he asked.

Stephen gave him a tired smile. 'Fighting,' he said. 'Grown up. Dead.'

'My papa's got a lot of sons.'

'So he has. He has the Devil's own good fortune.' Stephen glanced towards the tent entrance. 'Or perhaps he's the Devil himself,' he growled. 'Some of the bishops seem to think so.' He poured himself a cup of wine. 'I'll admit he has courage though. Trying to shift him is like trying to push a cart laden with boulders to the top of a mountain. If matters had been different . . .' He looked broodingly at William. 'I underestimated him. I won't do it again. I can't afford to.'

William didn't know what the King was talking about, only that it concerned his papa and it wasn't all good. He busied himself about the floor, collecting up plantains from among the newly cut meadow grass. The stalks and seed-heads somewhat resembled a lance with a fat tip.

452

'Do you want to play a game of knights?' he asked hopefully.

Stephen looked at William and the sad smile returned, although this time it was warmer. 'Why not, my little friend,' he said. 'What do I have to lose?'

William placed a handful in Stephen's lap and eyed him expectantly. 'Who has the first turn?' he asked. He knew it was polite to offer that privilege rather than to wade in himself.

Stephen's lips twitched. 'You do, since you gathered up the stalks,' he said, 'and you are my guest.' He held up one of the stalks and gave William the opportunity to try to knock off the seed-head, and as they played his smile continued to grow. William succeeded in knocking the head off the King's plantain stalk, which greatly delighted him and caused the King to chuckle. 'I should have known not to give the advantage to a Marshal,' he said.

They continued to play until William Martel arrived with Arundel to give a battle report. 'God knows how many arrows he's got stored in there,' Martel grumbled. 'Certainly he doesn't seem to be running out. I've lost another good man this afternoon.' He glared at William. 'We ought to bring the targes forward and strap the boy to them. That would give the bastards second thoughts.'

'You think so?' Stephen looked wry. 'I doubt it.' He leaned against the curved back of his chair. 'He doesn't have an endless supply and we'll draw all of his teeth in the end. Just wear him down with that trebuchet and keep your men behind the targes.'

'He put fire arrows through one this morning,' Martel said in an aggrieved voice. 'We can't get near enough to the structures and he's keeping them well wetted.'

'I well know how good John FitzGilbert is as a warrior and siege captain,' Stephen said, thin-lipped. 'I know it

453

won't be easy, but I am not prepared to have him sitting on my back when we ride for Wallingford. We have to take this place.'

They embarked on a discussion about bringing in more supplies. Feeling uncertain around Martel and growing bored, William went to look out of the tent entrance. Under an awning Stephen's guards and squires were tending to their weapons and talking to Martel's adjutants. In the tent next door, Stephen's cook was preparing a stew and roasting two hares on a spit. Standing talking to him was Tamkin, his citole case strapped across his back the way a soldier might strap his shield. His arms folded, he was deep in gossip with the cook.

Astonished and overjoyed, William called out and ran to him, flinging his arms around the musician's thighs. The knights turned and looked, curious. The cook stood still, his wooden ladle dripping fat over the hares, his eyes growing round. Tamkin leaned over William to embrace him. 'Your father says he is proud of you, that you are a true knight, and your mother the same,' he whispered against William's ear. 'They sent me to make sure you were well.'

William nodded. 'I'm playing with the King.' He showed the musician the bunch of wilting plantains he still held in his hand. 'I knocked the head off his knight. When can I go home?'

'Soon.' Tamkin's gaze flickered to the side. 'I have to go.' Disengaging from William he took off at a rapid walk.

'Know him, do you, boy?' asked Martel's knight.

'He's our musician.' William smiled. 'He sings in my mother's chamber.'

The knights exchanged glances and hastened off in the direction Tamkin had just taken.

A moment later Martel emerged from the tent and looked round for his men. 'Chasing a spy,' the cook

454

informed him. 'That singer who's been sniffing around. He's one of FitzGilbert's men.'

'If they catch him he'll hang,' Martel growled. 'I doubt the King will intervene this time.'

William felt worried. He didn't want them to catch and hang Tamkin. Stephen had heard the news through the open tent flaps and came to stand beside William.

'So,' he said, thoughtfully, 'your father cares for you more than he'd admit.'

'Perhaps we should string him up again,' Martel suggested. 'He and the musician could dance together for FitzGilbert's entertainment.'

Stephen wagged his forefinger. 'Don't taunt the boy. Done is done and I have made my decision on that score. Let this one have his future. Certainly if you catch the musician you may do as you will with him. I am sure that looking out for our young friend's welfare is not the only fish on his griddle. He'll have been relaying information to FitzGilbert and being paid for his tunes.'

'Oh, we'll catch him, and he'll dance,' Martel said, baring his teeth at William.

William looked back steadily, the way he knew his father would have done if thus confronted. He felt scared, but knew he mustn't show it.

Martel's complexion flushed. He made a sound in his throat and, turning on his heel, strode off. Stephen laid his hand lightly on William's shoulder. 'Don't concern yourself, lad,' he said. 'This is men's business. When you are a man you will understand.'

William looked round and up at the King. 'Do you still want to play at knights?' he asked, holding up the limp plantain heads.

'Another time, child,' Stephen said, his eyes deep wells of sadness. 'For now I have different games to see to.'

44

Hamstead, Berkshire, July 1152

The rain swept across the Kennet in thick curtains, heavy as link-mail. Sybilla walked the dogs past the lookout mounds, letting them sniff and meander where they would, rather like her thoughts. There had been no word from John. She had hoped to hear from him but had not counted on it. She knew he would have difficulty getting messengers out of the keep at Newbury, and would only concentrate on the essential ones. Telling her that he or William were safe was unlikely to be high on his agenda.

She had kept herself and the household busy, preparing lest Newbury did fall and Hamstead come next under siege. Gilbert and Walter had been taking out patrols and attending to matters of security around the demesne. Gilbert at eighteen and on the cusp of knighthood took his responsibilities seriously. He was, after all, John's heir and if Henry eventually became King, he would inherit the title of marshal in his father's wake. Fourteen-year-old Walter, quiet and slender in his brother's shadow, had a firm grasp of fiscal matters and a calculating mind. Those who initially overlooked him because of his slight build and understated ways soon found their notions disabused. They might not measure up when balanced against their father, but they had made a decent weight of their own and she was glad of their presence.

She kept herself occupied to hold at bay the raw, empty spaces in her chamber, but when she stopped, the pain encroached. No energetic small boy whooping around the room, leaving a trail of laughter and chaos. No tickles by the fire. No stories or music with him leaning against her side as she stroked his hair. Her older son was self-contained and less spontaneous, and although Sybilla loved him dearly, it was in a different way that didn't begin to fill the hole left by William.

And then there was her bed. It was not that she minded sleeping alone. John was often absent carrying out his duties and obligations, but before she had always been certain of his return. This time that conviction was absent.

The rain was soaking up through the hem of her gown and although her shoes were waxed, her feet were damp. She felt bereft and chilled. She knew she should turn back for the hall, but she had needed this moment alone, without her women or attendants, and the rain matched her mood. The urge to weep was a pressure behind her eyes.

Suddenly Doublet began to bark, swiftly followed by the other dogs, and Sybilla heard the thud of hooves on the road coming at a swift trot. One horse by the sounds of it. She calculated how far she was from the castle and knew she would be overtaken even if she ran hard. She felt apprehensive but not afraid. The dogs would protect her and she had both a knife and a hunting horn at her belt. All the same, she began to walk briskly towards home, casting constant glances over her shoulder.

The horse that came into view was a high-stepping black cob. Its coat gleamed in the rain and its feathered hooves were splashed to the cannon bones with mud.

Clinging to the reins and hunched over the saddle bow was Tamkin, his hair plastered to his head and his complexion grey. Sybilla gasped.

He looked up and she saw him summon his reserves. 'My lady!' He started to slide from the saddle and clung on. 'My lady, I am being chased! Go back, it is not safe!'

Sybilla unhooked the horn from her belt and blew on it three times. She didn't care if his pursuers heard her. She reasoned it would frighten them off if their quarry had company. They weren't to know she was a woman alone.

'Let me ride pillion,' she commanded.

He drew rein and she came to the horse, set her foot on his and hoisted herself up, straddling the beast in masculine fashion rather than perching sideways: what John with dark humour called 'doing an Empress'. 'Go!' she cried. She put her hands in his belt for purchase and heard him gasp, then felt the warm wetness against her palms.

'You're wounded!'

'Arrow,' he croaked and heeled the horse.

Hooves thundered on the track behind. Sybilla glanced over her shoulder and through the sheeting rain saw three horsemen bearing down on them. Tamkin heeled the cob again and it broke into a canter. Their pursuers were shouting but Sybilla couldn't make out the words. Then suddenly the men slewed to a halt, reined about, and spurred back the way they had come in a flurry of clods. Ahead of Tamkin and Sybilla, a dozen garrison soldiers had appeared at the run.

Tamkin released his grip on the reins and slowly toppled sideways into the arms of two of them. Sybilla allowed another serjeant to help her down from the saddle. 'Bring him to my chamber,' she commanded. 'Quickly, but be gentle with him.'

458

'What about—' A fourth soldier gestured down the track.

'Leave it,' she said. 'You'll not catch up with them and you may yourself be ambushed.'

In the solar, she flung off her wet cloak and had Tamkin placed on the bed and stripped to his braies. An ugly gash at his waistline was leaking blood and required stitching. At least no vital point appeared to be punctured. She sent for the keeper of the hounds since he was the most adept at sewing flesh together, having to do it regularly on the dogs.

'Bring wine,' she said. 'And lace it with sugar.'

Her women hastened to her bidding. The children's nurses took their charges to the far end of the room out of the way.

Tamkin's eyelids fluttered. 'It was an arrow, my lady,' he gasped. 'But it hit at a shallow angle and I was able to draw it free. Bled me like a stuck pig.'

'You're going to be all right. Herluin will stitch it.' She squeezed his hand.

He managed a faint smile. 'Stole a good horse though,' he said hoarsely. 'Belonged to William Martel, didn't it . . . son of a whore.'

'Which is probably why they chased you.' She pushed bolsters behind his back and made him drink the hot sugared wine that Lecia brought over.

'No, I stole the horse because I had to flee.' He took several swallows and a tinge of colour returned to his cheeks. 'Your son is well, madam, and your husband too.'

She leaned forward, her gaze suddenly intense. 'You have seen them both?'

He gave a wry grimace. 'Your son earlier today, madam. The King keeps him at his side and calls him his little friend. He seems most taken with him.'

Sybilla smiled and felt tearful with relief. Who would not be taken with William? she thought. 'And my husband?'

459

'Conducting a stout defence, my lady.'

She sensed an abrupt reticence in him. 'What are you not telling me?'

'Nothing, my lady, I swear it. My lord had bidden me keep an eye on the lad, to make sure he came to no harm, but I got too close and William saw me. He wasn't to know he shouldn't run to me, and I had to take my leave swiftly after that. I assure you he is safe with the King and not in any immediate danger.'

She was still not convinced he was giving her the whole story. His eyes were glassy with pain, but he was doing his best to avoid meeting hers. It wasn't consciousness of rank that was causing his behaviour, of that she was certain.

Herluin arrived to stitch the cut, bringing his wallet of iron needles, his fine silk thread and some unguent he swore by when it came to healing the dogs. Also some spiders' webs to clot the wound.

Tamkin grimaced. 'I always thought being a musician was a safer bet than being a soldier,' he said. 'Seems I was wrong.'

'Seems you were,' Herluin agreed cheerfully, drawing up a stool. 'At least you don't have a fur coat to shave off before I begin.'

Tamkin gave a weak grin.

Sybilla left Herluin to his task and joined her women and the children. 'William's safe,' she told young John, who had been very quiet since his little brother's departure – apart from a storm of tears on the day he had ridden away.

'Is he coming back soon?'

'Sweetheart, I hope so.' She kissed him.

'And my papa too?'

'Yes, and your papa too . . . God willing.'

460

45

Newbury Castle, Berkshire, September 1152

Together with Jaston, John heaved with all his might and felt the struts of the siege ladder shift against the palisade and then start to slip sideways with its burden of men. Next moment the structure toppled into the ditch, smashing and maiming the soldiers who had been clambering up its rungs. The occupants of another ladder had gained the battlements and John sprinted along the wall walk, back-swiped his sword across a serjeant's unprotected leg and, as the man dropped, crashed his shield into the face of the soldier next on the ladder, sending him down to join the others in the ditch. He clashed swords with a youngster, parried twice, then false-footed him and brought him down. The look of astonishment on the lad's face as he died joined the rest of the carnage of memories in John's mind. Just another bloody strand. Hack, parry, slash. Get the ladder off the battlements. Send it down into the ditch.

The archers had been conserving arrows for several days and were under instructions to make every hit count – to take the commanders and the senior serjeants. Even so, they would soon run out of shafts and their vulnerability would increase a hundredfold.

Breath sobbing in his throat, John helped the serjeants dislodge a third ladder and as it tumbled down, heard through a haze of exhaustion the sound of a horn blaring the retreat. The King's troops pulled back, dragging their dead and wounded with them, running with the ladders. The sun was low, only a few feet above the horizon, and the shadows were long. Which was just as well. John knew they couldn't have withstood another assault of this ferocity.

He cleaned his sword on a rag before sheathing it. Benet joined him, staggering slightly and bleeding from several superficial injuries.

'It's over,' John panted. 'I have held this place for longer than I thought possible, but next time they come, they will break us. I don't have enough men to hold them and there are no arrows left. He'll be able to bring his trebuchets in close and put a ram to the gate.'

'The morrow then.' Benet wiped at a persistent trickle of blood oozing from a cut on his chin. He gave John an intense look. 'What now?'

As they left the battlements, John gave the order to stand the men down apart from a token guard. 'I'll be damned if I'm going to surrender,' he growled.

'Then it's a fight to the death,' Benet said blankly.

John removed his helm and pushed down his coif and arming cap. 'No. That would be of benefit to no one but Stephen. When Henry does arrive he will need his field commanders and experienced troops.'

Benet eyed the determined set of John's lips and his mood lightened a little. His lord intended survival then, and wasn't expecting them all to go down in a final welter of gory heroics.

'We came in at night, we leave at night.' John rubbed his scar. 'On the morrow they can have this place.

462

Nothing we do will prevent it now. Let all the men eat and drink well tonight and prepare themselves. Whatever supplies we leave behind must be ruined so that Stephen cannot use them. Burn what we can, have the men use the barrels of salt pork and fish for their latrine. Scatter caltrops across the hall floor and set gin traps in the barn. Wherever they walk, I want them to find trouble.'

Benet gave a grim smile. 'Yes, my lord.'

Rubbing her arms, Sybilla fetched her cloak and, drawing it around her shoulders, sat before the hearth in her chamber. The September night was chilly and she felt as if cold fingers were stroking her bones. She threw another branch on the fire and watched the flames lick around the wood. It was pear from a rotten tree in the orchard and the wood carried a subtle fragrance that, as it burned, reminded her of other autumn nights. She carried a golden memory of sitting before the fire with John that first autumn of their marriage, roasting apples on the flames, drizzling them with honey, laughing as they tried to catch the drips and getting very sticky. Cleaning each other up. Sybilla smiled for a moment, but the memory, like a snatch of flame on a log, didn't last.

She had been in the saddle most of the day, returning from Salisbury, but although she was tired, she couldn't sleep because her thoughts were churning like an estuary mill when the tide was in. Newbury had been under siege for two months and she knew John must be growing ever more desperate. Occasionally he had managed to send a man over the palisade at night with a message and she had had her own scouts ride out to report from a distance on the state of the fight. Stephen obviously wasn't going to give up and march away; he was settled in for the

463

duration. Determined to do something, she had gone to Patrick to beg him to aid John, but the interview had been unproductive.

Patrick had been furious that she had dared the roads with the King's Flemings in the vicinity, and he had given her request short shrift.

'I cannot send aid to Newbury,' he had said, raking his hand through his hair. 'I've already spared as much as I can. I have to look to the defence of Salisbury.'

'But if the King takes Newbury, the road to Wallingford will be open,' she had protested.

'In that case Henry will have to come,' he had answered and then cleared his throat. 'Look, John's brave and I admire his stand, but that's his task: to stand. He chose it. I have to protect Salisbury and my lands for my son.' He cast a glance towards the corner of the room where a nurse was playing with a sturdy infant just learning to walk.

'And what of my son?' she demanded. 'What of William?'

Patrick gave her a perplexed look. 'You have another. He is not the only string to your bow. He's not even the heir to Ludgershall.'

'And that is all you think he is? Another string to my bow and expendable?'

'To put it in a commander's terms, yes. Ask your husband. He'd agree with me.'

She had felt like striking him but knew it would do no good except to confirm to him that she was a foolish, hysterical woman. 'How can I ask my husband when I do not know if I will see him again? At least give him and me that chance.'

She had seen the blankness fill his gaze. Even if she tore her hair, wept and clutched at his knees, she would not move him. 'I cannot, and were John in my position, he would give my wife the same answer. What I can do for you and your other children is offer you protection should the worst happen. As your nearest kin I am responsible for your welfare should you be widowed.'

In hindsight and knowing Patrick, Sybilla could see he had been trying to be reasonable, but at the time, she had called him a *nithing*, one of the English words borrowed from her father and his father before, meaning someone lacking all honour, someone who was literally nothing, and she had stormed out of Salisbury in enraged tears.

Now she set the poker in the fire and stirred the flaking, greying branch to show living embers of aromatic red. It had been a pointless exercise, she realised it now, but she had had to try.

A sudden rustle of straw and an anguished squeak proclaimed the hunting success of the now adolescent Lion. She watched him slink along in the semi-darkness near the shuttered windows, a mouse twitching in his jaws, his lithe body the colour of autumn leaves. Doublet had been stretched out by the hearth, and had lifted her grey muzzle at the sound. Her eyes were dimming and she might be too stiff for the hunt these days, but her hearing remained sharp. Awoken, she eased to her feet and limped to the door.

Sybilla rose too, pushed her feet into her shoes and went to let her out. The night was dark and the wind blustered with spatters of rain. Leaves rattled across the ward like lost souls. Doublet made her way down the steps and into the courtyard and Sybilla followed, shivering, arms folded inside her cloak. She began to regret not summoning one of her women to take the dog out. As she hopped from one foot to the other, Doublet barked and swung her nose towards the gate. The guards on duty made shrift to swing it open and she saw the troop enter the courtyard, the gleam of mail here and there illuminated by torch.

'John?' she breathed. 'Dear God, John!'

Frantically wagging her tail, Doublet limped across the ward as fast as she could and threw herself in ecstasy at him as he dismounted from a firelit Serjean. He spoke to the dog and the familiar voice wrenched through Sybilla. Suddenly she too was dashing across the ward and flinging herself upon him. She bounced off the rivets of his mail shirt and was pulled back into his arms. His kiss was as hard as the steel, the grip of his hands too.

'Oh God, oh God!' she gasped as he released her. 'I thought I wasn't going to—' Her throat closed.

'You should know that not even the Devil would have me. He took a taste once and spat me out of hell.' His own voice was gruff. He pulled her to him once more, his hand at the back of her neck beneath her hair, and kissed her again. When their lips finally parted, he held her away to look her up and down.

Sybilla suddenly realised she was standing before him clad in her chemise and open cloak, her hair streaming down for all to see. She gasped again, this time with embarrassed laughter, and became aware that several of John's knights were watching the exchange and grinning, some of them with open admiration. Hastily she folded her cloak around herself. 'Will you all want food and drink? Shall I rouse the household?'

'No,' he answered. 'Dawn will do and the men can bed down in the hall and make shrift for themselves for tonight. We ate and drank well before we set out. A bath wouldn't come amiss. I would hate to mire the bed.' He gave her his quick, knowing smile. 'Or you.'

*　　*　　*

466

Dewed with perspiration, panting, overwhelmed, Sybilla felt as if she had been caught outside and far from shelter in the middle of a violent thunderstorm and struck by lightning. The pleasure after two months of abstinence had been swift, jagged and intense – the first time. The second had been slower but no less powerful, and the third . . . She raised herself up to look at John. He was lying with his arm bent across his eyes, his chest and flanks still heaving and his body as wet as hers. He hadn't spoken of Newbury or what his arrival presaged. All had been submerged in the physical. She sensed that were he capable, he would still be at the centre of the storm – hiding. That's why his arm was across his face.

She left the bed and going to the tub, soaked a cloth in the by now tepid water and wiped herself down, then returned to the bed to do the same for him. His taut stomach muscles contracted at the first cold touch, and he unbent his arm and looked at her.

'Is it very bad?' she asked.

'It could be worse,' he said flatly. 'Is there any wine? I'm thirsty.'

'I'm not surprised.' She fetched cup and flagon from the sideboard.

He took the wine she poured for him, drank it down and held out the cup to be refilled. Having done so, Sybilla knelt on the bed and faced him. 'Tamkin told me that Stephen had taken William into his own tent,' she said.

A strange expression flickered across his face – fear, she would have said in another man. Apprehension certainly. 'Tamkin is here?'

Sybilla nodded. 'Only just. We almost lost him to blood loss and the wound fever.' She told him what had happened. 'He's recovered now. I sent him to Marlborough to sing for the garrison there and take messages. He rode on Martel's horse, naturally.'

'And all he said about William was that Stephen had him?'

'Yes, although I know he wasn't telling me everything, even as I can see that you are wondering how much you can escape without telling me. Whatever it is, I would know, no matter how bad.'

His expression grew bleak. After a long pause he said, 'Newbury is lost. We had run out of arrows and the men were exhausted. Stephen nearly breached us yesterday. We couldn't have fought off another assault so I gave the order to abandon the keep. We crept out after dark like thieves. There was nothing else I could have done except die at sunrise. The road to Wallingford is open, and Hamstead too should Stephen choose to come this way. On the morrow I'm pulling back to Marlborough and defending from there. It's my strongest keep.'

She gave a stiff nod. That was sensible. She could understand him being set down by defeat because he hated to lose, but knew there had to be more to it than that. 'What else is there?'

His face turned to stone. 'You do not want to know.'

'It's William, isn't it?' Her stomach began to churn. 'You haven't mentioned him once, and Tamkin was very careful about what he said too. Tell me!'

He swallowed and looked away.

'Tell me!' She pounded the coverlet with a clenched fist.

'If you must know,' he said in a hard, flat voice, 'Martel put a noose around his chest and hoisted him up on a gibbet. They threatened to kill him before the eyes of the garrison unless we yielded the keep.'

She let out a gasp and stared at him, appalled.

468

'I told them to do as they pleased – that he mattered not and I had the wherewithal to beget more sons. So Martel kindled a fire under him. I believe he thought it might break me because of what happened at Wherwell.'

Sybilla's gorge rose. She clapped a hand across her mouth.

'Stephen put a stop to it. Had the fire doused and William brought down unharmed, thank Christ. He's been with the King ever since.'

She swallowed hard but it was no use. She dived for the chamberpot and hung over it, retching.

John rose from the bed. 'Sybilla . . .'

She gestured him vigorously away.

Wearily he began to dress. 'I gambled William's life on the King's soft heart and I won, but the odds were too close for grace. If William hates me for it then so be it, and if you do too – well, I made my choice. If you want separate chambers at Marlborough, I'll make arrangements.'

Sybilla shuddered on all fours. 'I want my son in my arms, whole and unharmed,' she gasped. She deliberately used the word 'my' rather than 'our'. She wasn't sure John deserved that acknowledgement.

He buckled his belt and quietly left the room. She heard the heaviness of his usually light tread and sensed the weight on him. She was burdened herself and struggling. Did she hate him for doing what he had done? For saying what he had said, even if it was in bluff? She staggered back to the bed and collapsed upon it. Her stomach still quivered. She was numb and burning at the same time. She wanted to cry but the tears wouldn't come. Curling up amid the sheets that still bore a vestige of warmth from their bodies, she closed her eyes.

* * *

469

'When's William coming home?'

John looked round from inspecting Aranais in the stable yard and regarded his namesake. The boy was wearing his thick travelling cloak, leather hood and stout calfhide boots ready for the journey to Marlborough.

'That all depends on King Stephen. William's staying in his service for the time being.'

'I . . . I heard one of the soldiers say the King's men tried to hang William.'

John hesitated, then nodded. 'It was a trick to try to scare me into giving up Newbury. Your brother's safe now and he won't come to any harm.'

The boy twisted his hands together. 'Why are we going to Marlborough?'

'Because it's a while since I've been there. I need to check the defences.'

'Stephen's men won't c . . . come and hang me, will they?'

John's belly turned over at the question. God on the Cross, what strains had he set on his wife and family? 'Christ, boy, no. They'd gladly hang me but you can consider yourself safe.'

The lad gave a manful nod, but John could see he was not convinced.

Sybilla entered the stable, similarly clad in riding cloak and boots. She was wearing a gown with plenty of fabric in the skirts for riding astride and practical hose underneath. Her eyes were puffy as if she had been weeping, but they were dry now and the gaze she gave him was composed.

'Sweeting, go and find Gundred,' she said. 'I want a word with your father.'

The boy looked uncertainly between his parents. John ruffled the lad's hair. 'Go on,' he said. 'We'll talk later, I promise.'

470

'Yes, sir.' He left the stable, seven years old and walking as solemnly as an encumbered adult.

Lips compressed, John turned back to Aranais.

'I know you had no choice,' Sybilla said in a subdued tone. 'If you had surrendered Newbury at the outset, Stephen would have been on us like a plague of lice.'

He said nothing but busied himself checking the cinches on the girth strap.

He felt her step closer, barring his line of escape. 'You said once that either I trusted you or I didn't. I said then that I did . . . and for what it is worth, I still do – because if I don't, what is left to me but a wasteland?'

His breath caught at the note in her voice. There was fear, supplication and desolation. He had a sudden image of the two of them balancing on a high rope like the travelling players who came to entertain the castle folk at Christmas and midsummer, gambling their lives upon a narrow line of hemp strung between the courtyard buildings. He turned round, his throat working. His lips formed her name.

She stepped up to him, cupped his face in her hands, gently traced the line of his scar with her thumb. 'I have a wound that will not heal until William is returned to us whole and unharmed, but I realise that so have you.' She touched his breast, over his heart. 'You may have the wherewithal to beget other sons, as I have to bear them, but not without bleeding.'

Uttering a groan, he seized her in his embrace and kissed her again, fiercely, with a molten urgency as if last night's immolation between the sheets had only been a beginning.

Aranais snorted and butted John in the spine with his broad nose, causing him to bang teeth with Sybilla. John pulled back and looked round at the pawing stallion.

471

'I am reminded to put necessity ahead of need,' he said wryly and dabbed his upper lip on the back of his hand.

'Aranais is right,' she said with watering eyes. 'It wouldn't be practical.'

From somewhere he found the semblance of a smile. Taking the stallion's bridle, he led him out into the courtyard.

Sybilla licked her lips and found a small saltiness of blood upon them. She watched John gazing round the compound at the buildings and the defences and knew he was bidding them a mental farewell in case he never saw them again. It was one thing to gamble that the King had his gaze firmly fixed on Wallingford and would not come here, another to watch the dice roll and know that you were powerless. The lessons from Newbury were incised like number dots on a bone die for all of them. The consequences, too.

46

Siege of Wallingford, January 1153

William was thrilled by the new hood Mariette had fashioned for him out of sheepskins and coney fur. He had a pair of mittens to match too and socks made out of madder-red wool. She said it was to celebrate the season of Christ's birth and that he should have three gifts in memory of the gold, frankincense and myrrh that the three Magi gave to the baby Jesus.

'But I don't have three gifts for you,' he said as she arranged the hood over his shoulders and then, with a little laugh, pulled it up around his ears.

'Ah, *mijn kleine*, it doesn't matter. The Christ child didn't have gifts for the Magi. It is for the adults to give to the innocent children. A kiss will suffice.'

William obliged and received in return a familiar lye-scented hug.

'You make good use of these things, *ja*,' she said. 'There's snow in the sky.'

William peered out of the tent entrance. The earth was brown and muddy. Withy walkways had been cast down between the tents and the King's wooden siege towers to make walking easier for man and beast. He raised his nose and tested the air like a hound. 'What does snow smell like?'

'Cold, very cold. Like rain and like frost because it is both of them . . . and perhaps a little like white feathers, eh?' She gave a laugh to show she was jesting and tweaked the top of the hood.

In the early New Year the King was still besieging Wallingford with every hope that it would fall. Before Candlemas, he kept saying to his advisers. Henry was still bogged down in Normandy and it wasn't the season for winter sea crossings. By the time spring arrived, it would be too late. William had heard the talk round the fire in the King's chamber. There wasn't a lot of laughter, but he had sensed the grim determination of the lords. He knew if Wallingford did fall it would be a bad thing for his father, who had already lost Newbury; however, this was his life for the moment and he didn't feel sad or worried about it, just lived each day as it came.

A fanfare sounded as the King arrived on a blowing, sweating stallion. He'd been out riding and his face was flushed and his eyes bright.

'I have to go,' William said. 'It's my duty to warm his shoes.' He announced the latter with a proud lift of his chin. It was an important job – almost as important as keeping the King's belts cleaned and polished.

He managed to escape with another squeeze and a kiss, and had to promise to come and visit Mariette again soon. And then he was haring across the camp, leaping over puddles, dodging between the camp fires and running into the King's hall. The guards waved him through with grinning tolerance for they were accustomed to his comings and goings by now and he was something of a pet to most of them.

He was kneeling before the fire turning the King's soft

indoor shoes in front of the heat when Stephen entered the room, laughing at something one of the older squires had said. William Martel was with him and the Earls of Leicester and Arundel also.

'Hah, I haven't had a ride out like that in weeks, it does my heart good!' Stephen said with gusto. He removed his cloak, handed it to the youth and then threw himself down in his chair. The squire deposited the cloak and returned to remove Stephen's boots. With great solemnity, William came to kneel at Stephen's feet and slipped the warmed shoes on to them. The King was wearing similar socks to the ones Mariette had given him, except that Stephen's were made of silk not wool. The same colour though, a rich, warming red.

Stephen smiled at William. 'Ah lad, that's good. My feet were fairly frozen in the stirrups.' He glanced in amusement as he noticed the poker that William had thrust through his belt in imitation of a sword. 'Quite the little knight, aren't you, Willikin, hmm? Don't you go running off with the poker now; we'll need it for the fire.'

William made a slight face. To him it really was a sword. Nevertheless, he minded his manners and did as he was bidden. While he was still about the task with the shoes, a messenger was escorted into the room by Stephen's chamberlain.

'My lord, there is urgent news.' The messenger knelt and handed Stephen a letter. Stephen frowned as he took it and slit the seal tags. Rapidly he scanned what was written and in the next moment had risen to his feet in agitation. 'Henry of Anjou has landed at Wareham and struck at Malmesbury,' he said.

William pricked up his ears. His father and everyone had often talked about Prince Henry coming and making everything better again.

475

Martel swore and Arundel and Leicester exchanged glances. 'How many ships, sire?' Leicester asked.

'Fewer than two score and mainly mercenaries,' Stephen said. 'He'll have the usual suspects rallying to him – Gloucester, Hereford, Salisbury, Lincoln and FitzGilbert. I can't afford to let him take Malmesbury. We'll have to march to its relief before he grows too strong. Muster the troops.'

Leicester cleared his throat. 'Sire, might it not be better to remain here and continue the siege? Malmesbury is strongly built and surely can hold its own. If we leave now, Wallingford will be able to resupply in our rear. He is deliberately drawing you away for that to happen.'

Stephen shook his head. 'I dare not take the chance that Malmesbury will fall. I must deal with Henry before he establishes himself. If we can strike him swiftly, we may not even need to return to Wallingford.'

Arundel rubbed his jaw. 'He has troubles enough abroad. You might be able to persuade him to return there.'

'Bribe him, you mean?'

'You did it once before when he came across with mercenaries.'

'He was fourteen then, with barely a conroi to his name. Nor does paying him work. He keeps coming back. No, I will go to Malmesbury and confront him there.' He finished his wine and brusquely summoned William. 'Boy, find me a dry pair of riding boots and then go and tell the women we're striking camp.'

'Sire,' William said and, glad to have important tasks to do, hurried to obey the commands. Martel stuck out a foot to trip him up, but William leaped neatly over the extended boot, thereby earning a smile from the Earl of Arundel.

* * *

476

John emerged from his lodging in Malmesbury and hastened round to the stable yard. A bitter wind had got up in the night and now, just past the dawn, was flinging icy rain like a profligate guest hurling rice at a wedding. The pellets struck him full on as the wind veered and he gasped as they burned like cold fire upon his scar. He drew the hood of his cloak over his coif and hastened to where a groom was holding a sidling Aranais. A mail breast-band softly jinked across the stallion's chest and his face and neck were covered by a leather chamfron.

'Wants to turn round and go back in his stall,' announced the man.

'I don't blame him.' John hitched his sword out of the way and set his foot to the stirrup. In a practised move, the groom whipped the rug off the top of the high war saddle and John hauled himself astride and gathered up the reins. 'That's where we'd all be given the choice.'

'Nah, I'd be abed with two plump wenches to keep me warm.' The groom flashed him a broad smile.

John laughed. 'Now that sounds an even better idea,' he said as he pulled on his mittens. 'Certainly I'd rather be straddling a woman this morning than a saddle!'

Other soldiers were running out to their mounts, all swearing about the vile weather. John had to use his spur to nudge Aranais across the yard. Perhaps he should have ridden Serjean. The black was more stoical and placid, but Aranais, provided that he got over his irritable mood, was better in a fight and looked the part.

Another rug-clad stallion was being led from the stables, its harness ornate and its saddle cloth stitched with small golden leopards. An instant later, Prince Henry hastened from the hall, cramming a hunk of bread and cheese into his mouth. Chewing vigorously, food pouched in his cheek, he leaped to horse with agility. The blaze of his character almost seemed to illuminate the courtyard and John noticed how men's eyes were drawn to this energetic, red-haired young man. And why not? They had waited long enough for his arrival and now he was here, things could at least move forward . . . although today he'd have given up that moving forward to join the groom in his fantasy. It wasn't a morning to be abroad, let alone one for engaging in a pitched battle. Stephen had advanced rapidly from Wallingford to save the garrison at Malmesbury from Henry's concentrated assault. The stench of smoke still hung over the town which had been broached and looted by Henry's mercenaries. Only the castle held out and it was in difficult straits – as difficult as Wallingford's had been until Henry landed.

The scouts had sighted Stephen's force lining up across the river Avon and reported to Henry in the hall as he was breaking his fast. The call to mount up had gone out directly and now they were armed up and heading for confrontation.

'Stephen's got more men in the field than we have,' muttered Jaston as he took his customary position at John's left side.

John grunted. 'There's also a river in full spate between him and us. It'll be butchery if he tries to cross.'

'Some of the men are saying they'll refuse to fight.'

John gave him a keen look. 'Ours?'

'No, my lord, they trust you and will do your bidding. Some of Chester's men say their mounts are too weakened by privation and that they can't fight on the rations they've been living on.'

John gave a snort of contempt. 'Their rations are no different from ours and I can still wield a sword.' He pursed his lips, considering. 'If Chester's men are baulking, then it's likely there are men on Stephen's side who won't stand hard either.'

They rode down to the banks of the Avon. The wind was at their backs, shoving them forward with forceful gusts like an angry parent herding wayward children. 'Stephen's got the wind in his face,' John said. 'It's difficult for us, but twice as bad for them.' He watched flakes of wet snow land on his cloak and then melt away. The garment was double-thickness wool with an otter skin lining and designed to resist such conditions, but would eventually succumb.

The King's army was arrayed at the customary fording place on the far bank, scarcely fifty yards separating it from Henry's troops. Their banners were tearing in the violent wind and the mounted men were having difficulty controlling their horses. Scouts and footsoldiers probed the hurling spate of brown water with their spears, seeking a safe spot to cross. As John watched, one of them waded in with a rope attached to his waist, lost his footing and had to be hauled spluttering and saturated in to shore.

Henry rode to the front of his line and narrowed his eyes through the atrocious weather to the opposite side.

'They won't find a fording spot, sire!' John had to shout to be heard. 'Not today, anyway. Bring forward the archers. The wind's with us and against them. Anything we loose will plummet into their ranks, but if they use theirs, they'll just blow back on themselves.'

Henry nodded agreement. 'Yes,' he said. 'We'll give them a few volleys. Stir up some noise too.'

The archers were brought forward and Henry's smaller army began to beat their spears upon their shields and chant Henry's name. John tightened his hands on Aranais's reins as the sound prickled down his spine and ran like ice into his bones, reminding him of Newbury.

479

Stephen's army tried to chant a reply, but the wind snatched their voices and as the arrows rained down, the singing broke up in disarray. Horses were struck and went mad, plunging and bucking, careering into other horses. Men tried to scatter and were trampled. Others fell as they were pierced by the deadly rain from the far bank. Almost as if to aid Henry's cause, the wind increased and the wet snow became a blizzard. Visibility contracted down to a few yards of whirling whiteness and the river itself vanished. Henry rode up and down the line, his brown destrier bouncing along as if it were on cradle rockers. John was darkly amused to see that Henry had drawn his sword and was holding it aloft like a steel icicle. Even if there wasn't going to be a battle, Henry obviously wanted to be seen as a fighter as well as a battle commander.

The flurry eased. John stared across the sullen rushing water to the dim outlines of the other side and wondered if he was losing the sight in his good eye for where there had been men and horses, there were only a few humped shapes fading from his vision.

'Hah,' Jaston cried in triumph. 'They've given up. They're leaving! They haven't the belly for it!'

John shook his head. 'They can't get across with the river in spate. Nor can they pitch camp and wait out the weather in these conditions. They have no choice but to retreat.'

'You reckon they'll be back?'

'Who knows,' John replied and gave a dry smile, 'but the constable of Malmesbury will soon realise his relief column's abandoned him. It's going to make taking the place a deal easier.'

Sybilla puffed out her cheeks and flopped down on the bench in the small wall chamber she and John were using during the Prince's visit to Marlborough, having yielded the royal guest their room.

Her feet were aching and she was tired, but everything had gone very well to say she had had only half a day's notice of Henry's arrival to prepare hall, chambers and sleeping space for an army. The hall was packed to the rafters; so was the bailey and the town. Sybilla had had to find a night's rations for men and horses and doubted she and John would receive recompense – at least not in the near future. Having accepted the surrender of Malmesbury and secured castle and town to his own troops, Henry intended to make his winter quarters in Salisbury and there rest up his men. He was spending the night at Marlborough on his way. Sybilla supposed it was a mark of honour and trust, but it was also a drain on their supplies. At least Patrick, as Earl of Salisbury and sheriff of Wiltshire, had more resources to call upon than she and John did.

John entered the room, his own tread buoyant and a half-smile curving his lips. 'The Prince says he wants to be away at first light,' he said, 'but you never know with him. He may well linger until noon. He does it deliberately to upset everything. His grandsire would turn in his grave.' He sat down on the bench beside her and held out his hands to the heat of the firebox she'd had brought up to warm the room. 'Still, he'll be Patrick's bother after this.'

'I've told the kitchens to make extra bread and we have salmon and trout that can be turned into a reasonable dish for the high table should he choose to stay.' She removed her wimple and the fine net cap beneath to free her hair.

John took a long, dark tress and curled it round his hand. 'Do you know what Henry said to me as he was retiring?' He admired the dark gleam over his knuckles.

481

She shook her head. 'No, what?'

'That you reminded him of his wife.'

Sybilla gazed at him in surprise. 'In what way?'

'Apparently, you're both rare beauties of a similar age, you're both hot to handle with wits sharper than a honed blade, and you both make him laugh. He says he knows a thoroughbred when he sees one.' His lips twitched. 'He's grown into a discerning young man.'

Sybilla returned his smile. 'All I can say is thank the Virgin you do not remind me of him!'

John was highly amused. 'I take that as a compliment.'

'It's intended as one.'

He released her hair, lifted her legs into his lap and, having removed her shoes, began gently to rub her feet. Sybilla made a soft sound of pleasure but didn't entirely give herself up to it. There were things she wanted to discuss with him that she hadn't been able to during the hurly-burly of the day and their duties as host and hostess to royalty. 'King Stephen's army came up to face you across the river.'

'Yes, but they wouldn't cross it. The water was flowing too fast.' He stroked his thumb lightly back and forth over her ankle. 'You heard the details in the hall.'

'I just thought . . . I just wondered . . .' She shook her head and looked at him, her eyes suddenly bright with moisture. 'I am being foolish, I know. He wouldn't have brought William on a forced march.'

'We could barely see them or their horses, the conditions were so atrocious, let alone a baggage wain and a small boy. And you are right. Stephen would not have brought him. He will either have left him at Wallingford or sent him back to London. He'll be all right – and gaining a firm grounding in life at court.'

'My head tells me it is so, but my heart is less easily

persuaded.' She sighed and closed her eyes. It was point-less to keep harping upon the matter because it couldn't be altered. 'So what happens now?' she asked, changing the subject. 'It seems foolish putting the men into winter quarters when there is so much to accomplish.'

'You can only push troops so far before they break. A good commander knows that breaking point and stops before it happens. Everyone is exhausted and food supplies are short. A few weeks' warmth and respite will make all the difference. Stephen's retreated with the same notion in mind, I am sure. We have Malmesbury. Wallingford is still threatened but at least its garrison know we are here. A good commander also knows when to take advantage. Henry has his eye on gaining Southampton as a strategic port.' He circled his thumb lightly up her calf. 'Some of Stephen's barons appear to be weakening too. Come the spring, the tide may turn full measure . . . Winter is always a waiting time,' he added in a slumberous voice. 'The trees sleep, the ground lies dormant. Women spin and sew, men take respite and mend the tools of their trade . . . and sow autumn's harvest.'

Sybilla opened her mouth to say that no one sowed crops in January, but by then his dextrous touch had reached the back of her knees and he was shifting, pulling her into his lap, kissing her throat, and soon her lips were engaged in matters other than speech.

47

Gloucester, April 1153

Sybilla entered the abbey of Saint Peter and stood for a
moment in the vast nave with its magnificent Romanesque
columns and arches. Earlier, the church had been as closely
packed for the mass as a barrel of herrings. Gloucester
was one of the traditional places for crown-wearings and
court gatherings in full array. Since Henry wasn't a king,
he had refused to wear a diadem, but for once had put
aside his everyday tunic to don magnificent jewelled robes
and adorn his fingers with gold. He had milked each ritual
and ceremony for all it was worth, projecting the clear
message that he was the heir-in-waiting and considered
his moment not far off.

But now the church was empty apart from the occasional whispered footstep of a Benedictine monk. Small
motes of dust flickered and gleamed in the afternoon
sunlight slanting through the windows on to the tiled floor.
Sybilla paced slowly down the nave, and each breath she
drew brought her the scent of faded incense. Gundred
and a manservant walked quietly behind her, not intruding
on her wish for solitude. She knelt to pray, careful in her
movement. To the casual observer her manner was

graceful and deferential, but Sybilla was with child and sudden movements made her dizzy and nauseous.

Bowing her head, she repeated the paternoster and the creed, counting her prayer beads through her fingers. And then she said her personal prayers, for her husband, her children, her stepsons, the unborn child in her womb, and finally the special ones for William. It was close to his year day when he would turn six – God willing. He had been gone for ten months. She tried to carry his face in her memory, but it was like an imprint in mud that was gradually weathering and growing indistinct with time. She worried too that the face she was trying to remember would not be the one he wore when he returned. Just as Lion had been a fluffy kitten and was now a rangy young cat, more feral in his ways, so she knew there would be differences in William. Never again would he have that soft infant vulnerability and inno-cence. After what had happened to him, she knew he would be irrevocably changed.

She rose carefully to her feet and lit candles to send her prayers to heaven. She left silver in alms too and tried not to think she was bribing God. Emerging from the abbey, she saw the sun was low on the horizon and the shafts of sunlight cast the world in mellow tones of gold from pale primrose to deepest amber. A troop of horsemen ablaze with light was riding towards the palace close on the abbey. One of their number wore a gown of mulberry-red wool that must have cost the earth and his cloak was edged with sable. Although Sybilla had never seen Robert de Beaumont, Earl of Leicester, she was certain this was he. John had told her that delicate negotiations through intermediaries had been going on all through the season in winter quarters. A fortnight since at Stockbridge, de Beaumont's son had come to a parley and intimated that

485

his father was prepared to acknowledge Henry, not Stephen's son Eustace, as the heir to the throne. Since Leicester had already made pacts not to seek open confrontation with the likes of Roger of Hereford, William de Beauchamp and Ranulf of Chester, this latest step was a natural progression. John said Leicester was a wily politician who always knew where the sun was next going to shine on a mixed cloudy day.

She watched his troop ride past, then returned to the lodging John had acquired for their stay – a property that was usually occupied by a wool merchant, who, with an eye to his profit, had moved in with relatives for the duration of the court's visit. They were fortunate to have a roof over their heads in the fickle spring weather, but even so it was cramped accommodation and the servants and soldiers had to make do with straw pallets in goat shed and byre. Sybilla was glad they had left the younger children at Marlborough. Young John had sulked but his father had been adamant. Finding sleeping space in Gloucester for all who needed it would be nightmare enough without having to worry about his own household. Gilbert and Walter were here because in the fullness of time they would have positions at court and, with the latter in mind, it was useful to keep them in Henry's awareness. She was here because John had wanted her with him, saying not in so many words that he needed her, and Sybilla was keen to be at his side.

A maid was stirring a cauldron of mutton haricot over the fire and another servant had been out to a cookshop and obtained several simnel loaves. Sybilla had brought a stock of cheese and honey from Marlborough, and barrels of their own cider. She didn't know when John would be returning but thought it would be late, especially if Leicester had only just arrived. The Prince

486

was not one to keep regular hours either. She expected John to eat at court, and thus had the household summoned to dine; however, she had some titbits set aside under a cloth lest John should be peckish when he came back.

It was almost midnight when he arrived, and everyone was asleep apart from the watchman and Sybilla. His tread was soft, but she had sharp hearing and was alert. If not exactly on tenterhooks, she had begun to feel anxious. She started to pour him wine, then wrinkled her nose as he came to the trestle and lifted the cloth to see what was under it.

'You stink of attar of roses,' she said, anger uniting with her anxiety.

He sniffed his sleeve and grimaced. 'That would be one of the whores. She douses herself in the stuff.' He unfastened his tunic, pulled it over his head and tossed it on to the coffer.

Her grip tightened on the flagon. 'Is there any reason why I should not throw this wine in your face now?'

He gave her a long, steady look. 'The whores are part of my remit when I'm at court. It's a duty, like any other.'

'I am sure it is.'

He looked indignant. 'Do you think I would bring you to court and then futter other women under your nose?' Biting ravenously into a tart of minced venison and currants, he sat down on the edge of the bed. 'She was trying to inveigle her way into Henry's chamber and to do that she had to get around me and my ushers. She didn't succeed.' He added drily, 'I've been offered several interesting bribes and propositions tonight, but I've managed so far to resist.'

She gave him a narrow look. 'Just as long as you do not sample other wares when I am by.'

487

'I would never do that,' he said with affront. 'It would be dishonourable and lacking all respect.'

'Indeed it would.' Sybilla suspected that if she wasn't here, he might have been more susceptible to the goods on offer. By his code of honour, he was faithful to her. He didn't flaunt other women under her nose. Unlike many of his peers, he had neither a mistress nor bastards, which meant that if he did satisfy himself with others during a dry spell, he didn't give them his essence. Sybilla was pragmatic and knew how to value herself, but the overpowering perfume of attar of roses had still led to a moment of doubt.

'So,' she said, sitting beside him. 'While you weren't fending off whores who can afford to drown themselves in rose oil, what were you doing?'

He set his arm around her shoulders in a companionable manner that she suspected was an effort to be conciliatory. 'Making sure Leicester's household was shown to his lodgings, that everything was in order and that Leicester himself was given the warmest of welcomes.' His mouth twisted. 'He's the most astute man I know. We've been enemies for fifteen years. He's one of the reasons I swore for the Empress, but now I have to be practical and so does he. He no more wants to see Eustace take the throne when Stephen is dead than I do.'

'So Leicester has agreed to support Henry?'

His grimace remained. 'Not quite. Stephen, he says, is his liege lord and he will follow him until the day he dies, but he has agreed to swear for Henry as Stephen's heir, not Eustace, and he has promised to support Henry with men and money towards that end.'

She pursed her lips. 'What will Henry give him in exchange?'

'A prominent place in his government. The position of

488

justiciar, whatever other privileges de Beaumont thinks he can wangle.'

Sybilla frowned. 'So if you have to be at court with him and in the fullness of time have to work with him . . .'

He sighed. 'We're both older and wiser. Robert of Gloucester is no longer alive to be a source of friction between us. I dare say with Henry on the throne we'll find ourselves able to live and let live. We'll be working for a common goal.'

'So you are pleased?' She studied him thoughtfully.

'Cautiously optimistic. It's too soon to be pleased. Leicester's word isn't law and Stephen won't be prepared to acknowledge Henry as the next King.' He took a swallow of wine. 'Leicester's supposed to be here to offer Henry money to go away. He's not going to be returning with a message Stephen wants to hear – and Eustace will be incensed when he learns Leicester's going to support Henry's right to inherit the throne.'

'And Stephen won't turn against Leicester when he hears?'

'He can't afford to.' John was silent for a moment, then looked at her with a smile. 'Leicester had a private word with me before he retired to his lodging.'

'About what?'

'He tells me our son is doing well as the King's page and that he'll go far in royal service. Stephen apparently is very fond of him. Leicester says if William does not achieve his knighthood before next Christmas, it will not be for want of trying.'

Sybilla laughed, although her eyes filled with tears. 'I want him home with us by next Christmas,' she said with sudden fierceness. 'If Stephen is so fond of him then he ought to return him. He belongs at home with us.'

'I think it is perhaps because Stephen is not so fond of

489

me.' John's smile faded. 'I said one son more or less does not matter. Stephen probably thinks he is doing William a great favour by keeping him away from such a callous father – and who's to say he's wrong?'

'John . . .' She took his hand in hers.

He shook his head. 'Ah, I've drunk too much tonight, and I'm tired – – I'm not as young as I was. Come to bed. I've no doubt Henry will be abroad early in the morning and Leicester with him. I need to rest.'

She joined him on their travelling bed. He didn't often speak about William. Most of the time he guarded that part of him, but tonight, made vulnerable by weariness and drink, he had momentarily bared his fears and regrets.

'If William is doing well, it is because we have taught him well.' She slipped off her shoes, removed her dress and lay down beside him in her chemise.

He said nothing, but pulled her close.

'Your sleeve still smells of that accursed rose attar,' she complained.

He sat up and took off his shirt. 'Better?' he asked and she saw that although his face was tired, his smile was back. She looked at his musculature, which was still that of a young man: honed and smooth. Now her nose was filled with the scent of his skin, of healthy male sweat unadulterated by any flowery intrusions.

'Perfect,' she said, and leaned across him to pinch out the night candle.

48

Wallingford, Oxfordshire, August 1153

William liked riding with Stephen's army. It made him
feel grown up. He rode straight-backed, head high and
expression steely, carrying his shield on his back by its
long strap like a real soldier. There had been a gigantic
thunderstorm the day before and more rain was threatening in the sky, but he didn't mind. He knew if the
weather worsened he could always join the baggage train
and sit with one of the King's carters, or find Mariette,
who would shelter him in her laundry wagon.

King Stephen said he was going to fight Prince Henry
for the right to England's throne. His son Eustace was
with him too and very badly wanted there to be a battle.
Sitting before the hearth polishing the King's belt buckles
with a paste made from wine and cold ashes, William had
heard Eustace arguing they should fight. Something about
not being able to remove a deeply embedded thorn
without drawing blood. Eustace had been as red in the
face as Mariette on a laundry morning as he pounded
the table with a meaty fist. William had kept well out of
his way. Eustace was like Martel, swift to lash out in anger
at the nearest victim, be it dog, small child or hapless

491

servant. All the same, he liked to watch Eustace practise with his sword. He was very skilled with a blade and so strong he could cut the straw dummy on the training ground in two with a single blow.

The King had yielded to Eustace's persuasion and the two of them had left the tent together, the King staggering slightly as if he was very tired.

William jogged along on his pony, pretending it was a destrier. Chancing his luck, he pushed him into a canter and headed up the column towards the knights.

A hard hand suddenly clamped down on his shoulder. 'Where do you think you're going, young *meister*?' Henk growled, looking down at him from the saddle of his lean brown rouncy.

William widened his eyes. He had learned which particular expressions were the most appealing. 'I just wanted to look,' he said, adding hopefully as Henk inhaled to speak, 'I'm the King's attendant.'

'You're his hostage and his youngest page.' Henk was having none of it. 'You should be in the baggage train with the other non-fighters. Trust me, there's no place for shoe-warmers at the head of the line.'

'Can I stay with you then?'

'No, it's too dangerous.' Henk broke out of the column with a brief word to the mercenary riding at his side; taking William's bridle, he headed him back towards the baggage lines. 'There might be a big battle and the last place you want to be is among the fighting men. Stay with Mariette and if I see you coming riding up again, I'll kill you myself.'

'I heard the Earl of Leicester say to Arundel there wasn't going to be a fight,' William said.

Henk's expression sharpened. 'And just when did you hear that, my lad?'

492

'This morning when we were mounting. I was running errands for the King and I had to wait to give a message to the Earl of Leicester because he was busy.'

'What exactly did he say?'

William screwed up his face. 'That it was a good thing to take the army to meet Henry because then they could set about neg . . . nego . . .'

'Negotiating?'

William nodded. 'A truce.'

'You're sure you heard him say that?'

'Yes, sir. They were talking about how angry Eustace was going to be and Arundel said that he was sick of Eustace and didn't care whether he got angry or not. There was a real chance for peace and they had to take it.'

Henk made a considering sound in his throat. 'Well, that's interesting, my boy,' he said after a moment, 'but still no cause for you to be riding at the front. It could be all talk and no deed. You're to stay with Mariette. Understood?'

William heaved a resigned sigh, but nodded. 'I thought I might see my papa,' he said in a smaller voice.

Henk clapped him on the shoulder again. 'If he saw you at the front of the King's army among the knights, your father would—' Henk bit off the rest of what he had been going to say. John FitzGilbert had already seen his son in positions far more compromising and turned his back, the bastard. He didn't deserve the child's devotion. 'Go on,' he said gruffly. 'Go to Mariette. You'll see that father of yours soon enough.'

William did as he was bidden. No one seemed to be very keen on his papa. Whenever his name was mentioned, their voices would fall to whispers if he was by, but he was still aware of the words 'faithless' and 'mad' and

493

'hellspawn' being bandied around and it gave him a nasty feeling in his tummy because sometimes he thought it might be true.

Once again two armies faced each other across fast-flowing water, this time the Thames, and once again Henry was outnumbered, although not by as many this time. John sat his horse close to Henry because he had recently been discussing the supply situation. They were dangerously low on fodder for the horses and with scorched earth all around them it was going to be nigh on impossible to find more. Stephen at least had all of Kent to supply his troops. Something had to be finalised today, be it through battle or a refusal to fight. They were all punch-drunk and exhausted, reeling from skirmish to skirmish, losing a little bit more every time – even when they made gains there was a cost to the soul in scars that did not fade.

John checked the fastenings attaching scabbard to belt. He had sharpened the blade last night. Not that he'd be in the front rank if battle was joined. He had cracked his collar bone in a recent skirmish outside Oxford. The injury made it difficult for him to control his shield and horse and since it was his blind left side, he would be even more handicapped. Jaston had suffered a slash to his arm which was healing, but neither he nor John was at full fighting capacity. They would be at the back, responsible for guarding the baggage with the other semi-able wounded and the squires. If, of course, it came to battle. Leicester and Arundel had sworn it would not, but they had Eustace to contend with, and Stephen's Flemings for whom fighting was pay. Stephen's forces held the bridge over the Thames, but to reach Henry they had to cross it and that would make them vulnerable. If Henry took the initiative, he risked the same. There was too much at stake; too much to lose. William of Gloucester and Reginald of Cornwall were counselling caution. So too was Patrick. He might be rash when roused, but he had played both sides down the long years of conflict and had a strong streak of self-preservation.

Henry was frowning towards Stephen's army massed on the far side of the river. 'If not a fight, then we must have a decisive peace,' he said, tight-lipped. 'I will not ride away with a piddling broken-backed truce between us. I would rather fight single-handed to the death than come away from this with nothing.'

'Then it has to be peace, sire,' John said.

'That's rich, coming from you!' Patrick scoffed.

John slid his brother-in-law an irritated look. 'I made the choice to have peace with you,' he said.

'Hah, that was Gloucester's idea!'

'Was it?' John raised his brows, and turned his focus back to Henry. 'Unless we are assured of victory today, sire, we cannot afford to fight – nor can they. The only way they will give battle is if Eustace forces the issue, but Leicester won't follow him, nor will Arundel.'

Henry pursed his lips. 'And how many would follow me, I wonder?' He glanced over his shoulder at his assembled ranks. 'Very well. Let's see if we can run with a parley.' He turned to his uncle, Reginald of Cornwall. 'Go to the bridge under flag of truce with my lord of Gloucester and the marshal. Let Stephen take down his siege castles and depart from Wallingford, and I will withdraw from our entrenchments, but only if the King is willing to sit down with me and discuss a lasting alternative that will bring true peace to the land.'

'You were right, boy,' Henk said to William. 'There won't be a battle today – praise God. The lords have spoken between themselves and now Duke Henry and the King are talking.' He made a face as he threw down his lance and shield beside the baggage cart. 'No one wants to push his luck and I don't blame them. Course,' he added, 'there might be a battle between the King and his son. Can't see the lord Eustace going anywhere near peace talks with the man he's been trying to kill for the past several years.' He sat down by the edge of the cartwheel and took the horn of ale that Mariette gave to him.

'Well, hasn't Stephen been trying to kill Henry too?' Mariette asked.

'No, just shed him off his back like a burden.' Henk took a swallow of the ale and looked at William. 'Saw your father though.'

'Where?' William looked at him with anxious curiosity.

'On the bridge with a passel of other nobles before the King and the Duke came out to talk alone. Had his arm in a sling but it obviously wasn't a serious injury.'

Henk swilled down the rest of the ale. 'So that says something to me when a man the likes of your father, who's done what he's done to keep on fighting, suddenly comes forth to stand in no man's land and talk terms – eh?'

William nodded. He wasn't quite sure about the meaning of Henk's words, and he didn't like to think of his father being wounded, but at least he was all right. Perhaps he was meeting on the bridge to negotiate for William's return.

'So, are we staying, or are we going?' Mariette asked.

'How should I know, woman?' Henk flashed her an irascible look. 'All I can say is that unless matters change in a moment, we won't be fighting.'

'Might as well eat then.' Mariette went to fetch food from the back of the cart. William had been thinking

496

about going back to the King's baggage train, perhaps via a quick look at the front ranks to see if his father was still there, but decided to eat first. Mariette gave him bread and honey and a handful of early blackberries that she had plucked from a hedgerow.

William saved a piece of bread for his pony and was feeding it to him when shouting and the sudden thunder of hooves made him look up. Henk snatched his spear and shield from beside the cart and strode to William's side.

It was Eustace and his personal conroi. William watched the powerful roan stallion thunder down the pathway between the baggage tents, nostrils flaring red, mouth open against the bit. Eustace had spurred it so hard that there was a bleeding gouge on its flank. They were past in a flash, but William still had time to see that Eustace was very angry about something. He was so furious that he was ahead of his banner-bearer who was struggling to keep up.

'Hah, that answers it!' Henk laid down his weapons again. 'It's peace then.'

William wasn't sure he understood Henk, except that the word 'peace' might mean he was able to go home. Tentatively he voiced the notion as folk from the baggage section gathered to stand in Eustace's dust trail and watch the King's son gallop out.

Henk laid a hand on his shoulder and squeezed. 'I reckon you'll have to be patient a while longer, lad,' he said gently. 'We're not there yet, not by a long way.'

Unable to use his left arm, John had to mount his courser from the right-hand side, which proved awkward but manageable with the aid of a mounting block. All around him other lords were assembling their men and their

497

baggage, preparing to move out as the sun rose above the eastern horizon.

Stephen's army had departed the previous night. In this morning's dawn, all that remained was a detail of mercenaries and labourers, demolishing the siege towers at Crowmarsh. Supplies had been allowed into the beleaguered garrison at Wallingford and as Stephen's forces left, an almighty roar had swept from the walls to the Angevin army below.

Henry and Stephen had agreed a truce and, more than that, had agreed to meet and begin detailed peace discussions. It didn't mean that the struggle had stopped. The truce was fragile and was certain to be broken in places, but still there was optimism in the air – like the first awareness of returning light after a long winter. Precarious, cold and wan, but alleviating the darkness.

'Do you think it will last?'

John's lips thinned with irritation. Patrick had come up on his blind left side where he was further incapacitated by the injured clavicle. He suspected it was deliberate but forced himself to be civil. Awkwardly turning the horse using his right hand, he faced his brother-in-law. 'It will last providing we are resolved not to let it falter.' He pointed towards the siege works. 'That has to be a sign of commitment. Could you imagine this happening last year?'

Patrick looked. 'No,' he agreed.

'Last year I was under siege at Newbury and Stephen was determined to bring down Wallingford whatever the cost. Now what was the prize is no longer worth it. Men want peace now, not when they are laid in their graves.'

'Amen to that.' Patrick crossed himself. 'What about Eustace though? He's not for a settlement.'

'He'll have to be in the end. He can't hold out against everyone.'

498

Patrick tugged on his moustaches. He had started cultivating them in imitation of Ranulf of Chester's magnificent set of whiskers but with less success. 'His father will be stubborn about yielding up Eustace's right to be King. It won't be easy.'

'He'll do it though. He has no choice.' John looked at Patrick. 'What won't be easy is deciding who has what. Lands have changed ownership throughout the war. Men have had titles confirmed by one side and not the other. You were made Earl of Salisbury by the Empress, not Stephen.' He didn't add that as marshal to Stephen he had never been replaced and that his own position was currently more secure than Patrick's. So much was obvious without rubbing it in. If peace was made, then the exchequer would resume its routine business and he would be a vital part of it.

Patrick bristled. His stallion side-stepped and bucked, responding to his increased tension. 'But I will be confirmed,' he said forcefully.

John dipped his head. 'I have no doubt of it, but there are others in similar positions who are going to be disappointed and will have to make compromises. Some men have become too powerful in their small domains. There will also have to be agreement whereby adulterine fortifications are torn down or put into royal hands.'

Patrick gave him a sly glance. 'Well, that would include Newbury,' he said.

John studied the reins. 'If it does, it does. After the pounding it took there's not much of it left anyway.'

'And Ludgershall?'

He refused to rise to the bait. 'It's pointless speculating. Once we sit down to hammer out a truce, then we'll decide.' He looked again towards the siege castles on the Crowmarsh bank. He hadn't seen William yesterday,

499

although he had hoped for a glimpse. There had been several youngsters running around Stephen's camp as they made ready to leave. Any of them could have been William; he had been unable to tell from a distance. It would have been too easy to fix on one and comfort himself by pretending he recognised him. Besides, even at this stage it would be dangerous to show too much interest in his son's wellbeing before men of whose motives he was not sure.

'Hah,' he said to his horse, digging in his heels. Mercifully Patrick didn't follow him.

49

Marlborough, Wiltshire, August 1153

John crouched by the low mound of dark earth in the corner of Marlborough's bailey. It was a sunny spot where Doublet had been wont to sit on a summer's day, a marrow bone grasped between her forepaws as she rasped and gnawed at the contents. She had been a pup the year he defied Stephen. Fourteen years. A long life for a dog of her kind. 'She was the best,' he said. 'There won't be another like her.'

Sybilla touched his arm. 'No,' she agreed, not attempting to offer him platitudes. 'There won't.'

He rose to his feet. He had arrived home at dusk yesterday evening, and when Doublet had not hobbled to greet him, he had known with a pang of deep sadness that she was dead. Old and stiff as she was, her sudden departure in his absence had caught him off his guard. The other dogs had wagged to meet him, including three generations of her line, but it wasn't the same.

Margaret had laid a bunch of daisies on the grave together with a smooth stick of just the right size from a beech tree near the river. Her solemn gravitas was both touching and amusing, and he gently stroked her brown curls. Stuck in an army camp, forced to fight and discuss war and strategy day upon day upon day, he missed the tenderness of women in his life. Whores and washerwomen performed their functions, but it wasn't the same as being embraced by the joy and warmth of family. Sybilla was in the eighth month of her pregnancy and he had felt the baby in her womb throb and kick against the palm of his hand as they had lain in bed last night. Another boy, she said. Pray God for peace and a whole family by the time he was old enough to speak his first words.

They were returning to the keep, Sybilla's arm through his and Margaret skipping in front of them, when a messenger galloped through the gate, flinging down from the saddle even as he slewed to a halt. Sybilla's grip tightened and John's stomach somersaulted. He braced himself to withstand yet another blow.

'My lord, Eustace, Count of Boulogne, is dead!' the man gasped as he bowed. 'In Cambridge, at the hand of Saint Edmund!' He crossed himself.

John stared. *Dead? Eustace was dead?* The notion was as impossible to grasp as a wet eel.

'He raided the monastery at Bury and took away all the food in the monks' cellar for himself. When he sat down to dine on it, he suffered a seizure and died. Everyone said it was the wrath of the saint.'

Sybilla gave a shiver and crossed herself. John refused to be superstitious and didn't.

'They're bearing him to Faversham to lay him beside his lady mother. I've to carry the tidings to Salisbury next.'

Sybilla rallied and told the man to water his horse and go to the kitchens for bread and ale before he rode on. John gave him a silver penny for the news.

'Very fortuitous,' he said thoughtfully. 'Very fortuitous indeed.'

502

Sybilla gave him a quick look. 'You think he was poisoned?'

'It's as likely as falling victim to the wrath of a saint. I do not suppose men will investigate too closely . . . they didn't when old King Henry died.' He turned towards the keep. 'People will also say it's a sign that God favours the old King's grandson for the crown.' He slipped his arm lightly around Sybilla's waist. 'I think,' he said, 'in the light of what we've just heard, we might consider returning to Hamstead for your confinement.'

William lay on his pallet in the squires' tent and fidgeted. It was very late but he had left his toy sword in the King's pavilion and he knew he'd never be able to sleep unless he had it by his side. It made him feel safe and grown up, and pretending to be the latter helped him cope with all the bewildering things that were happening around him. There was supposed to be a truce, but even so, the fighting hadn't stopped. King Stephen and Duke Henry had just agreed to stay away from each other while their representatives held talks. Henk had told him that Henry was besieging somewhere called Stamford, and King Stephen wanted to teach Hugh Bigod of Norfolk a lesson and had brought his army to Ipswich. A lot of his earls had gone home, but Henk and the other mercenaries were still with him.

The other boys were all asleep. William pushed off his blanket and eased his feet into his shoes. Throwing his mantle over his chemise, he felt his way to the tent flap, the excuse ready on his tongue, should he be stopped, that he needed a piss. Outside the guards clustered around their camp fires, talking, mending their equipment, making music. Here and there the higher voice of a woman lifted on the air, and the occasional raucous laugh. William

503

slipped silently between the tents, pretending he was Lion. No one ever heard a hunting cat on the prowl.

The King's guards were standing to attention outside his pavilion, but William crept around the back. He tested the tent pegs until he found one that could be loosened and removed with a bit of tugging and pulling. If he had been able to yank Baldwin's sword from a targe last year, he wasn't going to be defeated by a common tent peg! It finally yielded to his determination, although not without toppling him over backwards and smearing his hands with mud. He wiped his palms down his cloak and, lying down in the dew-wet grass, wriggled under the gap he had made. It was a tight squeeze and for a moment he was afraid he was going to become stuck, half in and half out, but he sucked in his stomach and by moving the angle of his shoulders and pressing his cheek into the cold ground, he managed to wriggle through. A wall of thick woollen cloth faced him: the internal hangings for the King's tent, suspended by ring hooks from the top of the canvas. The hangings were dark red, woven with golden lions and almost as heavy as a mail shirt. Gingerly, he parted them and crawled into the main tent.

A fat candle burned on a wrought-iron stand, illuminating the detail that his sword wasn't beside the King's hauberk and big weapons where he'd left it. And then he saw the reason why and he caught his breath. King Stephen was sitting on his bed, turning the toy in his hand and staring at it with tears gleaming on his cheeks. William hadn't bargained for this. He had hoped to grab his sword and creep from the tent again unseen. Now he hesitated, torn between being bold and not being discovered. And then it was too late anyway, because the King looked up and saw him.

'What are you doing here, boy? Get up.'

504

Stephen's voice was all cracked and wobbly. William stood straight and pushed his hair out of his eyes with a mud-soiled hand. 'I came for my sword, sire,' he said. 'I . . . I forgot it.'

Stephen stared at the toy weapon. His shoulders shook, then shook harder and he raised a hand to cover his face. 'Ah, God help me, child, God help me! You come to me like a ghost!' He rocked back and forth and folded his other arm across his midriff as if he were in terrible pain, the sword pointing in William's direction.

William hesitated, uncertain what to do. It wasn't the first time Stephen had called him a ghost and he didn't like it. If he alerted the guards, they might think he had done this to the King and then they'd hang him over a fire again. 'I'm not a ghost, sire,' he said uncertainly. 'I only want my sword.'

Stephen shuddered. He used the cuff of his tunic to mop his face before turning a wet, red gaze on William. 'No, Willikin, you're not a ghost, but you remind me too much of Eustace and the swords he had before he took up the blade of manhood. Someone spent a long time crafting this . . . your father?'

William nodded.

'I made one for Eustace but it wasn't as fine as this . . .' The King swallowed hard. 'He's dead. He'll never hold a sword again, walk through that tent flap, or bring me grandchildren to sit at my knee. His offspring are dead in his loins – unbegotten.' With a shaking hand, he gave the sword to William. 'Your father does not know how fortunate he is still to have you.'

William felt uncomfortable. He didn't know what to say or do. He wrapped his hand around the leather grip and took reassurance from the familiar feel.

'Men say it's God's judgement on me for taking a crown

505

that wasn't mine and for breaking my oath that I would support the Empress. But oaths taken under duress are not binding. Surely God sees and knows what is in a man's heart?' He pushed his hands through his thinning hair in a distracted gesture. 'But how can a man see and know what is in God's? It is forbidden to him to know the purpose of the Almighty.'

'Do you want me to warm your shoes or pour you wine?' William asked.

Stephen sighed, and wiped his eyes again. 'You're a good boy, Willikin.' A smile twisted his lips. 'But warm shoes and all the wine in the world will neither comfort nor drown my grief. Your father has thrown away what I could not keep no matter how I tried. It's finished, and I never told him . . . that I . . .' He clenched his fists. 'Holy Christ . . .' His shoulders began to shake again.

William looked down at the sword in his hand, wanting to help but not knowing how. 'Shall I guard you?'

Stephen made a sound, half broken laugh, half sob. 'Why not?' He waved his hand. 'You can do no worse than the grown men. I have received a mortal wound despite all their efforts. Pull a pallet across the tent entrance and use my cloak for a blanket. You can sleep there with your sword at the ready.'

William did as he was bidden with alacrity. The King's cloak was lined with ermine tails and very soft and fine. The hay stuffing of the pallet was new and sweet-smelling and he was suddenly very tired, but knew he should wash his hands and face first and say his prayers.

The King let him use his jug and ewer, and said the paternoster with him, then arranged the cloak as William lay down. 'I once did this for Eustace,' Stephen said. 'It was long ago, but it feels like yesterday. I wish it was.'

William fell asleep, his hand still curled possessively

around the grip of his sword. Gazing down at him, Stephen was silent, but the light from the candle caught the glimmer of new tears as they ran down his cheeks.

50

Winchester, November 1153

Sybilla gazed around the main chamber in what, until
recently, had been her husband's house in the city and
was still reserved for him to use when he had need of a
place to stay. He had given it to the Church when Stephen
had taken Winchester and he thought he might never
return.

The servants were still unloading the baggage from
the packhorses and bringing it to the room. The travelling bed with its two mattresses and thick woollen hangings; the coffer containing sheets and napery. Blankets
and coverlets, clothing chests, cushions and caskets.
Hangings, cups and platters. The shouts of the grooms
busy with the horses, together with the noise of a household still arriving, wafted up through the open shutters
and she went to look out into the yard at the string of
pack ponies. The afternoon was raw and dank and the
breath of men and animals puffed in the air like smoke.
John was busy talking to the caretaker from Troarn Abbey,
who had had custody of the keys. Young John stood
solemnly at his father's side, head up and expression
manly and serious.

Sybilla turned back into the room. Margaret was sitting beside the cradle watching over her baby brother.

'He's asleep,' Margaret said a trifle wistfully. She found the baby infinitely more interesting than her little sister Sybilla, who was at the blundering toddler stage and a nuisance.

'No surprise, sweetheart, since he was awake all through the journey,' Sybilla answered with a smile. 'Small babies always sleep a lot.'

'Why?'

That particular word was constantly on Margaret's lips and finding answers could be wearing. Sybilla glanced round as John entered the room, keys in hand. 'Tell your daughter why small babies always sleep a lot,' she said.

'I hadn't noticed that they did.' He glanced thoughtfully into the cradle. 'Because they have a lot of thinking and growing to do,' he said.

Margaret nodded. 'What do they think about?'

'Salted herrings mostly,' John replied seriously, then, as Sybilla had done, went to look out of the window.

Sybilla eyed their daughter who was looking extremely puzzled. Joining her husband, she gave him a dig in the ribs.

His lips twitched. 'It might even be true. Who is going to gainsay me? Gilbert and Walter have taken the boy for a look around the city. Since I have a day's grace before the negotiating begins at the castle, I thought you might want to wait until the morrow.'

'You wouldn't want to let your wife loose among the booths and stalls on her own,' she said with a straight face.

His smile deepened before fading to pensive. 'Not until the terms have been agreed. I'm hoping there won't be any serious difficulties, but it's still no good counting eggs

509

before the hens have laid them. If things go well, there'll be a full peace agreed, to be ratified at Westminster next month. Henry will be confirmed as Stephen's heir and do him homage and I'll be able to return my hauberk to its bag and my sword to its scabbard.'

Sybilla was not fooled by the lightness in his tone. She could see the strain in his jaw and the hand he had braced against the wall was tight with tension. She stroked the soft blue wool of his sleeve.

He continued to look pensive. 'Many of us are going to have to put the past behind us. Stephen never replaced me as marshal. I have no doubt he will take me back, and Henry will expect the same duties from me. My sons will follow where I tread; I have their careers to broker through the court.' He gave a twisted smile. 'Everything changes while it stays the same, doesn't it?'

'What's troubling you?' she asked. She tried to concentrate on him, but nevertheless had to bite her lip as she heard Margaret loudly asking her nursemaid why babies thought about salted herrings all the time.

He sighed. 'Everything will be returned to as it was on the day that the old King died. Some men will have their lands restored; others will have to forfeit their gains. Castles built without permission will be demolished. We could find ourselves stripped of Wexcombe and Cherhill. Marlborough could be taken away, and Ludgershall. Newbury too.' He gave a sour grin. 'I will still keep the post of marshal because I'm too good at the job to be replaced and I had the office in the old King's time – so at least we'll keep Hamstead and Tidworth.'

Sybilla felt queasy. 'Surely that won't happen?'

'Who can say? I would hope not, but there's nothing I can do except lobby and persuade. Many others will be caught in the same predicament, your brother included.

510

He spent a lot of time and effort extending the castle at Salisbury, but it will all have to be razed and the land returned to the cathedral.'

'Well yes, but that's more blatant.'

'Mayhap, but it comes out of the same basket. I—' Suddenly he stopped speaking and went very still.

'What?' Sybilla looked out of the window into the courtyard. A hard-faced man clad in a quilted tunic was dismounting from a loose-limbed rouncy. Beside him on a brown pony was a boy with sun-bleached brown hair. The latter dismounted with a lithe hop and Sybilla's heart started to pound. It couldn't be William. It couldn't be. The child she was looking at was far too tall. The man spoke to him and unfastened a baggage roll from the back of his horse, and the boy replied, then turned round and, facing the window, looked up.

'Jesu God!' Sybilla gasped. Gathering her skirts in her hands, she ran to the door leading to the outer stairs.

John remained rooted to the spot, unable to move. He was no coward, could stand hard in the face of impossible odds and the likelihood of death, but what faced him now was a test of courage he thought he might fail. How could he look William in the eyes, having denied him at Newbury and abandoned him to the whim of his enemies? And how would William look at him? The father who had turned his back and said he did not matter?

Sybilla had reached the foot of the stairs and without hesitating had swept William into her embrace, picking him up, hugging him, twirling him round. John swallowed to see the eager joy and brightness in both their faces. He wanted to hide, to bury himself under a cloak, shut himself away. But if he yielded to that impulse, gave in to cowardice, then to the outside world, to his son, it would confirm the impression that he thought him of no

511

consequence, when in truth William was perhaps the most important thing in his life just now. Until he paid that debt there could be no balance – and in hesitating he was already almost too late.

Drawing a deep breath, John went to the door, then made his way down the stairs, his hand gripping the rope support rail against the wall. He knew William might reject him and was anticipating a rebuff, perhaps even hatred.

The soldier who had escorted William bowed to him, but the gesture lacked deference and John caught a glimpse of utter contempt in the man's eyes before he lowered them. Tears running down her face, Sybilla released William, and father and son faced each other at the foot of the steps. William had grown so much he was almost the same height as his older brother. Long legs, long arms. The little boy had gone. Beneath his sun-streaked fringe, William's stare was steady and level – almost adult in its gravity. John could feel himself being measured, weighed, assessed.

'There are times when I have not been proud of myself, son,' John said hoarsely, 'but I have always been proud of you.' He took William in his arms and embraced him like a soldier, acknowledging that it was man to man and not man to boy. 'Well done!'

William embraced him back, and the gesture wasn't that of a clinging child, but of a peer. John's vision blurred and he had to fight the constriction in his throat.

'The King asked me if I wanted to stay with him or return to my family,' William announced as John drew back. 'I said I wanted to come home.' He turned to his escort. 'This is Henk.'

The man bowed again and John nodded acknowledgement. From the looks of him and his name, he was one of Stephen's Flemings. 'I thank you for bringing him to us.'

'It was the King's will and, more than that, the boy's,' the man growled in accented French. 'I did as I was bidden. My woman wanted to keep him, and had it been down to me I would have let her.'

A bold speech. Here was the hostile resentment John had half expected from his son.

'But then,' Henk added, 'I remind myself that even if a stoat is always a stoat, its colour changes in winter.'

'Your point?' John asked curtly, his arm still around William.

'The stoat does so in order to survive and to fool its enemy. I see in you now what I did not see before because you hid it too well. For what it's worth though, I tell you that you have already hammered out the best – and forged it in the fire.'

John gave him a sharp look, but found a mordant smile. 'An apt comparison,' he said. 'And you are right. I couldn't make this one over again.'

By the soft light of a ceramic candle torch, Sybilla looked down at William, slumbering on a pallet beside his older brother. John joined her, slipping his arm around her waist, and for a long moment they gazed in silence at the child-adult lying in the stead of the little boy they had given to Stephen, his wooden sword and shield propped at his bedside. Then before the light could disturb his sleep, Sybilla lit the way to their bed, set the torch in the canopy holder and drew the hangings fast around her and John.

'He is changed, but in the way that a shoot grows stronger and becomes a sapling,' she murmured as she unpinned her veil and removed her hair net. 'He's learned

513

to hold things inside and to sit still and listen for a minute, and that is not all to the bad.' Her tone was steady, although it took an effort. She was still reeling from the emotional impact of having William suddenly returned to them. From being half empty she was suddenly full to overflowing and striving to adjust.

John said nothing, his expression closed.

'He is resilient, more so than us, my love.' She set her hand over his and squeezed. 'He doesn't have guilt to deal with as we do.'

John looked down and linked his fingers through hers. 'It was when he asked where Doublet was . . . Christ . . .'

'Yes, it's the small cuts that come the keenest.' Her throat tightened. 'He is past the time and age now to sit in my lap. Before he stood by my side as a small boy and held my hand. Now he's taken steps away from me on the road to manhood. Someone else has had that part of his life and it will always be a hole within me.' Through the threat of tears she forced a smile. 'For him it's different. He's a hero home from adventuring – and ready to set out again come the dawn. I can see it in him.'

They finished undressing in silence. Beyond the bed curtains, one of the younger children whimpered in sleep and was soothed by the soft murmur of a nurse.

Sybilla prepared to snuff the torch, but John caught her back and drew her down to him. 'Leave it,' he said.

Sybilla leaned over him. The light fell upon the left side of his face and she traced the damage with gentle fingertips. The past was indelibly marked in the thick ridges of scar tissue, still anger-red. And contrasting with it, the fine-grained skin still taut to cheekbone and jaw. The straight nose, the firm mouth that had a soldier's uncompromising line, yet could be as subtle as silk upon her skin. It was several weeks since Ancel's birth and much longer than that since they had lain together. 'John?' she breathed as he bit down gently on her forefinger.

He reached to stroke her hair and, like his lips, the fingers that could grip and wield a sword to such devastating effect were now tender and slow-moving. 'Comfort me,' he entreated. 'Make me believe this night is a new beginning and not the end.'

'There has to be an end to what is begun,' she whispered, her breath in his. 'Surely you have the stamina to finish – and then start again.'

He laughed softly at the innuendo. 'With you, yes. But . . .'

'Then you believe already,' she said, 'but since there is still the matter of comfort . . .' She kissed him. 'Whatever happens, we'll survive.'

Epilogue

April sunshine spilled across the grass in pale gold streamers of light. For the first time since winter, there was true warmth in the rays and the air had a balmy feel that said spring was finally here.

Holding his stallion's bridle, John stood in the place where a year and a half ago a mass of siege tents had faced his keep at Newbury. There was nothing to show. The grass had grown back and sheep cropped the area. Most of the villagers were going about their normal business – relearning it after the years of uncertainty. A contingent of men, youths and small boys were busy at work on the keep. An ox team was hauling away timbers and the industrious sound of hammering and general demolition carried across the ditch to John.

William and his older brother ran across the grass, play-fighting with their swords. A black adolescent pup gambolled in their wake, trying to nip at their heels. John watched the older boy create unnecessary flourishes and the younger one go straight in with elegance and economy. Add that to the promise of height and strength and one day William was going to be utterly formidable. One day

. . . John glanced uneasily at the patch of ground to his right where the gallows had stood. Nothing remained, but he could still feel the shadow of a life almost ended before it was begun – and at his behest.

Sybilla joined him, wrapping her arm around his. 'It will soon all be gone,' she said. 'Every last timber and stone. In time even the memory will fade.'

'I won't be sorry,' he said. 'I am glad to set an example for the peace and see it torn down.' It had been a relief to receive the joint command from Henry and Stephen to demolish Newbury. Almost as much of a relief as the permission to retain Ludgershall as it was, to remain castellan of Marlborough at least for now, and to keep for his lifetime the manors he held in royal demesne. His position as hereditary marshal had been confirmed. He was to sit at the exchequer in Westminster when the next session was held, and the cogs of organised government would begin to turn again in earnest. His eldest sons would come with him to court and learn the tasks and duties of the Marshalsea. His namesake would be trained in knighthood and governance so that he could take on the duties of Ludgershall and the lands his mother had brought to the marriage. And William . . . He watched the child stop on the perimeter of the ditch and stare up at the castle, then, with a joyful yell at the top of his lungs, leap down and begin scrambling up the other side, the pup striving at his heels. His older brother hesitated but after a moment followed.

'He's a natural leader,' Sybilla said with pride in her voice. 'And fearless.'

'A woman at a fair once told me I would beget greatness,' John mused. 'I thought she was a mad old hag in search of favour, but now I wonder if she was right. I feel that he is marked by fate.'

517

Sybilla shook her head. 'Not so.' She smiled at him. 'Like his father, he will carve his own – they all will. Of that I am certain.'

Having gained the palisade at the top of the bank, William turned and waved to them.

'You see,' Sybilla said, her voice filled with strength and optimism. 'This is a new beginning for all.'

He made an amused sound, but inside he was touched and proud . . . and a little humbled. In mutual companionship, they moved towards the diminishing remains of Newbury and let their mounts crop the fresh grass along the top of the ditch.

Author's Note

While writing two novels about the life of the great William Marshal, *The Greatest Knight* and *The Scarlet Lion*, I had read about his father, John FitzGilbert the Marshal, as part of my research. I began to ponder upon the man who had fathered William and it wasn't long before that pondering became a stronger notion that really he deserved a novel of his own.

John is, of course, notorious for that famous 'anvils and hammers' speech in *L'Histoire de Guillaume le Maréchal*: 'Mais ils dist ke ne li chaleit de l'enfant, quer encore aveit les enclumes e les marteals dun forgereit de plus beals.' ('He said that he didn't care about the child because he still had the anvils and hammers to forge even finer ones.') At first glance, it didn't look promising as a character study – a father who could give up his son, watch him being led to the gibbet and speak of him with such indifference. Many people will have looked on John Marshal with disgust for those words and will have perhaps concluded that children in the twelfth century were an expendable commodity. However, there is much more to that speech and to John Marshal than meets

519

the eye, and it was the story behind the story that I set out to tell.

The conventional sources show John as the senior royal marshal from the year 1130 when he would have been about twenty-five years old. His father, Gilbert, was the marshal before him. The pair of them had fought against two challengers in a public trial by combat to prove their right to the title some time before this, and had won. So John was not only an able administrator, but skilled in combat too. His duties as marshal were many and varied and included keeping order at court, organising transport and lodging when the court was on the move, responsibility for the royal kennels, stables and mews, keeping tallies of wages owed to the King's mercenaries and taking custody of debtors at the exchequer. He was also responsible for the keeping and the regulation of the royal prostitutes. Later in his career, chroniclers would call him 'cunning' and marvel at his abilities as a builder of castles, a deviser of strategies and as a hard soldier in the field. The *Gesta Stephani* forthrightly calls him a 'scion of hell and root of evil' but, it has to be said, is somewhat biased in its reportage. It may just have something to do with his extracting tribute and labour from the Church lands within his jurisdiction, not to mention being a supporter of the Empress rather than Stephen for whom the *Gesta* has a bias.

In the twelfth century, aristocratic marriages were a matter of business. One looked for a partner with advantageous lands and prospects. Often there was strong competition for the most likely heirs and heiresses. Love and affection were bonuses and not part of the equation. When John FitzGilbert married Aline Pipard, he was doing the best he could for himself at that time in his career and with the resources available. Had the war between Stephen

520

and Matilda not taken place, he would, in all probability, have lived out his life with her. However, desperate times call forth desperate measures. Faced with his eventual destruction at the hands of a more powerful enemy, John took the expedient of divorcing Aline and marrying into his opponent's family. By doing this, John took the pressure off himself and his lands. The inheritance of his two sons by Aline Pipard remained stable and Aline herself was not disparaged when she remarried Stephen de Gai, uncle to the Earl of Gloucester. Had John not made the alliance with Patrick of Salisbury, it would almost certainly have led to his death and his sons, small boys at the time, would have been put in uncertain wardship. By making the new marriage, he stayed in control.

John's stand at Wherwell Abbey is another incident in his life that is often remarked upon by historians. Versions of the event in primary sources are confusing, and in the secondary ones they are numerous, as everyone has an opinion on the subject. This being fiction, I have chosen to pick my way through the differing accounts in a way that best suits my narrative. One version (*L'Histoire*) suggests that the Empress was at Wherwell and that John was supervising her retreat. Another account says that she was nowhere near the abbey and that John was at Wherwell trying to get supplies through to Winchester when events overtook him. What is certain is that John lost an eye in an intense and literal firefight at the abbey with the men of Stephen's mercenary captain William D'Ypres.

Coming to the famous and infamous events at Newbury, there is strong speculation that Newbury Castle was in fact Hamstead Marshal, which lies only four miles to the west of Newbury today. Archaeological digs in the Newbury area have yet to turn up any sign of a castle site. However, I have gone with the older traditional notion of there having been a castle at Newbury, although I have been deliberately vague about naming its site. Many of the castles from the troubled years of Stephen's reign were temporary edifices, hastily thrown up to combat local threats or extend power bases. As soon as a peace was agreed, these 'adulterine' castles were ordered to be torn down. I suspect that if Newbury Castle did exist (which I like to think it did), it was one of these adulterine fortresses. It wouldn't have stood for long – a couple of years at the most – and would therefore have left little mark on the landscape. I have said John was known as a man with a talent for castle-building, and therefore he must have been seen to be doing so. I suspect Newbury was one of his many projects.

Concerning John's behaviour towards his small son William as a hostage, the evidence is interesting. Stephen is known by history to have been gentle and chivalrous towards women and children. John would have associated with Stephen at the court of Henry I when Stephen was still Count of Mortain. After Stephen became King, John served as his marshal for several years before their rift. He would have been well aware of Stephen's nature and that knowledge would have lessened the gamble he took with William. While William was a hostage, a Marshal retainer was sent to the camp in secret with a brief to keep an eye on the little boy. I have called the servant Tamkin in the novel, although his name appears to have been 'Wilikin'. This is purely in the interests of avoiding confusion with William, whom Stephen called 'Willikin' too. Sending a trusted servant to keep an eye on William is not the act of someone immersed in callous indifference. My own belief is that John found himself between a rock and a hard place and did the best he could in the circumstances. He had to act for the good of the majority.

522

The 'anvils and hammers' speech has more going on in it than first meets the eye. John was the master marshal, as his father had been before him. Originally, the royal marshals had been much concerned with the equine side of matters. Indeed, many of their rights and privileges in the King's court go back to these beginnings (when a young man was knighted in the royal court, he was obliged to give the master marshal either a palfrey or a saddle). A marshal or *marescallus* was also a name for a farrier or a blacksmith, and the tools of the trade were the anvil and the hammer. When John Marshal said those words, he was referring not only to his personal virility, but also to the traditional symbols of the marshal's occupation. Having associated with him at court, Stephen would know of John's dealings with the court prostitutes and this would have emphasised the sexual connotations of that speech. John Marshal did indeed have the 'anvils' and 'hammers', he knew how to use them, and Stephen knew he knew!

Readers who are acquainted with my novels *The Greatest Knight* and *The Scarlet Lion* will know that little William survived his ordeal to become a celebrated tourney champion, guardian of kings, Earl of Pembroke and finally regent of England. John was not to see his fourth son's rise to greatness as he died in 1165 when William was eighteen years old and training to knighthood in the house of Guillaume de Tancarville, chamberlain of Normandy: a position John had secured for him – surely a sign that he was not indifferent.

Concerning other matters, readers may want to know if Henry I was indeed murdered by poison. The answer is no one knows. All that can be said for certain is that he was taken violently ill at Lyons-la-Forêt and died a few days later. I think it not implausible that he was helped

523

on his way, and this being a work of fiction, I was able to explore that notion.

I have conducted the solid backbone of my research by using the main primary sources and various academic secondary sources, which I have listed below. Less conventionally, I have augmented the above by using what is sometimes known as the Akashic Record to access the personalities of the characters and events in their lives. This is a belief that each person leaves behind an indelible record of themselves impressed upon sub-atomic material – what mystics might call the consciousness of the universe. These recorded emotions, thoughts, feelings and actions can be accessed if one has the ability – rather like seeing past events as one would see a film.

I have found this resource invaluable for gaining insights into the life of John Marshal. It has been particularly useful in fleshing out the personalities and lives of John's wives Aline and Sybilla, about whom history has left us very little detail. Were I a historian, such archives would be inadmissible, but as a writer of historical fiction without such academic restraints, I have found them extremely useful and enlightening. If one believes in their existence, then they are a unique way of accessing the past. If they come from the subconscious, then they are still a fabulous creative tool. What I can say is that the combination of all the strands of my research have shown me in John FitzGilbert the Marshal a resourceful, charismatic man of fierce courage and high standards, a man of intelligence, pragmatism and understated humour who showed a resolute refusal to accept pity or self-pity, however dire the circumstances in which he found himself. A man who battled the odds and won through to give his descendants their opportunity to reach for the stars.

Select Bibliography

Bradbury, Jim, *Stephen and Matilda: The Civil War of 1139–53* (Sutton, 2005, ISBN 0 7509 3793 9)

Chibnall, Marjorie, *The Empress Matilda: Queen Consort, Queen Mother and Lady of the English* (Blackwell, 1999 edn, ISBN 0 631 19028 7)

The Chronicle of John of Worcester, vol. III, ed. and trans. by P. McGurk (Oxford Medieval Texts, Clarendon Press, 1998, ISBN 0 19 820702 6)

Crouch, David, *The Reign of King Stephen 1135–1154* (Longman, 2000, ISBN 0 582 22657 0)

Crouch, David, *William Marshal, Knighthood, War and Chivalry, 1147–1219* (Longman, 2nd edn, 2002, ISBN 0 582 77222 2)

Davis, R. H. C., *King Stephen* (Longman, 1990 edn, ISBN 0 582 04000 0)

Dialogus de Scaccario and Constitutio Domus Regis, ed. and trans. by Charles Johnson (Oxford Medieval Texts, Clarendon Press, 1983, ISBN 0 19 822268 8)

Gesta Stephani, ed. and trans. by K. R. Potter (Oxford Medieval Texts, Clarendon Press, 1976, ISBN 0 19 822234 3)

The Historia Novella of William of Malmesbury, ed. by K. R. Potter (Nelson, 1955)

History of William Marshal, Vol. 1, ed. by A. J. Holden with English translation by S. Gregory and historical notes by D. Crouch (Anglo-Norman Text Society Occasional Publications series 4, 2002 , ISBN 0 905474 42 2)

Hollister, C. Warren, *Henry I* (Yale University Press, 2001, ISBN 0 300 08858 2)

Huntingdon, Henry of, *The History of the English People 1000–1154*, trans. from the Latin by Diana Greenway (Oxford University Press, 2002 edn, ISBN 0 19 284075 4)

The Letters and Charters of Gilbert Foliot, ed. by Adrian Morey and C. N. L. Brooke (Cambridge University Press, 1967)

Painter, Sidney, *William Marshal, Knight Errant, Baron and Regent of England* (Johns Hopkins University Press, 1949)

Tyerman, Christopher, *Who's Who in Early Medieval England* (Shepheard Walwyn, 1996, ISBN 0 85683 132 8)

Warren, W. L., *Henry II* (Eyre Methuen, 1977 edn, ISBN 0 413 38390 3)

White, Graeme J., *Restoration and Reform 1153–1165: Recovery from Civil War in England* (Cambridge University Press, 2006 edn, ISBN 0 521 02658 X)

Articles and Related Items

Armstrong, Catherine, 'John fitz Gilbert; the Marshal', http://www.castlewales.com/jf_gilbt.html

Crouch, David, 'Robert Earl of Gloucester's Mother and Sexual Politics in Norman Oxfordshire', *Historical Research*, 72, 1999

Farrer, W., 'An Outline Itinerary of King Henry the First Part II', *English Historical Review*, Vol. 34, No. 135, July 1919

Hill, Rosalind, 'The Battle of Stockbridge 1141', article in *Studies in Medieval History Presented to R. Allen Brown*, ed. by Christopher Harper-Bill, Christopher J. Holdsworth and Janet L. Nelson (Boydell Press, 1989, ISBN 0 85115 512 X)

King, Alison, Akashic Records Consultant

Mooers, Stephanie L., 'Patronage in the Pipe Roll of 1130', *Speculum*, Vol. 59, No. 2, April 1984

Painter, Sidney, 'The Rout of Winchester', *Speculum*, Vol. 7., No. 1, January 1932

Prestwich, J. O., 'The Military Household of the Norman Kings', *English Historical Review*, Vol. 96, No. 378, January 1981

Stacey, N. E., 'Henry of Blois and the Lordship of Glastonbury', *English Historical Review*, Vol. 114, No. 455, February 1999

As always I welcome comments and I can be contacted through my website at www.elizabethchadwick.com or by e-mail to elizabeth.chadwick@btinternet.com

I also post regular updates about my writing and research on my blog at http://livingthehistoryelizabeth chadwick.blogspot.com. There is also a friendly, informal discussion list at ElizabethChadwick@yahoogroups.com, which readers are very welcome to join.